A Hidden Fire

Helen Cannam is the author of more than twenty published works of fiction, most of which are now available in ebook form. For many years she lived on the edge of Weardale, where much of the action of this novel takes place. She now lives in Durham city.

A Hidden Fire

Helen Cannam

Though many of the characters in this novel are known to history, those living in Meadhope, Holywell, Haroby or Silworth, or closely connected to them, are all imaginary and not based on any individuals alive or dead.

PART ONE

1604

Chapter One

Her brother, her darling brother, was coming home. He would be here today *(God willing!)* riding back into her life as he had not done for so many years.

She'd known a man once, struck by lightning and lived, she didn't know how. He'd been her grandmother's groom, here at Holywell. She, Kate, had been a child then—eight or nine perhaps—but she remembered it well. He'd told how after the first moments it was as if he'd been filled with the Holy Spirit, fired to his very soul with new vigour, new life; born again for some good purpose, so he'd claimed. He'd ended his life a drunkard, so there'd been no lasting change, but still.

That was how it had always felt to her when Nicholas came home, like forked lightning, bright, fierce, turning every corner of their lives upside down, bringing excitement, delight; but no change for good, only unseemly laughter and a sense of danger.

Yet after so long—would it still be the same? She'd had no news of him for ten long years, no knowledge of where he'd been or what he'd been doing, even if he was still alive. And then, last week, a messenger had come with a letter in that oh-so-familiar scrawl, telling her he had *'returned from the wars'*, though which wars, in what land, he did not say, nor why he had returned. Two other things he did say, however: that being at present in York, he would be with her at Holywell on the Eve of the Ascension, this very day;

1

and that in one essential way he had changed beyond words.

Would there still be the same excitement at his coming? Or would he be a different person, changed from the wild younger brother she remembered and loved, turned to sobriety, orderliness, become like everyone else?

The question shamed her. It was what she'd longed for, this thing that had happened to him. As his elder by five years, she'd pleaded with him, admonished him, prayed most earnestly for his endangered soul. His letter had even acknowledged the power of her intercession: *'Your prayers have been answered, sweet sister. I have found my way home, to the true faith.'*

Well, she would know soon enough what he had become, before the end of this day that was just beginning, if all went well.

Moments earlier, on first waking into the darkness of the spring dawn, she'd lain as usual, propped on pillows, eyes closed, fighting the urge simply to stay where she was, deferring the day and its duties for as long as possible; even to sleep again. But beyond the heavy folds of the bed curtains everything was quiet, so Jane must be up, her truckle bed empty, the blanket and linen folded in the neat way Jane did everything. Very likely she was already rousing Mariana and the boys from their beds. Outside, the birds were singing, greeting the dawn even before its light reached the room. Before long, Alice would have revived the kitchen fire, Cecily fetched water from the well, Moll set the dough to rise for the day's bread, Sarah milked the cows. It was not right that Kate should linger in bed while all that was going on.

Then she'd remembered. This would not be like other days, marked out by routines that must be followed no matter how tired she was. This was to be a day like no other, set aside, made special from the moment the letter had reached her, telling her that Nicholas would be here, that they would meet again after all the years of silence.

Joy exploded through her. She pushed aside the bed covers, reached to pull the curtains back, just as Jane took hold of them at the other side, her round face lit by a smile.

'Good morning, madam. I let you lie a bit. You didn't sleep so well, I think. Over-tired from yesterday.' So many preparations, so much to do, that they had not had one moment's respite, and Kate's mind had continued to turn over and over long after she was in bed.

'As I guess you were too, and here you are up and dressed!' She took Jane's hand and slid to her feet. An astringent perfume reached her, from the bowl of warm water Jane had put ready on the chest at the foot of the bed. 'Rosemary! To liven the brain. That's just what I need.'

'Though not, I think, for remembrance?'

'As if I could ever forget Nicholas!'

'No one did, who knew him.'

Kate gave her a sharp look. 'You sound disapproving.'

'I think even you who loved him so much did not

always approve of what he did. He was a troubled lad, not easy.'

Knowing it was true, she could hardly protest. 'Not any more, from what he wrote.'

'We shall see. But I think today will be good. It's even stopped raining.'

Kate glanced out of the window at the flush of Maytime green revealed by the dawn: new leaves, fresh grass, colour surging up through the dun of winter. Joy drove out the last traces of weariness, the ache in her unrested limbs. Her heart singing, she washed face and hands, rubbed her teeth with a rag, combed her hair before covering it with a clean coif, pulled on fresh linen, fastened bodice and kirtle, with Jane's help. Joy gave fervour to her brief morning devotions. Joy took her on winged feet (though always—*careful now!*—with decorum, an outward appearance of calm and dignity, fitting for the mistress of her household), down the stairs to the hall, where, slowly, reluctantly her family was gathering.

Tousled, sleep-frowsty servants crept yawning into the room, rubbing their eyes: Alice, Moll and Cecily from the kitchen; Sarah the dairymaid; the boy Will, whose mind would always be that of a child; John Emerson, a part of Holywell as long as Kate could remember. Roused from their beds by Jane, the children were dressed and standing in a dutiful line: twelve-year-old Edward, twins Philip and Mariana, nine years old; and—

No, not Toby, again! Kate caught Jane's rueful look,

and the faint shake of the head. Yesterday she would have been (had been) angry and disappointed. Today there was no room for anything but an inward shrug at the inevitable. Time enough for Toby later.

The routine prayers took on new life, new meaning today: the *Pater Noster* and *Ave Maria*, a passage in English from the Papally approved New Testament, prayers for an old servant who was sick, and for the absent Toby, and for the day ahead of them all, ending with the Grace before they were all dismissed to the day's duties and activities.

Once everyone else had gone, she turned to Jane. 'Toby?'

'He rode out early, madam. He would not say where, just went.'

'To the Hall, I suppose.' Kate sighed. 'And then, I trust, to his lessons. But he should have stayed for prayers, he knows that. What can we do?'

Jane shook her head. 'I don't know, madam. But it's often so with lads of his age. Nothing but trouble, yet they grow into fine men in time.'

As Nicholas had done, it seemed. Toby at fourteen was an exasperating reminder of his uncle at that age. But did she have to wait so long for him to change, doing nothing meanwhile to hasten the process?

'I had hoped, after all I said to him last week, after what he did. I thought he'd taken it to heart, that he'd mend his ways at last. And he knows how important today is. If he should not be here when my brother comes...'

'He'll be here, you wait and see, once his lessons are done. To go to church, that was bad of him. But just a bit of youthful rebellion, I'd guess. Or maybe there's a girl he has his eye on. As for today, he'll surely be home for his dinner. You know how he looks forward to his uncle's coming.' As he did, Kate knew, guessing at a kindred spirit in the turbulent young man he scarcely remembered.

Jane ran a consoling hand down Kate's arm. 'Today's for good things.'

'It is. And Toby will love my brother, I know. He could not fail to.'

But there would still be hours to pass before Nicholas could be expected to arrive, long slow hours. Kate heard the young ones read and recite their catechism, as far as they were able; helped Mariana with her embroidery (a piece of work by now grubby from long reluctant hours of sewing, dotted with stains where the child had pricked her finger. Mariana hated embroidery); spent a profitable hour in the stillroom making sweetmeats with some of her precious supply of sugar, and checked that there was enough beer in the brewhouse. After that, she went to the kitchen to supervise the preparation of dinner. Would Nicholas be here to share it with them? She hoped so, very much, and had arranged for something better to be prepared than their usual oatcakes and pottage: a hen (rather old, but palatable enough stewed slowly with onions and good herbs) and a brace of rabbits from the Holywell lands. Tomorrow they would feast indeed, but she wanted

6

today's meal to be a little celebratory too. Please God Nicholas would not arrive too late to enjoy it!

Noon came, their usual time for dinner. The food was ready, the table set in the hall, but there was no sign of Nicholas. Mariana, never patient where her stomach was concerned, whined that she was hungry.

'You will have to wait a little longer.'

'What if he doesn't come for hours?'

'Then we shall have to eat without him. Meanwhile, you must show a little maidenly restraint. Take Philip into the garden. Running around will stop you thinking of your belly.'

But by the middle of the afternoon, with still no sign of their guest (or of Toby), Kate gave in and sat the household down to dinner.

'My brother will have a hard journey, after all the rain.' In telling Jane she was trying to convince herself. 'The roads will be bad, flooded perhaps. I hope no harm's come to him.'

'There's hours of daylight left yet.'

'And still no Toby. Surely he can't mean to spend all day with Hal Featherstone?'

'It wouldn't be the first time.' Jane rested a hand on her arm. 'Never fear, madam. All your menfolk will be safe here by nightfall, I'm sure of it.'

But when dusk came—later than usual, for the day had been bright—there was still no sign of Nicholas. Anxious, deeply disappointed (what if he should not come at all today?) Kate made yet another foray into the kitchen, to check that there was food enough for a late supper, should it be needed, and was making her way back across the passage that ran the length of the house, when Toby burst through the door, stripping his hands of his worn leather gloves.

He saw her, slithered to a halt, pulled off his hat, bowed, then raised anxious eyes to her face; anxious, yes, but with mischief lurking there too.

'Toby, what is the meaning of this? You were not at prayers, nor at dinner. Where have you been?'

'Oh, riding, with Hal.' He bowed his head again, in a gesture that could have been seen as an apology, had it not been for his sly grin. 'For all you know I said my prayers as I rode.'

'I wish I didn't know you better than that.' She gazed at him, shook her head. 'Oh, Toby, I despair sometimes! You know how earnestly I pray for you. I had hoped—If you would only try, really try to do better.'

'Ah, but mother, just think: poor Father Fielding must have something to do when he comes. One of us must have something big to confess, or he'll feel he's wasting his time.' His smile was engaging, wheedling. Against all her righteous instincts, Kate found herself smiling too.

Oh how like Nicholas he was, at this same age, excusing himself for some escapade! Though in Nicholas's case it would likely have been very much worse than simply missing prayers. *Oh, my dear brother! And this dear son, this beloved wayward son...*

'I should punish you.' She failed completely to sound as stern as she ought. 'But your uncle will be here soon, please God, and you not fit to welcome him. Go and make yourself ready.'

He grinned again, accentuating the dimples in his cheeks, sure of himself, of her love for him, a love that would forgive anything.

As she had so often forgiven her brother.

Her late husband had believed in the use of the rod to correct and guide his children, and had made frequent use of it. She had never been able to bring herself to do the same, for all his rebukes for her frailty, though there was very little else in which she'd dared to defy him in life. It was as well he'd regarded her reluctance as a sign of womanly weakness, only to be expected, and taken the painful duty on himself. Or had he found it painful? She had never been sure. He was always so cold about it, so calculating.

As for her, she shrank at the very thought of scarring the tender flesh of her little ones, these precious children, so easily hurt, so easily struck down by illness or accident: fire, a fall from a horse, drowning, too long exposure to cold and hunger. How could she add to their pains? For their soul's sake she would guide and direct them, but gently, keeping their bodies safe and whole. As once she had failed to do, to her eternal regret.

Now, sometimes, faced with Toby's waywardness, she

wondered if she'd been wrong, if she'd been too gentle, too forgiving, if his father's approach would have achieved a better outcome. Yet Nicholas had been beaten in boyhood, with no apparent good effect. Unless—perhaps in the end, this late conversion was part of it, a long matured result. How could she tell?

If only he would come! The old Nicholas had been wholly unreliable. For him to be late or not to arrive at all, would have been almost routine. He would turn up days after he was expected, full of wheedling smiles, the most lame of excuses (if any at all) and the certainty that she would forgive him anything. But that was the old Nicholas. What of the man he had become? Had he really changed so much? Oh, what was he like now, this brother she loved so much?

Very soon she would have to send the children to bed and bar the doors for the night. Perhaps, as she'd hinted to Jane, he'd been delayed for some unavoidable reason: a lame horse, a flooded river; an accident, sickness or worse —Oh, please, not that! Anxiety gnawed at her, along with a flash of anger, that he should do this to her, when she'd so much longed for this day, prepared for it with such loving care. She'd imagined how he would step into the house, impressed by the calm and orderly household over which she presided, warmed by her welcome, feeling that he had come home. Then there was tomorrow: what might this delay mean for tomorrow's plans?

Toby emerged, washed, hair combed, a clean shirt

under his best doublet. The other children gathered with him in the hall, where a supper of bread and cheese was put ready for them. She could delay no longer; she could not have her whole household put to inconvenience because of one predictably unreliable young man. She caught Jane's eye, saw her nod. 'I'll call them to table.'

They took their seats, family and servants together, the hungry children reaching for the food with unmannerly eagerness, Toby muttering under his breath. 'All this trouble, for nothing!'

Kate was on the point of rebuking him when Mariana, whose hearing was sharpest, cried: 'A horse!' Trusty, the house dog, leapt barking to his feet; and a moment later they all heard it, the clatter of hooves in the courtyard.

He was here at last!

Chapter Two

He was a stranger, the mud-spattered man dismounting from his horse. Lean, dark, bearded, he bore no resemblance to the lively fresh-faced boy who had ridden out of Kate's life ten years before.

She made no move towards him, simply stood watching from the doorway with her children beside her, straining to see the least sign of the man she remembered.

John Emerson led the horse away. The stranger stepped towards them, his expression closed, his eyes watchful beneath the brim of his hat.

Little sounds broke into the taut silence: the stamping of the horse as John rubbed him down, the wind in the trees, the restless movement of the children. The thud of Kate's heart sounded loud in her ears. Could this indeed be Nicholas?

He pulled off his hat, held out his arms, smiled —'Sister! Kate!'—and she ran to his embrace.

He *was* the same beloved brother, she knew that now, as he kissed her again and again, held her close; released her so he could turn and swing the younger children in his arms in an exuberant display of affection. Older, leaner, his voice deeper than she remembered, his face scarred and grooved with the years and many unknown cares, he was yet the same dear brother who had parted from her at Haroby on the day she'd watched him go and felt abandoned, alone, bereft.

The same? No, she was wrong. He'd told her he'd changed, and the next moment she knew how much. Once he'd embraced Toby—'Such a fine tall young man, nephew!'—Nicholas stood back, quiet, the laughter gone.

'I would wish to thank God for my safe arrival in this place, dear sister.'

Kate just had time to glimpse the astonishment, even dismay, on Toby's face, before he bent his head over dutifully clasped hands, as she did herself. They all followed her example, standing just where they were in the windy yard, an untidy circle, silent, waiting.

Nicholas drew a deep slow breath, as if gathering all his strength before releasing it in a flow of words. Kate understood enough Latin to know he was thanking God and the Blessed Virgin for his safe arrival, asking for a benediction on his sister's house. It gave her an odd sensation, hearing the holy words from her brother's mouth. So unlike him.

But so like Father Fielding's prayers, on his rare visits to Holywell.

A startling thought shot through Kate. She cast a furtive glance at her brother, seeing the face of a man absorbed in fluent prayer, remote, closed off from any distraction. Could it be—?

She pushed the question aside, deferring hope and fear alike. Perhaps, later on, when she found time to be alone with him, to talk at length and learn what was in his mind and his heart, perhaps then he would tell her, let her know precisely what had brought him to Holywell after all this time, what were his hopes for the days to come. For now, as the prayer ended, there were other more worldly matters to concern her.

'Dear Nicholas, come inside.' She took his hand to lead him indoors. 'You must be tired, and hungry.' She could see how very weary he was, now the first joy of their meeting had faded a little.

'Seeing you again has restored me, Kate, and being here. It's been a long time.' He looked around him at the hall lit with tallow candles (and close by, just a few of the expensive sweet-smelling waxen ones), the worn hangings, the floor strewn with herbs amongst the rushes, the log fire blazing in the great hearth; he was not to know they used peat for everyday warmth, like the poorest of her tenants. 'I can still remember; the feel, the smell. Like coming home. Changed, but not changed.'

As perhaps she could say of him; she had yet to find out. 'Will you eat now, or later?'

He cast a rueful glance at his muddied clothes. 'I think it best if I tidy myself first. But I see you were at supper. Don't let me keep you from it. I shall eat when I'm more fit for company.'

Kate showed him to the best bedchamber (wax candles here too), where she'd ordered a fire to be lit, and lavender-scented water brought to him. 'When you are ready, there'll be supper for you in the parlour.'

* * *

By the time Nicholas joined her in the small painted parlour on the first floor, household prayers had been said and Jane had ushered the children, complaining volubly, to their beds. 'There'll be time enough to enjoy your uncle's company tomorrow.'

Meanwhile, this was Kate's time. She waited while Nicholas, in famished silence, devoured bread and cheese and the remains of a rabbit pie. Washed, hair combed, freshly dressed, he looked almost like the brother she remembered; and yet oddly less so. The way he ate, greedily, as if he had not eaten for days, was just like eighteen-year-old Nicholas: he had always been a boy of fierce appetites. But afterwards, when he took his seat on the richly cushioned chair at the fireside, there was something withdrawn in his expression, a sense of emotion fiercely held back, which was quite unlike the impulsive openness of the lad she had known.

Sitting facing him on a carved chair ungraced with cushions, her hands occupied with her sewing, she watched him, trying to find the right words to put all the questions she longed to ask.

In the end, it was he who spoke first. He reached out and fingered the heavy embroidered damask draped over his sister's lap. 'I would guess this beautiful work is to be a priestly vestment.'

That was something the old Nicholas would not have noticed. 'Yes. Though to an outsider it's a gown for my own use. In fact, it *was* a gown of mine, long ago, a very fine one. But the vestments we had are threadbare and this fabric is still good.'

'And you have no wish now for vain adornments. I see that, in the modesty of your dress.'

She could have said that she had little occasion to wear the few fine clothes that were left to her, but thought better of it, while feeling a twinge of irritation at his comment about her modest dress. The dark velvet she wore was her very best gown, the ruff crisply white and starched, all put on in his honour.

Nicholas fell silent again, but it was a contented silence. Having taken a slow reflective drink of their best ale, he laid the tankard down on a nearby table, stretched his legs towards the fire, flung his arms back to clasp hands behind his head.

'Oh, it's good to be here!' His gaze was full of tenderness. Silence, then: 'I think this might be the moment.' He reached under the chair and took out a package wrapped in cloth, which he handed to her. 'A fitting gift for a dear sister, to whom I owe so much.'

'There was no need! It's enough that you're here. But thank you.' She unwrapped the package, disclosing a little book: *A Short Rule of Good Life. Newly Set Forth According to the Authours Direction before His Death*. 'Oh!' She gave Nicholas a questioning look.

'It was written by the blessed martyr Father Robert Southwell.' He saw that the name meant nothing to her. 'Of the Society of Jesus. He was cruelly tortured by that devil Topcliffe, and martyred at Tyburn in '95, in February. You must have had news of him!'

Every Catholic knew of Topcliffe, Queen Elizabeth's notorious torturer, but of this one of his victims—no. Her thoughts rolled back. Nine years ago…

'That winter, Sir Thomas had just died. I was brought to bed with the twins.' It was as if a dark shadow had fallen over her. She shivered. 'It was then—'

'Of course. You had other concerns at the time. I understand.' His hand closed over hers. 'Now you can make the acquaintance of the holy author of this book. It was printed secretly in London. Guard it well! And I urge you to read it and make it the pattern for your life. Guided by it, your home will surely become a place of order and peace and piety.' He hesitated, his eyes on her face, perhaps gauging something of her astonishment at the way he spoke, her prickle of resentment at his exhortation, she who through his troubled youth had tried to be his guide and protector, as far as she was able.

'Oh, I'm sure this place is already such a household!' he put in quickly, before continuing in the careful considered manner that was so unlike his old impetuous speech. 'But I think there are none of us so perfect that we cannot benefit from the teaching of a saint. Father Southwell offers a guide for each moment of every day, so that all may be made holy, as in a monastery.' He took the book from her, turning the pages, pausing now and then to read a sentence or show her a particularly impressive passage. 'He wrote for just such women as you, Catholic wives and mothers, or holy widows, in whose hands lie the spiritual welfare of their children and their households, establishing there a fortress against the heretic world outside. I know myself, from my own experience, what such an example can do, for which I cannot find words to thank you enough. That is how it ought to be in every household that calls itself Catholic. Holy lives, filled with prayer and lived without compromise, with the sacraments at their heart.'

'When we can get them,' Kate put in wryly. 'It's more than a year now since any priest came near us.'

'Ah, I hoped you had a more frequent ministry!'

'Our priest Father Fielding does what he can, though he's no longer a young man. But he lodges mostly in Northumberland, and has many households to visit.'

'Is there not a priest at Ashburn Hall? The Wynyards have not turned apostate, surely?'

'There's only old Mistress Wynyard left. She keeps herself to herself, and has a name for watching every penny. There's a nephew will inherit one day, I believe, though I know nothing of him. Father Fielding calls on her too, but he's hardly made welcome.'

'And you haven't the means to provide safe lodging for a priest—which you would do if you could, I know that. But even without that blessing, this household of yours can offer a faint reflection of our eternal home; indeed, I feel sure it does already. Tell me, are you much troubled by pursuivants, or the penal laws in general?'

'Not at all, thank God, not since we came here!' She shivered, memory pierced by visions of soldiers coming in the night, flaming torches casting long leaping shadows; the house ransacked, the days of work it took to put things right; the fear left behind, even when no incriminating trace of their Catholic faith had been found. It had happened twice to her, at her uncle's house before she was married, and again at Haroby in the year of the Armada, occasions seared on her memory. 'Our neighbour Sir Cuthbert Featherstone, though a magistrate, has always sheltered us from persecution, perhaps because he was reared a Catholic. We have never even been fined for non-attendance at church. The best of neighbours and a good man, if any Protestant can be called so.'

'Hmm. An apostate.'

Kate heard the disapproval in his voice. There were, she knew, some Catholics who abhorred any compromise with Protestants, even the least contact. Afraid of finding Nicholas was of that kind, she changed the subject.

'I have so many questions. You said nothing in your letter, except that you were coming to visit us here. Not even why you were coming.'

'Is it not enough that I wish to see you?' He gave a rueful half-smile.

'Of course. More than enough. Yet—Well, we've heard nothing from you for years. Since before…Not since we came here.'

'Nor I from you.'

She felt a tremor of irritation. 'How could you, when I had no idea where you were? You just disappeared.'

'At Sir Thomas's bidding.'

'He's been dead these nine years.'

There was a pause, then: 'For a long time I did not know what had become of you. I came back to Haroby once, to find you gone and the place deserted. No one would tell me anything, except that Sir Thomas was dead. So, failing all else, I went for a soldier, to Flanders, until two months gone.'

'Then how did you know where to find me this time?'

'Oh, I went to Ashby.'

'Ashby?'

'Ashby St Ledgers, where I live now.' He must have seen the question in her eyes. 'You know Great Ashby, the home of the Vaux sisters?'

'I know of it, yes.'

'It's not far from there, in Northamptonshire. Closer to Haroby, in fact.'

She had no recollection of the place. 'What took you there?'

'I serve in the household of Lady Anne Catesby. You know she's some kind of kin to the Vauxs? I met her son Robert, by chance, in London, on my return to England. He like me has found his way back to the church.' All at once his face looked as if a light had somehow been lit beneath the skin. 'Perhaps that's what he saw in me, something of himself. I'm thankful he did. Ashby is like Holywell, a haven for those of our faith.'

'I don't remember them, the Catesbys.'

'No, they would not have been at Ashby then. Lady Anne went there on her widowhood, five years ago, as you came here: it was her jointure. As well as the Vauxs, the Catesbys are kin to the Throckmortons at Coughton.'

'I see.' Now and then a priest harboured by the Throckmorton family, or by one of their numerous Catholic relations, had made a furtive visit to Haroby, tolerated, just, by Sir Thomas. Which reminded her of the question that had slipped into her mind at supper. Unsure what answer she hoped to hear, she drew a deep breath. 'Nicholas, you've said nothing of any woman, nor of marriage.'

'Oh, there have been—well, not anything fit to speak of before my sister. And marriage, no. I have never had the means, nor the opportunity. Nor perhaps the inclination.'

Then, the question she had been working towards: 'Have you thoughts of entering the priesthood?'

She saw a startled look in his eyes and decided she'd been completely mistaken. Then he said slowly: 'It has been in my mind. I have prayed for guidance. I'm still not sure.'

Fear clutched at her; she knew only too well, as he must too, how hazardous was the life of a priest in England, how often short and full of suffering. The book Nicholas had given her, the work of a martyred priest, underlined the dangers.

Yet the same prospect offered possibilities. 'You could come and live here, as a priest. No one would think anything of it, my brother under my roof. You could act as my steward! Oh, I know accounts were never your strong point, but you would only need to be a steward in name. I am not truly in need of one.'

'I suppose there was a steward cared for the place before you came here. You kept him on then?'

Cold hooded eyes, giving nothing away; a thin pale face...She gave a little shiver. 'No, William Fowler was too much my husband's man. It was he—Enough to say I could not keep him on. I manage without.'

'You don't have a steward! It's heavy work for a lone woman, looking after your estate.'

'It's not so great an estate. It never has been. I have a bailiff, who collects the rents for me. Andrew Wardle, at Low Burnside Farm.'

'One of your farms? Is he trustworthy?'

She felt a quiver of resentment that he should question her so closely, as if he mistrusted her judgement. She was annoyed to find herself colouring. 'He's—well, honest, loyal, a good Catholic, a man who understands husbandry. But not greatly lettered, nor skilled with accounts.'

'I see. That must make hard work for you.'

'There is someone who oversees him, and advises me, when I am in need: Master Gervase Langley.'

'A steward then, surely?'

'He is a neighbour. A good man and a good friend. But —' She hesitated, wary of his reaction. 'He is the parish— the protestant parson of Meadhope, the rector.'

'That's not good. For such a man to have power over your tenants.' The cold blast of his disapproval hit her, though his voice was quiet enough. 'Do you not fear for the example to them? Worse, to your children?'

She felt her heart thump. What would he say if she were to tell him the rector of Meadhope was also tutor to Toby and Edward, as well as to Sir Cuthbert's son? 'He is discreet and knows he must not trouble them nor me. He is a man of wide views. He is celibate, and I wonder even if he has Catholic sympathies at heart, though kept well hidden, naturally.'

'Then he perjures his immortal soul.' Nicholas frowned. 'I hadn't expected this. It almost makes me think I should accept what you suggest, to keep you safe from the taint of heresy. But I'm not sure. I need time, and prayer. And there are other concerns. I shall stay here with you for a time, though I think it best that I return to Ashby before too long, until the way becomes clear and we see how the land lies.'

She caught at a possible meaning behind his words. 'Oh, do you mean toleration, if it comes? Do you think it's true what they've been saying? I heard it from Father Fielding, who was sure of it. He says this new Scottish King will allow us to worship without vexation, as soon as the times are right.'

'So he promised. We had it on the best authority. But the signs are not good, and in any case mere toleration is not enough. Our aim must always be to have England restored to the true faith.'

'I pray for it daily, of course.' It was the appropriate response, but so remote a possibility that she did not really believe it would ever come about. 'But just to have things a little easier, so we can live at peace…Only sometimes it seems that just when everything looks more hopeful, somebody does something really stupid and it all gets difficult again for us.'

'Ah, you're thinking of that affair last year. It was an ill-conceived plot by a tiny faction, led by a lunatic in the guise of a priest. It was never going to work. But I do believe better times will come, somehow. There is still a faint hope that King James may have a change of heart; he has scarcely been a year on the throne. And the Queen is of our faith, it seems, though she keeps it quiet. And remember who his mother was. That must mean something to him.'

The hope of so many English Catholics, Mary Queen of Scots, who ended her life imprisoned and condemned by her cousin Queen Elizabeth: 'He was taken from her as a child, and raised a Protestant. I know better than most how little his mother may now be to him.' It was not quite the same, but there were parallels.

It did not need the rough edge to her voice to remind Nicholas what she meant, what she was feeling. 'Nor do you know what Thomas truly thinks and believes. He is not free now to act as he wishes, but the heart is hidden. When the day comes, then—' He broke off, paused, then went on in quite another tone, brisk, matter-of-fact, as if he wanted to get it over with: 'Did you know he was wed last month?'

The words stabbed her to the heart. She drew a sharp breath against the pain, her hands stilled, her eyes on her brother's grave face. 'Who…?' Faltering, she found she could not shape the question.

'Mistress Lucy Machyn.'

Of course; his guardian's daughter, almost certainly a Protestant like her father. Had Thomas at nineteen years old had any say in the matter? Probably not. Did he retain any knowledge of the faith in which, until his eleventh year, she had so carefully nurtured him, and to which he'd promised he'd always be true? She had no idea. As Nicholas had said, one could not know what lay in his heart. As for the marriage, she had guessed long ago, as perhaps even his father had intended, that this marriage would be his eventual fate. How could Tom's guardian resist the opportunity to unite two great estates, by marrying his only daughter to his dead kinsman's heir?

Nothing was said for what seemed an age. Kate returned her gaze to her needlework, though she made no attempt to take it up again. So many memories suddenly brought to life, turning in her head!

Draining the last dregs from his tankard, Nicholas watched her.

'Tom's still young. There's still time for him to return to the church. Perhaps at heart he has always been faithful.'

She raised her eyes again, hungry for consolation. 'Do you ever see him?' He'd said that Ashby St Ledgers was not far from Haroby; near enough indeed for him to have news from there.

'I'm sorry, no. We move in different circles. And he lives at Silworth, at Roger Machyn's place, not at Haroby. It's further from Ashby.' He changed the subject. 'And what of my other nephews and nieces? What hopes do you have for them?'

'The greatest hope is that King James will allow us to live free of persecution.'

'Amen to that. But we must not ask for ease, or perhaps even hope for it.'

'No.' *Yet why not?* she asked herself. Life had been hard enough, still was in many ways, and Toby at least would be much easier to handle if their Catholicism were no obstacle to a normal life. But she sensed that to say this would risk destroying her brother's admiring view of her, and she did not want that. For he was right, as the church had always taught: suffering was to be welcomed, making the sufferer more sure of bliss in the next world.

'You'll remember Margaret?'

'Thin little thing, a bit younger than Tom? Not much to say for herself.'

'But always devout and eager for the religious life. She's already overseas, with the Benedictines in Brussels. Edward is soon to go overseas too. Father Fielding found a kind benefactress, a widow of some means in Newcastle. She will pay for Edward's journey and all that is needful. She did the same for Margaret.'

'That was generous of her.'

'Indeed. As for the twins, I don't know. Philip—well, you must have seen.'

'I have the impression he is not strong, neither in body nor perhaps in mind.' All at once, Nicholas's voice was very gentle.

'No. I think—I know—the journey here, when he was just a babe. He nearly died. And since, well!' The old guilt pierced her, though she tried not to let it show. She cleared her throat. 'As for Mariana, I think she is unlikely to have a calling to the religious life.'

'People can change.' He was smiling a little. 'She is young yet.'

'That's true. We shall have to see.' She hoped he hadn't noticed that she'd completely failed to mention Toby, whose latest escapade had been to attend Sunday worship at the heretic village church.

'And if there comes a day when they're off your hands, into God's care, if you are still living on that day—what then? The religious life for you too? I would pray for such an outcome.'

I would not! The thought, unbidden, startled her. What could be more desirable, for a widow with no other demands on her time and energy, than a life given over to prayer, to poverty, chastity and obedience? It was the last of the monastic vows that made her shudder. Here at Holywell she might be poor, dependant often on the charity of neighbours; she might inevitably be chaste, the late Sir Thomas having left her with little inclination for sharing her bed with anyone, even had she had the opportunity. But the one thing she most valued was that here there was no one to command her, to tell her what she must do, how she must run her household or rear her children; to rule her life, as her husband once had done. She might sometimes feel weary of the endless demands on her time, the daily need to make decisions for her household, but she had no wish to yield that responsibility to anyone else.

'I think I am not called to such a life.' She chose the words with care.

'Then I think perhaps I see a better future for you, once the children are grown and out of your care.' Nicholas took her hands in his, his voice warm with a strange kind of passion, his brown eyes lit with an intense gleam far removed from the dancing brightness of the old days. His gaze seemed to read her very soul in a way she found increasingly uncomfortable. 'The gift I gave you will show you the way, as I've already hinted. Holywell is surely destined to become a haven for priests, a centre for worship. If you like, a monastery in all but name, a place apart. I have seen the good such places do, the example they show the heretics. You may already be close to establishing such a place with your little flock. It could be so much more when you have no other call on your resources, and only your own safety to consider.'

'Perhaps.' Why did the very thought chill her? What better aim could she have, as a Catholic widow?

Something must have shown on her face, for Nicholas released her hands and straightened. 'Dear sister, we've sat up long enough, I think.'

'Oh, forgive me! After such a long journey, I should not have kept you talking so late.'

'No—no! I'm so glad to have had this time. I hope we shall have many more such while I am here. But for now...'

'Time for bed.' She laid her sewing aside, wrapping it carefully in clean linen, placing it on top of the book he had given her.

He got to his feet. 'And tomorrow is the feast of the Ascension. But there will be no Mass celebrated here?'

'I'm afraid not. But we'll have music at our morning prayers. We've been practising hard. And we'll have a feast too, in honour of the day, to make up for your scanty meal this evening. We're bidden to Meadhope Hall, to dine with Sir Cuthbert Featherstone and his family.'

She knew then how completely she'd misjudged the situation. She felt the shift in the atmosphere before ever Nicholas turned his fierce frowning gaze on her.

'I will not break bread with apostates and heretics.'

Shocked, not fully understanding, she stared at him. 'They are our good neighbours, our friends.'

'That you can speak of them so, think of this so lightly

—that shocks me, Kate.'

She forced herself to return his gaze, though its intensity chilled her. 'But you must surely sometimes gather with your neighbours? We did often at Haroby. And even our uncle, who was so strict…'

'I will sit at table with heretics and apostates only if the needs of the church demand it, and then unwillingly. But not ever in friendship or what you call neighbourliness.'

'Never? Not ever?'

'Did I not make myself clear?' His eyes glittered, his voice was taut with anger. 'I fear you have fallen away somewhat. I thought better of you than this.'

She tried to push aside a tremor of guilt, but her voice had all the defensiveness of a naughty child. 'I only do what we always did.'

'You saw what that led to. Why else did you snatch your little ones from Haroby and come here? For the safety of their souls, was it not?'

She bent her head, her fingers twisting together in her lap. Memories: terror, hunger, sickness—and Philip, her daily reminder. 'It did not save Tom. They nearly died, because of me.'

'Better that than to burn in hell for ever.'

She shivered. So she had thought once, in the madness of that time.

'Would you do otherwise now? Surely not!'

She looked up at him, meeting his gaze, implacable, searching. 'I don't know. I think perhaps—I don't know.'

Then: 'Nicholas, they're expecting us, tomorrow.'

'Then you may go, if you must. I shall not. I would sooner eat plain food here at Holywell than share a feast with heretics.'

This was not what she'd planned or hoped for. But what could she do? She was too weary and troubled to argue further. 'Perhaps we should speak again in the morning, when we've slept. We're both tired. Let's say goodnight for now.'

'And pray earnestly to do what's right.' His expression abruptly softening, Nicholas embraced her. 'Good night, dear Kate. God give you quiet rest.'

Kate knew quite well that she had no hope of any kind of rest, quiet or otherwise, for all her bodily weariness.

As she stepped into her bedchamber, she hoped to find that Jane was still awake. She wanted so much to talk over this evening, to try and settle her mind. But Jane was sleeping soundly, though she'd left a candle burning on the small table beside the bed, enough to light the way as Kate undressed and slipped under the covers, to lie there with her head spinning, anxiety and doubt and heartache tumbling over and over one another.

What was she to do about tomorrow's planned feast, if after a night's reflection Nicholas still refused to go? It would be disrespectful to her kind neighbours to turn down their invitation at the very last minute. She had at first planned to invite them all to dine at Holywell, to make her brother's acquaintance. What would Nicholas have done if that had been the arrangement? Refused to come to table in her own house? It was as well perhaps that Sir Cuthbert, mindful as always of her limited means, had instead suggested they come to Meadhope, but that did not make it very much easier. She could hardly leave her brother to dine here alone on his very first day at Holywell. She felt angry with Nicholas for putting her in so difficult a position, and yet guilty too. Was he right, and ought she to have kept herself apart from her heretic neighbours? She had blamed her husband for the compromises that had led to the ultimate betrayal, but she had never thought that she might now be leading her family on the same path, for she herself had never compromised in the things that mattered.

Only there was Toby, going to church...

Her thoughts churned in her mind, finding no solution, beyond hoping that by morning Nicholas would have relented, softened by a good night's sleep. The wayward boy seemed to have become a rigidly principled man. Her prayers had been answered, but she was not sure she welcomed the result. She wished she could have seen some sign left of the boy she had once known so well.

And there was that other boy who had grown up in ways she could only guess at. Nicholas's news of Tom had caught her unawares, savagely prodding an old wound to searing life. It had always been there, for nine long years, but she had somehow learned to live with it, to push it away from the forefront of her mind. Until tonight, when

Nicholas spoke of where he lived now; and what he had learned.

She tried to pray, tried to offer her grief to God, but nothing seemed to break through the relentless turmoil of her thoughts, her revived memories. Prayer eluded her as much as sleep.

A grey rain-washed dawn was already breaking when she gave up and crept into the tiny panelled closet off her bedchamber which was her private retreat, and knelt there at the prie-dieu, the prayer desk where morning and evening she offered her dutiful private devotions. She'd brought her rosary with her from under her pillow, letting the beads drop mechanically, silently, through her fingers, while her body ached and her thoughts raged and churned with the news that Nicholas had brought.

Her own son, her firstborn, and she had not even seen him wed!

She had not even *seen* him for years, nor put her arms about him, touched his thick brown hair, heard how his voice sounded now it would have settled into the deep tones of manhood. Would she even know him were they ever to meet again?

She opened her eyes and raised her head. Against the rain, snaking in miniature rivers down the uneven window pane, she seemed to see his face, the beloved features caught for an instant and then gone. If she could have held on to it, the face would have been the one she had seen turned for one last look on the day they took him away, not the face of the man he had become, the man she did not know.

A boy of eleven, taken from her on June 13th, the feast of St Anthony of Padua—two weeks today, coming round again as it did every year to jolt her into recollection. Not that she ever quite forgot, even though there had been nothing at all in the long years to bring him to mind, no letter, no news even; until yesterday. Sometimes she'd even found herself wondering if his death would have been easier to bear. Had he died, she would have had the rituals of death for consolation, as she had for the other little ones who had died in infancy, Frances and John and her stepdaughter Anne, snatched from her by that terrible fever. For them she'd had Masses said, and their graves though far from here were places she was free to visit. Where Tom was concerned she'd been left only with her private devotions and a perpetual ache of loss, an open wound that had never quite healed, made worse by her fear for his immortal soul. No, death would not be better, if she could not be sure his soul was safe.

Blessed St Anthony, seek out my lost son. Mother of God, have pity on me and on my dear son. Bring him home: home to the true faith, home to his grieving mother.

And please let Nicholas come with us to Meadhope tomorrow, so I don't have to offend anyone!

Chapter Three

'We'll manage fine.' This was Jane's response when told that they would stay at Holywell today, as Nicholas was resolute in his refusal to go to Meadhope. 'Good thing we have that suckling pig ready. There's just time to get it roasted. There'll be enough for us to have a good feast.'

'I've sent word to Sir Cuthbert.'

'That your brother was weary from his journey, so you'd sooner dine quietly at home?' Head tilted sideways, wry smile, raised eyebrows: it was clear that Jane did not give credit to any of it. That was no surprise, since Nicholas had emerged from his room this morning with no visible trace of yesterday's weariness; unlike Kate, who felt irritable and exhausted. Later perhaps she would tell Jane the true reason, which she could not possibly have given to their neighbour.

Jane's pragmatic response to the change of plans was consoling, as was her conviction that Sir Cuthbert would think none the worse of her for it—which was proved when John, returning from delivering the message to Meadhope Hall, presented her with a massive venison pie, compliments of Sir Cuthbert, bringing tears of gratitude to Kate's eyes.

As for the children, she took them on one side when Nicholas was out of earshot and told them the same lie, knowing how disappointed they would be. They'd looked forward to feasting with the Featherstones, whose hospitality was generous and their cook truly accomplished.

'We shall have our own special feast here, with your uncle.' She'd already given orders for the suckling pig to be put on the spit, and other delicacies to be prepared. She hoped it would be enough to mollify them.

After breakfast, as already planned, there was the morning worship for Ascension Day. As she'd told Nicholas, they had been practising the music, *Haec Dies* by William Byrd, its six parts somehow mangled into four, to suit their limited skills. 'I know it's meant for Easter, but I don't think that matters.' Nicholas knew the work too, his voice tunefully augmenting the lower notes; and he read the appropriate Bible passages with great expression, which must, Kate thought, have brought their meaning home to the little ones—even to Toby, who seemed more attentive than usual.

There were no lessons today, for the festival, so the children were despatched to the garden after the service, while Kate supervised preparations in the kitchen. Nicholas disappeared to his room, to pray, he told Kate. Toby, who had looked forward to begging soldiers' tales from his uncle, shrugged off his disappointment and went outside to romp with the younger children, as if he were himself a child again.

It *had* been for the best after all. Casting a last critical eye over the tables made ready for the feast, confident that the food was fit to be served, Kate was glad that they were to dine at home. She was glad that her brother would be able to see how capable a housewife she was, she who had ruled over her small fiefdom for nine years without the aid of husband, father or brother. This rapidly prepared feast would be as enjoyable and happy an occasion as any at Meadhope Hall; those she loved best in all the world gathered to eat together under her roof, provided for by her household. Well, not quite every one, but as nearly so as she could hope for.

Tidy, dressed in their best, the family assembled in the hall. Nicholas came to take his place beside her at the top table, where the children too would be seated, as they would not have been allowed to do among the greater number of adults at Meadhope. Nicholas remained on his feet beside his chair, laying a hand on Kate's shoulder.

'Allow me to say grace before we eat.'

Since her husband's death, this had been Kate's duty. For a moment she hesitated, fighting a quiver of indignation. But what could be more seemly than for Nicholas to do it, as the senior male family member at the table? 'Of course. Please do.'

She always took care to keep her graces short, as Nicholas surely would too. She remembered how he used to complain vociferously about Sir Thomas's long prayers.

But if Kate remembered, it seemed her brother had forgotten, or now thought very differently about it. The old Nicholas would have hated the long Latin grace that the new Nicholas poured out over the still empty table, while

Alice and Moll hovered in the doorway with the dishes to be served, the cooked meats rapidly cooling. Even to Kate, it seemed to drag on interminably, as her stomach growled and churned. She heard Toby shuffle restlessly; his foot hit the table leg—by mistake, or in protest? He coughed, fidgeted again; Nicholas went smoothly on, as if he'd heard nothing. A repeat performance from Toby: should she look up, frown at him? Would he notice if she did?

There was a pause in the flow of words. The end? *Thank the*—! No, for he resumed, as if he'd simply been drawing breath to give impetus to the elaborate sentences that followed. On, and on, and on. Would he never finish?

At last! *'Gloria Patri et Filio, et Spiritui Sancto. Amen.'*

She heard Toby's very audible sigh of relief, but when she tried to catch his eye he deliberately avoided her gaze.

They took their seats on the benches about the table, while the servants laid out the dishes. Nicholas, in the armchair at the table's centre, looked from one end to the other, taking in the cooked meats (salt beef, roast pork, the venison pie, the inevitable rabbits), the fine white bread, the buttered leeks and turnips, all presented as decoratively as the skills of Holywell permitted. 'Well, sister, this is a fine spread! This is what every soldier dreams of!'

Was there just a trace of disapproval in his voice? She cast an anxious glance in his direction, but his eyes told her that he knew this was something out of the ordinary and not their usual plain fare.

She ventured a light-hearted response. 'Ah, is that why

you've graced Holywell with your presence? You've tired of army rations and come home to fatten yourself!'

She thought for a horrible moment that he was offended by her teasing, for there was no answering smile. A pause, while she watched him, saw with relief that there was after all a rueful twist to his mouth. 'You know me too well, dear sister!' He tore a hunk of bread in pieces, dunked one in the meat juices on his plate (they were using the best pewter plates, not the everyday wooden ones).

'Sir, what do you eat in the army?' That was Mariana, who loved her food and sometimes seemed to think of little else. Kate wondered whether to rebuke the child for intruding into adult conversation without permission, but stayed silent, seeing that Nicholas was smiling at his niece.

'Oh, whatever we could get. Rats, dogs, cats.' He grinned at her screwed up face. 'Sometimes good food, but not often. And never as good as this. You eat well at Holywell, little mistress.'

'Is that really why you gave up soldiering, sir, because of the food?'

'Have you left the army, sir?' Toby was gazing at him in dismay. 'Why would you do that? Is it not a fine way of life?'

'It is very fine to fight with all one's heart and soul for a good cause. Spain's campaign against the heretic rebels in Flanders—to me, once, that was a clear cause for which a man would gladly lay down his life. But there are many temptations, many evil things done in war. It is not all clean and honourable, by no means. And there are other ways to serve. Times are changing, have changed.'

'Were you a captain? Did you lead your men in battle?'

'That is in the past, Toby. I do not ask to lead, nor ever have; rather to be led, by the example of Our Lady and the blessed Saints, walking in their footsteps.'

Kate thought she saw a flicker of distaste in Toby's eyes. 'I just wanted to know, that's all.' He frowned. 'I'd wish to be a soldier, one day. There isn't anything else I'll be fit for.'

'Who knows, nephew? Pray for guidance, ask to be shown the way. Don't assume you know it for yourself.'

'Why did *you* go for a soldier?'

'It was, I fear, by my own selfish will, even from rage. I thought life had treated me harshly, that it was unfair. Perhaps you have some such feeling sometimes. But by the intercessions of your mother and those who truly cared for me I was led through God's grace into a new and better life. Now I know that to follow my will is not the way.'

'But how do you know when it's not just your will?'

'Pray earnestly and often. Be guided by your mother, and above all your confessor. Then you will know.'

That silenced Toby, who gazed truculently at his plate, scooping food into his mouth as if to feed his angry disappointment. It did not help that Edward, usually the least assertive of the children, began a pious exchange with his uncle, about how he had been guided to seek his vocation as a priest. Nicholas's approval filled his voice with warmth and affection.

'There's no higher calling, as I'm sure you know. Are you bound for the seminary at Douai?'

Edward cast an enquiring glance at his mother. 'I don't think so. Father Fielding says—'

'It is not yet finally decided. We will be guided by Father Fielding.' Who detested what he called 'the Jesuit faction' that dominated the seminary in the Low Countries where priests for the English mission field were trained: some protective instinct told Kate it was better left at that, as far as her brother was concerned. Last night's conversation had made her wary.

'Please God that by the time you are ordained priest, England will be Catholic once again, the churches cleansed of heresy, acceptable for our use.'

'Oh that would be wonderful, sir.' Edward's eyes were shining. 'Do you think it possible?'

'Anything is p—'

Toby gulped a mouthful of meat; broke in: 'Once you rode your horse right into the hall at Haroby. A big black horse.'

He flinched in the face of Nicholas's scowl.

'I'd have thought you too young to remember that.'

'Oh, but there was such a commotion. My father was *so* angry!'

At that moment Kate glanced along the table to where the servants were seated at the far end of the hall, catching Jane's eye, and her faint smile. She remembered that day so well! Sir Thomas had indeed been furious; the more so because many of the servants, his children and even (he feared) his wife had found it hilarious.

Returning her gaze to her brother she saw that Nicholas now took a very different view of the escapade. 'You would do well to forget that incident. The devil and his angels had me in their clutches for many years. It is a matter for great thankfulness that I have been wrested from their grasp. I have long since repented of the offences of my youth, and done due penance for them. If I could wipe them from all memory, I would be content. Above all, I would not have anyone led into sin by my example.'

Toby relapsed into a sullen silence. There was for a time no sound but the clatter of spoons on pewter, drinks being gulped, the steps of servants bringing more food, removing empty dishes. Kate's spirits plummeted. She had hoped for so much from this reunion, yet now the air seemed full of hostility and disappointment. She searched her mind for something to say that might lighten the mood about the table, but it was Nicholas who spoke first.

'Do you ever have readings while you eat, sister?'

'Not often. Sometimes. Always in Holy Week.'

'The lives of the saints.' Toby's voice was heavy with boredom. 'The same old things, over and over.'

'Toby! Any more talk like that and you'll be sent from the table.'

'Your pardon, mother.' His shrug rather belied the apology.

Kate, troubled, watched her son. She knew how much he'd been looking forward to this visit, as she had done, though she guessed there'd been an element of hero-worship in his anticipation, based on little more than knowing that his uncle was a soldier and had led a wild youth. She had not thought he would have any memory of such things; he'd been only five years old when Nicholas had left Haroby for the last time.

Stirring within her was an uneasy sense that she too, like Toby, was regretful for the loss of the old Nicholas. But surely not? How could she even begin to think that, she who had prayed and prayed that her wild brother would find the right path, as he so clearly had?

Yet, he seemed so different, this young man who had so newly arrived. After the first joyous moments, she'd found it hard to know what manner of man he had become, how much, if anything, was left of the old Nicholas. Had the little brother she'd so deeply loved, who had brought such joy into her life even as she despaired of his wild ways, been replaced by a grimly censorious young man by whom she felt judged and found wanting?

Of course not, she told herself. The very idea was ridiculous! He was still Nicholas; she had only to get to know him all over again. The brother she remembered, whom she'd loved and cared for and tried to guide, and who loved her, was still there, but changed for the better in a way that could only make her love him the more, once he allowed her into his heart.

'Now, little mistress Mariana, tell me what story you like best, of all those you've heard?'

That was better! Nicholas was clearly trying to ease the strained atmosphere that had fallen over the company.

'I like Jane's stories best. She used to tell us about—'

'Sir, I like the story of Saint Godric. John told us about him.'

'Ah, Master Edward, I'm glad that you favour your local saints. And this man John, who told you the tale? That's John Emerson?' His glance took in Kate's confirmatory nod. 'Now, tell me, what is it that so attracts you about Saint Godric?'

'Oh, he had adventures, and then he was holy too.'

Kate saw Toby scowl, but was glad that Nicholas seemed to have enticed the usually reticent Edward into easy conversation, even if it was not of a kind likely to appeal to his older brother. She could see that Mariana too was feeling rebuffed and ignored, but then as a girl she must expect such treatment, a sad but necessary fact of life.

Having recounted what he recalled of the life of Saint Godric, Edward was once more consumed with shyness. Into the silence that followed, Nicholas returned his attention to Kate. 'Your sons do not wait at table, yet Toby is of an age to do so. Do you not require that of them?'

She felt herself colouring, swept again by the uncomfortable sense that she was being scolded, that she had fallen short of her brother's expectations of her. She forced a confident reply. 'I expect it, very often. But today I thought it an occasion for us all to be seated together.'

An occasion filled with love and laughter, a family reunited—and instead she had this, an awkward, uneasy meal that was nothing like Kate had imagined or hoped for. More dishes were brought to the table, cups were filled and emptied and filled again (though she saw that Nicholas drank little), while the conversation jolted spasmodically from one topic to another, interspersed with uncomfortable silences.

A solid lump of disappointment grew and set inside Kate, so that by the end of the meal she was close to tears. She forced them back, determined that something should be salvaged from the ruins of her hopes.

She rose from her seat and clapped her hands. 'Now, I think, for some dancing!'

There would be dancing at Meadhope Hall today, but she did not see why the children should miss that too. She saw the delight on their faces, sweeping away all the restraint of the meal. The tables were cleared and pushed aside, John Emerson brought out his fiddle and the dancing began. Kate had feared that her brother would find some excuse not to join them, but instead he took the twins' hands in his and led them onto the floor. Feeling her spirits lift, she reached out to Toby, who still hung back, looking morose.

Another reluctant shrug, though he came to her side. 'There'll be better dancing at the Hall. Much better.'

'You are not at the Hall. So you'll just have to make the

best of it.' She took his hand. 'Come now. You know how you love to dance.'

She was relieved that his sullen mood was not long resistant to the lilt of the music.

'It was a good day, in the end.' Kate's thoughts were full of the dancing, of her brother restored to the boy she remembered, enjoying every moment, laughing and teasing.

Jane studied her face, as far as she could make out its features in the flickering candlelight. 'Master Toby cast off his sulks for a bit. And did you see Mariana? She loves dancing, that one.'

'We all do.' Kate sighed, reluctantly admitting the truth. 'But without that—and at prayers…I would wish Toby would be more mannerly.'

Her son had not even tried to hide his boredom at evening prayers, all his resentment returning to the surface.

'He's only as his uncle used to be.' Kate, on a stool by the window of the bedchamber, had her head bent, so Jane could not read her expression. She said carefully, 'Perhaps you would hope he would one day be as Master Nicholas is now.' It was, Kate knew, a question, if she chose to take it as such.

She looked up. 'I don't know. I ought to wish it, I think. But—oh, I knew he'd changed. He told me so. But sometimes I've felt there's nothing left, just a stranger.'

'He was a boy when he went away. He's a man now.

You could not expect him to stay the same, whatever happened.' Jane ventured to sit beside her. 'The pretext you gave, for dining here today instead of at Meadhope: that was not the real reason, was it? He was a good deal fresher than you this morning, not like a man in need of rest.'

'I had to give a reason that could be spoken in public. But no, it was not true. An excuse, that's all.'

'He would not go? Not from weariness.'

'No, for conscience sake. He would not eat with heretics, he said.'

Jane gave a soundless whistle. 'That's harsh! You'd soon have no friends outside these walls. Or do you think him reasonable?'

'No, how could I?' She sighed. 'I don't know, to tell the truth. It troubles my conscience. I don't know what to think.'

'You're tired. You need sleep. It may be that everything will seem different in the morning.' She ran a consoling hand down Kate's arm. 'I know what store you set by his coming.'

'Too much, I think.' A little later, as Jane pulled the curtains about the bed, Kate added, 'The strangest thing, is to have him rebuke me: Nicholas, of all people! Perhaps I've been too long without a man to guide me.'

'Nonsense. You've managed fine. You need no man to tell you what's right.'

'Just you then?'

'Now that makes more sense!'

Chapter Four

'Allow me to lead our devotions this morning, sister.'

Neither Nicholas's tone nor his expression invited the possibility of a polite refusal, so Kate agreed, though she saw how Toby scowled at the prospect. She, like her son, would have welcomed a brief session today, and she guessed that was not what would follow, even though there was no longer the excuse of a major festival.

She was right. There in the dim and chilly hall the prayers seemed to go on and on, interminably. Kate tried to force her mind to follow them, to offer her own devotions alongside her brother's words, but she was too conscious of the cold, of her weariness, of the tension in the air from the unwilling listeners.

Toby shifted restlessly from foot to foot, yawning ostentatiously and increasingly loudly, a form of protest that the twins began covertly to imitate, with suppressed giggles. Kate frowned at them, laid a warning hand on Mariana's head, which silenced the twins though had no effect on Toby, who kept his head bent through it all, deliberately avoiding her gaze. When prayers were over and the household dismissed, Kate held him back.

'That was unmannerly of you, Toby.'

'What was?' His eyes were bland.

'You know precisely what. You made no effort to join your prayers with those of the rest of us. You did not even try to pay attention. You set a bad example to the children and showed great discourtesy to your uncle.'

'Why did he have to be so long about it? It was the same yesterday. And all in Latin too.'

'You know your Latin.'

'I have enough of it in lessons.'

'Whatever you feel, while your uncle is here you will treat him with courtesy. You will keep your impatience to yourself, and pray about it.' *As I failed to do just now*, she thought ruefully.

'Yes, mother.' There was no teasing smile, no attempt to mollify her. Instead, he turned away. 'I'll be late for my lessons.'

'Today's to be a holiday. Did you not hear me say so?'

'I'd rather be at my lessons.' On his way to the door, he swung round. 'Is my uncle staying long?'

A pang shot through her. She had so much wanted these two beloved men in her life to love one another. 'I don't know. He only came a day since. Toby, you could learn much from him.'

He shrugged and left the house.

He had never shown any enthusiasm for his lessons before, which only demonstrated how much he resented his uncle's visit, however eagerly he had anticipated it beforehand. Heavy-hearted, she stood gazing after him.

'Where's he going so early?' Nicholas, coming up behind her, startled her.

'To his lessons.'

'But I thought—?'

'It was to be a holiday. Yes. But it seems he prefers to be learning.'

'He must have an inspiring tutor.' Nicholas's voice had a sceptical edge. Did he guess why Toby had been so eager to leave?

'Oh—oh, yes, I suppose…He has lessons along with Hal Featherstone, Sir Cuthbert's son. As does Edward.'

'Is that wise?'

She sighed. 'Perhaps not.'

'I think you did not speak of your hopes for him. Do you think of the priesthood for him too? I know he spoke of the army, but—'

'Of one thing I'm quite clear: Toby is not priest material. Not unless he changes a great deal. You can't force these things.' She gave a rueful smile, though it gained no response from her brother, who simply continued to look very grave, with that strange manner, taut and restless, as if from some sort of repressed anger. It brought to life all her unease.

'Would you like me to have a talk with him? When does he come home?'

'At dinner time. But, no, I don't think it would help. Or not at present, the mood he's in.' What could Nicholas possibly say to Toby that would not simply make things worse? Perhaps she should trust him to understand the frame of mind of a rebellious boy, but she wondered now if he truly remembered what that had been like. She realised how little she knew of this changed man beside her. So far nothing gave her any hope that he would be able to influence Toby for the good.

Within an hour, the rain had ceased, the sun came out, and Nicholas overturned all her doubts by taking the younger boys under his wing, asking them to show him how well they rode; and Edward and Philip spent a thoroughly happy few hours displaying their skills before him, while being gently instructed in ways they might improve. He was as he had been at the dancing yesterday, warm, laughing, flinging her a grin of triumph when he guided timorous Philip to a successful manoeuvre. If only Toby had stayed to join them! He would so much have loved showing off his horsemanship, finding it being taken seriously by a knowledgable adult.

As it was, Kate could only stand and look on, hand in hand with Mariana, who was furiously jealous of all the attention being lavished on her brothers.

'I can ride too, better than Ned. And *much* better than Philip. John told me so. Why can't I ride with my uncle?'

'Because it would only show him how unmaidenly you are. I'm sorry, my pet, but that is how it is. I do understand, for I used to love to ride too when I was your age. But we are women and it is not for us.' And how as a child she had envied her brother's freedom to ride as and when he chose!

'Dame Juliana rides. She goes hunting.'

'Dame Juliana is a heretic.' She wondered how far the fact that Sir Cuthbert Featherstone's wife was not a Catholic was of any relevance to her argument, but brushed the thought aside. 'I tell you what we shall do: we shall go to the stillroom and make some of those delicious almond cakes. I'm sure your uncle will like them as much as you do. So long,' she added, 'as you don't eat them all before they get to the table.'

They ate Mariana's favourite cakes in the garden, before Jane took the children to be washed and tidied for dinner, leaving Kate alone with Nicholas.

'They're good children, on the whole. You've done well.'

'On the whole'—what did that mean? Her younger brother, that once wild young man, was talking to her as if he were her father or her uncle; or even her confessor. But then if he were to become a priest, she would have to get used to it, to learn to defer to him, as indeed she supposed she ought to do simply because he was a man and she a mere woman. She gave a wan smile and changed the subject. 'Do you remember Holywell at all?' Only the first three years of his life had been spent here in the home of their grandparents.

'I don't think so, apart from the hall, when I first came in. I have no memory of our father.'

'He was scarcely here, until the end. And even I have little memory of our mother. She was always sick. Do you remember our grandmother?'

'No, I can't say I do. There's one thing, though, a tiny thing. Was there a pony, a fat black pony?'

Delight lit her face. 'Oh, that would be Pitty! He was meant to be 'Petit', but we never got it right. You had your first ride on him. You were fearless.'

'Ah, so that's why I remember! Just an impression, as if I'd caught a glimpse from the corner of my eye. But it's a memory of something happy, I do know that much.'

'You loved horses even then. We both did. I was so proud of you.'

'And now I have better loves.'

She was sad that this moment of shared reminiscence should have been cut short. But she told herself he was right: to dwell on the past was to waste precious time in vain things that did not matter.

Yet she could not help but remember. After her marriage, Nicholas had come often to visit them at Haroby, causing the sort of havoc and disruption that then always attended him, trailed after him like a spangled cloak. Following the death of their uncle, he had even lived with them for a time, since he had nowhere else to go, his own small estate having been sold to settle a string of debts. It had not taken long for her husband's patience to wear thin at his constant pranks, the one Toby had so unfortunately recalled being almost the last.

But in being banished from Haroby, he had taken laughter with him, leaving the place darker, more sombre than before, at least as far as Kate was concerned.

So many memories...If he'd only waited! Just a few weeks before Sir Thomas died he'd come to bid her farewell; for good, so he'd said. *'I guess it's the wars for me, Kate. I can think of nothing else.'* She recalled the bitterness in his voice. She had known for a long time that he resented his lack of both prospects and wealth; with no land, little education, marked with the brand of an alien religion and with no inclination for a quiet life, there was no obvious career for him to follow. Perhaps, she thought now, that had been the root of his wildness, fed by anger and a sense of worthlessness. Well, she could not deny that this at least had changed, for the better. Except that oddly she still had a sense of a different sort of anger, held fiercely in check.

'You never did tell me how you found I'd come here,' she prompted him.

'It was at Ashby. They'd heard things. How it was after your husband died, how he died apostate, so it was said, how you disappeared; how young Tom was in his kinsman's care at Silworth. So I thought, where would she go? There was only one possible answer.' He smiled faintly.

'I suppose there was.'

'I would wish you'd been able to send for me at the time, to help you, rather than risk so hazardous a journey. A lone woman, with a host of little ones, a newborn infant.'

'Two newborn infants.' She forced her thoughts back to the choice she'd made, the decision to risk everything in flight. The memory still made her shudder. 'I had to act quickly. Or so it seemed to me then.' She studied his face. 'Would you have helped me if you'd been there?'

'Of course.' There was something wry about the half-smile on his lips, something rueful. 'But it would have been for the wrong reason.'

'Oh?'

'I would have done it for the dislike I had of Sir Thomas, not for what ought to have been the purpose: to snatch the souls of your little ones from the devil's snare.'

It was the right answer, yet it chilled her. *Why do I feel like this, when he says things that should make me rejoice? He is only showing how much he has changed for the better. I should be thankful. His right reason is the same reason I had at the time. Yet—*

'It did not work though. Or not for Tom.'

'If you had taken refuge somewhere else, not in the obvious place?'

'Oh, where else could I have gone, a lone woman, as you said yourself, with only Jane for company and all those little ones in my care?' Yet she had asked herself that very question often enough.

'I see the difficulty. The Thorntons at York perhaps?' The Thornton matriarch, Dame Frances, was a distant relation of their grandmother.

'We rested with them on our way, where we were welcomed with great kindness. But it was well enough known they were our kin. If we'd stayed there, I doubt that would have been any better in the end.'

'Perhaps not.' He bent his head, frowning, and then abruptly looked up again. 'Do you ever see them?'

'Not for a long time. The last time was—oh, eight years past, when I went to York to bring the twins from their wet nurse. Otherwise, no. Though I did have word last year that Sir Arthur had died.'

'I called there on my way north. It was from there I wrote to you. You know I lodged with them when I was at St Peter's school?'

Nicholas's schooling had been spasmodic, broken by frequent expulsions, his time at St Peter's being no exception. 'You said they were kind to you.'

'And good Catholics, though I did not then see it as a matter in their favour. Only—their son Richard, Dame Frances' stepson—we were schoolfellows, you know, though he was my elder by a year. Then, he was the more sober and obedient of us. Now, I feel he's showing signs of rather too flexible a conscience. But I may have misjudged him.'

Into Kate's mind flashed a memory of a boy with calm grey eyes, and a smile that lit his face; even now, the thought warmed her. 'He was good with the little ones, when we were there. That I remember.'

She turned to lead her brother about the garden, through the sheltered walled plot where she grew her precious herbs. Here, always, she felt calmed and content. It was her haven.

'I've wondered sometimes—why was it called Holywell? Is there a well?'

'There's one at Meadhope. Some people still go there, though it was desecrated long since. But here— Grandmother always said there used to be one, but it dried up the day Queen Mary died, for shame at what had come over England.' She gave a rueful smile.

Once, Nicholas would have made a joke of that, mocking his grandmother's gullibility. This time he did not even return her smile. 'An apt symbol, for we are now in a very desert. Where was it? Do you know?'

'I'll show you, if I can still find the place.' She led him through the garden gate, over a field providing grazing for their small herd of milch cows, to the border of a wood, where she gestured towards a ruined heap of stones. 'There, you see. That was the stonework round it once. There's nothing left.' Just a tangle of brambles over dry ground; or as dry as any ground in this time of near-incessant rain.

Nicholas stood gazing down with a sombre expression. What was he thinking? How sad it was? How trivial an expression of a greater loss?

She remembered standing here beside her dear grandmother as she told her the story of the well, and how it had vanished so suddenly.

'Folk used to come from miles around to pray and make offerings. I came here on the day I wed your grandfather, to lay flowers and pray for a fruitful marriage. It never dried up, not once. Then, just like that, gone! The very day Queen Mary died, though we didn't realise that till afterwards, when the news came. A sure sign...'

Kate had been struck then by the solemnity of the story, its meaning piercing her consciousness. She'd felt a terrible sadness, tears rising to her eyes, as they were now. She glanced at her brother, taking in his stillness, his grim expression.

'To whom was it dedicated? Do you know?'

'Grandmother didn't say. She said they always prayed to Our Lady here. So perhaps that was it.'

Nicholas stood gazing at the place in silence, his face sombre. She watched him, wondering what he was thinking.

All at once he moved, tipped his head on one side as if something had caught his ear; and then strode away from her towards the ruined parapet that had once sheltered the well, peering behind it. 'There's a stream over here. Has it always been here?'

She followed him and looked where he pointed, over the wall at the tiny burn that splashed down beyond it, out onto a stony bed running through the field below, until it disappeared into the ground at the side of the track leading to the house from the main road. 'I think so. I don't remember it not being here. But I've never thought about it much. Or not until it washed some of the road away last winter. That's when John built the little bridge over.'

Nicholas turned on her with an odd glint in his eyes. 'Don't you see, sister? I think our grandmother saw only part of the story, the sad part, but not the hope it offered, the path to a new way. I would wager anything that this little stream was not here when the well flourished. I would guess it once fed the well, keeping it alive. Then, at that very moment, on that very day when our land was forced again to turn its back on the true faith, at that very same moment, the water changed course, abandoned the well and ran freely along another, stronger course.'

She knew he was trying to tell her something, willing her to see where his thoughts were leading him. 'That's what I told you.'

'No, don't you see?' He sounded impatient. 'It's clear to me, so clear. Like the ancient churches of this land, the holy well is now an empty shell, meaningless, without any holiness about it. But here, beside it, the water is running freely on another course, carrying refreshment to the soul in a new channel. As we must do, we who still serve the true God, the true faith. We are exiled from the old symbols of our faith, the old buildings, the empty temples, but we carry the truth with us. *We* are this stream, Kate, *we* are the vessels that carry the true word of God.'

She was moved by his passion, by the intense light in his eyes, though it did not quite make sense to her. She was not much given to flights of fancy. 'I see. I think I see. Yes.'

He grasped her hands and stood facing her. '*We* are the remnant of Holy Church in this land. It is in our hands to bring it back to the true path, so that the wells may be filled again, the temples cleansed and re-dressed in glory.'

She was not sure how to respond. 'It's a lot to ask.'

'With God nothing is impossible. With a steadfast dedication to the cause of His service—' She felt the urgency, the way his voice shook with emotion, reflecting the light in his eyes. 'It's in our hands, and the hands of all of our faith. You can see that, I know you can!'

'Yes.' She tried to show him that she understood, though she felt a little like a slow-witted scholar trying to find an answer that would please a rigorous schoolmaster. 'For me, it's to raise my children in the fear of God, in the true faith, to be loyal servants of Holy Church, to be ready to face any trial that may lie before them, without flinching.'

'That's precisely so. That's right!' He swung her arms, then kissed her. For an instant she had another glimpse of the warm laughing brother who'd danced in the hall yesterday. The next moment he was once again a didactic young man, tense with the fervour of his new-found faith. 'You will raise soldiers for his army, girded with the armour of Christ! I am convinced that your sons have it in them, all of them, even Toby—perhaps Toby especially, for I see in him something of what I was; and I know what I am now, by God's grace and your prayers.'

For a moment, just for a tiny fraction of time, she had a mental picture of her scapegrace son as Nicholas appeared to see him, an ardent Christian soldier. It was all she could do not to laugh, or make a joke of it. But that would have been unseemly in a respectable woman, and in any case she sensed that her brother was in no mood for jokes and would be deeply offended by any attempt to make light of what he said. She schooled her expression to something matching his own solemnity. 'Yes, brother. I'm sure you're right. God willing.'

'As He surely is. With our help—*my* help, if I can find a

way.'

She flashed a look at him, questioning. 'Oh?'

'I shall pray about it.' Rather to her relief, he visibly relaxed. 'What I should like for the present is to know more of your little estate.'

Again she had that sense of being assessed, examined for her fitness to guide her household. 'There's not time now. After dinner perhaps.' She tilted her head, trying to force light-heartedness into her tone. 'Is this in case you should one day find yourself my steward?'

He did not return her smile. 'For the love I bear you, I wish to see for myself that all is well with you.'

She was not sure quite what he meant by that. She was beginning to realise that there were often hidden meanings to his words, that nothing was said lightly. But she made no comment, simply led the way back to the house, while all the time something stirred uneasily in her. She wanted to share her brother's enthusiasm, his passion. She was thankful that he'd found his way back to the church. But she felt she no longer quite understood him, that his response to anything she might say or do was no longer at all predictable.

Yet what he'd said at the holy well, what he'd seen there, its symbolism: that was to find hope in desolation. How could she fail to be moved by it, by his certainty?

They went in to dinner, where everyone was gathering in the hall, servants and children together. All but one.

Nicholas looked round at the company. 'Toby's not

here.'

Kate caught Jane's eye, saw the faint shake of the head.

'Is he all day at his lessons?'

She resisted the temptation to say 'yes', but could not quite bring herself to tell a lie. 'They will have ended by now. I'm afraid that sometimes when he's with Hal he forgets the time. It may be they've gone hawking.'

'It's not the hawking season.'

'Well, riding then. As soon as he gets hungry he'll remember the time and come home.' She tried to sound untroubled, as if it did not matter, though she could see only too well that Nicholas thought it ought to matter. She felt angry with Toby for bringing her brother's tacit disapproval on her head.

Toby was not with Hal; or not any longer.

'Come back with me,' his friend had invited, once their lessons at the rectory were over. 'Have dinner with us.'

Toby knew he was expected at home, that with his behaviour this morning he had already exceeded even his mother's gentle limits. He ought to go home. But he did not hesitate.

'Anything to escape my uncle's preaching and praying!' The two boys turned their horses' heads towards Meadhope Hall. 'It's like living in a monastery.'

'You said he'd be fun. You talked of nothing else, until I was sick of the very sound of him.' They exchanged grins, though Toby's scowl returned almost at once.

'He's changed. Mother said he had, and by God she's right! He's nothing like I remember, not one bit. You should have heard the grace before dinner yesterday, when we could have been here with you. He went on and on and on until I was faint with hunger, and then this morning too. We did have some dancing yesterday, but what's the fun in prancing round the room with your little sisters and brothers, when you could have—Well!'

'We missed you too. It was all a bit, well, flat without you. But I guess your uncle had a long journey, the day before.'

'All that about being weary from travel. I don't believe a word of it.'

Hal's eyes widened. 'Why then?'

'Don't know. Unless he wants us to be all monastic and pious.' He gave a sudden involuntary tug on his horse's reins, which caused the animal to come to a complete halt. 'Oh, Hal, you don't know what it's like to be always reminded that we're different, we can't do what everyone else does, we're right and everyone else is wrong, even you and your family. Maybe if my father had lived—' He turned bright brown eyes on his friend. 'You are so lucky!'

Further disappointment lay in wait for him at Meadhope, once dinner was over, for Hal's fencing master arrived unexpectedly to give the boy a lesson. As Sir Cuthbert directed his son, Toby lingered, hoping Hal's father would invite him to take part in the lesson, but no such offer came. Clearly, receiving a gentlemanly education in Latin and Philosophy was one thing; but for a young Catholic to be taught any of the warlike arts—that was quite another matter.

'I shan't be that long,' Hal assured him. 'Go and take a look at the new horse I told you about. I'll come and find you in the stables when I'm done.'

Toby ought to have said, 'No, I'd better go home.' But he went instead to the kitchen, where he begged a slice of yesterday's venison pie from Nan the kitchen maid, who was fond of him, before wandering aimlessly towards the side door, full of rage at the world's unfairness, yet hoping that a chance encounter might improve the day, if his luck was in.

It was, at last. The passage leading from the kitchen towards the stable yard ran past various adjoining rooms given over to food preparation—dairy, pantry, wine store, brewery—and out towards an open door; where Bess's unmistakably alluring figure was outlined, dark against the sunlight, blocking his way, her hair, as fiery as Hal's, lit from behind like a halo. A year older than her brother (and so of Toby), Hal's sister Elizabeth was a pretty young woman, with enticing curves of mouth and body, who had some time ago made it very plain to Toby that she admired him.

'Toby!' Her voice was soft, completely of a piece with the curves of her body. She took a step nearer, so that he caught the scent of her, a light perfume, fabric warmed by the body beneath it; the scent of a young woman, eager for his company. 'You're not going yet?'

He knew quite well what she wanted and what would happen next, as it had once or twice before in ways he had never been able to forget and ached to have repeated.

'Not if—' He found it hard to speak; his voice, never reliable these days, emerged as a breathy squeak.

'Shh!' She laid a finger on his lips, took his arm and drew him aside through an adjoining door, which she closed behind them. He was vaguely aware, from the jars and bottles ranged on shelves, the pestle and mortar, the scent of herbs, that they were in the stillroom. But it could have been anywhere for all he cared.

'No one will find us here. Not while my mother has Mistress Anderson visiting.' She reached up to draw his mouth towards her, then her hand moved down, touched him. *Oh!*

His hands slid round her tight-laced waist, its unforgiving rigidity, tried to pull her nearer, though the starched folds of her ruff kept her at a tantalising distance.

'Wait!' She tugged at the strings holding the ruff in place and pulled it off, then nestled close to him, though her other hand stayed—agonisingly, wonderfully, urgently —where it was.

He moved his hands to her shoulders, pale, smooth as silk; felt his way beneath the heavy fabric to close his fingers over her breast. He heard her gasp at his touch, felt her lips part against his mouth. 'Oh Toby!'

'Oh Bess!'

He pushed her back against the cold shelf. He felt her

tug at the hooks and lacings of her bodice, loosen the ties at the neck of her chemise, further freeing her breasts to the touch of his hands and mouth. They sank down bit by bit to the floor, too much lost in the delight of each other's bodies to care how cold and hard it was. He lay over her, tilting her farthingale behind her like a fan, his thighs pressed against her heavy skirts. Even through the layers of petticoat he could feel that she had parted her legs. He resisted a fierce urge to reach down, to lift her skirts, work his way up her leg. *Above the waist*—they must stay above the waist! That was what Jane had told him, and Hal too had hinted. Not that Bess appeared to have been taught that lesson.

With one hand she was stroking him beneath his shirt, while with the other she caressed that other place. He felt an explosion in his body, heard her breathing wildly beneath him. They clung together for long throbbing moments, finding some kind of inadequate release. 'Oh Bess, I want you!'

'Oh and I want you too!'

'Marry me!'

She giggled. 'Don't be silly!'

He sat up, suddenly deadly serious. 'I'm not being silly. I love you.'

'You know that's not enough for marriage.'

'We're of good family. Your father's neighbours.'

'And Papists and landless, all but. You know what my father would say to that.'

'Let me try him at least! You're not his son and heir. It can't matter so much who you marry.' He kissed her again, little kisses all over her face, then moved down. He could feel her responding as before, her breathing quickening.

She managed to say, 'Anyway, you're only a boy.'

'Don't you love me then?'

She took his face in her hands, held it so she could study it, planting a kiss on his mouth between each sentence. 'I love you. I want you. But marriage—well, that's a serious business. In any case, my father has someone in mind for me.'

Shock drove out desire, like a deluge of cold water. 'Who is it?'

'No one you know. He's heir to good estates over beyond Houghton-le-Spring. The right religion. Twenty or so. Presentable enough.'

'Then I'm just someone to pass the time with?'

She ran a finger down his cheek. 'For that, you are much more agreeable than Will Fenwick. You know how to kiss, and what to do with your hands. He hasn't the first idea.'

Toby drew away from her, swept by a surge of anger; one that was becoming only too familiar of late. She enjoyed what he did to her, but that was it, at least as far as she was concerned. He was a nonentity, a plaything, someone beneath serious consideration. Would she even recall who he was, in years to come? He doubted it. *Papists and landless, all but*—that was how she'd described him.

Feeling utterly humiliated, all passion drained away, he rose to his feet. 'I'm wanted at home. I should have been back long since.'

Conscious of the change in his tone and manner, Bess reached up and clasped his arm. 'Toby, I don't love you the less for what you are. It's the way it is, that's all. You must see that.'

'Oh, I do!' Touched by what he felt was a real affection for him, he softened a little, began to plead. 'Then wait for me, Bess! Don't let your father marry you off, not yet. Surely he won't force you, if you hold firm? I'll make my fortune somehow, prove I'm worthy of you, so even your father will see it!'

'You'll be a Papist still, won't you? That will always hold you back.'

'If I stay a Papist.' He shivered a little as he said it. Was that the devil on his shoulder, whispering temptation in his ear? At least his mother was not around to hear him. 'After all, your father was raised one, wasn't he?'

'After a fashion.' She tilted her head to one side, a smile just lifting the corners of her delectable mouth. 'I know you've been to church at least once. I saw you. Would you do it again? Give up everything? Would you do that for me?'

Did Eve look so, tempting Adam to taste the apple? Was that what led him to give up his soul, to give up all hope of Paradise? He longed to whisper 'yes', to kiss her again, to tell her he would do anything at all for her, *anything* to make sure of her as his wife, swept as he was by so many conflicting emotions: longing for Bess, longing to be part of the normal life of this neighbourhood, to take his place as his friend Hal would do one day, as a respected gentleman, a figure of authority, a man of standing in the country in which he lived; a man that any father would welcome as a husband for his daughter. Yet...to condemn his soul to Hell for eternity—was that a price worth paying?

Perhaps he could conform just as far as was absolutely necessary, while always reserving something for the true faith, with the expectation that as his life ended he would return to his true home? If there was time, if that was permitted him: that was the fear, of course. Not everyone was allowed time for penitence at the end.

He let the devil in, and kissed her. 'I would do anything for you! Anything!'

After that they lay back down on the floor and began all over again; emerging at last, hastily trying to repair their dishevelled clothing, to find that Hal had long since finished his lesson and come looking for Toby. Bess slipped away just before her brother reached them. Toby hoped they'd not been seen. He didn't think even Hal would approve of what they'd been doing.

Chapter Five

After dinner, because Nicholas asked to see them, Kate spread the account books and ledgers on the parlour table. 'You'll find them dry enough. I know how impatient you always were when anyone tried to interest you in the matter of your expenditure.'

There was no answering grin. 'Do not judge me on what I was, but on what I am now, through God's mercy.' He gave the two weighty ledgers a hurried look. 'These are not the current ones, I think. Where are the rest? Or have you fallen behind?'

'Master Langley has the latest one.' She felt a pang of unease at bringing the rector's name into the conversation, aware as she was of her brother's disapproval. 'I asked him to check the figures before the Whitsun rents become due.'

'I see.' He gazed at her for what seemed a long time, while she thought he was about to make some disparaging remark, but instead he began to turn over the pages of the books, asking her to explain this detail and that, talking over the estate's past receipts and expenses and inquiring about its current financial position.

Once more Kate felt like a neglectful pupil being examined by a stern tutor, afraid of having her idleness exposed; yet this was Nicholas, her dear brother, who loved her. She wanted to enjoy his company, not resent it.

'Nicholas, it's a beautiful afternoon. Please don't let us waste the day over these old accounts. Let's go for a ride.'

'Simply for idle pleasure?'

That was precisely what she'd had in mind, but she added hastily, 'I thought you'd wish to see the extent of my land.'

But it *was* a pleasure, to be out in the sunshine and clear air, even on her aged mount that struggled to keep up with Nicholas's more showy animal.

She led the way round the boundaries of her estate, calling at the Holywell Mill, pointing out herds and flocks, the few struggling crops they grew, almost all on land worked on her behalf by Holywell's tenant farmers, some of whom came out to greet them and offer refreshment, home brewed ale, dense rye bread, hard end-of-season cheese. They passed an agreeable half hour at Low Burnside Farm, where Andrew Wardle, the genial Holywell bailiff, welcomed them most warmly.

'Hm, not the sharpest of minds, I think.' Nicholas said, as they rode away. He directed a disapproving look at his sister, who ignored it. 'However, you seem well known and loved.'

'I try to earn the respect of my tenants, to be just and compassionate.'

'How many are of our faith?'

'Most of them. Not quite all. Those that are come to Holywell when we are able to have Mass said.'

'That's good.'

They had followed a track for some way up the northern slope of the dale, beside a burn that tumbled down towards the river. Ahead of them, the track entered a small scrubby wood: alder, hawthorn, birch, the occasional graceful ash, underlaid with brambles.

Kate gestured vaguely towards the northern horizon. 'There's more of my estate beyond there, but not much. One small farm. After that, there's the fell, common land. Like everyone else, we graze our sheep there in the summer. They went up two months since.'

'Then let's take a look, sister. I wouldn't wish to leave out any part of your property.'

Knowing full well what lay on the far side of the wood, Kate had hoped for a different response. Fighting an urge simply to suggest that they turn round and go home, ignoring the existence of the most troublesome of her tenants, she led the way through the wood into the neglected fields beyond, rank with weeds or grazed by a few scrawny animals. She was conscious all the time of Nicholas's censorious gaze sweeping over them, though he said nothing. The farmhouse came within sight, though the stench of it reached them almost before they saw the filthy yard and rotting heather thatch.

Nicholas drew rein, looking it over with an expression of distaste. 'So this is one of yours?'

Again, that sense of guilt, of not meeting her brother's expectations: 'I'm afraid so. This is High Intake Farm.'

'Ah, the place that is so negligent with the rent! What's the name of the man? Stobbs, is that it?'

'Henry Stobbs, yes. He has a large family and small

means.' She did not add that he was also a quarrelsome drunkard. She hoped he was not at home this afternoon, for he could not be trusted to show her proper respect.

'That is not, I think, sufficient excuse for such clear neglect. Is he a Catholic?'

'What has that—? Not openly, certainly, though he's not much of a churchgoer either.'

'Then surely you owe him no leniency. Better turn him out and let the place to someone of our faith. Or does your heretic counsellor advise otherwise?' His voice was heavy with sarcasm.

'It's not as easy as that. In the end, it's my decision, but I don't take it lightly.' And she did not intend to spoil the day by going into the intricate details of a complicated situation, and her feelings about it. She was weary of being made to feel like a naughty child. She reminded herself that Nicholas was her junior by many years and only newly come to any kind of virtue. He also lacked any experience of managing an estate, as far as she knew.

She became aware of a clattering noise from within the house and a face peering out through the dirty cloth that served as a window pane. Even from this distance she sensed the hostility of the watcher. She shivered and turned her horse's head. 'Let's go home. You've not yet seen my stables. I'd like your advice about the horses. We have few enough, and small means for buying more, but I'd like to make the best of what we have.'

It was the surest way of distracting Nicholas from the

shortcomings of the Holywell estate and her management of it, for he had always been knowledgable and skilled in anything to do with horses. As they approached the house she saw John leading the plough horse out from the stables. Reaching him, they halted and Nicholas began an animated conversation with the older man, ranging over the sturdiness of this animal, the virtues of horses in general, and John's memories of Nicholas as a small child.

Kate, waiting patiently, feeling happier (if a little bored), had her attention caught by a movement in the stable yard. Someone had entered it from the far side—no, two people. Her gaze sharpened, watching: Toby and Hal, riding together. They disappeared round the corner of the building.

'I'd like to check on something,' she murmured, though Nicholas barely acknowledged her words. 'I'll see you in the stable yard.' She left the two men talking while she rode down to the yard, dismounting at its entrance.

Youthful laughter drew her to a stall where Toby and Hal were inspecting her son's horse for possible lameness. Toby had mentioned it to her two days ago, she recalled, though John had assured her there was nothing wrong, beyond the undoubted fact that the horse was old and ill-formed.

As she came nearer, she heard Toby's voice. 'There'll be a saint I can pray to I guess. Saint Bellyfull of the Bare Bodkin. A sure cure for any horse's ills. Maybe if we can get hold of a relic—a saint's pizzle: there must be a good few of them, never used. That should do it! Who needs good horses with help like that?'

Shocked to the core, Kate came to a standstill. It was not just the words, the derision, but the bitterness in his voice…Where and how had her son, so carefully raised, learned to speak like that, as if he were as much a heretic as his friend? He was a little wild sometimes, she knew, and far from biddable; he had even committed the sin of putting in an appearance at the parish church. *Just to see what it was like,'* he'd told her, when she'd found out from the wife of one of her tenants. *'Every bit as boring as I thought!'* he'd added. But this was different, and far worse. To sneer at holy things, to think them a matter for ridicule—! The answer seemed obvious enough, though she'd hoped that, from respect for her and for her faith, Sir Cuthbert would have frowned on such open mockery from one of his family and taught his son an equal respect.

She took a deep breath to calm herself and stepped into the stall, her feet rustling in the straw, warning them of her coming. She knew that Toby, seeing the severity of her expression, would know at once that she'd overheard him. But all she said was, 'Hal, you will I think be late for supper. You, Toby, should have been home hours ago.'

Toby pulled off his hat, all at once the dutiful son. 'I beg your pardon, madam.' The fact that he sounded entirely in earnest told her that he knew she was too angry to be mollified by his usual teasing excuses.

Hal, conscious of the atmosphere that had arisen, if

not its cause, bowed to her, mounted his own handsome beast and rode away.

As soon as he was out of earshot, Kate said: 'Toby, I never want to hear such talk from you again. Many sons would be beaten for such filthiness, for such it is.'

She saw how deeply he had coloured. He did not even try to deny anything or to excuse himself.

'If that is how you behave in Hal Featherstone's company, then I must forbid you to meet with him.'

'Oh!' His eyes flew to her face, scanning it to see if she were in earnest. 'Oh, mother, no!' Seeing no softening, he went on, 'I know it was wrong. I should not…Madam, even Hal doesn't say such things, or not often, and then it's only when there are others—well, not all his friends are so considerate of my feelings.'

'*Your* feelings! It was you I heard speaking, not Hal!'

'I know. I am sorry, truly sorry. If I hurt you—'

'The hurt to me is nothing. The hurt to God and His saints, whom you derided, the hurt to your immortal soul, that is what is at issue here.'

He bit his lip, clearly trying to think of some appropriate response, as if he sensed that for once his wheedling smile was not going to be enough, or even acceptable. 'I will remember, when I am next at confession.'

'So I should hope. But for now you must pray earnestly in your heart for true contrition, and for the strength to resist the example of your so-called friends.'

'Yes, mother.'

'Go to my closet. I will come to you very soon.'

As she watched him go, she heard Nicholas ride into the yard, where he dismounted just outside the stable door.

'Trouble?'

Had he heard anything, or was he simply forewarned by her expression? 'Oh, just Toby being Toby.'

But it was much more than that. The thought burned in her mind as she tried to appear light-hearted, while they discussed the horses; coming to no helpful conclusion, since only an impossible expenditure could adequately supply Holywell's stables. Should she tell Nicholas what she'd heard, and how much it disturbed her? Not yet, not now. She needed to ponder the incident and work out for herself what was the best approach, how to deal with it.

Back in the house, she found an excuse to leave her brother in conversation with Edward (always ready for an earnest discussion of religious matters), and then made her way upstairs to her closet, where Toby, all sullen misery, sat slumped on a stool.

He stood up as she came in. 'I am sorry, mother, so sorry. I beg you to forgive me!'

He *was* sorry, she saw that, but she feared it was rather because he had distressed her than for the fault itself. 'We will kneel down and pray together, Toby.'

They knelt side by side on the hard floor. She waited for him to be still, while she collected her thoughts, sought for the right words. She urged him to confess to God, as he would if a priest were hearing him, and ask for mercy and the intercession of the Saints, and heard his mumbled, unhappy confession, there in the semi-darkness of the room.

Was this, she wondered, how it was for a priest hearing the confession of a penitent? What a responsibility, to wait in silence to hear what was said, to give due weight to the secrets of a penitent's heart, to offer a means of recompense by some appropriate penance, to channel God's forgiveness!

But no, she was allowing her thoughts to wander into shameful territory, even putting herself, a mere woman, in the place of God's priest. Women were the temptresses, so she had been told by every priest she had ever met; children of Eve, the creatures who, without guidance, without the submissive obedience that was the supreme quality of Our Lady, were doomed to lead men astray.

So, as Toby murmured his contrition, she prayed earnestly for the intervention of the blessed Mother of God on his behalf, and on hers too. Even after he'd gone meekly on his way, head bent, shoulders hunched, she continued her prayers, for herself alone, that she might guide her son rightly in the future.

Would she be able to do it? Was she even the right person, in the absence of a priest, to guide him in his faith, when he was otherwise offered examples only of heretic males? If things went on like this, he would so easily go astray, easily be encouraged in occasional distaste and perhaps at last wholesale rejection of all she'd tried to instil in him; it was happening already, if today was anything to go by. She prayed earnestly that he might be kept on the right path, that some way would be found to stop him from straying, but she could see no clear way ahead. Most boys of his age would by now have long since left home, to serve in a suitable household; or as Hal Featherstone was soon to do, to go to university. She had known for a long time that she ought to have made some such arrangement, while always putting off the decision. And now this had happened, to bring her failure home to her!

Could it be that Nicholas was in fact the answer to her prayers? Whatever unease she might feel about him, however little she might as yet have come to know the man he had become, he had certainly been brought back to the true path after his wayward youth. Might he offer Toby an example her son would willingly follow, if he were to stay here, ordained or not, to act as her steward? Could she persuade him? The keen interest he'd shown in Holywell's affairs could be viewed as a hopeful sign.

Unfortunately, so far Toby seemed utterly impervious to his uncle's good qualities; but then he'd seen very little of him. It was natural enough that he should find the long prayers tried his patience. They did hers too, though she felt guilty about it. She felt too that it was her fault he'd been absent for most of the time since her brother came to Holywell. She ought surely to have been able to force him to stay at home, though instinct told her he would have found a way to disobey her whatever she did or said. Perhaps the shock of this afternoon would make him more biddable. She could only hope so.

There came a light tap on the door of her closet. 'Mother?'

It was Toby again, edging his way in. 'I forgot. Sir Cuthbert gave me a message. Will we please to come to dine at the Hall on Sunday, now that my uncle is well rested?'

As if she hadn't enough to trouble her at the moment! Kate sighed. 'Thank you, Toby.'

'We will go, won't we? I know, after today...But it's not Hal's fault, or Sir Cuthbert's.'

'I think it will not be possible. But we shall see. I'll send my answer when I've considered the matter.' To refuse one kind invitation from her neighbour, on what might seem reasonable grounds, that was one thing; but to do so twice, without very good reason—that would be another matter.

Why oh why did her brother have to be so unreasonable? She could not see that eating with her neighbours, heretic or not, was likely in any way to imperil the souls of her family. On the other hand, in view of the way Toby had behaved today, perhaps he had a point. Perhaps he was right.

Oh, why did it all have to be so hard?

Toby was a different person at supper, offering to serve at table and doing so almost without fault, as if to demonstrate the exemplary nature of his mother's teaching. Afterwards, at evening prayer, there was a moment when Kate thought he was about to show his impatience with his uncle's long devotions, but the scowl was quickly suppressed and he stilled and kept his head bowed.

Nicholas must have seen how anxiously Kate watched her son, for after prayers he murmured, 'You have concerns about Toby. Let me speak to him.' Thinking he was about to follow Toby from the room, she laid a hand on his arm.

'No, Nicholas. Not now. It's not the moment.'

She hoped he would leave her then, but instead he waited at her side until they were left alone in the hall.

'You are troubled about Toby, I can see that. You must realise, as is clear to me, that he's too old, too active and virile, to be still under petticoat rule, however holy, however virtuous.'

Kate felt herself blushing. Had he read her thoughts? Some instinct made her want to contradict him, but how could she when he'd simply put into words what was on her mind?

'I know. He needs firm guidance, firm *masculine* guidance. I'm afraid I find it hard. The only men he has to look up to here—apart from John Emerson—they are all heretics, as is his closest friend. It's natural enough he should want to fit in with them, that he should even resent the restrictions the Catholic faith puts on his life.'

'I know how that feels. It was how I was, once. It almost led me to reject all of it, to lose my very soul for worldly things.' He shook his head. 'You haven't thought to send him to some other household for his education?'

'I know it's expected. But where? Who could—? Besides, I could not bear to lose him. And at least here I can hope to have some control over his daily life.' Though she knew as she said it how close she had already come to losing that control.

'Yet you let him take lessons from a heretic? I presume his tutor is not of our faith?'

Please don't let him learn the truth! 'No, but I trust him. He teaches only safe things, Latin, Greek.'

'How can you be sure? And what of the company the boy keeps, his closest friend: the Featherstone boy, isn't it?'

She had no argument against that implied accusation, especially today. She could see the reproof in her brother's eyes, hear it in his voice, while wanting to fend it off, to find some valid excuse for her handling of her son, but she could think of none.

'You should have sent him away from such temptations long since, while he was still a child. At fourteen he's almost a man.'

She was weary of his lecturing, weary of his disapproval. He might be putting into words precisely what she felt herself, but she was unreasonably irritated by it. It was not her brother's didacticism she needed now, but Jane's common sense. 'It's getting late. We'll talk of this another time.'

'And meanwhile offer our prayers for God's guidance.'

Then, with a knot of anxiety turning inside her, she remembered that there was another far more contentious matter to face. 'Nicholas, we have another invitation to dine at Meadhope Hall. On Sunday.' Today was Friday. 'I have to send my answer in the morning.'

'Surely there is no question? You know my thoughts on that.'

'Could you not relent a little? Just for the one time, that's all I ask. Then you will be able to judge for yourself what kind of neighbours I have.' *The kind who led Toby to speak so crudely of holy things?* Unease stirred in her. 'You might think more kindly…' She faltered into silence before the cold rejection in his face.

'I do not change my mind. For yourself, do as you please, but I shall not think the better of you for it.'

After that, she could barely bring herself to say good night with any warmth.

She closed her bedchamber door with relief. Shaking her head, Jane rose from unfolding the truckle bed. 'Master Nicholas has been having words again.'

Kate's smile was rueful. 'You read me like a book, Jane. I should not mind. He means well. He only has our welfare at heart.'

'That can rile you the most.'

'Yes. Especially when it means turning down another invitation from Sir Cuthbert. I fear I shall have to tell him the truth this time.'

'That's not all is it? There's something happened with Toby today. Enough to make him put on on his very best behaviour at supper. I noted it.'

The lightness left Kate's face. She told Jane what had happened, while the servant listened attentively. 'You told this to your brother?'

'No. No more than to hint. He guessed there was something amiss, but—'

Jane watched her, head tilted sideways. 'You did not wish to tell him?'

'I don't know. Not yet. He—Oh, I'm not sure! Perhaps Toby will come to like his uncle better, and pay heed to what he says. Nicholas was good with the little ones today.'

'He was. It warmed my heart to see it. It could be he feels strange. He doesn't know how he should be with you, not any longer. You were his guide and teacher for so long. Now it's all changed, turned round the other way, or that's maybe how he'll see it. He's a man after all. Perhaps he'll find a gentler way, in time.'

'Oh I hope so.' Kate began to undress. 'Toby's wildness made me think of Nicholas, and wish that he too would change, like his uncle. Now I'm not sure I want him to follow such a pattern. I don't know why, not really. I don't know what to do for the best.'

'Toby's not as wild as Master Nicholas was. At heart he loves you and wants to please you. Master Nicholas never cared what anyone thought that I recall.'

'Then you don't think Nicholas wants to please me? Or

ever did?' The thought surprised her. She had always been certain of his love for her. Was not that the same thing?

'Once, maybe. Now I would guess he's sure of himself, so sure he needs no one's approval. Except perhaps of that gentleman at Ashby he speaks of.'

Kate shot her a startled questioning look.

'That Master Robert Catesby. I saw how he changed when he spoke of him at supper tonight. Like a candle lit behind his eyes.'

That was exactly right, Kate acknowledged. She had seen it for herself, but was surprised that it had been so clear to Jane too. But then Jane had always been a shrewd judge of character. Was she right in the other things she'd said?

'I hope it's true that Toby wants to please me. In the end, it should make it easier for me to guide him.'

Chapter Six

As if to prove the rightness of Jane's argument, Toby, washed, brushed, impeccably dressed, was first in the hall next morning. He bowed to his mother and then stood ready for prayers, head already bent, eyes closed. Kate, less attentive than she should be to her brother's long devotions, watched Toby as his lips followed the words, showing no sign of impatience or restlessness. She felt a glow of gratitude and love. Perhaps after all he was not beyond the reach of her authority; perhaps there was hope that she could guide him on the right path. She was glad that Nicholas was able to see that all was well, with no cause for anxiety.

Prayers ended, the household dispersed to their daily duties, and Kate caught Toby's eye, returning his smile, open, affectionate, without guile.

'A word, nephew!'

Nicholas strode forward, laid a hand on Toby's shoulder.

Kate caught her breath. What was this? Approval from his uncle? If so, the scowl clouding Toby's face did not bode well.

Nor did her brother's manner. Nicholas had lowered his voice, but she could hear every admonitory word. 'You have caused hurt to your mother. You consort with heretics and apostates. Don't turn from me. Hear what I have to say! You are a man now—'

Toby wrenched his shoulder away. 'Let me alone! It's none of your business!' The look he threw at his mother was full of cold fury. 'You had no right to tell him! How could you?'

He swung round and ran from the room.

'I'll go to him.' Jane's soft voice broke through Kate's dismay, then she was gone.

Enraged, Kate swung round on her brother. 'I asked you not to speak to him! There was no need.'

'Allow me to be the judge of that.' His eyes were cold, implacable. 'He is clearly grown too headstrong for you to handle. He needs a man's authority. As you said yourself, he has no pattern to follow, such as a young boy needs.'

'He was behaving perfectly well this morning. You know nothing of what passed between us yesterday. You had no right to speak to him without my permission.'

'It is you who should have my permission, may I remind you, as your brother and the senior man of the family. And you ought to have told me of his errors yesterday, whatever they were.'

She caught her breath, bit back a furious retort, while struggling to think of a reply that would not enrage her brother further but would remind him that this was her house and they were speaking of her son. What made it harder was that there was nothing in Nicholas's expression to suggest he was in any way moved by her objections.

'I passed much of the night in prayer.' His tone had softened just a little. 'I am troubled by your difficulties. You carry too great a burden for one woman to bear. The rearing of boys should be in the hands of men, once they are grown beyond infancy, but Toby has been raised without such guidance, to his obvious harm. You yourself acknowledged such to me last night.'

And how I wish I hadn't! 'That did not give you the right to interfere.'

'May I remind you that you invited me to remain here as your steward, precisely to provide a remedy for what is lacking in your household. That is so, is it not?'

How could she deny what was so obviously true? If only she had been less precipitate, less swept away by her love for her brother, before she had taken time to get to know him again, to understand what kind of man he had become, to realise that there were unplumbed complexities to his nature!

'Through the night I gave strenuous thought and prayer to this matter. And it seems to me that it is right that I do indeed offer my services as your steward. It is right that there should be a gentleman to direct your household and guide your children.' Again his expression softened a little. Taking her hands, he even smiled faintly. 'So, Kate, I accept your offer. I shall come to live at Holywell as your steward, in deed as well as in name. That will be for the best, I think. You will no longer have to carry the burden alone, for I will be there to carry it for you. Now, what do you say?'

I will carry it for you, he said; not *with* you. It would not be a shared duty, but one handed over completely to her brother. She could sense that he was utterly sure of her compliance. How could it be otherwise, when she had so impulsively, so hastily made that offer to him?

'I don't know. You have been here less than two days. I know you so little now.'

She could see that she had astonished him. 'Are you saying you don't want me to come here? That it was no firm offer? I don't understand. I know women are given to caprices and strange notions, but to change your tune so suddenly, after everything! What is this?'

'What I said, what I offered—it was a thought that came to me, but without due consideration. I—'

'Which you now withdraw?' His voice was cold with displeasure.

'No, not entirely. Perhaps not at all. But I need time to think what would be for the best. You saw for yourself how Toby is with you.'

'Because he has not been well raised.'

That stung her. 'I thought I was the pattern of holy motherhood!'

'He is no longer in need of a mother. He needs a firm masculine hand, which is what I offer.'

'But if he will not accept it?'

'He must be made to do so.'

Miserable at the great gulf that seemed to have opened between them, Kate softened her voice. 'Nicholas, I ask only that we wait a little before we decide what is best. Try a gentler way with Toby; that's all I ask for now. He needs praise as well as blame, and encouragement. If he could only have been with you yesterday, when you rode with the young ones. He would have loved you then.'

He stood gazing at her, frowning. Was he about to admit that he had indeed been too hasty in speaking to Toby this morning?

No, for his tone was grudging, reluctant. 'Very well, let us leave the matter for now. We'll speak of it again another time.'

'Thank you.' She braced herself to face the next problem that confronted her. 'You won't change your mind about dinner tomorrow?'

'You know I won't. But you know too that you ought to follow my lead in this.'

This time, she sent no message but set out after breakfast to ride to Meadhope to see Sir Cuthbert for herself, though she still had no very clear idea what she was going to say to him.

She had just crossed the boundary of her own land when she saw a big fair man on a good horse approaching her at a stiff trot. She drew rein and waited until he reached her, doffing his hat as he did so. 'Madam! Good day. I was on my way to call on you.'

'And I to call on you.' Should she invite Sir Cuthbert to continue on his way to Holywell, risking an uncomfortable meeting with her brother? It would be unneighbourly not to do so; yet she was no longer sure where lay the limits of neighbourliness. 'Your kind invitation—'

'Ah, that! I fear we are fated not to be able to dine together. My dear wife is indisposed. A rheum merely, but enough to keep her from company.' He spread his hands. 'I know, she never ails—and now this!'

The relief set her shaking. No need then to explain! 'Which I regret most deeply, as I would wish very much to meet with your brother.' There was an oddly jocular note in his voice. 'He has cost me a deal of trouble, I should tell you.'

'Oh?' Could they have met already, and had Nicholas treated their neighbour with discourtesy, which to her brother would not be discourtesy at all?

'I had a visit from Henry Stobbs yesterday. Told me there was a Papist priest at Holywell.' He studied her face, though beneath his bristling brows his eyes were lit with laughter. 'I take it this was not the case? A lean dark foreign-seeming man perhaps?'

She understood him. 'Oh! We rode by High Intake yesterday. He must have seen my brother, and thought—I see!'

'So I told him. I take it your brother has not turned priest?' From the amused glint in his eyes it was obvious he expected a negative answer.

'Indeed not!' She tried to make her tone light, as if she saw the joke. 'Not in the least!'

'Henry Stobbs is not easily gainsaid, as you know. But it was clear it was all malice.' The light abruptly left his face.

'You need to have a care of him.'

'I know. He gets no better.'

'It's fortunate he has no friends. I think I satisfied him —I hope so. I didn't want him taking his complaint to those who might take him more seriously. You wouldn't want pursuivants at your door.'

She shivered. 'No. I thank you most warmly.'

After this, she could not ignore the demands of hospitality. 'Will you ride with me back to Holywell, to take some refreshment?'

'Gladly. I was on my way to call on you, for there's another matter I would talk over with you, of greater importance.'

She turned her horse back the way they had come. 'Oh?'

'It concerns your boy Toby.'

She caught her breath. 'Oh, what has he done now?'

'Nothing amiss, I'm sure.' *I wish I could be so confident,* was Kate's rueful thought. 'It's my belief he has the makings of a fine man. I would wish to have a hand in the accomplishment of that end.'

She gave him a questioning look.

'I will tell you all when we're indoors out of this wind. I wager you'll like what I have to say, and young Toby too.' He caught her eye, smiled, then changed the subject. 'I see you've got your ploughing done. The sowing too?'

Within sight of the house, Kate found her heart beginning to pound. Would Nicholas be there, and how would he greet their guest?

'The children are in the garden with Jane,' John Emerson told her as they dismounted in the yard. 'I was about to ride with Master Toby.'

'And my brother?'

'In his chamber, I believe.'

That was a relief in a way, though she'd half hoped that Nicholas would have taken the opportunity to ride with Toby this morning, as a first step towards mending their fractured relationship.

She led their guest upstairs to the parlour, where some of Holywell's precious store of sack was brought to them, with the last of the almond cakes.

Sir Cuthbert leaned back in his chair, took a sip of the wine. 'Now, madam—'

Behind Kate, the door opened. She looked round to see Nicholas standing there. 'I heard you had returned, sister.' He broke off. 'Sir?'

Anxiety thudded freshly through her. 'Nicholas, this is Sir Cuthbert Featherstone, our dear neighbour and friend. Sir Cuthbert, my brother Nicholas Gaunt.'

Rather than the customary bow, Nicholas managed only the very slightest inclination of the head. 'Sir!' Not *'Your servant, sir!'* as ought to have been the greeting to his social superior. His expression only too clearly showed his distaste.

'Do take a seat, Nicholas. Some wine?' She hoped the tremor in her voice was not too audible to her guest. Part of her hoped her brother would accept the invitation; another that he would refuse it completely and leave the room.

He sat down, at some distance from them both. 'No wine, I thank you.'

What now? She was anxious to hear what Sir Cuthbert wanted to tell her, but with Nicholas there it had all become so awkward and uncomfortable. She drew a deep breath, forced a lightness of tone she did not feel. 'Sir Cuthbert tells me you are suspected of being a priest in disguise.'

There was no softening in Nicholas's voice. 'Oh? Is that what brought you here?'

'No, only in part. Your sister has a troublesome tenant, who reported this from malice. But that was of no great importance. I came to rescind the invitation to dine, due to my wife's indisposition. And to make an offer, which I think will be acceptable to your sister and her son.' There was no response from Nicholas. Sir Cuthbert cleared his throat, as if aware of a chill in the atmosphere, then turned all his attention to Kate.

'You know my son Hal is to go to Cambridge this coming Michaelmas?'

'I think Toby mentioned it.' As he had indeed, more than once, with a piercing envy in his voice, for yet another privilege that their faith denied him.

'How would you feel if your boy were to go with him?'

She stared at him, trying to take in what he was saying. Nothing in their conversation this morning had prepared her for this.

'I'd pay for his keep, all that he needs, as I would do for my own flesh and blood. That's the offer.'

'A very generous one!' She dared not look at Nicholas, though she could feel the hostility that emanated from him as if it had taken physical shape.

Perhaps Sir Cuthbert had seen something in his face, and hers too, for he added, 'Oh, I know you have worries about the oath. I assure you, he'd have no need to take his degree. That's done all the time by those of your faith. I know all that business, swearing against the Pope—you won't want that for him. But he would have the studies behind him, to help him on his way in life.'

'If he left the place without contamination.' Nicholas's voice was icy.

A little silence, while Sir Cuthbert pondered the matter. Then: 'I think he would be pleased by the proposal.'

Of that Kate had no doubt: Toby would be rapturous, entranced. 'You have not mentioned this to him, I hope?'

'Not as yet. I had thought to speak of it when you dined with us, but as it happens...'

She felt swept by relief. 'Please, I beg you not to speak of it to Toby, not for the time being.'

'Not at all!' Nicholas rose to his feet, all cold formality. 'We thank you for your offer, which is I am sure meant kindly. We will give it due consideration.'

Rage swept through Kate. Her response to Sir Cuthbert would have been very much the same, for the offer had taken her by surprise and she needed time to consider all its implications and decide what to do. But for Nicholas to take it on himself to speak for her, as if the decision lay entirely with him—that infuriated her, though she tried to repress the feeling.

Furthermore, his tone and manner made it very clear that this was a dismissal, a signal for Sir Cuthbert to leave. Their neighbour might not be the most sensitive of men, but he could hardly miss the implication, and he was not one to outstay his welcome.

He gulped down the last of his wine and stood up. 'Time I was on my way, my dear madam.' He bowed to Kate. 'Let me know what you wish me to do. I think it just the thing for the boy.'

She took his hand, the warmth of her voice making up (she hoped) for her brother's churlishness. 'I can't thank you enough for your generosity.'

Relieved that Nicholas made no attempt to follow, she went with Sir Cuthbert to the yard, standing by until he had mounted his horse. 'Forgive my brother if he seemed a little less than grateful. He does not know you as I do.'

'Nor I him. I'm sorry not to have made better acquaintance with him. Another time perhaps.'

Could he really mean that? His face gave nothing away. 'Thank you sir. God speed.'

Once he'd gone, she stood where she was, trying to bring herself under control, fighting anger, resentment and a conflicting sense that there was no logical reason for her to quarrel with her brother. He'd said nothing that she would not have said herself if he had left it to her. Which was precisely the point: he had taken it on himself to speak for her, without her agreement.

He met her in the passageway. 'An impertinent offer, a dangerous one—and one you should have refused instantly.'

'He meant it kindly. He has a generous heart. It's no small thing.'

'No small thing! He aims to lure your son to his heretic church.'

Was that true? 'If Toby does not take his degree, as Sir Cuthbert suggested, he would not have to swear the Oath of Supremacy.'

'Our kinsman Richard Thornton did just that, and now I fear his faith is wavering. Yet I'd have sworn he was immoveable. Toby is, I think, less steady, more easily swayed.'

She had no means of knowing if he was right about Richard Thornton. But to deny her son so great an opportunity, a chance to leave home and begin to make his own way in the world, as a young man—could she do it? And if, as she feared, word of the offer were to reach him somehow, what would his reaction be? She could imagine only too well.

'You can't think of accepting this proposition, surely?'

'I need to consider it. I cannot take it lightly.'

'Indeed not, for I'm convinced it is not lightly made.

On the contrary! Pray about it, Kate. That will put you right.' He straightened, drew himself up to his full height, took a deep breath. 'One thing is sure. This changes everything. It would not be enough for me to come here as your steward. That will solve nothing, so long as Toby mingles with such as the Featherstones. There is too much temptation by far. You will assuredly lose him. He will as certainly be lost to the Church.'

She had been uneasy at her brother's decision to come and live at Holywell. Now that he had with equal suddenness changed his mind, she felt bewildered, unsure of herself. Perhaps they were more alike than she had thought, both given to making impulsive decisions and then regretting them soon afterwards. A part of her felt relieved that the complications of that first decision would be avoided: Toby's inevitable resistance, her own resentment (however sinful) at submitting herself to her brother's control. But she was wary of what might follow. 'Then what will you do?'

'I have a thought, but it's too soon. I need to consider what is best, with the greatest urgency. When I know, I will tell you. Meanwhile—' He took her hands in his, his gaze burning on her face. 'Kate, I beg you for the sake of your soul and those of your children, cut yourself off from your neighbours, have dealings only with those of our faith! That is the only way to be safe.'

She felt a knot tighten inside her. 'You make it sound so easy. My whole life is bound up with our friends.'

'As it should never have been, from the start. Why else come here?'

She had no argument to offer. She simply felt very tired, weary of the whole thing. 'I will pray about it, of course. I always would have done. We shall see.'

He was not pleased, but he let it go; temporarily, she knew. 'And I shall pray, of course. There must be a way.'

All she knew was that it would not be a way that would offer Toby the opportunity he would so much have welcomed.

That was Jane's view too, when later Kate found a moment to tell her of it. 'Master Toby would be overjoyed. He'd like nothing better. But you?'

'It's the risk to his faith, the danger to his soul.'

'You don't trust him?'

The question startled Kate. How could Jane think otherwise, knowing Toby so well? 'Would you?'

'I think I'd leave it in God's hands.'

Kate gazed at the other woman's calm face. She had not heard Jane speak quite like this before. Always dutifully observant of the demands of their faith, she had never as far as Kate recalled shown much of what lay below the surface. 'Is that enough?' Realising what she was saying, Kate pressed her hand to her mouth. 'Oh! Of course, it must be. But isn't it wrong to put temptation in his way?'

''He doesn't know about it?'

'Not yet. Only I don't altogether trust that none of Sir Cuthbert's household will let it slip.'

'And if you were then to refuse? That would bring a storm on your head.'

'I know.'

The following morning Kate woke from a troubled sleep to Jane's usual greeting; only it was not as usual, for she could see at once that something had driven out all Jane's customary calmness.

'Madam, you should know. It seems…your brother. He's gone.'

Kate slid from the bed, began hurriedly to dress. 'Gone? Gone where?'

'I don't know, madam. John said he heard him long before dawn, saddling his horse. He got up to see what was amiss, but Master Nicholas said only that he had a matter to attend to.'

She struggled to understand, to take it all in. Was this what Nicholas had meant when he said he 'had a thought'? Where could he have gone?

'He left this, madam.' Jane held out a piece of paper, which Kate shakily unfolded.

My most dear sister,

I pray you will forgive my hasty departure. It is for a short time only. There is something I must do, which I trust will be to your advantage, for the good of your son's soul. You must refuse that devil's offer, as Eve should have refused the apple. At the very least make no decision, take no action before I return, as I shall do, God willing, in less than seven days.

Your brother, N

Kate handed the message to Jane, who read it. 'The devil's offer? That's Sir Cuthbert's offer to Master Toby? Hmm.'

'He hints that he has something else in mind. But what? To go so suddenly, with no word to me at all. I don't understand him.' Head whirling, she finished dressing, trying to calm herself. 'We shall know in time, I suppose. Meanwhile, to prayers.'

Descending the stairs, she braced herself for Toby's anticipated delight at his uncle's departure, while being guiltily aware that her son was not the only one to feel a sense of relief. She herself was conscious of the easing of a tension she'd barely known was there. Life was so much simpler without the need to conform to her brother's rigid standards, to steel herself to argue against them, to defend the choices she made, to soothe Toby's anger.

And meanwhile they were free to resume their normal routines. As soon as Dame Juliana's indisposition had ended they dined at Meadhope Hall; from which happy gathering Toby returned full of excitement. 'Mother, Hal says his father will pay for me to go to Cambridge, when he goes up, this very Michaelmas!'

So much for Nicholas's warnings! It was as she had feared: in that easy-going household where few had ever felt the need to watch their tongues, there was little hope of keeping the matter secret.

Kate sighed. 'I asked Sir Cuthbert to say nothing to

you for the moment.'

'Hal said he'd been told not to. But why shouldn't he? It's what I'd like above everything. I can go, can't I, mother?' He studied his mother's face, all the excitement slowly fading from his expression. 'You wouldn't refuse me this?'

'I think you know why I have doubts about it, Toby. I need time to consider it, and even then…You must be patient, and not hope too much. It is likely enough it will not happen.' She laid a hand on his shoulder. 'Nothing's decided yet, not for certain.'

She saw he was close to tears.

'I'll do anything you want, I promise. I'll seek out somewhere I can go to Mass, as much as I can. And I'll never ever speak loosely of holy things. I'll keep away from bad company. Anything. Please let me go! I want it so much.'

'I know. I know. We shall see.'

Oh, if only he had not made that stupid joke the other day! Toby felt deeply ashamed—or at least ashamed his mother should have heard it. He knew too how much he'd hurt her, and he did not like the feeling. More to the point, if he'd known this offer was to come from Sir Cuthbert he would have been so much more careful. He was thankful that (according to Jane and contrary to his assumption) his uncle had not been told of the incident, for he guessed that Nicholas would use every argument possible to prevent him from going to Cambridge. He was grateful to his mother for that, and just hoped it was not too late to convince her that he could be trusted.

Yet part of him resented the need for it. Why shouldn't he make jokes with his friends, like any normal boy of his age? The unfairness of being so set apart that he could not share the common daily talk of other boys; that was a constant sore. How could they be friends in earnest, if this thing was always to stand between them? How could he ever be accepted by his contemporaries, when his whole life was tainted by the fate his birth had decreed for him?

Still, his uncle had gone, taking his malign influence with him, the dreary preachiness, the scowls of disapproval. How long he would be away, Toby did not know. His mother had said only that he would soon return. He knew he must do everything he could as speedily as possible to show his mother that he could be trusted, that he could go to Cambridge and still remain as staunch a Catholic as she would wish.

There was, too, at the back of his mind, the thought that if he were to make a success of his time there, even take his degree and afterwards forge a career for himself, then Sir Cuthbert might look favourably on him as a potential son-in-law. How he was to achieve this in the short time before Bess would inevitably be married off to someone else he did not quite know, but the thought was there, a possibility he knew he could never speak of before his mother.

So, he was scrupulous at attending prayers, being in

time always for meals, helping to serve at table with unusual eagerness, caring for the younger ones, taking them riding, even including Mariana in that privilege. She was in fact a better rider than either of his brothers, and much more fun to ride with, so the concession was easily made. He began to enjoy the feeling of being the good older brother, worthy of the respect and even adoration of his juniors. It brought a dim far-distant memory to his mind. Long ago, he had been cared for by a beloved older brother exactly as he was doing now. Once, he had ridden in Tom's protective company. He'd been just a small child then, barely breeched, but some sort of memory had stayed with him, a warm memory tinged with pain.

Only on two occasions did he meet Bess, both times by chance, though he had a suspicion that she had deliberately put herself in his way. He made the most of each opportunity, carefully avoiding any discussion of the future, simply enjoying the moment.

He rode home after their second meeting feeling happy and optimistic. His uncle had been gone for three weeks now, and Toby suspected that even his mother had begun to think he would not return, or so Jane had told him. It was a bright day, and his mother had been intending to spend the afternoon preparing herbs in the stillroom, something she always enjoyed. Now might be the moment to find her alone and win her over; to entice her to say yes to his going to Cambridge.

He was whistling as he rode into the stable yard, where

John was rubbing down a sturdy brown horse, a strange horse, not one of theirs. No, not strange: he'd seen it before, ridden by his uncle.

Toby dragged his own beast to a halt (not difficult, when it was within sight of a stall and food). John looked up. 'Master Gaunt has returned.'

Toby fought an urge to turn his horse round and ride away, anywhere beyond his uncle's reach. But that would solve nothing. The most urgent thing was to get his mother to agree to Sir Cuthbert's plan before his uncle could work on her. If he'd just arrived, he'd likely go to tidy himself before spending time with her, or so Toby hoped. If only he'd tackled her yesterday or the day before, not put it off until what seemed the perfect moment.

He dismounted, stabled his horse, noting that the adjacent stall was occupied by a mare he had most definitely not seen before, a well-made strawberry roan. 'Master Gaunt brought that one with him,' John told him. Toby would have liked to ask more, to look the horse over, but that must wait until another time.

He braced himself and went into the house, looking for his mother. Not in the stillroom, or the kitchen or the garden…He was making his way to the parlour when he met Jane. 'Your uncle is with her. She asked not to be disturbed.'

His heart sank. It looked as if he was too late. Or was there still hope? He sent up a little prayer and went in search of his brothers and sister, who were at their lessons.

'Uncle Nicholas is back.' Edward spoke as if it was a matter for rejoicing.

'I know. Where has he been? Where did he go?'

'Don't know. He went straight to talk with mother. He was in a good mood.'

The thought of Nicholas in a good mood was not, for Toby, a happy one.

In the parlour, Kate, who had faced her brother's return with mixed feelings, was finding herself more surprised with every moment.

Even as he'd embraced her out in the yard, she'd been aware of some subtle change in him, though she could not quite think what. 'Dear Kate! Forgive me, I had not meant to be away so long, but there were things—Well, I have much to tell you.'

She drew away from his embrace, unsure how she felt, unsure of him. 'Have you eaten? You must be tired.'

'I dined on the way, not to put you to too much trouble. I can wait until supper time. But first, dear Kate, there is something I must say to you.'

In the privacy of the parlour, he took her hands, while she braced herself for one of his admonitions.

'Kate, I have been wrong, harsh even. I have judged you by what ought to be, in a perfect world, not by what is, by what you have endured as a lone woman.'

She stared at him, bewildered. 'I don't understand?'

'Let's sit down, then.' He took his seat across the

hearth. 'What I saw here, when I first came back—it was what I wished to see, what I hoped to see. And when I realised it was not quite so, I judged you harshly, as I would a man. I made no allowance for all you have suffered, all you have done, the many demands upon you, a mere woman. Further than that, I was wrong in how I handled your son. You urged me to approach him differently, more gently and kindly, and you were right. I see that now. So I ask your forgiveness, for the love you bear me, for all you have done for me. For the love I bear you.'

It took her some time, through her astonishment, to find the right words. But how could she reject him, after that rush of feeling? 'Of course I forgive you, if indeed there is anything to forgive.'

'Oh indeed there is, and you will see it in my amendment of life, in the way I behave towards you and towards all your household.'

Tears came to her eyes. This new humble, loving man beside her was offering a fresh start to their revived relationship, as if those awkward uncomfortable past days were to be wiped out. Or so it seemed. Was that really possible? 'What has brought this about?'

'In this case, I sought counsel from one, a priest of the Jesuit order, whom I regard as the wisest and most holy of men.' A faint smile. 'It could be that your prayers also reached me, as before.' He released her hands. 'But that's enough of that. I have a matter of the gravest importance that I wish to put before you. It concerns Toby.'

Her heart thudded. 'Ah! I should warn you—he knows of Sir Cuthbert's offer. Young Hal let it slip.'

'That's most unfortunate. How did he take your refusal?'

She hesitated, trying to find a reply that would not anger him or deepen the frown of disapproval barring his brow. 'I have not yet told him. I was not quite sure.'

'How could you be unsure? There can be no question —' He fell silent, took a deep breath, as if reminding himself that he claimed to have changed; spoke more slowly. 'I hope that what I have to offer will eclipse that proposal.'

She could not imagine what would be more likely to appeal to Toby than the prospect of going to university with his dearest friend. 'If it comes from you, he may not like it, on principle.'

'I know. I have work to do there. But you will see the change I shall bring about.' His eyes held hers, full of excitement, while he paused as if seeking the right words for what he wanted to say.

'I cannot think what you have in mind, unless it's to repeat your intention to come to live here, if not as my steward, then in some other capacity.' But Toby would hate that, unless Nicholas had indeed changed very much. It was hardly a solution.

'No, that isn't at all what I have in mind. He must of course leave Holywell and all its temptations.' He paused, as if conscious once again that he had been reverting to an approach he had renounced. When he spoke next it was slowly, softly. 'I think you will agree that it would be for the best were he to be removed from all contact with heretics, so long as he is sufficiently content with the arrangement.'

'You may be right, but I can't see how that's possible. As I said, I'm sure he has no vocation for the priesthood, so sending him overseas wouldn't do. And in my view he's too young to go as a soldier.'

'Oh, much too young, Kate. I wouldn't wish for that for him. No, I have a better idea. Hear me!'

Chapter Seven

Seething with resentment, Toby stood with bent head among the household gathered for prayers. Nicholas began, his voice grating on Toby's nerves.

There was something different, a warmth in the tone, a short prayer in English. Then: *'Gloria Patri et Filio, et Spiritui Sancto. Amen.'*

Toby shot a look at his uncle. Surely he couldn't have reached the end so soon?

He had, for he'd raised his head and was exchanging a remark with Edward, who was standing beside him. Toby caught his mother's eye. She had a faint smile, a knowing smile, as if she understood Toby's astonishment, but had expected this to happen.

What now? It was a Saturday, so he could hardly hurry away to his lessons. Could he approach his mother, asking for a quiet word? Perhaps that smile offered hope that she was going to give him what he so longed for.

He felt a hand on his arm.

'Toby, I would show you something. I think it will please you.'

I doubt it, thought Toby, but after glancing at his mother, who was watching him in an anxious manner that only made him more uneasy, he followed his uncle out into the yard and across to the stables.

'I have seen that you lack a good horse.'

Toby caught his breath. The strange horse, the roan

he'd seen yesterday afternoon—could it be…? No, surely not. Such things did not happen to him, especially not at the hands of his uncle. Heart thudding, he went with Nicholas until he came to a halt right in front of the roan's stall.

'Take a look at this beast. Tell me what you think. You ride a good deal with young Featherstone—he has access to a decent stable, so I understand. John Emerson tells me you have the makings of a good horseman, though sadly you've not given me any opportunity to observe that for myself. I think you will have picked up some knowledge over time.' Toby glanced at Nicholas, who was smiling. 'Go ahead. Look her over. Bring her into the daylight.'

The mare was not showy nor especially spirited, but she was, Toby thought, a good solid riding horse, reliable and steadfast, in appearance at least. Once out in the yard, he ran his hands over the animal's legs, led her around to examine her gait, looked in her mouth, hoping all the time that he gave the impression of knowing what he was doing.

'Well, what do you think?'

'She's a good horse, sir.' He waited, heart thudding. 'You brought her here?'

'I did. I thought her likely to suit you. Make use of her while I'm here. And afterwards, keep her for your future use, if all goes well.'

At Cambridge? He knew he would need a horse there, yet he could hardly deprive his mother's household of one of their few useable beasts. He shot a look at his uncle, trying to read his expression. Was this the explanation of his changed manner, that he had come round to accepting the idea?

Toby was torn between mistrust and hope, wondering whether to say more, to bring his questions into the open. 'I thank you, sir.' He longed to ask for a fuller explanation, but dared not; not yet.

'I think you will wish to try this creature's paces. She's called Ruby. Not very original, but there we are.'

Toby saddled the horse, mounted, gave his uncle one last questioning look—'Off you go! Then tell me what you think!'—and left the stable yard at a brisk trot.

He had sometimes been allowed to ride one of the Meadhope horses, but to ride a good horse, knowing that it might be his, at least for a time: the enjoyment was beyond words. He could feel the reserves of strength and stamina, the animal's eager response to his direction. It was a huge pleasure. If only it had not been offered to him by Nicholas! And if only he did not fear that there would inevitably be a price to be paid for this unexpected gift, not in money but in some commitment on his part.

'I like her very much, sir,' he told his uncle on returning to the yard. Such cold words, when he was flooded with delight!

'Then make use of her while you can. After that, then we shall see.'

He hated that phrase when his mother used it; even more now, from his uncle. Suddenly tired of all the hints, the prevarications, he drew a deep breath. 'I will need a horse at Cambridge. She will be perfect for me.'

He swung from the saddle, finding himself eye to eye with Nicholas, seeing the coldness in the man's gaze; and knew then, at once, that any hope he might have felt had been utterly misplaced.

'Oh no, Toby. Cambridge is out of the question. You must surely be aware of that?'

He was plunged into despair. Oh, he had been right to mistrust his uncle! All that softness, the shorter prayers, the friendly manner; the gift of the horse—they were all designed to lead up to some other end, one Nicholas knew full well that Toby would dislike.

'It's for my mother to say.' His tone was truculent, defiant.

'Your mother agrees with me.'

'Then I shall ask her!'

'Do. But bear in mind that I am the head of the family now, as your closest male relative.'

He seemed impervious to Toby's glowering look. 'Shall we ride together? It's a fine day for a ride.'

Toby flung the reins towards his uncle. 'I'll not ride with you! I'm—I'm...' What? He had no idea what to do now. Saddle up his old horse and ride that sorry beast instead? That would be very hard. 'I've got other things to do.'

He strode away, angry, despairing, loathing his uncle.

* * *

After that Toby gave up trying to please anyone. It had got him nowhere so why should he make the effort? He was present at prayer and meal times only sufficiently often to keep him from too much in the way of a reprimand. He even stopped trying to please his mother. He noticed with a sense of triumphant justification that his uncle's prayers grew imperceptibly longer, day by day. He was clearly reverting to his old ways, a sure sign that he had not really changed at all. It had been a ruse to win Toby over, nothing more. A couple of times Nicholas tried to entice him to join in some activity with the other children, and once, by himself. But Toby refused to be cajoled. When he needed a horse, he rode his old unsatisfactory beast, while painfully conscious of the roan mare waiting in her stall. 'She needs exercise, Toby,' his uncle told him one day. 'You should ride her.'

'Ride her yourself!' he threw back at him, though longing tore at him.

It was just after prayers on the following Friday, a week after Nicholas's return, that he overheard a brief exchange between his uncle and his mother. 'I can delay no longer, Kate. I am needed there.'

Delay no longer? Needed there? Try as he would, Toby was not able to hear any more, but his heart leapt. It was clear (wasn't it?) that Nicholas was saying he was about to leave Holywell, perhaps for good. Once he was gone, surely his mother could be won over, would relent, would allow him to go to Cambridge? He was as certain as he could be of anything that it was his uncle who was preventing him from taking up the offer. He just had to be patient a little longer.

'Toby, your uncle wishes to speak to you.'

Having just returned from a particularly agreeable session with Bess Featherstone (in the Featherstone orchard, this time), Toby stared stupidly at his mother, while a cold shiver travelled the length of his spine. Could they possibly have found out?

'In the parlour, in private.'

'But—Why?'

With a gentle smile, his mother laid a hand on his arm. 'The reason will please you, I'm sure. But tidy yourself a little first.'

'Yes, mother.'

Not at all reassured, he went to change into a clean shirt, resentment seething inside him.

He found his brothers in their room, looking over some music together.

'Uncle Nicholas wants us to sing tomorrow.' The next day was a Sunday, when, in the absence of a priest to say Mass, their mother alway led them in more celebratory prayers, with singing for festive occasions. 'You should come and practise with us.'

He had no intention of doing so. 'It'll go on for ever. Last Sunday was bad enough.'

Edward looked shocked. 'I don't know how you can say that. I love to hear Uncle Nicholas.'

'As far as I'm concerned he can't leave too soon.'

'He does go on a bit sometimes, but not as much as he used to. And when he rides with us—You don't know what you're missing, Toby.'

Oh yes I do, thought Toby. *And I know what I'm gaining: Hal's company and (with luck) a few more moments with Bess...* The very thought excited him so much that he had to turn away from his brothers, trying to calm his quickened breathing.

The thought of the roan mare slipped tantalisingly into his mind, but he pushed it aside. He still had no clear idea why Nicholas had offered it to him, but that was beside the point. He wanted nothing at his uncle's hands.

He guessed there would be a long lecture on how he ought to behave, perhaps a reiteration of the refusal to allow him to go to Cambridge. He braced himself for it as he made his way to the parlour. He would endure it, while telling himself it would all soon be at an end. This must surely be Nicholas's final harangue before leaving Holywell.

Outside the parlour he paused, took a deep breath and then pushed open the door. His uncle stood by the window.

'Sit down, nephew.'

Toby sat on the fringed stool his uncle had indicated, very upright, hands clasped in his lap, trying not to look as nervous as he felt.

'Have you any clear thoughts about your future?'

To marry Bess? To go to Cambridge? To live the normal life of a country gentleman? There was no point at all in saying any of that, or not to his uncle at least. He would save it for his mother, when Nicholas had gone.

He shrugged. 'Nothing much, I suppose.'

There was a little silence, while Nicholas studied his face and Toby simply felt uncomfortable and irritated, wishing this was over and he could leave the room.

'I understand you.'

Do you? How could you possibly?

'You are angry with the Church. But it is the injustice of the laws that should anger you, not the demands made by our faith. The churches are rightfully ours, as were the monasteries and their lands taken from us by unjust monarchs, desecrated and ruined by evil men. That is what should make you angry.'

'What use would that be? It doesn't change anything.'

There was a pause, which made Toby think his words had struck home.

'It could change everything, in time, with discretion and skill and courage.' Nicholas gave a faint smile. 'Oh, I know it seems hard to you here, where to be faithful seems always to mean poverty and discomfort, to be set apart from your neighbours. True, such a life is no less a calling than the heroic vocation to martyrdom, but at your age it's hard to see the truth of that. I know this only too well, for at your age I thought as you do. But were you to find yourself among others who shared your faith, who could work together for the conversion of England, who would face any danger, any hazard to achieve that end, then you would not seek to turn your back on the Church.'

In spite of himself, the words tugged at something deep inside Toby, but he pushed them aside. As he struggled to find the right thing to say, his uncle went on. 'Let me put a proposal to you. One that I think will give purpose to your life and offer you prospects that you may not have considered.'

Toby had an appalling vision of being shipped overseas, along with Edward, to a life of abstinence and prayer. He straightened, ready to fend off any such suggestion, his face guarded, his voice cold. 'Sir?'

'I shall return to Ashby St Ledgers in a few days'— Toby's heart leapt. *Deo Gratias!*—'and would wish to take you with me. Your mother agrees.'

It was a different vision, but every bit as bad, to be every moment in the company of this pious, preachy, joyless uncle of his. 'Sir—I—No—' What could he say? Was he free to refuse?

'Your mother is greatly approving of the proposal. It seems to her to offer the perfect solution to your future.'

To leave Holywell, and Hal, and Bess; to give up all hope of living a normal life, until such time as he could make his escape from his uncle's clutches? No! The thought was unendurable. 'I do not think, sir...'

Nicholas held up a hand. 'Wait, Toby. Hear me out. You would be part of the household at Ashby, where you will always find the resources of our faith: priests to say Mass and hear confessions and offer guidance, the finest priests in the mission field, of the Jesuit order.'

'Father Fielding doesn't like the Jesuits. He says they're trouble-makers.'

Nicholas frowned, though his voice remained gentle. 'I would suggest Father Fielding knows little of them. You would soon find how mistaken he is. That's not all. Lady Anne Catesby, a most holy gentlewoman, the lady of the house, she sets the tone of the place. But it is her son Robert Catesby—He is...well, you will discover what manner of man he is. I can barely find the words. You could not fail to love him, as do all who meet him.' Nicholas's face was rapt, lit with enthusiasm. The tenderness in his voice astonished Toby. 'He would take you under his wing as far as the martial arts are concerned. Should you one day wish to become a soldier—you are young yet, I know, and it's too soon to map out your path. But to be taught by a master in horsemanship and swordsmanship, as well as being educated in the manners and virtues of a gentleman: I think you would find that to your taste. Is that not so, Toby?'

It did not sound so bad, on the surface. It even sounded enticing in a way, just the sort of thing that would have appealed to him, in normal circumstances. If anyone else had offered him such a prospect, he would have been tempted. But from his uncle—well, that was quite another matter.

He straightened, trying to look like a responsible young man, well able to make a sound decision about his future. 'I think I would rather go to Cambridge, sir.'

There was a silence, while Nicholas studied Toby's face in a way that made the boy feel acutely uncomfortable. It was almost as if he could read everything that was going on in his mind. When he spoke again his tone was gentle, even kindly. 'Toby, I have been where you are now, resentful of all our faith demands of us, restless, unhappy, not knowing where to turn. I understand you so well, better than you realise. At Ashby you will find a man who can be your guide, show you the way, set you on the right path. I would be honoured to be the one to lead you into his household.' He laid a hand on Toby's arm. 'It is what your mother wishes too.'

It was she who had sent him to this meeting! The realisation struck him at last that he could no longer hope for any help from his mother. He felt, bleakly, as if a trap had closed over him. 'Do I have any choice, sir?'

'We all have free will. But in this case—' He shrugged. 'However, we will speak again in the morning, when you have had time to think, and pray.'

In the darkness before dawn Toby slipped from the house, saddled his horse and rode away from Holywell. He had no idea where he was going, no plans, no thought in his head except to ride and ride and put as much distance as possible between himself and his hated uncle. It was an escape from prison, a flight to freedom.

But it was pouring with rain and his thick cloak soon

became a sodden weight on his back and shoulders. It grew a little less dark, the air thickening with the scent of newly-revived fires in cottages and houses from which sometimes lights glowed. In them would be warmth and food, and people who cared for one another, really cared.

It was far too early to go to Meadhope Hall. Very likely Hal, with the rest of the household, would still be asleep. For a moment his imagination hovered on Bess, all soft rosy warmth in a bed rich with the scent of her. Oh, to be lying beside her now!

Stupid even to dream of it…

He drew rein as he came within sight of the Hall, toying with the idea of making his way to the kitchen, in the hope that someone there would be awake and take pity on him. But he thought better of it, knowing that he would find only the most menial kitchen servants about, lighting the fires before the cook was up.

Not far from the Hall was the church, whose door was never locked. It would offer some kind of shelter. He dismounted, paused. Someone was crossing the churchyard, coming his way.

He slipped back behind the building, watching. Master Langley—of course, it was Sunday! He would be going to make ready for the day's services.

Toby waited until the rector had disappeared into the church before mounting his horse again.

There was nothing for it now but to have a vigorous ride, without aim or object, trying to keep to the most sheltered ways, until he and his horse were exhausted and hunger had become an agony for him. So he dug in his heels and rode, on and on, without thinking where he was going.

In time the rain ceased and the sun rose, with a drying wind. Time passed: he had no idea how much, but hunger told him it was a very long time since he'd eaten. From the angle of the sun he thought it was nearly midday.

He had no intention of going home, not under any circumstances. So it must be the Hall, where by now the household would have returned from church. Perhaps he could appeal to Sir Cuthbert, asking him for shelter from his mother and his uncle.

Stupid idea—would Hal's father ever encourage disobedience to one's parents and superiors? Unlikely, surely. But possible, just possible.

He handed his horse to a groom in the stable yard and then wondered what to do next. Would they all be at dinner? Could he make his presence known and still be sure of a welcome, on this day when he would not be expected?

Unsure, he put his head round the kitchen door and found his favourite kitchen maid cutting bread. Almost before he spoke she'd handed him a large crust to eat. Not wanting to impose on her or get her into trouble by begging more food, he took the bread and wandered into the herb plot at the further end of the garden, where the sun had woken the scents to life; and—joy of joys!—he found Bess wandering the paths.

A swift glance round told him she was alone. 'Bess!'

She turned at his hoarse whisper. 'Toby! What are you doing here?'

He put his finger to his lips. She gestured towards the honeysuckle-draped arbour that filled a corner of the garden and he followed her there, taking a seat beside her on the stone bench. It was not quite large enough for two when one of them was wearing her best farthingale, so they were very close. He could feel his breathing quicken, more so as she took his hand in hers. 'Did you come to see me?'

The truth? No. 'Of course.' He leaned closer to her, found her receptive mouth, slid his hand under the low neck of her gown. Oh, this was what he needed, even if he had not known it, his Bess in his arms, the world shut out. Nothing else mattered.

'What—? Bess! Toby!'

They sprang apart. Toby, jumping to his feet, met the furious gaze of his friend, his dear friend Hal, looking as he had never looked before.

'What in God's name do you think you're doing with my sister?'

Bess laid a hand on her brother's arm. She looked remarkably calm. 'Hal, it's nothing. He's my friend too, you know.'

Hal scowled at her. 'You'd best go in, Bess. Mother sent me to find find you. It's dinner time.' He might be her junior, but in this she obeyed him, looking a little subdued, though she turned on her way to blow a furtive kiss to Toby, who dared not return it.

The two boys stood facing one another, Hal's face set in severe lines that made him look years older and caused Toby to feel like a chidden child. Hal was quivering with rage, his fists clenched at his sides, as if to prevent himself from hitting his friend.

'What do you think you were doing with my sister?'

Toby cleared his throat, trying to find an assertive voice. 'I love her.'

'Don't be stupid, Toby. She's not a kitchen wench for you to dally with. I thought better of you than that. It's an insult, a real insult.'

'Why? Am I not worthy of her?'

'You're a Catholic, a recusant. You've no money and no land and no prospects. You can't possibly have imagined she could be anything to you!'

Coming from his dearest friend this was unbearably hurtful. If only he could have prevented the hot colour from flooding his face! 'I meant no harm. She did not seem...' No, he could not even hint, as he'd been about to do, that she had encouraged him, for that would bring shame on her.

'You'd best go. I wish we didn't have to meet again, ever. I shan't say anything to my parents, for my sister's sake, but I won't be talking to you at our lessons. If you can find a way not to come to them, that would be the honourable thing.'

Oh, I can find a way! Toby thought as he rode back to Holywell, angry, sick, miserable, drenched with a sense of abandonment.

Do I have any choice? He'd asked his uncle yesterday. Now he knew the answer.

Chapter Eight

It was the right choice, the right decision; of course it was! She had thought and prayed about it for the two long weeks since Nicholas had put the proposal before her.

Yet a heavy weight of dread crouched inside Kate as she made her way downstairs on the morning of Toby's departure. One glance at his face as he stepped into the screen passage, arms full of his few belongings, made her feel no better. He did not look in the least like a lad about to embark on an exciting new phase of his life.

She could not bear it, to see him go like this, locked into some miserable world of his own, with no trace left of the impish humour, the wayward charm that had always both exasperated and delighted her. She had lost one son on a day of grief and pain; she could not endure losing another the same way.

She went to him. 'Toby—'

'I'm taking these out to my saddle bags.' His voice was expressionless; his eyes did not meet hers.

'Have you eaten?'

'I'm not hungry.'

'You must eat. You've a long journey ahead of you.'

He turned from her with a shrug. She reached out and took his arm.

'Toby, it's for the best. You will have a happy and useful life.' How could she be sure of this? She had thought her doubts had been laid to rest, but now...

'I expect so.' He freed himself. 'Did you send word to Master Langley?' So cold!

The previous day the rector had sent to ask if Toby was ill, since he had failed to turn up for his lessons.

'John took my letter.' She had sent another to Sir Cuthbert, thanking him for all his kindness to her son, explaining only that Toby was to go away with his uncle, to further his education.

Toby moved to the door, dropping a soft red shoe as he went. Kate picked it up. She'd had shoes made for each of the children, for their occasional dancing lessons. From the very first, Toby had danced well, eyes sparkling, full of mischief and happiness.

As they had not sparkled all week, since last Sunday; the day when, late again, he'd agreed to go with his uncle, and—suddenly meticulously dutiful—lost all the light from his eyes. Oh, what had she done, by falling in with Nicholas's plan?

'You dropped this, Toby. Let me help!'

'I can manage, thank you, mother.'

She tucked the shoe into the random cluster of belongings in his arms. So many questions crowded her head, but she had no idea how to begin to ask them. On the two occasions during the past week when she'd tried to prompt him into confiding in her, she'd been sharply rebuffed. Instinct told her it would be the same this morning. She was about to try one last time, when Nicholas emerged from the hall.

'We're all gathered for prayers, sister. You take your place. I'll bring Toby.'

As she entered the hall, Kate passed Jane, who reached out and, briefly, took her hand. Their eyes met; two women about to say farewell to the boy they loved. Kate squeezed Jane's hand before releasing it and going to take her place before the assembled household.

It was fully daylight by the time the travellers were ready to leave. In the yard, damp with mist, John held the horses, Nicholas's solid brown gelding and the roan mare he had so generously brought for an ungrateful Toby.

'Don't leave it so long before you come again.' Kate embraced her brother, though it was not *his* departure that filled her thoughts.

'That's in God's hands.'

'Not entirely.' Then, when he said nothing, 'Toby seems very unhappy.'

'We are not called to be happy. Be thankful the wildness has left him. I've seen the change these past days.'

Was this what she wanted, to see Toby remade in Nicholas's image, if that was what it was?

He held her a little away from him. 'You know you can safely entrust your son to my care. For his soul's sake.'

'Have a care for his body too!' Her voice shook, though she tried to keep it light.

'You can be sure of that. He will be cared for as I care for myself.'

'I don't find that very reassuring.' She forced a tremulous smile.

He kissed her. 'Be sure, dear sister, his welfare is everything to me. A sacred trust. I promise you that.'

'Make sure he writes!'

Ignoring her words, he took her face in his hands, lowering his voice to an urgent murmur. 'As for you, dear Kate, consider all I have said. If it seems hard, remember it is only for your own spiritual welfare, which is as dear to me as my own. Think to keep yourself and your household safe from the snares of the heretics, whatever the cost in falling out with neighbours, the loss of those you call friends. Believe me, no price is too high to pay for purity of religion.' He gazed at her a little longer, as if expecting some response, but when she said nothing kissed her again.

He called to Toby, who had simply walked past them to stand ready by his horse. 'Come and bid farewell to your mother, Toby!' He smiled at Kate. 'You see, he's eager to be on his way.'

Only perhaps in the sense that he wanted to get the leaving over with, or so it seemed to Kate. Toby—obedient, changeling Toby, his mouth set in taut lines—came to her, pulling off his hat as if about to kneel for her blessing; hesitated. And was in her arms, clinging to her.

She stroked his hair, trying to choke back her tears. 'God bless you, my dear son. Be a credit to your name, to your uncle and to Holywell.'

'I will, mother, I promise.' He drew back, looked into

her face. 'Mother, forgive me for the pains I've caused you.'

Oh, Toby, this pain today is the worst of all! 'I forgive you, as God does, so long as you try earnestly to live by His light.' She rested her hand on his hair and closed her eyes. 'May God and His Holy Angels and His Blessed Mother go with you.'

She released him, but only to the arms of Jane, who was hovering nearby, ready to clasp him as close as his mother had done and for almost as long.

At last he freed himself and walked away, with a furtive rub of his sleeve over his eyes. He mounted his horse. His uncle, already mounted, gestured for them to move off.

They neither of them looked back, not once.

Tom had looked back, that day nine years ago, his face white, strained in the torchlight...Two sons lost, two different kinsmen...Had she indeed lost Toby as surely as she had lost his brother, never even to have news of him until he'd grown to manhood?

'It's going to be very quiet here at Holywell, madam.' Jane's voice, like hers, was rough with unshed tears.

Was there just a hint of reproach in Jane's tone, or did she imagine it? She watched the other woman lead the younger children away, leaving her alone with her thoughts.

In the mental turmoil that followed her brother's proposal she had several times been on the point of talking it all over with Jane, kind, sensible Jane who so often proved remarkably astute where the motives of others were concerned, and who loved Toby as she did herself.

But something had held her back. A sense that Jane would not approve? That she saw no harm in Sir Cuthbert's offer? For whatever reason, Kate kept silent and instead spent long hours in her closet, praying, pondering, questioning.

It should have been the answer to her prayers for Toby, that her devout brother should take care of him. Especially as he had shown this new softer side of himself, had clearly come to see things through her eyes, had genuinely tried to win Toby over. He'd told her what had happened about the horse, so she knew how very hard he'd tried, though it was to her entirely predictable that Toby had reacted as he had.

Which was one thing that had given her pause. How could she send Toby away with Nicholas when he clearly disliked his uncle so much and Nicholas was still very far from winning his trust, still less his affection? Could he ever be won over?

She accepted that the offer he'd made was on the surface what any mother in her position would wish for her son. In any other circumstances it would have appealed to Toby as well. It would remove him from all the temptations to heresy, while offering him the manly training he would surely enjoy.

Yet—could she trust Nicholas?

She was shocked she could admit such a thought, even for a moment. Nicholas as he had been in his youth? No, she would no more have entrusted Toby to him than to a wild beast. But now, when he was so clearly a changed man, changed for the better, why did she hesitate?

Days had passed, while she saw increasing evidence of how Nicholas's manner had changed; and her brother's impatience with her grew.

'Sister, I need your answer. I don't understand why you hesitate. I've a mind to take it into my own hands, as the head of the family. It is only for the love and respect I bear you that I do not do so. As a woman, you know you must allow yourself to be guided by me.'

Which was true, according to all she had been taught, even if in the eyes of the law Nicholas could have no rightful claim to authority over her household, Roger Machyn being still legally the guardian of her children. Men, rational beings, were better able to make wise decisions than were the weaker sex. And in this case, she understood it was a priest who had given the proposal his blessing, albeit one of those Jesuits that Father Fielding so disliked. Nicholas had told her of the long and profound conversation he'd held with the priest at Ashby St Ledgers, and how it had influenced his change of heart.

So in the end she'd yielded to Nicholas's urging, and given in.

Then she'd told Jane.

'So, you see, Toby is to go to Ashby St Ledgers with my brother.'

'I see.' Then: 'I saw you were troubled, madam.'

Kate was on the point of saying, *You don't approve? You think it wrong?* but bit back the words. She had made her decision. There was no going back, no point in regret. 'Nicholas will take good care of him.'

A tiny pause. 'Yes, madam. But is it not over-near to Haroby?'

That was another thing that had given her pause, though she'd tried to dismiss it, as Nicholas had when she'd put it to him. 'Roger Machyn's estate is at Silworth.'

'That's near enough still.'

'My brother assures me there is no intimacy with them. The Catesbys keep themselves to their own circle.'

Again that momentary pause, before Jane said, 'If you're at ease in your mind, then that's all that's needful.'

'Indeed. Nicholas will make sure he's safe. That's the whole purpose of it.'

But in spite of everything doubt still lingered, along with her grief at Toby's going. In the end, there was only one place that offered solace.

In the garden the sun drew earthy scents from the box that lined the beds, the only sounds the distant rush of the river, the chatter of sparrows in the orchard trees, the constant dale wind; and far off, a cuckoo calling. Now and then, Kate stooped to pull up a weed, or to run her hands over a bush of rosemary or sage, wakening perfume to soothe her jangling nerves.

'I thought I'd find you here.'

She stood up, stretching a little to ease her back. 'You know me too well.'

'You always loved this place best.' Jane's smile was like a caress, consoling, warm; yet her eyes were red-rimmed, as if she'd been weeping.

'The children?'

'With John, riding. That's not why I was seeking you.'

'Something's amiss?'

'Moll's toothache is worse. Her face is swelled up like a football. I put oil of cloves to it and she's gone back to bed. I've sent for Peter Nattrass to pull it.' Peter Nattrass was the Meadhope barber-surgeon.

'Oh, I'll go—'

'No, madam, there's nothing to do, not till afterwards. I thought you should know, that's all.'

And you knew I'd be in need of comfort, Kate thought. *As you are too.*

Jane relaxed a little, looked round the garden. 'You wouldn't think it was the same.' She answered the question in Kate's eyes. 'This place: do you mind how it was when we came, that day? All brambles and ruin. You could scarce tell it had ever been a garden. And now…'

'Yes, I do remember.' Oh, so long ago! Yet all at once as if it had been only yesterday: she felt again the chill of the air, the desolation, the exhaustion tempered only a little by relief at having come at last to a place of safety. 'All we went through to come here, you most of all. To come so far from all you knew, leaving everything behind.'

'I had nothing to leave. All I had was with you.'

Jane, newly widowed and delivered of a stillborn child,

134

had come to them as a wet-nurse when Toby was born; and proved to be so capable, so kind, that she had stayed with the family long after her nursling was weaned, caring for all Kate's children as they grew. But Toby had been her first. He was, in a way, as much her child as Kate's.

'We would never have come safe here without you, any of us. In such a time of cold and famine, so many dangers! You warned me how foolish it was, even insane. You were right. We came close to perishing, so close.' She shivered. 'Do you remember that place we came to, the second day?'

'And Master Tom—' Jane broke off, as if recognising she was treading on dangerous ground.

A day Kate had pushed to the back of her mind because of what came after: Tom, a boy of ten, suddenly become their protector, their guide.

They had skirted the place as dawn broke, a decaying hamlet, its few houses roofed with mouldering thatch, its stink reaching their nostrils almost before it came in sight. Fearful of being seen, they'd made their way across a weedy field towards the woods that fringed it.

But someone had seen. They'd heard a shout, glanced round, found a gang of men running after them.

'We'll never outpace them!'

'Stones!' That was Tom. 'Let's all get stones!'

He'd spotted a heap of stones, cleared from the field in some earlier time when someone had cared. He directed the younger ones to take the heaviest stone they could lift; Jane and Kate did the same. 'Line up, like soldiers. Get ready to throw.' A hand raised. 'Not yet! When I say the word!'

Bunched together, just spaced enough to give them freedom of movement, they'd watched the men come nearer; five of them, armed with cudgels, more than a match for two women, four children and the infant twins. Kate had felt her heart pound, her breath held. She'd felt sick, terrified. They were almost on them.

'Now!'

They threw, with all their might. Some of the stones fell short, but Tom and Toby aimed well, and Jane too, and Kate had been good at games as a child. She saw the men hesitate, taken by surprise. One fell, his companion halting to bend over him.

'Again!'

They'd grabbed more stones, aimed again. This time they hit two more of them, bent for more stones, threw and bent, threw and bent, took aim again. One or two of the men threw a stone in return, but without harm. The barrage from Tom's little army continued relentlessly. And at last the men gave up and fled.

'Oh, thank God!' Kate had turned and hugged her son. 'Oh, Tom thank you! You were wonderful!'

'Like a real soldier!' agreed Toby, gazing at his brother with eyes full of worship.

'No time to hang about,' said Tom briskly, resisting emotion, though Kate could see how pleased and proud he was. 'We need to get away, quick. They might have friends to call on.'

'Why would they chase us?' Toby wondered. 'We haven't got any riches.'

'They won't know that will they?'

Which was true, but Kate recognised that two unattended women might offer other temptations to such men; and the children...

She shuddered even now, remembering. 'He was brave, Tom.'

Against all decorum, all dutiful respect, Jane put her arms about Kate. 'Brave, and good. I'd guess he's never lost that. Nor will Master Toby.'

Kate rested her head on Jane's shoulder. 'He's not gone for ever, not like Tom. He'll visit us, and write. I'll show you his letters, I promise.' It was one of the surprising things about Jane, that she'd learned to read before ever she came to Kate's household.

'They all have to leave us, one day. We're blessed we had him so long.'

Kate freed herself, managing a wintry smile. 'I know. At least he's safe with Nicholas, body and soul.'

There was just a hint of a pause, a look, before Jane was once again the respectful servant. 'Amen to that, madam.' Then: 'I must go and see if Peter Nattrass has come.'

Kate caught her hand as she turned to go. 'Thank you, Jane.'

Alone again, she wandered on along the paths, her

mind full of memories.

The day after their arrival, she had found this ruin of a garden, discovering a rose withered but still blooming among the brambles, sweetly scented even so late in the winter. The plant was still there now, a vigorous shrub, green with leaves; and a first rosebud close to opening.

Nine years and more since they had come here, fleeing the consequences of her husband's death...

Chapter Nine

She'd been near her time with the twins. Already confined to her darkened bedchamber, warmed against the February cold by a great fire, she'd had the constant protective company of attentive servants and visiting neighbours, matronly women who'd borne children themselves. She'd known that this birth would be different, and very likely difficult. Heavy, lethargic and very bored, she'd simply prayed for it all to be over.

Then Jane had come to tell her that Sir Thomas had been taken ill while out riding. 'An apoplexy, madam. They said we should keep it from you, but I knew you'd not want that.'

Nor had she. Ignoring the protests of her other attendants, she'd hurried to his bedside.

Sir Thomas was not a young man, but had always seemed stronger than most, never ailing, always active and busy. Now, stretched on his great bed, he'd looked shrunken, shockingly diminished, his left side immobile, his face twisted and strange. As the surgeon and physician, hastily summoned, argued in low voices about the different treatments they favoured, she'd leaned over and whispered that she'd send for a priest. He'd raised his right hand, his brows struggling to form a frown. His lips had moved, the words slurred but unmistakable: 'No—! No!'

Perhaps, she thought, he was not yet ready to acknowledge his danger. She'd try again another time. For now, he must be left to the ministrations of the medical men, bleeding and blistering and cupping, the nauseating medicines, none of which had so far been of any use against the repeated fits.

Then her pains had begun. The twins had come into the world more easily than she'd feared, and been carried at once to their father's bedside, so he could acknowledge their arrival. Urged by Kate, Jane had again made that whispered offer to send for a priest, and once again it had been rebuffed.

It may be he doesn't know what he's doing, Kate had thought. Should she send anyway? But to ask a priest to risk making the journey, to risk his life, when she could not be certain how he would be received, if he would be received at all…?

In the end she did send a message to their Throckmorton neighbours at Coughton. A priest had come to baptise the twins, but was then refused entry to Sir Thomas's room. She could do no more.

Two days later they'd told her he was dead.

She was still only nine days into her lying in, but she'd brushed aside the objections of her attendants, washed and dressed and gone to the room where her husband's corpse lay, surrounded by candles and praying servants, household officials and the dead man's three older children, Tom, Margaret and Toby.

She'd knelt among them, her head bent in prayer, her fingers slipping over the beads of the rosary one by one, though there were no words of prayer in her head, only a shameful sense of relief.

She'd known she ought to grieve for this man she had been duty-bound to love. A moody and exacting man, Sir Thomas Machyn had yet been a good husband, as the world saw it. He would do what was right and even kind, but sometimes in such a way, in such a manner, that she'd found it hard to be grateful.

In the candlelight, his beard jutted assertively into the air from the waxen face, a sort of living excrescence screening the gaping mouth; chestnut streaked with grey—more grey than there'd been on their wedding day twelve years before, when, a frightened fourteen-year-old, she'd stood at his side before the priest. An old man he'd seemed then, as indeed he was at forty three, with frowning lines between his brows, discontent marking his mouth in repose. But a good Catholic, her Uncle Gaunt had told her when he'd made the arrangements, and a man of wealth, twice married, twice widowed, with a daughter just two years old, in need of a stepmother's care.

He'd been the one to seek the union, approaching Uncle Gaunt, making it clear from the start that he desired her enough to brush aside her lack of wealth. His eager bedding of her had proved that, often several times in the one night, with a voracious appetite that had left her sore and aching. And endlessly pregnant. Perhaps he'd loved her in his way, as she'd never been able to love him.

In this bed where he lay in death, each act that had led to the conception of their children had taken place, acts she had no wish to recall. As soon as she'd recovered from the birth of one child, the next was conceived. They said a woman must take pleasure in the act to be able to conceive, but if he'd ever heard that he'd not heeded it; his own pleasure was enough. She'd done her duty, accepted her husband's demands, borne his children, cared for her step-daughter until fever had carried her off, along with two of her own children; done everything a good wife should.

Except in that one last thing, which she'd thought was what he wanted, but then began to doubt. Why otherwise had he refused the ministrations of a priest? True, for all the twelve years of their marriage, and especially since the threat from the Spanish Armada had inflamed suspicion against Catholics, he'd been sufficiently regular in attendance at the parish church to avoid the attention of the authorities and keep himself out of trouble. But he'd often been present at Mass when a priest was in the house; though not lately, not in recent years, now she came to think of it. She'd thought it was chance, that he'd happened to be absent from home on each occasion. Now she wondered. To pay lip service to a heretic church during his life, to keep his family safe, that was natural enough in its way, and something many men did, with property and family to protect. She'd always assumed that, faced with death, the ultimate moment of truth, he would long to make his peace with the true Church, to confess and be absolved and so die in peace. The only fear he must have had, so she'd thought, was that he would not be given time to do that essential thing.

But he'd had time, and opportunity, yet he'd failed to make use of it.

What did that mean? That he'd come over the years to accept the heretic teaching of the established church, that he'd turned his back on the faith of his childhood and youth; apostatised? It was a terrible thought, not only when she looked back over the years she had known him, but for the future, for his ultimate destination. And for the example it gave to their children. Perhaps she would tell the children that he had in fact died shriven. She would have a Mass said for his soul. Must the children ever know the truth? Would she wish them to know it?

Slowly, the realisation had crept over her that it was in her hands, to tell them or no. There was now no man at Haroby with the authority to instruct or guide her. Sir Thomas was dead. She was no longer subject to his control. She was a widow, with six young children to raise and vast estates to manage. It was a huge responsibility. But somewhere in her obedient, dutiful soul something stirred, some sense of excitement and hope for the future. Widowhood brought freedom, independence, responsibility. Her duty now was not to a husband, but to her household and her children. And always, first and above all, to their souls.

Jane had come softly in, hesitating near the door for fear of disturbing her prayers. Kate turned her head.

'Madam, Master Turner's still here. He wishes a word

with you before he goes. I've told him you're not long brought to bed of twins, but—'

'I'll see him.'

Sir Thomas had refused to admit a priest, but had sent for his lawyer who, she understood, had for many hours been alone with him, making (she presumed) some final arrangement of his affairs.

She went to where the man waited in the parlour downstairs.

'Madam, forgive me for troubling you at such a time, but I thought it right that you should know how Sir Thomas left matters. You will know soon enough, but I think you should be forewarned.'

She'd felt a little chill, though could not think why. 'All goes to Tom, I think.'

'Indeed, madam. But Master Thomas is not of age, being a child still.'

She'd begun to guess, but did not dare to put it into words.

'Your husband named his cousin as guardian, for his sons.'

'His cousin?' She'd tried to think who that might be. She could recall no talk of cousins, no visits.

'Roger Machyn, of Silworth.'

She did remember then, though she knew him largely by repute: a distant cousin, a heretic, Justice of the Peace, oppressor of Catholics. It was he who had authorised the terrifying night-time search of her uncle's house in the year before her marriage. She had even suspected he was responsible for a later ransacking of Haroby. He was the last person any good Catholic would want as guardian of his children. She'd felt sick at the very thought that he should have any influence over hers.

She'd realised that the lawyer was speaking again.

'*Sole* guardian, madam. He is to take them into his household. But you are not to go with them, nor to have any say in how they are educated. All communication with them must be at an end.'

She stood frozen, staring at him, trying to make sense of it. And it did make sense, terrible sense. Put together with the way he'd died, she saw it now only too clearly: Sir Thomas had turned his back once and for all on the faith in which he'd been raised, her faith, the true faith. He wanted his children raised in the heresy he had chosen.

She drew a deep breath. 'Can I object to that?'

'I think not, madam. As a Papist—'

Papist! He'd called her a Papist, that term of abuse used in the world beyond these walls but never before inside them, to her knowledge. Oh how very far Sir Thomas had gone from the safe place where she'd thought him to be!

Then something shot into her mind. 'Does this Roger Machyn know how things are left?'

'I think Sir Thomas had left him to understand—But he will not yet know of Sir Thomas's death, I think. I am about to go to him.'

There was no time to lose. As soon as the lawyer had

gone, fired by a storm of energy that swept away all the lassitude of childbirth, she'd summoned Jane.

'Tell no one, let no one know! Help me pack a few necessities for a journey, all the things that matter. I'm leaving tonight, as soon as we're ready. I'm taking the children.'

'Leaving? Madam, you're still lying in. You cannot— Where do you mean to go?'

'To Holywell.' She'd seen the blank look on Jane's face. 'In the Bishopric of Durham. My jointure, so it's mine for my lifetime.'

'But—Sir Thomas is not yet buried.'

'He wanted no Requiem Mass, no holy rites. Let the heretics bury him.' She'd explained about the boys, and their new guardian. 'I'm not going to allow them to be taken from me. Holywell's a long way off. God grant we'll be safe there!'

Chapter Ten

'My dear madam, you're feverish. You wouldn't otherwise even think of such a thing. It's madness, truly!'

Jane had been quite right. It was foolish beyond all reason. Only just delivered of twins, newly a widow, Kate should have been resting in her darkened bedchamber with her neighbours about her, supported and cared for until she was free of the dangers that hung over every new mother. To have dismissed all those attentive neighbours, to be out of bed, frantically packing, her mind fixed on making a long and hazardous journey all on her own with six young children—it *was* madness.

But for Kate that was nothing set against the deadly threat to the souls of her children. What was present discomfort against the near-certainty of hellfire to come? Was Sir Thomas by his will to drag her children after him to that dreadful fate? Was she meekly to give up her beloved little ones to a heretic stranger?

Scarcely pausing for breath, she'd tried to explain all this to Jane, as the other woman helped her choose what to take and what to leave. Whenever she could insert a word, Jane had tried and tried to convince her to give up the whole idea.

'You are weak still. It's not safe for you, nor for the children. From what you say it's a long way, and so cold. After the winter we've had, the roads will be bad. Hunger and disease, they make men desperate. Two women and all the little children—No, madam, this is some sick frenzy. I beg you not to do it.'

Two women, she'd said. 'I don't ask you to come with us.'

'You know I wouldn't have you go alone.'

Kate had raised her eyes from the heap of clothes she'd been gathering together. 'You'd do that, come all that way, so far from all you know? Oh, Jane, I can't ask that of you!'

'You're not asking. I'm saying. *Whither thou goest, I will go...thy people shall be my people, and thy God my God...*'

'What's that?'

'Ruth, in the Bible, when—' Jane coloured. 'Never mind.'

Kate stared at her. 'Is that the Protestant Bible?'

'I wasn't always of your faith, before...But that's by the by. I beg you not to go! You could find a way, talk to this Roger Machyn. You may find him more kindly than you fear. He doesn't have to do what Sir Thomas wished, not to the letter.'

'I daren't risk it. My husband cared for the children's bodies, in his way. My duty is to nurture their souls. It's for that I'm going.'

Over and over Jane had argued with her, tried to make her see sense; over and over Kate had stubbornly refused to listen until, too exhausted to say more than 'Enough, Jane! I am going, with the children,' she'd sunk down on the bed.

'You see, madam—'

Kate held up a hand. 'No, Jane. No more!'

'Then let us at least take a man with us, to keep us safe.'

'What man? Who can I trust at Haroby, not to betray us?'

Jane could think of no one. Even the most devoutly Catholic members of the household had been loyal servants of Sir Thomas. But she'd found one final objection: 'The babes, madam. They're too young. They'd be safer left here, with their wet nurse.' The wet nurse had been chosen, but in the upheaval of their father's death, the twins were still with their mother.

'We can't risk the delay, taking them to the nurse. I've fed them myself up to now. I'll do it as long as I have milk.' She'd taken a deep breath, found renewed energy from somewhere. 'Don't look so troubled, Jane. God and our blessed Lady will watch over us.'

She'd thought Jane was about to make some retort, but she must have thought better of it, for she'd said no more.

After that, there was Tom. At dusk, Kate had summoned him to her, telling him to dress in his warmest clothes and help the younger ones make ready for a journey. Usually an obedient child, and a loving one, he'd gazed at Kate with disbelief and resistance warring in his eyes.

'Where are we going? Why?'

'There's no time for explanations. Just do as I say. I'll tell you as we go.'

He'd stared at her a moment longer—and then, to her

relief, done as she'd ordered.

They'd set out as darkness fell, with two horses to carry the younger children and the packed saddle bags. The swaddled infants were strapped to Kate's chest. But when, an hour from Haroby, where they'd halted in the uncertain shelter of a dense wood, Kate had tried to explain the reason for their journey, Tom's reaction was very far from what she'd hoped it would be.

'But if it was his will, what my father wanted, we should have stayed. I'm his heir. Haroby is mine, or will be when I'm of age.'

'And meanwhile it is under Roger Machyn's control. As you would be if you had not come away.'

'It's what my father wanted. We should have stayed. I should have led the mourners. It's not right.'

She'd feared he might turn round and leave them, but she'd urged on him her reasons, silently praying he would understand. She'd thought he had not loved his father—Sir Thomas was not easily loved—but he had respected him, looked up to him.

'It is for your immortal soul, for the souls of you and your brothers.'

'Do you think I'm so weak that a heretic guardian would turn me heretic too?'

'You are young. The pressures would be very great. There would be no good influences about you at Silworth.' Fearful for him, and for all of them (what if he should return to Haroby and set the authorities after them?) she'd tried another angle. 'Think of your brothers. Their souls too are at risk. Would you endanger them? You may be strong enough to resist, with God's help, but they are very young, easily led astray.'

She was not sure she'd convinced him, but at least he'd stayed with them, riding in silence through the night (thank God the moon was almost full!), looking after the younger ones with a surly compliance that showed how little he relished the journey. She'd prayed that as they travelled he would come to see she was right, that she had no other choice.

Then came what, afterwards, they called the 'victory of the stones'. At the end of it, triumphant, full of a sense of his own power, Tom had seemed to shed all his doubts about the journey. He became the leader of their defenceless party, the protector of frail women and children. 'Never fear, mother,' he'd told her a mile or so on from the incident, as she sank wearily to the ground, her back against the trunk of a beech tree. 'We'll come safe to Holywell!'

The place he'd never known, never visited, reached by a road even more unknown to him than it was to his mother...Dizzy with exhaustion, Kate had smiled at him, though her mouth had felt strained, as if she'd almost lost the power to move it, to move any part of her. Now that the excitement was over, now they were safe (for the moment at least) her body was giving her a stark reminder that she'd risen too soon from childbed.

'God and His blessed angels are with us. We're doing God's work.' The words, spoken without thought, had sounded odd to her, as if her voice came from a long way off, a meaningless repetition.

Nine years on from that time, her memory of the journey was shredded into tiny particles, a haze of fever and exhaustion pierced by nightmare moments of terror: dogs set on them, slobbering mouths with savage teeth; aggressive beggar gangs; the sound of hooves thudding nearer and nearer as the little company shivered in the shelter of a holly that dripped icily on them, tormented them with prickles. And always hunger and bitter cold.

They'd travelled under cover of darkness, sleeping through the day as best they could in any shelter they could find—dense woodland, derelict barns—huddled together for warmth.

Kate had seen herself as directing their journey, but she'd had no idea how long it would take them to reach Holywell, had known little more of the route than that they must keep travelling north. It was as if they'd launched out onto a limitless ocean without sail or pilot, utterly at the mercy of the wind and waves.

Very soon Kate had come to depend utterly on Tom; and on Jane.

Jane, the steady calm servant she'd scarcely known, except as a dependable, dutiful member of her household —she'd become their rock. Unfailingly cheerful, always encouraging, she'd foraged food from the hedgerows, found shelter, kept the little ones quiet when they feared discovery, amused them with stories and invented games. Above all, she'd cared for Kate, made sure she ate as far as anyone did, kept her warm while she snatched at sleep; and never once complained.

One act of kindness had lit the days of fear and suspicion: a woman, finding them sheltering in her byre, had invited them in to her fireside, no questions asked, bringing broth, and bread fresh from the oven. Rested and refreshed, it was only as they were about to set out again that they'd learned she was the wife of a heretic parson. Kate, repelled by the thought of a married priest, prayed that at the moment of death the woman's kindness might count in the balance against her damnable beliefs.

Spring retreated as they travelled north, the flowers in the meadows those of a few weeks earlier, the trees still struggling into leaf. The air grew colder, the rain heavier and sometimes falling as snow. Kate's milk began to fail, leaving the babies constantly hungry. When she could walk no further, Jane and Tom lifted her onto the back of one of the horses.

She had little recollection of what came after, beyond a tiny image that lingered still, like a cruel parody of a family portrait. She'd seemed to look down on it, on her own self, grey-faced, eyes closed, with the two babes clutched to her shrunken breasts, Mariana's crying reduced to a fretful whimper, Philip white, inert; and huddled under Jane's sheltering arms, her other children crushed into silence, hollow-eyed, so cold they were beyond shivering. That image had haunted her nightmares for years afterwards.

She had a faint memory of what happened next: a sign seen, York mentioned, Tom urgently questioning. She thought she'd told him of their kin in that city; must have done, for the next thing she remembered with any clarity was that they were there, in the home of her grandmother's distant cousin Dame Frances Thornton and her husband Sir Arthur. For her, there was the utter bliss of a soft bed. For the twins, a wet nurse speedily found by Dame Frances; for the older children, the kindness beyond his years of their son Richard; for all of them, warmth, food and rest, two whole weeks of care to restore them enough to face the final days of their journey.

And so at last, three days from York, they rode in sharp winter sunlight down the hill towards Holywell: her childhood home, her domain.

Here she had once known laughter and freedom, the joys of the changing seasons, springtime and harvest, Christmas feasts and friendly neighbours, and above all the unconditional love of her beloved grandmother.

Even the pain of their leaving, she and Nicholas, two bewildered children, nine and three years old, taken away by her Uncle Gaunt after their grandmother's death; even that memory could not wipe out the years before. Corners of it had always lingered in her mind, to be stirred to life by some small thing: a scent suddenly caught, a taste, the way the light fell on a hidden corner.

And here it was again, Holywell, nestled in the shelter of the hills on land sloping down to the river, a weathered grey building distinguished only by the squat tower at its western end, and somehow looking much smaller than she recalled, after years spent in the grandeur of Haroby.

Her golden memories shrivelled and fled.

This was no great house, but a small manor—and one, she'd soon learned, in a terrible state of disrepair. The fields were waterlogged or rank with weeds, the barns empty, damp filled the rooms with the stink of decay. She had no idea what they would do for food. Her husband's appointed steward William Fowler, living in comfort in Durham city, had clearly done no more than ensure the rents were collected, such as they were. Only one servant remained, the others having long since gone in search of more profitable employment: John Emerson, whom she dimly recalled as a name and a fresh young face, was now a wiry bent dour man, who lived on in his stable loft because he had nowhere else to go, and was still, in spite of everything, resolutely Catholic in his allegiance. He'd come to see who had clattered into the yard so late in the day, but when he knew who they were gave them a silent, unemotional welcome, opening doors, seeing to the weary horses, telling Kate, 'Tomorrow I'll seek a woman to give a hand.'

As he'd kindled a fire in the kitchen and brought hay

(only a little damp) to make beds for them near its furtive warmth, he'd said, 'There were men came a week past, looking for you.'

Kate's heart had thudded: Roger Machyn, it must be, or men in his pay! 'What happened? What did you tell them?'

'The truth. That I'd heard nowt of you since you left here, way back. They had a look around, then went away.'

Thank God they'd stayed at York for so long! Without that...Kate had shuddered at what might have been, had they had an easier journey.

Later, when the children were asleep, she'd lain wakeful, thinking over what John had told them. If their pursuers had called a week ago, then they could not have been following any trail they themselves had left. Rather, Roger Machyn must have assumed that, since Holywell was her jointure, Kate had taken the children there. So it had not after all been the safest choice! Except that, taking so long about the journey, with so many wrong turns, so many delays, they had ensured that Roger Machyn would assume he'd been mistaken and direct his search elsewhere, or give it up altogether. Were they by chance safer now than they ever had been? She could only hope so.

She'd glanced at the faces of the sleeping children, peaceful in the firelight, praying that nothing would harm them. *Holy Mother of God, keep them safe! Let them not be taken from me!*

Then she'd seen that Tom's eyes were watching her; he

at least was not yet asleep. She reached out and took his hand. 'It will all come right, I'm sure of it.'

She saw that he smiled a little. 'I know. Goodnight, mother.'

In the end, it *had* come right, or almost so, in the ambiguous way these things happened. All these years later, safely established among kind neighbours, able to live at peace—something good had been snatched from that desperate time.

Yet: was Nicholas right? Had that peace been gained by the same precarious compromise she had condemned in her husband, the very thing she had fled here to escape?

Chapter Eleven

Coming downstairs at dawn next morning, heavy-headed from lack of sleep, Kate found Philip curled up by the embers of the fire, his head resting on Trusty, the mastiff. The boy was fast asleep.

The dog opened an eye, stirred his tail, but otherwise did not move, mindful not to wake the child.

Kate felt a rush of emotion. The dog had been brought to them by Sir Cuthbert nine years ago as a lively puppy, a gift on their arrival at Holywell, and another reminder of the kindness of their neighbour.

All the small things over the years, the gestures of friendship, all that made her feel part of this place— Nicholas would say they did not stem from affection or friendship, that they were all prompted by a desire to lure her from her faith. Yet Sir Cuthbert had never seemed to her to be a man who took his religion very seriously. He would likely have been content to bend with whichever way the wind was blowing, to follow whatever faith his monarch asked of him, not so much from an instinct for self-preservation as from loyalty and decency. She guessed he was not a man who would either die or kill for his beliefs. Was that so very wrong?

Of course it was! She knew that, in her head if not with her heart. And in the past her care for her children's souls had driven her from all worldly comfort and safety.

As Philip's condition had daily reminded her, from the

moment she'd brought him home from York and through the years after as, often ailing, he'd learned only very slowly to walk and talk.

Guilt had been her constant companion since those days. She had surely been right to bring the older children here. But the twins—should she have left them at Haroby, rather than risk everything on the journey north?

She did not know. Jane had never said to her 'I told you so,' though Kate wondered sometimes if that was what she thought. Once, when Kate's sense of guilt had broken out in words, Jane had said only, 'He was never the strongest, even when he was first born. It's likely he would always have been like this.' She did not add, *That was why he should have been left behind.* She did not need to, for Kate felt it always, every single day when she saw how frail he was, how damaged in mind and body.

Jane, uncomplaining, without a word of blame, had simply done her best to care for the ailing toddler when he'd been brought to Holywell, helped him with infinite patience and gentleness to walk and talk as best he could, to make such small improvements as lay within his ability. His own twin sometimes lost patience with him, but never Jane.

Kate had tried to tell herself that it had all been for the good, that she could have done no other. She'd believed that firmly when she first came to Holywell, for all the cold, the exhaustion, the lack of food they'd found on their arrival. They were safe; by God's goodness they had evaded Roger Machyn's men, and very soon she knew that they'd fallen amongst good neighbours, who were kind, sustaining, making life easier for them all.

And Nicholas too was sure she'd done right to flee from Haroby, even though she'd not in the end been able to keep Tom safe; in spite of the damage to Philip.

'Staying, you would have been contaminated, most surely, and so would your little ones.'

But he'd said that on the first evening, before he knew how much her life, all their lives, meshed with those of their neighbours. Once he learned the truth, he'd made it only too clear what he thought of it.

As the household gathered in the hall before his departure, the words of his prayers had been flames, burning themselves in her memory. She knew they had been directed at her as much as the Almighty—solely to her perhaps.

'We are a people apart, a holy remnant.' His voice had trembled with emotion. 'We have in our hands the conversion of this land to the true faith. To do this we must keep ourselves uncontaminated by the lures of the heretic so-called church. We are entrusted with the cherishing of your church in this land. Holy Mother of God, pray for us when we fail, give us the courage and strength to take the hard path!'

And then there had been his parting words, at the very moment of leaving Holywell, leaning down from the saddle to speak to her alone: 'No price is too high for purity of religion.'

She'd felt a surge of anger. He wanted her to be some kind of saint, she who was just an ordinary mother, an ordinary woman.

Yet he was right, of course he was. Even Father Fielding, that gentle undemanding old man, would have agreed that such was the best path, while accepting that it might sometimes be an unrealistic ideal.

Philip woke, the dog stirred, rose, shook himself. The dwindling company of her dear ones gathered for prayers, which she recited mechanically, her head a whirl of doubts and questions without resolution.

In Nicholas's eyes she was almost a schismatic, an apostate, because she lived on good terms with her neighbours. Could he be right? She did not want to think so, she did not want anything to disturb the way of life she had made for herself and her family.

And then she remembered Toby, going to church, making foul blasphemous jokes. He was already half way to being tainted—No, more than tainted, lured into the deepest of sins. In the end it was for this reason she'd yielded to her brother's plan to take her son with him to Ashby.

Was that what had happened to her husband, that he'd made what he thought of as small gestures to protect himself, and then found himself lured ever further into heretic ways until at last he'd become one of them, irrevocably, so that even in death he was not able to extricate himself? And Tom, was he too lost for ever?

Yet: could she turn her back on Sir Cuthbert's kindness, on the friendship that had supported and protected her through the past nine years, since the morning, two days after their arrival at Holywell, when he'd ridden into the yard to make himself known to them?

She'd been aware that he'd called, as a good magistrate should, to discover what kind of person had come to take up residence there. She'd known he would be expected to take note of any recusant tendencies, any sign that she was a Catholic, and her household too. But from the first he had been kindly, even understanding. He'd told her that Roger Machyn's men had called at Meadhope Hall, applying to him as magistrate for information about her, to which he'd truthfully replied that he knew nothing of her and that Holywell was uninhabited, as far as he knew. At that point he had not even known of Sir Thomas's death.

'As well your pursuers did not come any later!' he'd added at the end of his visit, before he assured her that she could turn to him for any help she needed.

And so it had proved, for he had protected her, supported her, helped her in so many ways. How could she think it right to cut herself off from all contact with him? Surely it was because of him and those around him that she had survived, succeeded in providing her children with a home, done her best to raise them?

Yet Nicholas was so certain she was wrong. In all her life she had never heard anyone speak with such passion of what he believed, of how that belief must change his life, all their lives. For years she'd prayed for his conversion. Now that it had come, now that her prayers had been answered, could she turn her back on what it confronted her with?

Had Nicholas come by chance, by God's grace, to a closer understanding of their faith than she had, after years of devotion? Should she allow herself to be guided by him? The fact that something inside her rebelled at the very thought was no indication that she should not accept his guidance. His faith had been forged in a greater fire than hers, and was perhaps the more true for that.

She ought to accept what he'd said, she was sure of it. Yet...

As she dismissed the household from the hall, saw Edward leave for his lessons with the rector, she felt close to tears, filled with a sense of failure, of helplessness. What was the right way? The one Nicholas advocated so fiercely, to cut herself off, as far as was humanly possible, from all contact with the heretic world? Or to go on as she always had, living as best she could in harmony with her neighbours while still trying to keep the flame of faith alive within her household, her family?

Instead of making her usual inspection of the kitchen and the other working rooms, instead of summoning the twins to her for their lessons (or rather, Mariana for hers), she sent the children to play in the garden ('It's such a fine day. It will do you good.') and made her way to her closet, to try and gather her thoughts.

On impulse she went to the chest, covered with a heavy piece of old tapestry, that stood by the window, providing an occasional seat; and a false bottom in which any incriminatory items could be stored: the vestments and altar cloths to be used in celebrating the Mass, her Book of Hours, a rosary, a crucifix—and the book Nicholas had give her on his arrival at Holywell.

This showed her what he had prayed for. Here, surely, she would find strength to help her on the lonely, difficult path. She turned the pages, reading at random: to dress simply, decently, frugally; to avoid idleness; to teach the children to pray; to give to the poor—all this she did, one way and another.

The Christian, she read, *is not come to a play, pastime or pleasure, but to continual rough battle and fight, against unplacable and spiteful enemies and…must resolve never in this world to look for quiet and peace…*

It was Nicholas's voice speaking to her, urging, admonishing. She slammed the book shut, thrust it back in its hiding place.

Oh why did she feel so angry, so rebellious, when she knew at heart he was right? Because she was a weak woman, too ready to take the easy path?

She was still struggling to pray about it all when, close to dinner time, Jane came in search of her.

'Master Langley is here, madam. He came with Master Edward, when the lessons ended.'

'I'll come.'

Kate found she was trembling as she followed Jane towards the spiral stair that led down to the hall.

This was a sure sign that her brother was right, that here, today, was the moment when she must take the first decisive step towards severing all but the most superficial connection with her heretic neighbours.

Yet she felt sick at the very thought of it. Mind and body alike rebelled at doing what Nicholas urged so passionately.

Though the sun was shining, the air soft, it was cold in the hall, and the rector sat close to the inadequate glow of the peat fire, rising to his feet as she came towards him, his blue eyes level with hers. He was a neat spare man, immaculate linen at neck and wrist, his small beard clean and well-trimmed. He pulled off his hat and inclined his head, his smile at once wry and warm, lighting his eyes. 'Madam. I trust I find you well.'

Oh how could she believe even for a moment that this man was in any way a threat to her or her family?

Yet he was, he surely was, if only because he had won her friendship. This was how Satan most easily found a way in.

And here, now, laid before her, was the perfect opportunity to send him on his way for good, out of her life and that of her children.

She found herself exchanging pleasantries. 'We are all well, I thank you.' Then: 'I see you have brought the book. Shall we sit here?'

She gestured towards the table, taking her seat beside him, where he set down the ledger.

'I had meant to call last week, but thought it best to wait for your brother's departure. I knew you'd have other things on your mind, the more especially when I learned your son was to leave you too. I shall miss him, for all he was not always the most biddable of students. I was a little sad I had no opportunity to say goodbye.'

She tried to repress a stir of guilt, telling herself this man was her enemy, and Toby's too. It was fitting that all relations should be severed between them. Soon, she would ensure the same for Edward.

'It must have been a joy to you, to meet again with your brother after so long apart.'

Joy! Had there been any joy in Nicholas's visit? In the first moments, yes, of course; but rather more of trouble, and pain. Was that her fault?

She went on quickly: 'Do you remember him at all, as a little boy?'

'Ah, no, you'd long gone when I came here, in '90, that was. It would be Sir Arthur Weir who was here in your grandmother's time. Nearly fifty years he served this parish, right from King Henry's day, before all the changes. He would have baptised you, and your brother.'

She remembered then, the old, old man. She thought she'd even been to church with her grandmother from time to time, but not in the last few years before she died. 'He must have seen a lot of changes.'

'Indeed.'

'But he became a heretic at last.'

He cast a sharp glance in her direction. 'I don't think he changed much. He simply went on serving the parish and its people as he always had. The words changed, from Latin to English, he wore different vestments, the statues went from the church, but I would guess his beliefs remained the same, at heart.'

Would Nicholas have condemned him too? The complexity of it all made her head ache.

She realised Gervase Langley was speaking again.

'I shall miss young Toby, but it's time he took steps into manhood. And I always had doubts about Cambridge for him. He's no scholar.'

'Yes. No.'

Again the keen glance that seemed to read what lay behind her words, though kindly, with a gentle understanding. He cleared his throat, spread the account book on the table. 'To business then, madam. Andrew Wardle and I have put our heads together over the figures. He would have called with me today, but he begs to be excused. He has a return of his old trouble.'

A severe looseness of the bowels, she recalled, coming on very suddenly. 'Poor man. I'll call on him.'

'We went over the figures together yesterday. We think you will find all in order. You will rejoice to learn that all the Whitsun rents are paid, save for those due from Henry Stobbs at High Intake.'

She sighed. 'And we'd be foolish to think he'd ever pay them. That's two years now since he's paid anything. Andrew will need to call on him again, when he's recovered.'

'I fear that won't serve. He's already called several times, and had only a mouthful of cursing for his pains. The last time Stobbs set the dogs on him. He claimed it was not deliberate, but you know the man.' He studied her appalled face. 'Perhaps Francis Steadman could be asked to intervene. I'm certain Sir Cuthbert would allow it.'

Francis Steadman was Sir Cuthbert's steward, a man of implacable authority—and, of course, a heretic. In this small thing at least she could refuse without a pang, though all she said was, 'Not yet. Let's see, shall we?'

'Times are hard. The harvest was poor again last year. If we have more favourable weather, it may be that things will improve. But I fear Henry Stobbs will never be a prudent man nor a sound husbandman. Nothing like his father, sadly.' He sighed. 'I gave my word to Andrew Wardle that I'd remind you of this, that you'd be within your rights to turn him out at the next Quarter Day. If you were to give him a final warning at Lammas tide…'

'But that's Wardle's counsel, not yours?'

'Stobbs has a sickly wife and many children. They are not to blame for his sins.'

'I know. Cecily Stobbs, his second child—she's in my household. I can see for myself how hard things are at home. Which is why I've done nothing so far.' She paused, trying to gather strength, to fortify her will. 'My brother urged his eviction, as not being of our faith.'

She felt the the rector's close scrutiny.

'Is that what you wish?'

It ought to be. 'I think it would not help our neighbours to think kindly of those of our faith, were I to let that direct my judgement.' Oh how far she was still from her brother's command!

'Indeed. Though none would blame you for losing patience with Henry Stobbs. On the other hand, he could, I think, be a dangerous enemy.'

'Oh?' She remembered Sir Cuthbert's warning, and shivered a little. 'So that is a good reason to let him stay where he is?'

'Perhaps. It's hard to know what's best. He is malicious, but he has few friends. However…' He drew a deep breath. 'Enough of that! There's one thing Andrew Wardle told me. Holywell Mill is doing good business, since the mill at Ashburn ceased working.'

'Then let's have some refreshment and drink to that! Better still, you will, I hope, stay and dine with us?'

She had not done it. Not the right moment—or cowardice? She knew what Nicholas would say. In memory she saw the frown between his dark brows, heard the reprimand, the disappointment at her weakness.

She told herself she'd only deferred the moment of decision, that it would come, it must come, when the time was right.

Like a lightning strike, Nicholas had left her with all that was familiar, all that made her feel secure, shrivelled and scorched to nothing. She had somehow to find the courage to start again, on the right path.

Later that day, upstairs in the parlour, she glanced out of the window and saw a dark figure on a bony horse crossing the field beyond the stable yard; someone returning from the river, from the Mill perhaps, by a circuitous route? Watching him, she thought there was something familiar about him—yes, it looked like Henry Stobbs. Or was it just that he was on her mind, following the rector's visit? Even if it was her tenant, then he might simply have been calling on his daughter. Not that he had so far shown any evidence of affection for her, or interest in her well-being. On the contrary.

'He is malicious,' Gervase Langley had warned, and she knew how true that was.

Thank God, then, that the magistrate was their good friend Cuthbert Featherstone. If they had not been on friendly terms, then Holywell would already have endured a visit from the pursuivants, following Stobbs' report of a priest glimpsed at Holywell. Surely she was right to wish to shield her household from such a fate?

Chapter Twelve

Leaving home was very much harder than Toby had expected. Anger had made him give in, forced him to turn his back on Holywell, but from the moment he left it behind he felt torn in pieces by conflicting emotions. It had been his home since he was five years old, almost as long as he could remember, and though he'd chafed at its restrictions, he found that with every mile he rode the leaving of it grew more painful.

Tears pressed against his lids, his throat ached. He rubbed his sleeve over his eyes, furtively, but his uncle must have caught the movement.

'Weeping, Toby?'

'No! No, of course not!'

'No indeed.' There was irony in Nicholas's voice. 'You are a man now, all but. Most lads your age would already have been years away from home.'

There was no need to remind him of that. It was one of the many things that had chafed him back at Holywell, one of the many reasons to feel shame at what fate had forced upon him. But now—there was so much left behind! Bess, for whom his heart longed and his body ached, Hal too (if he could be forgiven), the house, his sister and brothers, Jane, his mother, all of them increasingly enfolded in a recollected glow of warmth and kindliness with every step his horse took away from them. Would he ever see any of them again in this life? Would he ever be happy again?

'The road's better here.' His uncle's voice, brisk, matter of fact, broke in on his misery. 'Let's give our beasts their heads.'

Toby gave his uncle a questioning look. Nicholas turned away and with a shout urged his horse into a gallop. A moment of hesitation, while Toby watched; and then excitement caught him. Unable to help himself, he dug in his heels and gave his own horse its head. The thud of hooves filled him, shuddered through body and mind, drove out everything else. They covered several miles, the speed exhilarating, hooves thundering at a gallop over the well-paved, well-drained portion of road.

When at last they drew rein, faced with a swollen stream approached through deep mud, Nicholas gave his nephew an appraising look. 'You manage your horse well enough. But your seat could be improved. See! Look how I sit, the legs so, the feet, and your hands too, thus.'

Excitement fled. Toby seethed with indignation on behalf of John Emerson, who had done his very best, in his taciturn but kindly way, to teach him what he knew. It was not John's fault that he was not a gentlemen born, with a gentleman's knowledge of all the finer points of horsemanship. Yet Toby had been conscious for a long time, comparing himself with Hal, that he lacked many of the necessary skills. He'd tried to get his friend to pass on some of what he'd learned at home, but Hal was no tutor and had little conscious recollection of anything he'd been told; he was also inclined to take risks and show off in a way Toby could not begin to follow. Toby wanted to improve, of course he did, but not like this. Just for a moment he considered pretending not to have heard his uncle's advice. Casting a single brief glance at Nicholas, he turned his gaze rigidly to the front.

'You'll not see what I mean that way.' There was a teasing note in Nicholas's voice, which did not make Toby feel any better.

But he had seen enough to know how to adjust his position, which he did, as unobtrusively as possible, hoping his uncle would not notice.

'That's better! Now let's get safely through this water!' Nicholas led the way with such skill that Toby could not help but feel a twinge of admiration.

After that, Nicholas said no more about Toby's horsemanship, but instead became a knowledgeable guide, pointing out places he knew, telling him something of their history: the ruins of a once great monastery, the house where a fine and saintly man had lived before he'd faced a terrible execution in the reign of King Henry VIII. He proved to be an unexpectedly fine story-teller. Though Toby tried very hard not to show it, he often found his interest caught and held, enough for a time to keep his homesickness at bay.

They set out at dawn each day, with few breaks of any kind until dusk. As they travelled further south, the air grew warmer, the landscape softened, became more lush and wooded.

'We'll be at Ashby tonight,' Nicholas said, on the morning of the fourth day. *'Deo volente.'*

Toby did not know whether to be glad or sorry. He would never have admitted it, but in spite of himself he had begun (almost!) to enjoy the journey. He gave a faint smile, but said nothing.

'Ashby is only ten miles or so from Haroby. Do you remember much of your time there? You were very young when you left—not even breeched, I guess.'

The familiar irritation surged through Toby. 'I'd been breeched long since.' This was not strictly true, for the ceremony that marked the change from infancy to boyhood had taken place at Christmas time, just weeks before his father's death. He'd been proud of the manly clothes replacing the cumbersome skirts still worn by his younger brother Edward. He'd felt suddenly closer than ever to Tom, his hero; on the way to manhood, as his brother was.

Nicholas gave him a keen sideways look. 'Do you remember much of your life there? Of your older brother, for instance?'

Could his uncle read his mind? He tried to sound casual. 'Tom? Aye, a little.' The thought still sent a pang through him.

'You were close perhaps?'

Why was his uncle asking all this, when he ought to guess that it would hurt? 'It was a long time ago.'

If Nicholas noticed the mulish set of his mouth, he ignored it. 'Your cousin Roger took him from Holywell, I think. That was not long after you reached there?'

'Aye.' He had no wish to say more, but he could not so easily shut out the memory: the clatter of hooves in the moonlit yard; clubs thundering on the door, shouting, armed men crowding the hall, faces lurid in the torchlight.

Jane and John had hurried the children up to the attics, leaving their mother alone to confront the enemy. Toby had held no memory, as his mother did, of any past visit from pursuivants who came seeking priests, but his mother told him it was very like this. Though in the end there was no captive priest, only Tom taken prisoner. Once they had him, they'd abandoned the search, as if that was enough for them. Tom's siblings had emerged from their cramped and airless hiding place in an old chest upstairs to find their brother gone.

He had promised to be faithful, their mother had said. He had been brave, self-controlled.

And Toby had felt the loss of him ever since.

'You've had no word of him from that time?'

'No.'

'He's been raised at Roger Machyn's place at Silworth, not at your old home at Haroby. He will be of age before very long, and come into his inheritance.'

Toby shot a look at his uncle, but bit back the urge to ask more.

'Wed now, and a heretic, an apostate.' A pause. 'So it's said.'

In spite of himself, Toby yielded to curiosity. 'You've

seen him?'

'Not I, no. I doubt Roger Machyn would look kindly on any such meeting.'

'Does he still see himself as my guardian?'

'By law, yes, so he is. A reason to keep away from your brother.'

Then why all this talk of Tom? To remind him to be careful? He felt only bewildered and sad, the ache of loss that had never quite healed stirred to fresh life.

As Nicholas had predicted they reached Ashby St Ledgers towards the end of the day. Yet another establishment, thought Toby with renewed resentment, run by a devout woman. Like Holywell, but without his family, without Bess.

Someone had arrived just before them, his horse already handed over to the groom, with whom he was in animated conversation, though he looked round as they approached; a short, sturdy round-faced man, a little older than Nicholas.

'Nick! If it isn't old Nick!' Face alight, he came to lock Nicholas in a warm embrace.

'Tom Wintour! I didn't think to find you here!'

'Ah, I have the advantage of you then. I expected to find you returned.' The stranger's bright friendly eyes turned on Toby.

'My nephew, Toby Machyn. Toby, this is my good friend and erstwhile comrade in arms, Tom Wintour. We met long since, in Flanders.'

'On the wrong side, the first time. But we found our way back, the two of us.'

Somehow Toby found it easy to believe that this vigorously muscular man had been a soldier, for all that he was more gaudily dressed than Nicholas, a flamboyant figure in contrast to the younger man's sobriety.

'What brings you here? A foolish question! Robin has returned?'

The other man shook his head. 'Sadly, no. I've come from a visit to my brother, thinking to find Robin home.' His expression was rueful. 'A house full of infants—you can imagine! I hoped for the antidote of some sane masculine company, but it seems Robin's still from home. As always, elusive.'

'He was in London a month since.'

'I know. I was with him there.' He shrugged. 'Aye well, there we are.'

'Will you stay until he returns?'

'Perhaps. We shall see. At least I'll have the pleasure of your company, old Nick.' He grinned at Toby. 'So we knew him in the army, though he's long since turned his back on Satan's wiles. Now, tell me, Nick…'

The voices of the two men echoed in his head as Toby followed them into the house. His weary brain took in panelled walls, the gleam of oak floors (no rushes here), fine hangings, solid furniture, the scent of wax candles—no stink of tallow, no underlying mustiness, no draughts, and everywhere, it seemed, servants busy with their tasks. It seemed that Ashby was not after all so very much like Holywell; outwardly at least it reminded him rather of Meadhope Hall.

They were bidden at once to supper. Tomorrow, Toby gathered, he would be waiting at table with the other young boys who served them this evening. For now, he was consigned to the most lowly table, just able to glimpse his uncle far off, still in animated conversation with his old friend. Toby was too weary to talk to his table-fellows, who in any case showed little overt interest in him. At least the food was good and plentiful.

The household's night prayers followed almost at once, led by Lady Anne Catesby; Toby's first glimpse of the mistress of the house. His head spinning with exhaustion and strangeness, he scarcely took in the prayers, though the words were familiar enough. He felt sick with a boredom sharpened by anger. What, he thought, was the point of coming here, if he had simply exchanged one tediously religious household—and that a safe and loving one, with friends close at hand—for an identical but alien one? His uncle's promises of a manly education, of vigorous male company, had not tempted him even at his most resentful of the constraints of home. Now he felt sure it had all been a ruse, a deception, to lure him away from Holywell.

The next day, dragged early from the bed he shared with three other boys, lined up for morning prayers, he felt little better. The prayers seemed interminable, just as they had at home when Nicholas had led them. Afterwards he was summoned by the lady of the house, to be given an austere welcome. 'I hear much good of you, Toby Machyn. I pray that here you will grow in faith and wisdom.'

He murmured something incoherent, bowed, and was led away to a breakfast of bread and small beer, eaten in a sleepy silence. He cast a furtive glance at his companions, with a pang of longing for Hal, intensified by the memory of how bitterly they had parted. Could any of these boys offer him any kind of compensatory friendship? Most of them were much younger than he was, but one, a lanky boy whose limpid blue eyes peered out under an unruly thatch of blond hair, looked to be about his own age, and once even cast a faint smile in his direction.

No talking was allowed during the morning hours, which were filled with the usual academic subjects, with which Toby was only too familiar: Latin, grammar, rhetoric and logic, taught much as Gervase Langley had taught them. He was relieved to find he could hold his own (more or less) with these subjects, but when it came to arithmetic, geometry, astronomy and music he felt stupid, ill-educated.

Dinner time was no better, for then he found himself waiting at table with the other boys, something he had done often enough at home, but his mother's rule had never been as rigorous as it was here, where the smallest detail had a right and a wrong way and the house steward kept a sternly watchful eye for the least mistake.

Trying to follow what the others did, Toby fumbled

with the linen napkin half-draped over his arm.

'Like this!' murmured a voice next to him.

His eyes met the blue gaze of the blonde boy. 'Thank you!' he mouthed.

'Silence!' They exchanged sheepish grins, before beginning their dignified walk into the hall.

By the time the tables had been cleared and the boys allowed to sit down to eat, Toby was ravenously hungry. Beside him, a thin red-head asked, 'Is it right Master Catesby will be here tomorrow?'

'My grandam's not had word.' That was the youngest boy among them, about the same age as the twins, Toby guessed, a solid child with thick chestnut hair. His 'grandam'—that must be Lady Anne. Did that make him Master Catesby's son?

'Oh, I wish he'd come back! It's far the best when he's here!' There was rapture in the voice of the third speaker.

Toby thought they talked of the absent Robert Catesby as they might speak of a beloved saint, with just the same note he'd heard in his uncle's voice. He wondered what it was about Lady Anne's son that drew such universal near-adoration. He was pretty sure that he would hate Robert Catesby. No one could be that perfect, without also being unbearable.

The afternoon was devoted to instruction of a physical kind: swordplay, horsemanship, and dancing. Toby danced well, but he lacked knowledge of the finer points of horsemanship and he'd never been taught to use a sword.

He'd been pleased to find the soldierly Tom Wintour was to teach them, but very soon he heard two of the other boys laughing at his clumsiness and felt ashamed. Wintour, observing it, clapped him on the shoulder. 'We'll make a swordsman of you yet, my lad!'

At supper time, when the household had dispersed and the boys sat down to their meal, Toby found himself next to the boy who'd helped him at dinner time.

'I'm Humphrey.'

'I'm Toby.'

'You're Master Gaunt's nephew? Just come?'

His mouth full of rather good beef pie, Toby nodded.

'I've been here close on two years. It's strange when you first come, knowing no one.' He lowered his voice a little, to name their companions one by one. Toby tried to commit their names to memory, but there was only one he could be sure of, the boy who had spoken of his 'grandam'.

'That's Rob Catesby, the lady's grandson. And Master Catesby's son.' Again there was that rapt look. 'What I'd give to have such a father!'

'My father's dead.'

'Aye well, so might mine be, for all the—no, that's not just. He does at least acknowledge me.' He caught Toby's questioning look. 'He's kin to Master Catesby, a gentleman, but my mother was his kitchen wench. I'm base-born.'

'Ah, I see!' But he did not, quite; except to guess that it must make life hard for Humphrey. Perhaps he himself was not so hard done by after all.

And now he felt he had the beginning of a friendship. After evening prayers, he ventured, 'I wish they wouldn't go on so long!' and then saw at once that he'd misjudged his companion.

'I like these times.' The quietly spoken words were like a rebuke.

Toby felt disappointment, and an uncharacteristic quiver of shame. Yet how could an energetic engaging lad like Humphrey think this way? How unlike Hal!

The other boy smiled. 'I would go for the priesthood, but they don't take bastards.'

Toby did not quite know how to respond to that, so contented himself with what he hoped was a sympathetic murmur.

He learned quickly which subjects were best not spoken of to Humphrey, while in other ways their acquaintance did grow into friendship. His homesickness lessened, and his sense of resentment.

The days were so packed with activity that there was scarcely time to think, still less to brood, and he slept well at night. Holywell began to seem very far away, lost in a past that was fast slipping from his memory.

It was well into August, at the end of an oppressively hot day, that Toby became conscious of a stir of excitement among the boys waiting to serve the supper table.

'Master Greenway's come!' murmured young Rob.

Toby peered round the door at the top table, where a

sturdy rosy-faced brown-bearded man had taken the place of honour beside Lady Anne, who had previously always taken her meals in her own parlour.

'Look at that coat! Oh, I'd give my right arm for one so fine!' That was Wat, who had a taste for fine clothes and (to Toby) an extraordinarily wide knowledge of what was in fashion. 'They call that the Italian style, you know.'

Master Greenway's clothing certainly looked fine enough, rich with embroidery and gold lace.

'Quiet there! Do your duty!'

They moved forward with the first dishes for the top table (roast meats of many kinds) though Humphrey managed a final whisper. 'It's the Feast of the Assumption tomorrow. That's why he's come.'

Toby pushed the apparently irrelevant remark from his head, but it came back to him at evening prayers, as Master Greenway, in all his finery, took his place to lead their devotions. Staring so long that Humphrey had to nudge him to bow his head, Toby understood at last. Of course! Master Greenway must be a priest. But how utterly unlike Father Fielding, whose manner was as homespun as his shabby food-stained clothes!

Tonight, the resonant voice lent music to the familiar words. At the end, when Latin gave way to English, Toby was struck by a familiar lilt; in that at least there was a faint likeness to Father Fielding.

This man, this priest, was urging them all to come to him tomorrow to make their confessions; and first to pass the night in earnest contemplation of their sins.

Toby glanced at Humphrey, who was clearly taking this admonition very seriously, as indeed were the other boys. No point turning to them for sympathy then. But one thing he knew for certain: he was not going to confess to this elegant gentleman, or to anyone else for that matter. If anybody had sinned, it was his uncle in bringing him here, his mother in letting her brother have his way.

Prayers over, he turned to make his way to bed. 'Toby Machyn!'

It was the priest's voice. Hesitating, only just rejecting an urge to refuse the call, he shrugged and went to stand before Master Greenway.

'You are newly come here, my son. From my own home country, I learn, or near enough. I was born a little further north than Holywell. But we are alike north country men.'

Toby was not going to allow himself to be won over so easily. But the man was a priest after all, and so merited the minimum of respect. He was trying to think of some suitably neutral response, when the other man said,

'I would welcome news of my birth country. We can talk perhaps when tomorrow's celebrations are done?' A pause, as if seeking Toby's face for some hint of a friendly response. 'But first, my son, I wish you a holy night. I will hear your confession in the morning.'

Oh no you won't! Toby did not dare say the words aloud, but simply took his leave with the barest courtesy and went upstairs to his shared bed.

Later, as he began to drift into sleep, he heard an excited whisper from the far side of the bed, 'My father's here! He's just come, tonight!'

Chapter Thirteen

'Master Catesby, my nephew Toby.'

Nicholas gestured for Toby to come further into the room, towards the tall silhouette against the window.

Head high, jaw firm, braced to dislike—even hate— Toby took a step nearer, and another, gradually making out the showy red velvet doublet, the tanned face, neatly bearded.

A well-made, brown-haired man in the prime of life, with hazel eyes that seemed to see into his very soul…

He felt all at once exposed, naked, very small, as if a brilliant light shone on him, revealing every defect.

'Ah, the newcomer to our family! Welcome, my boy. Your uncle has told me great things of you.' Toby shot a startled glance over his shoulder; Nicholas gave a faint smile. 'You have the makings of a fine man, I understand. Tell me how you like it here. And what you hope for.'

Toby fumbled for the stool the man indicated, pulling it towards him and then, misjudging the height of it, sat down with a thump, almost toppling it. He righted himself, drew a deep breath, searched his confused mind for some suitable reply.

'I like it well enough, sir.' It was a schoolboy's response, the answer good manners required. He found himself concerned lest Master Catesby should think this a half-hearted reply, that he would disapprove. Yet why should he want this man's approval? His coming here was hardly a free choice.

He heard the click of the latch as his uncle left the room, at which his companion took a seat nearby, lowering himself to Toby's level.

'So, what pleases you most of all? Or do you compare this place unfavourably with the home you have left behind you?'

He did not know how it happened, or why, but the gently spoken enquiry changed something in Toby, loosened his tongue. He found himself talking of his hopes and fears, even about his rebellious feelings back home in Holywell, things he had not told his uncle, even on their journey south when his feelings towards Nicholas Gaunt had begun to soften a little.

It was as if all his thoughts were already visible, his motives open like a book for this man to read, so that there was no point in trying to hide anything. At the same time, he was certain that Master Catesby understood him, cared about him, truly wished to know what he thought and felt. The man asked few questions, but when they came each one was perfectly pitched to nudge him into further confidences: how he loved dancing, but hated Latin, how he struggled with the new-fangled arithmetic, how he longed to be a better horseman and skilled with the sword.

'A man of action, I see. That's good. This land of ours has need of such as you, with your youth and energy. Tell me, who were your teachers at Holywell?'

Toby talked of John Emerson, and even (in an

unguarded moment) of Gervase Langley, relieved to see there was no disapproving scowl. He talked of Hal, though not how they parted, and of his growing friendship with Humphrey.

When at last he faltered into silence, with 'Sir, forgive me, I talk too much,' Master Catesby began to talk to him in his deep resonant voice, telling him what he could hope for from this place, how he could learn to set his sights higher than he had ever dreamed, how that here it was hoped he would find a place to nurture his soul as well as his body. He would grow into a man clearly made in God's image, in the service of the Blessed Virgin His Mother. He would flourish like a young tree, putting forth blossom, bearing rich fruit. Catesby spoke in earnest, but not solemnly. There was passion in his voice, fire in his eyes.

'Oh, Toby, I know how you have chafed at the cruelties inflicted upon those of our faith. But tonight, this very night, Holy Mass will be celebrated under this roof. There we will all be able to dedicate ourselves anew to the service of our mother Church.'

Oh yes! leapt his heart.

He thought: *What has happened? What has he done to me?*

He was being dismissed, walking away into the everyday dimness of the house, his eyes still somehow dazzled, his head spinning.

He scarcely saw his uncle, who was hovering outside the room as he emerged. 'Well, Toby, how was it? What do you think of our Master Catesby?'

He stared at Nicholas as if he could make no sense of the question. 'I—well—I have to go, uncle.'

Freeing himself from the heavy hand on his shoulder, he went to his room, where he found Humphrey kneeling in prayer at the bedside. He hesitated, on the point of retreating, when the other boy turned his head, smiled, rose to his feet.

'You've met Master Catesby. I can see it in your face.'

'Aye.' He stood gazing stupidly at his friend, not sure what to say next. There were too many things jostling for attention in his head.

'Father Tes—Master Greenway is still upstairs, if you want to see him before Mass.'

To make his confession? Yesterday he'd repudiated the very idea. Now? Something had changed, but in what way? He did not know.

'I always find it a comfort.'

'I'm not you.' Even to his ears his voice sounded awkward, rough.

'No, indeed not. And all the better for it.' Humphrey grinned. 'Soon be dinner time. It will be good today, with the Master here.'

It *was* good. Lady Anne joined her son and the priest at the high table, to which the boys carried the most lavish and delicious of dishes. And there was more than enough left over for their own dinner, once the tables were cleared. Yesterday, Toby would have fallen upon the food with his usual voracious appetite, as the other boys were doing now, joining in the joking exuberance of their laughter.

But today was different. He barely noticed the splendour of the food or the talk around him. His appetite seemed to have fled. He ate little, and it could have been stale bread for all the savour it offered.

'Toby! Wake up! Did you not hear me?'

He turned dazed eyes on Wat's questioning face. 'No— no. What did you say?'

Wat's companion, a lanky boy named Arthur, nudged him. 'He's in love, can't you see? Off in a lovesick world of his own!'

'Aye, so he is! Not eating, with all this fine food before us! Oh, Toby Machyn, who's the wench then?'

'Let him alone, Wat.' That was Humphrey's gentle intervention, and since even the most boisterous of his companions liked Humphrey (who in any case deftly changed the subject) they did let Toby alone.

As soon as dinner was over, he made his way to the small upstairs room set aside for Master Greenway to hear the household's confessions, and there made his own confession with a seriousness he had never felt before. He even found himself telling of his concupiscence with Bess, his attendance at the heretic church, two things he had scarcely been able to admit, even to himself, as being sinful.

Unlike Father Fielding, this priest took him very seriously, probing his motives and his feelings, waking in him new layers of shame and contrition. For his penance, he was told he must fast for two days and pass each subsequent night in constant prayer. He felt a combination of shock and exaltation that something so hard should be asked of him. After that, the words of absolution seemed to wash away all the past, set him on a new path.

He began on his penance at once. That evening, when the tables had been cleared after supper and the boys sat down to eat, Toby left them and took himself upstairs, ignoring the growling of a stomach deprived of anything substantial since breakfast.

And then came the Mass, which bore no resemblance, apart from the words, to the few furtive hasty Masses at Holywell, held in a darkened room with his mother's makeshift vestments the only adornment. Here Mass was celebrated in a room that was hidden, yet made as fit for the purpose as any chapel, lit with abundant wax candles, the priest dressed in the most gloriously rich vestments, the words sung to heart-touching music (in which both Robert Catesby and Nicholas Gaunt took their parts). It was like nothing Toby had ever experienced in all his life. There was no danger of boredom here, only a wish that he might be worthy of what was offered.

At the end, standing in the emptying room in a glow of rapture (intensified by the light-headedness of hunger), he felt a hand on his shoulder.

'The first day of our acquaintance, Toby Machyn, and I know already that you are to be a blessing on our household.'

Toby turned his head and met the warm penetrating

gaze of Robert Catesby. Colour flooded him from head to toe. 'I thank you, sir.'

The man gave his shoulder a little shake, smiled, and left him. Toby gazed after him until the sound of his footsteps had long faded from his hearing.

From that day the household was utterly transformed. It seemed as if Robert Catesby brought a special illumination with him, a glow that lit up everything around him, yet drew all eyes to the place where he was, the focus of all their hopes and ambitions. When he spoke, his voice seemed to enter one's very soul, drawing from it all that was good. How could one meet Robert Catesby and not want at once to be like him, to follow him to the ends of the earth?

For days afterwards Toby could not sleep, could scarcely eat; mind and body fizzed with excitement. Wat had not been so far out when he accused Toby of being in love. It *was* like falling in love, without the shameful feelings that went with it, a kind of spiritual glow. He was held in an enchantment, in which he lived for those moments, at some point each day, when the tall scarlet-clad figure would seek him out, hold his hand, lay an arm across his shoulder, and always gaze at him with the intentness of one who found his every word worth hearing, who cared about him above all. Yet watching with jealous eyes when the man talked to his son, to Nicholas, to the lady of the house, to the many visitors who called there, even to the most menial of servants, he saw that this was a man to whom *everyone* mattered, who cared about each person he came across. Toby had known no one like him.

He was a fine horseman too, and Toby loved the days when the boys rode with Robert Catesby through the lanes, over the fields; or when Catesby joined the younger members of the household at their lessons, offering a gentle hint there, or more strident advice, precisely as it was needed. In a softer mode, they would sometimes sing together of an evening, while those most skilled (which Toby was not) accompanied them on lute or virginals.

In the afternoons, if rain kept the boys from their outdoor pursuits, Robert Catesby summoned the older ones among them to debate together. Eager to stir them to argument, he encouraged them to consider the deepest matters, to put their thoughts and questions into words.

They talked of authority, and its limits: the King's, their schoolmaster's, even the Pope's. They talked of truth and lies, and whether sometimes it was right and good to lie. 'If, say, you have a priest hidden in your house, and the pursuivants come, how do you answer their questions, knowing what the cost of truth may be?'

Well, that was easy enough, Toby thought.

But there were other things that seemed less easy, things that this new life had brought forcefully to mind, though it took some courage to put them into words; such as something the rector had once put to him.

'Sir, there was a man, a heretic, said to me once, 'Do we not all worship the same God, at heart? It is only the

Bishop of Rome, his Holiness the Pope, *his* power that stands between us.' So he said.'

He held his breath. Had he said too much? Robert Catesby waited until he'd finished speaking and then was silent, considering what he'd said with an expression of great seriousness. At last, speaking with his usual intensity, he said,

'And the sacrifice of the Mass? The very heart of our faith? Does that mean so little, to become a matter of indifference?'

'No, no. But—Well…'

'Ah, Toby, it is a matter of regret that there are fine men—fine in a worldly sense—who are not of our faith.' That was Master Greenway (whom Toby now knew to be Father Oswald Tesimond, one of those Jesuits whom Father Fielding so detested). 'But as you say yourself, they are guilty of heresy. Unless they repent before their lives end, they are most certainly bound for Hell. You must pray for their conversion, work for it in every way you can. We all must so do. But we cannot ever allow ourselves to be seduced by their arguments.'

Afterwards, Humphrey, who had listened attentively to the discussion, but taken no part in it, came alongside him as they went to supper. 'It's hard, isn't it? You were thinking of your brother.' The previous evening he'd told Humphrey about his lost brother, and Tom had indeed been one of those in his mind when he put the question to the group. 'I would wish we'd all escape Hell, or nearly all. And when there's one you care for, and you know—Well!'

It *was* hard to accept, yet it made sense to Toby, touching him as no argument put by his mother or Father Fielding ever had. He was convinced. Here, in this house, he had found his faith—not rediscovered it, but *found* it as he'd never known it before, in his very heart and soul; come home to it as he never had at Holywell.

He no longer wished he could be like Hal or Bess. He felt ashamed of the mocking talk he'd been a part of, ashamed that he had ever derided any aspect of this ancient true devotion, sullying its purity with such behaviour, sullying his very soul. He'd felt that it made him a part of their lives, cemented into their friendship, sharing their ways; but he saw now that Satan had lured him, led him astray, and he'd only too willingly given in. He no longer even wanted to belong to his old life, in any way.

This was better by far, an atmosphere of devotion and excitement that surrounded him, caught him up, seeped into his bones.

There came a night when, exhausted from a day of vigorous exercise, he sank at once into a profound sleep; then stirred, disturbed by some distant sound, and fell again to sleep. And this time to dream. He knew he was lying on straw in the byre at Meadhope's Home Farm (though it didn't look much like it), where he was roused from sleep to find Bess stooping over him, so close that he could see the rounds of her breasts above the low neck of her gown. He reached out and drew her to him, tugging at her clothes, pressing her against the straw, reaching where he had never before dared to reach. As they lay together he entered her, abandoned to passion, possessed by it, until he moaned his pleasure and she cried his name and they moved apart to lie side by side. And he woke.

It was dark, still, only the hooting of an owl disturbing the night silence, though already there was a hint of dawn light in the quality of the darkness. Soon it would be time to get up for the first prayers of the day.

And he had woken from a filthy dream! Shame swept over him. How could he bring that past sinfulness to this place, how could he even dream of such a thing? What did that mean for the state of his soul? That after all—in spite of his most sincere confession, in spite of his prayerful intentions, in spite of the holy influence of this place—he had somehow failed to slough off the evil things he had done at Holywell, the person he had been there?

He moaned, rolled over with his face in his hands and tried to offer prayers. But he felt sleep steal over him again, bringing visions of Bess's sweet tempting form, his body aching for the wicked consolations he'd found in his dream. He slid from the bed and knelt on the hard floor, hands tight clasped, trying to ignore the chill that crept through his shirt to his shrinking flesh, and implored the Holy Virgin to shield him from sin; and most of all from wicked thoughts and imaginings, from the desires that still throbbed through his rebellious body.

He did not go back to bed that night, though there was

still an hour or so left for sleep. Instead he went outside to the yard and washed at the well, stripping in the frosty dawn, scrubbing at his body, allowing the freezing water to drive out all filthiness, all desire, all lewdness; and as he did so murmuring the words of the *Pater Noster* and the *Ave Maria* over and over, to force his thoughts where they ought to be.

He felt the more ashamed when Master Catesby emerged from the house and saw him. 'You're up early, Toby.'

His smile filled Toby with a confused mixture of shame and devotion. Faced with his own sinfulness, who would not thrust it aside, feel renewed and restored, transformed by that alluring, overwhelming smile, by the presence of this man?

He felt himself blushing. Suddenly conscious of his nakedness, be pulled on his breeches and shirt. 'I woke, sir. So I thought—' He found he could not tell an outright lie with that searching gaze upon him. But neither could he tell the truth, such as it was. Suddenly it all seemed less than he'd thought, a dream he had not chosen. He was ashamed that there was still something in him that had allowed the dream to invade him, but it was over. It would not happen again. Bess was nothing to him in this place, a part of his lewd youth.

Another smile, a hand laid on his shoulder, giving it a gentle shake. 'More ready than any of us to face the day. That's good. Let's to prayers.'

He joined the reciting of the psalms with all his heart: *Deus misereatur nostri, et benedicat nobis...* 'God be merciful unto us and bless us...' The words in English seeped into his memory, the gentle tones of Gervase Langley threading its way through the Latin. Oh, his past sins were hard to drive away today! He forced himself to concentrate, to listen to Robert Catesby's strong voice leading the alternate verses, following that lead with the other men and women and children of the household. This was the voice that would lead him now, on to the right path, the path that led not to Hell but, in time, to Paradise, God willing.

This world he'd found at Ashby was another world from his childhood home, an adult world. He had left behind the wayward boy whose only guide was his mother's gentle rule. Here in this household he felt as if he had found himself, found a fuller, maturer life.

He had found a friend too, one worthy to replace Hal in his heart, a friend he could wholly respect as well as love. He could never have dreamed of joking with Humphrey as he had with Hal. There would have been no point, for such unseemly talk would have sullied their friendship. Yet Humphrey's gravity when faced with serious matters was nothing like his brother Edward's rigid piety, nor much like his uncle's, but was essential to his very self.

So busy was Toby's life these days that he saw little of his uncle. At first, full of resentment against him, still fighting homesickness, that had been a relief. But once he'd met Robert Catesby his feelings changed. Without

Nicholas's intervention he would never have come here.

One morning, meeting him by chance in the passage as he made his way to the stables for a riding lesson, he pulled off his hat in greeting.

'How goes it with you, Toby?'

'Oh, it's more than I—Oh, I thank you for bringing me here! I never thought—'

'A little taste of how life ought to be, in all this land, if only England would return to her true allegiance?'

Toby had not looked at life at Ashby in quite that way. He considered the matter. 'Aye, I suppose it is. We don't have to hide anything. No one's afraid.'

'That's not quite so, sadly. It's not like Holywell, where you were hemmed in by heretics, but even here we're not wholly safe from disturbance. Imagine how it would be if the parish churches were ours again, our cathedrals glorious, shrines restored, monasteries rebuilt and offering hourly praise to God from the lips of men and women with lives given up to His service. Just imagine how that would be!'

Toby tried to stretch his imagination to include all those apparently limitless possibilities; then found himself caught against an apparent stumbling block. He thought of Hal, Sir Cuthbert, his mother's heretic neighbours; and Tom. That they were bound for Hell was a tragic reality. But that they should be endangered in this life too, that was another matter. 'Wouldn't that mean making enemies of a lot of people? The people who don't want the old faith back again?'

'Only in the same way as they see us at present, as their enemies.'

'But that's because it's the law. It's what the King wants.'

'But if we had a king who felt otherwise, a king schooled in the true faith? Or a queen?'

'We haven't though. You said, the King is not so favourable to Catholics as you thought he would be.'

'If there were another monarch on the throne?'

Toby was struck by the note in his uncle's voice, almost urgent, fervent, not simply speculative, but putting forward a possibility, something that could be a reality one day. His uncle had served in the armies of Spain, Catholic Spain, which had once sent an Armada to restore the true faith to England. Could it be that he had knowledge of some future Spanish plan, one that might yet succeed? 'You think it could happen.'

'I do. And before long, please God.' Nicholas gave him a sideways look. 'But that's not talk for public ears. You know that.'

'Of course. I'm not stupid.' Toby grinned. 'But if it came about, we could say what we liked.'

'Indeed.'

Later, he told Humphrey what his uncle had said. 'He seems to think things might change, soon.'

Beneath Humphrey's thick fringe he glimpsed a frown. 'Hopes? Or believes?'

'Believes. So I thought he meant. Don't you think it's possible?' He'd found that Humphrey liked to learn what went on in the world beyond Ashby, reading and listening to keep himself abreast of the news; which he would then pass on to Toby, who was, on the whole, not much interested.

'I don't know.' He seemed to be giving the matter careful thought. 'The King is working to make peace with Spain, so I heard, so they will not come to our rescue. Unless they make it a condition of peace, to restore the true faith. But I do not think the King would agree. We can pray for it, I suppose.' Which, Toby thought, was not quite what his uncle had meant.

Robert Catesby's return quickly brought another change to the orderly household at Ashby St Ledgers, along with the light and excitement of his presence. For the boys, life continued much as usual, but as the days passed they saw rather less of him. There was a constant bustle of arrival in the yard, as yet more visitors rode in, always men, much of an age with Master Catesby, bringing with them an atmosphere of purpose, of intent. Many of them were kinsmen (like Tom Wintour, whose brother Robert soon joined him), others close friends. The Catesby household was part of a whole interconnected community of devoted Catholics, in an area where there were few who had apostatised, and Robert Catesby had many friends—of course he did, for who, meeting him, could not feel he had found a friend, a person he could respect and love and trust with his very life? Gradually Toby came to recognise some of these visitors, who would spend hours together shut in the small room over the porch of the house which Robert clearly used as a kind of study.

There was Robert's cousin Francis Tresham, the Wintour brothers and John Grant, all connected one way and another by marriage or by blood, and Kit Wright, whose brother Jack, a superb swordsman, gave the older boys occasional lessons in swordsmanship. But that was a sideshow, for they came, he saw, for quite another purpose: for talk long into the night in the privileged heart of the household, his uncle among them. Toby yearned to know what kept them talking so long, but all he heard were indistinct voices, sometimes low and sombre, sometimes raised, and occasional laughter; the unfamiliar smell of tobacco lingering; the sight of servants taking food and drink to the men—or rather one servant, Thomas Bates, Catesby's devoted manservant. He felt sore that he was not even an important enough servant to play that part. He was forced to recognise that he was only on the fringe of the enchanted heart of this house, a very junior member.

At bedtime one night he stood for a long time gazing out at the point where the light from the porch window fell on the path outside, until Humphrey, wondering what he was looking at, rose from the bed to join him.

'They're talking late tonight.' Humphrey's voice was soft, concerned not to rouse their sleeping companions.

'I wish we could be there to hear them. My uncle says I must be patient, that I'm too young, that there are things it's best not to know yet. But that great things are coming.'

'He said that?' Humphrey's voice was sharp with unease.

Toby turned to look at his friend. 'Why, what's wrong with that?'

'Nothing. Nothing at all.' But the disquiet was still there. He put a hand on Toby's shoulder. 'Better pray about it. There's nothing else for us to do.'

Just for a moment a little tremor of anxiety troubled Toby's exhilarating sense of being on the edge of great things. But later, in bed, all doubt left him. What his uncle had hinted must surely have something to do with restoring England to her lost faith. If anyone could bring that about, then Robert Catesby and his friends were the ones to do it, of that Toby was quite sure. And he prayed that he might be a part of it.

The following morning, Catesby had gone, and the company with him. Even Toby's uncle, bidding him a hasty farewell, rode after them.

The house seemed dark, empty, hollowed out.

PART TWO

1605

Chapter Fourteen

It did not help at all, to be once again scouring the stock of larders, pantry and dairy for something to turn into a celebratory meal. Nothing had changed since her last inspection, two days before.

Autumn winds, a long winter with snow and bitter cold yielding only slowly to a laggard spring had brought hunger to Holywell. Lent was long past, but Easter had brought no end to fasting and their stores had lessened even more in the two weeks since.

There was a small stock of oatmeal, past its best, though it had provided the usual potage for breakfast today, along with small beer: not much for men and women with a day's work before them. Otherwise, there was cheese, hardening fast (the cows, starved of grass, were giving little milk), and the remnants of their last ham.

'There'll be no feast tomorrow.' Kate's tone was resigned. This was, after all, what she had expected.

'No, madam, but we'll do what we can.'

Jane could often work wonders with limited resources, but even she had her limits. Kate smiled, straightened her shoulders. 'We shall have a feast for our souls. That will suffice.'

She saw from the the look in her eyes that Jane was not convinced.

It seemed like an answer to prayer, a small miracle, when, a short time later, Cuthbert Featherstone rode over

('Passing your door, I thought to call') with a haunch of venison in his saddle bag. Kate knew, though he did not say so, that he was perfectly well aware of how things stood with them. For a moment, with a tremor of apprehension, she wondered if somehow he knew everything, knew what this evening would bring; but no, how could he? This was simply an act of kindness from a generous neighbour.

And by no means the first. As she took the venison from him, feeling its weight, the smell of it, the texture of the cloth in which it was wrapped, she had a sudden flash of memory, of another such moment long ago. 'All your years of kindness to us. When we first came here—Do you remember?'

She could see he was struggling to recall what she meant.

'We'd been here only a few days. We had nothing, then you came by, to welcome us with just such a gift as this.'

'That must be ten years gone, just about. A long time.'

'You told me you remembered my grandmother.'

He beamed at that. 'She was a kind lady, to a little boy. Well loved. I was glad Holywell was occupied again.' Then he frowned. 'But you thought I'd betrayed you?'

She shook her head. 'That was afterwards. And only for a moment. I soon knew better. It was William Fowler, I'm sure of it.'

'Ah, the steward here?'

'My husband's steward, until then. He was dishonest as well as malicious.' She handed the venison to Jane, who was hovering near her.

'Shall I bring something, madam?'

Kate turned to Sir Cuthbert. 'You'll take a glass of sack?'

She led their neighbour into the parlour, where Jane soon brought some of the precious wine, running low like everything else, but rarely called upon these days, except on such occasions.

'Have you good news of young Toby?'

'None, I fear, good or bad.' She tried to sound calm, untroubled, but the hurt of it pierced her, along with the usual twinge of anxiety. 'I would guess time passes swiftly for him, with so much that is new and so much to learn.' But it was nearly a year now. Nicholas had written once, briefly, to say that the two of them had reached Ashby St Ledgers after an uneventful journey and were in good health, but that was all, in spite of the promises he'd made. There had not even been a message from Toby, passed on to show he still thought of them kindly, or thought of them at all.

'A good lad. I would—But you know what I would have wished for him. That's in the past. He will one day, please God, become a fine man and a credit to you.'

Rather, to his faith, she thought but did not say. It brought to mind again the struggle with her conscience that had tormented her after Nicholas's visit, a struggle she'd thought concluded, but which still darted to the surface when she least expected it. The closest she'd come to complying with his strictures was to distance herself just a little from her neighbours, fewer deliberate meetings, fewer shared meals. She knew that was not enough.

'Your younger boy, Edward—our good rector tells me his lessons have ceased. You have other plans for him perhaps?'

The question seared her, as if her neighbour could read the answer in her eyes. She felt herself colour, knowing the truth; knowing too how near it was, how fully in her thoughts. What could she say, without revealing what must be hidden?

To her relief Sir Cuthbert spoke again, before she could think of a response.

'A very different lad, I feel, from his brother. Hard to get to know. Perhaps his uncle will provide for him too?'

She tried to steady her voice, though her heart thudded so much that she feared Sir Cuthbert could see it. 'As you say, he is a very different boy.' *If I had cut myself off from the Featherstones, there would be nothing to hide. He would neither know nor care what was to become of Edward.* But she had not cut herself off, so she must somehow change the subject. 'I hope the Lady Juliana is well?'

'Is she ever anything else? Strong as a horse, my dear wife. Thank God!'

'Would she like the image?' Kate's smile was sly, warm with relief.

'Oh, she'd delight in it. To her a horse is finer than any human. We men are mere clods.'

By some hidden train of thought he came to another matter: 'You know Henry Stobbs has been struck with the cattle plague? His cattle, that is.'

'I'd heard it. I sent Andrew Wardle to let him know we'd cancel his debt for the rent.'

'That was generous!' Sir Cuthbert's eyebrows seemed to grow like a springtime hedgerow.

'On condition that he pays at least some of the Whitsun rent, when it's due.'

'You think he will?"

'I doubt it very much. But this is no time for harshness.' Especially when so important a guest was expected at Holywell...Once, Henry Stobbs had informed on her to Sir Cuthbert, taking her brother for a visiting priest. That had been a matter for laughter. But if he were to choose from malice to keep watch on Holywell again? She shivered, adding casually, 'Your cattle are clear, I hope?'

'So far, thank God. Yours looked in fair fettle when I came by, in spite of the winter.'

At the end of a rather laboured half hour of talk, she went out with Sir Cuthbert to the courtyard, where young Will held his horse. She repeated her thanks for his kindness, and once he'd ridden away stood for a little longer, breathing in the scent of the stables, lingering to give Toby's old horse a consoling word or two before returning to the house to discuss the preparation and cooking of the precious venison. They would dine well tomorrow after all. How fitting that Sir Cuthbert had unwittingly made this generous gesture on this most special of days!

As she stepped into the kitchen, someone came in from the yard, carrying a pail of water. For a moment Kate did not recognise her; then with a sense of shock, she did.

Cecily Stobbs had never been plump or robust, like the other girls. Today she looked thinner than ever, stooped as if expecting a blow; with reason perhaps, as there was a fresh red bruise marking one side of her face, already blotched with darker shades, the skin split at its centre. She halted, slumped against the doorpost as if to stop herself from falling, as if simply keeping on her feet was beyond her. Jane ran to seize the pail before it spilled; Kate took Cicely's arm.

'I'm in need of help in the stillroom. Please to come with me.'

To work in the stillroom was an honour accorded only to the most privileged servants, and the most skilled. Kate was well aware that Moll and Alice would resent furiously that she should extend this invitation to their unsavoury workmate. She would deal with them later, on the quiet.

Once in the stillroom, she closed the door. 'First, you need something for that bruise.' She dipped a cloth into a ewer of water.

Cecily put a hand to her face. 'I fell, madam.'

'Indeed? Is that so?' She sat the girl down on a stool and put the cold wet cloth against her face. 'Hold this there.'

212

She reached to take down a flask from one of the shelves. 'There's mullein and lavender in this, for healing and soothing. It will help ease the worst of it.'

As soon as the chill had gone from the cloth, she bathed the bruise with the lotion.

'Now, what's going on? Did I not bid you stay at home until Friday?' She had wanted to make sure that any of the household who were less than devout (or less than discreet) were not at Holywell during these two days.

She had not thought Cecily could look any more frightened, but now she did. She was visibly shaking.

'Aye, madam. But…'

Kate sighed. 'No matter. Did this happen to you here, this morning?' Unlikely, and she guessed the answer. It would not be the first time.

'I—no—yes.'

'You are not well. You should go home and rest.'

'No—no, madam! I wish to stay! I beg you!'

Cecily made a panicked move to stand, tottered, would have fallen had Kate not held her, lowering her gently back to her seat.

She looked into the girl's frightened imploring eyes, trying to read what lay behind her plea. Did she know what was to happen and long to be a part of it? She always seemed attentive and respectful during household prayers, but her father at least had no such loyalties and if she were to go home now and tell what she knew…if she did know.

'If you do not go home now, then I must ask you to stay

213

until Friday.'

'Oh I thank you, madam!' Relief coloured Cecily's face, though Kate felt a twinge of apprehension.

She handed the girl into Jane's care. 'I'll keep an eye on her,' Jane promised. 'For now, she needs sleep and rest.'

Back in the kitchen, Kate told Moll and Alice only that she had summoned Cecily so she could bathe her bruise.

'Aye, well, that'll be her Dad's doing,' said Moll. 'Always was over-ready with his fists.'

Kate was sure that was the case, but made no comment.

Alice gave an exaggerated shudder. 'He followed me all the way back from market last week. He's creepy.'

'I've seen him a good few times, watching us— watching John Emerson too.'

Trying to reassure them, Kate said, 'He'll not see anything to catch his interest.'

Except today, if he were to think to pass by. Would he care that his daughter did not come home? Kate went to have a word with John, to ask him to let her know if he saw the man about the place. John would in any case be on the watch as their guests flocked to the house, tenants and friends: Andrew Wardle her steward and his wife, Peter Gibson, near neighbour to Henry Stobbs, and even old Mistress Wynyard from Ashburn Hall, emerging grudgingly from her solitude; all those who had waited two long years for this day, and for the most special guest of all.

* * *

He rode into the courtyard at dusk, shrouded in an ancient cloak, thick against the rain. If he'd been asked who he was, he would have answered, 'William Sutton, scrivener.' John Emerson, knowing the truth, hurried to greet him and take his horse to a quiet corner of the stables, as Kate opened the door to usher him into the house. Hushed darkness fell over the courtyard, while in the hall the company gathered in silence for the visitor's blessing.

A simple supper, then one by one the entire household made their way in turn to Kate's closet, where the man they knew as Father Fielding—rounder, more lined, his sober clothes more stained than ever—waited to hear their confessions and give spiritual guidance with his usual gentle pragmatism. When her turn came, Kate took courage to speak of her brother's counsel, though fearful that the priest would only reinforce it. No, certain that he would.

He was silent for what seemed a very long time after she told him of her dilemma, and at last asked her searching questions about Nicholas's conversion, and who had played a part in it. As soon as she spoke of the Jesuit priests her brother so admired, she saw the old priest's expression change.

'The Jesuits would have us live in constant warfare with the authorities, removing all hope of a peacable and holy life.' He spat out the word *Jesuits* as if it contaminated his mouth. 'We are not asked to *seek* martyrdom. Does our Lord not command us to render *quae sunt Caesaris Caesari et quae sunt Dei Deo?* Give to Caesar what is Caesar's, to God what is God's.'

Kate was not sure how this admonition applied to dining with her neighbours, but felt consoled that Father Fielding took a less rigid view than did her brother. He himself might not seek martyrdom, but in serving his scattered flock he daily faced the possibility of capture and an appalling death.

Few of the household slept much that night. To Kate, the air seemed to be strung like a lute, taut, yet threatening at any moment to slip out of tune; resonant with song and terror, the two inseparable threads of these times. Even the youngest of them knew what it meant, knew their celebrations must be secret, hidden, for they were about to collude in breaking the law, for which the penalties were no light matter.

Shortly before dawn they crowded into the windowless attic room, where all but the shortest of them had to stoop a little under the low ceiling. There the makeshift altar was ready, and the vestments so carefully fashioned from Kate's best gown. Father Fielding blessed them, before robing to begin the Mass.

As the familiar, longed-for words filled the room, Kate tried to concentrate her mind, to shut out fear, to stop herself from listening for any untoward sound—approaching horsemen, clubs hammering on the doors, steps on the spiral stair that led up from below. Twice in her life it had happened, once in her girlhood, the other as a young wife, when the pursuivants had ridden to the house and scoured it for signs of their faith. The first time, the priest had fled from the house just in time; at Haroby there had been a priest's hole, where the visiting officiant had hidden safely. But the terror of it all had clung to her memory, haunting her ever after.

Slowly tonight the fear left her, the solemnity of the occasion caught and held her. There was singing, ragged and tuneless, but the best they could manage, rapt faces caught in the candlelight. She glimpsed Moll and Alice and Sarah, full of uncharacteristic solemnity; Cecily, who had begged to be here (so she had known about it after all!), and seemed held in enchantment. And Edward, utterly absorbed in what was happening, offering up the days that lay ahead of him, as she too tried to do. For that was the second reason for Father Fielding's visit: once the Mass had ended and the day's feasting was over, he would take Edward with him to the ship that would carry him to the Low Countries, to the seminary where he would train as a priest.

'God go with you, Edward. May His blessed Mother watch over you and guide you and keep you safe.'

Edward raised his head as she withdrew her hand from his hair. His face was calm, half-smiling; no trace of tears. 'I thank you, madam my mother.' He rose to his feet, then turned away to his hired horse. She watched him mount.

Another departure, another child gone from her. But she could not grieve for Edward's going, whose reason was what any good Catholic mother would desire for her child.

A week ago, Kate had called her son to her in her closet, to hear him as he stood before her, eyes meeting her gaze, unwavering, assuring her that yes, he did indeed feel called to the priesthood, and yes, he was content to go from home to serve in that capacity. That assurance had relieved her of a certain stirring of unease. Yet, afterwards, she'd felt unease of another kind. No, regret, for this son whom in some ways she felt she scarcely knew, perhaps because he'd given her so little trouble, always devout, always obedient, quiet, reserved, a child who had never seemed very childlike.

It was too late for any such regrets. If she had somehow been a less than devoted mother, she could not now begin to make restitution for any lack he might have felt. In any case, he showed no sign of resentment or reproach towards her, but simply knelt to ask for her blessing, begged her to pray for him, and accepted her embrace in his usual calm way.

And this morning at the moment of parting he seemed only quietly happy at the prospect before him, hugging his younger siblings, promising to write when he could, *if* he could, and hoping one day they might meet again. 'When England returns to her true allegiance, perhaps? Who knows?' he added, while Father Fielding nodded his approval, adding, *'Deo volente!* God willing'

Katharine went back into the house, Jane at her side.

'Another of our little flock gone.' She wondered if Jane

felt more sadness at this departure than she did. 'Just the twins now.'

'You've no thoughts for their future?'

'Not yet. Not really. Mariana—well, for her a good marriage would be best, but with no dowry worth speaking of, and he would have to be a Catholic...' Jane was murmuring her agreement, but Kate thought there was an odd light in her eyes, almost questioning. Something held her back from probing its cause. 'As for Philip—it could be that my brother will help to find a household fit for his needs. We shall see.' She sighed. 'I would feel happier at such a prospect if only Toby had written.'

'It's the not knowing. But you'd have heard if all was not well. If he was sick, or—'

'I know. I'm sure of it.' But she wasn't sure, not quite.

The twins were in the garden, walking steadily along the paths between the beds of herbs, the dog at their heels, Philip clutching Mariana's hand while she chattered away to him, kindly, patiently.

Kate summoned them to her. 'It is time now for your lessons.'

Mariana protested, but they followed her meekly enough into the house, to the parlour. There Kate gave Philip a hornbook in the hope that today might be the day when he at last began to grasp his letters, even start to read. As she heard Mariana falter over her Latin, she found herself wondering again what was to become of these two youngest children of hers. They were not pious children.

They showed no sign that they might either of them be suited to the religious life, as Edward so clearly was, and Philip was perhaps too damaged ever to be suited to any occupation. For Mariana, as she'd said to Jane, marriage would be the obvious solution, but a Catholic husband willing to take on a near-dowerless wife would be very hard to find. Kate's uncle had struggled to find her a husband, even with her modest dowry. She herself had been fortunate that for some reason Sir Thomas had taken a fancy to her, young though she was. Like her daughter, she had not been suited to the religious life, though she'd feared sometimes that this would inevitably be her fate if a husband did not come forward. Sometimes, later, while Sir Thomas was alive, she'd found herself wondering if that fate might have been the better one after all.

She forced herself to concentrate on the lesson. Time enough for all this, as they grew. God would provide a way, enlighten the path for them. All she could do was to make time later in the day to pray for her children and ask Our Lady and the Saints to intercede for her and for them.

It was nearly supper time when Jane interrupted her earnest prayers. 'Madam, Master Wardle is here. He begs for a word with you.'

It was barely four hours since he'd left the house! What could possibly bring him back again so soon?

She made her way to the hall, where her bailiff waited. With him, ominously, was the rector.

Andrew Wardle's big red hands pulled at his hat. 'It's Henry Stobbs, madam.'

It would be!

'He's laid hands on Peter Gibson's beasts, best part of a score of them, and all healthy animals. First thing this morning, before it was light.' While Peter Gibson was at Holywell, at the forbidden Mass. Had his neighbour known of it and seized his chance, thinking that so dangerous a secret would keep him safe from retribution?

Kate sighed. 'Those two have been at loggerheads for ever. But Henry Stobbs's cattle have the plague, so I was told.'

'Aye. Peter Gibson's are clear. It's come to blows and Stobbs is brought before Sir Cuthbert, locked up for now.'

'It's a hanging offence, stealing cattle.'

'The cattle are back where they came from. Peter Gibson made sure of that. So it's his word against Stobbs's as to what happened.'

'I know who I'd believe.'

'Aye, there's no doubt of that. But it's my guess Stobbs will get away with it. Maybe a whipping, at most. It's his way.' Andrew Wardle shifted his large ungainly frame as if bracing himself for what he had to say next. Kate knew what was coming before he continued. 'This time, madam —well, it's my thought Stobbs has come to the end, after this.'

'He was hit hard with the sickness.'

'He's had every chance, madam. More than any man

could hope for. You've been, well—soft, sometimes, I reckon. He's a bad neighbour, always has been. He neglects his land and his stock, he's always behind with the rent. There's no way he'll change for the better now.'

'He has a wife, and children.'

'Aye, and they'll be a charge on the parish. Can't be helped.'

The rector broke in. 'I will do what I can to make sure they are cared for. But I think with Andrew here that you cannot continue to ignore what he has done. You have a charitable heart, which is to your credit, but you do him no favours, or yourself.'

Kate stirred uneasily, knowing that charity played very little part in her leniency towards her tenant. Fear for what he might do in revenge, for his malice; that was a much greater consideration.

'We'll be a laughing stock if he's let get away with this. That's my view.'

'I fear the time has come,' the rector agreed.

She burst out: 'Oh, I hate these things! To have to play so with men's lives, when it hurts so many!'

'But he is the one hurting their lives, not you, madam. His neighbours are suffering all this time for want of a solution. Andrew here has done all he can, and you know how often I myself have spoken with him, admonished him.'

'I know.' She gazed at the two men, with a sense of utter weariness. Andrew Wardle had been very patient with her softness, as he put it. The rector had supported her as far as he could and was staunch in his advice and support, but it was for her alone to make the ultimate decision and face the consequences.

The thought came fleetingly to her that Henry Stobbs, almost alone among her tenants, was not a Catholic, even nominally. She knew instinctively what Nicholas would say: 'Cut him from your life! He is bound for Hell whatever you do.'

To see things so clearly, so much in black and white—that must make life so much easier. Was it womanly weakness that prevented her from doing so, as Nicholas would surely have said? She was not so sure.

She took a deep breath, forced herself to sit more upright, to brace herself for what had to be done. 'That is decided then. He must be turned out, at Whitsun. We'll draw up the notice, you and I, Andrew.'

It was raining on the day the Stobbs family were evicted from their house. Kate forced herself to ride with Andrew Wardle, John Emerson and the handful of other men gathered to carry out the duty, armed with cudgels, just in case. The rector, unarmed, rode with them.

She'd feared that Henry Stobbs, released after a brief imprisonment, would greet them with violence; at the very least, set his ill-tempered dogs on them. To her surprise they found the dogs tied up, the family standing in the cold drizzle with their goods at their feet, meekly awaiting their fate, the gaunt mother and four of their children. Cecily, told of what was to happen, had been assured of a home at Holywell and had remained there today. Kate did not know what the girl thought about it all.

Henry Stobbs alone showed no sign of meekness, for all that he stood with the rest of his family. As they came near, he met Kate's gaze, unwavering, with an implacable expression that spoke of hate and anger and malice and made her shiver.

The rector went to shepherd the mother and children to the rectory, where he'd undertaken to give them shelter until a more secure home was found for them. Henry Stobbs slung his packs on the back of his bony horse, cast one last icy glance at Kate and walked away, pausing to spit at her feet as he passed.

Chapter Fifteen

'You haven't heard a word I've said!'

Humphrey was in an odd mood this morning, had been for several days in fact. Never voluble, he was generally more inclined to listen than to talk. But today he seemed caught up in some world of his own, far away from what was usually a companionable time together at the end of the day, before evening prayers.

Now, he turned his head (they were sitting on a sunlit bench in the stable yard), gave a vague smile, as if he'd still not quite taken in what Toby had said to him. 'I beg your pardon, Toby. Did you say something?'

'You know I did. What's eating you?'

'Oh, nothing, I guess.'

'You can't fob me off with that. I know you too well.'

The other boy shrugged. 'It's something and nothing. Just on my mind, that's all.'

'What is?'

Humphrey was silent for some time, as if choosing the right words, before he spoke again, very slowly. 'You know that little chamber by the dairy, just before you get to that door?' He gestured towards a low door at the far side of the yard.

'Can't say I do. I never use it. What about it?'

'You know I lost a glove yesterday? I thought I might have dropped it in the stable, so I went that way to look for it. It was late, after supper and getting dark. It was open, the door to the chamber. I don't recall ever seeing it open before. The back door was open too, and they were carrying boxes in from outside, stowing them in the chamber. Your uncle and Tom Bates. Heavy boxes.'

'Stores for the house?'

'Toby, I saw muskets! Inside the chamber, stacked against the far wall. And pistols. And the way they carried the boxes, carefully, looking about them all the while, as if to make sure they weren't seen. I don't think they saw me. There wasn't much light, and I hung back. It just didn't feel right.'

Toby considered the matter, trying to think of some simple explanation. 'Are you sure about it—the weapons, I mean?'

'Quite sure.'

'Rob says his father told him he's getting a troop together to fight in the Low Countries. That'll be what they're for, I'd guess.'

There was no sign of the expected relief on Humphrey's face. 'I've heard that. I don't believe a word of it. I think it's a story to cover for something else.'

'But why? It sounds likely to me.'

'What, when Spain is in peace talks with King James? If there's no war, you don't need arms or soldiers. It doesn't make sense, not to me.' Beneath the blonde fringe the frown intensified. 'It's not just that. There's something not right, something more. I've felt it for a while. You've noticed too—last time Master Catesby was home, when we went past the parlour?'

'You mean when we heard him wrangling with his mother about something?'

'About selling land, and she refusing. Why would he need the money so much? If the story about the troop for Spain isn't true, I mean?'

'Recusancy fines perhaps?'

'Maybe. But there's been no word he was in trouble lately. I think there's something else, and I don't much like the thought of it.'

A shiver ran the length of Toby's spine. Fear? Excitement? Or a little of each?

'Haven't you felt it? Something in the air, something wrong?'

He knew exactly what his friend meant, though he would not have put it in quite those words. Ever since he first became settled at Ashby, for more than a year now, he'd sensed an undercurrent of excitement growing beneath the orderly daily routine, especially when Robert Catesby was in the house—as he had not been for some weeks now, since the time when the altercation with his mother had been overheard. But to Toby the tension, the sense of something brewing, swelling, was a positive thing, to be welcomed, embraced; something he longed to be a part of. His uncle's occasional guarded hints only added to his eagerness.

'You can't think there'd be anything wrong, Humphrey. We're talking about Master Catesby here!'

'I know; I know. Once, I would have thought…Oh well, I hope you're right! Anyway, if you want to see what's in that little chamber I told you about, take a walk that way, some time when it's quiet. See if you can see anything.'

The very next morning, in the dark before breakfast, Toby made his way to the little-used passage Humphrey had mentioned. There was no one about and little light to show the way, and no sign of anything untoward—just a succession of closed doors, most of which opened to the usual sights: shelves of cheeses, hams hanging from a vaulted ceiling, beer barrels filling the air with their tang. The door next to the outer door, Humphrey had said: Toby laid his hand on the latch. Unlike the others, it would not budge; locked, clearly.

He tried again.

'Toby!'

His hand jerked back as if the latch had scorched it. He swung round, mouth open, to where a candle illuminated its bearer.

'What are you doing here?' His uncle's tone was accusatory.

'Er—I…' He grasped at what Humphrey had told him. 'I dropped a glove. I thought—'

It was clear that Nicholas did not believe him. He braced himself to receive a furious rebuke, in the coldly relentless manner that had once been only too familar. Instead, he saw Nicholas draw himself up, take a deep breath; and when he spoke again it was calmly.

'I came in search of you. I have an errand for you, thinking you could be trusted.'

'You know I can.' He was glad he was too far from the candle flame for his uncle to see how deeply he had coloured.

Unfortunately, that was not enough. 'I'm troubled, Toby. What are you doing here? That farradiddle about a lost glove. You'd not have dropped it here, even if it were true. And why try that door, pray?'

Should he make an attempt to bluff his way out of the difficulty? Would his uncle be deceived? Better perhaps to be completely honest, showing himself entirely worthy of trust. But he was anxious not to shift any of the blame onto Humphrey. 'Someone told me they'd seen arms stacked in this room.' He held his breath, waiting for a possible explosion.

Nicholas came nearer, holding the candle high, illuminating his own grave expression. 'What if there were?'

Toby sought the right response. 'You said there'd be great things coming, one day. Maybe it's to do with that.'

'So there will, a great enterprise. But for now it's better you don't know too much. If you have questions, ask me, by all means. But do not talk of it to others, no matter what they say. Promise me that!'

Feeling important, Toby met his uncle's questioning gaze. 'I promise. You can trust me, uncle.'

'Good. I do believe I can. Now, I have need of a

message to be carried to Norbrook, to Master Grant's house.'

John Grant was one of the family network around the Catesbys, an irascible man, married to the Wintour brothers' sister. 'Oh yes, of course! I'll be glad to take it.'

'You must go now, immediately. I'll give you directions. And Toby, remember this is a most secret errand. You must speak of it to no one. No one at all. You understand?'

Heart thudding, pride swelling in him that he should be so trusted, Toby nodded. 'Yes, uncle.'

'Good.' Nicholas glanced round, as if checking that no one was lurking in the empty passage to overhear what he had to say, though when he spoke it was so quietly that Toby himself scarcely caught the words. 'Ask to speak to Master Grant in person, no one else. Tell him that the cargo will be with him at midnight tonight, without fail. Now, repeat what I have just told you!'

Toby did so, though he felt that for something so apparently urgent the message sounded disappointingly mundane. But if the 'cargo' should be some religious item, then there would certainly be a need for secrecy.

Or a crate of arms, muskets and pistols, such as Humphrey claimed to have seen.

He longed to ask, but dared not.

'Leave at once, without delay. The steward has been told you are sick, and will not be at breakfast or attending to your duties today. Take your own horse, saddle him yourself.'

'I'll get my cloak.'

Meeting Humphrey on the stairs, he longed to be able to confide in his friend, to discuss what had happened, but he recalled his uncle's warning. 'I don't feel so good,' was all he said, hobbling past the other boy, as if he were indeed unwell, and uneasily conscious that Humphrey was watching him with concern.

It was late morning by the time Toby reached Norbrook. He left his horse in the stable, where his attention was caught by the other occupants of the stalls, the finest, most powerful horses he had ever seen: coursers, of the kind used in war. Exactly the kind of mounts you would need for a troop destined for the Low Countries, or so he would have thought before yesterday's conversation with Humphrey. Could his friend be wrong, for all his awareness of what was happening in the wider world beyond Ashby? He longed to spend some time looking at the horses, even talking about them with the groom who took charge of Ruby, but instead asked for the master of the house.

He was admitted to John Grant's office, where he gave his message to his silent host. John Grant gave a cursory nod. 'So they've reached Ashby. Good!'

Did this confirm his suspicion that the 'cargo' consisted of the crates Humphrey had seen?

'I thank you. You may go on your way.'

Not even an offer of food, though he'd ridden half a day with no breakfast and it was now dinner time! It was a poor reward for his trouble.

But he had a few coins in his purse, and there must be an inn or alehouse on the way back to Ashby where he could buy something to eat.

He rode slowly, looking about him for a likely place. Ah, a building glimpsed through the trees!

No, just the gatehouse to a rambling stone house, a gentleman's dwelling. Earlier in the day, on his way to Norbrook, he'd been too concerned with his errand to notice what he passed. Now, something made him draw rein, something that snagged at his memory. The shape of the gatehouse, the colour of the stone, the way the trees sheltered the short drive that led to to the house—surely he had known it once, passed this way long ago, maybe even ridden under the arch into the courtyard beyond? Or had it been a similar but more extensive property, the one he remembered? If so, why did this still seem familiar?

He searched his mind, but unable to grasp at anything tangible, caught by the gnawing pangs of hunger, he shrugged and followed the road round the next bend.

And there at last was a scattered hamlet, with an inn, the *Red Lion*. His money would stretch only to bread and cheese, and hay for Ruby, but he sat down and ate hungrily. An old man sitting nearby (eating a pie whose savoury smell drew Toby's envious gaze) tried to engage him in conversation, asking where he'd come from and where he was going. To fend off questions he had no intention of answering, Toby asked one himself. 'That house back there, with the big gatehouse? What is it, do you know?'

'Oh, that's the Machyn place. Haroby.'

How could he not have known? A wave of emotion swamped him, shutting out the rest of the old man's words.

He gulped down the last of his food, went in search of his horse, and rode slowly back the way he'd come, drawing rein by the gatehouse—so much smaller than the vast edifice in his memory, which had dwarfed modest Holywell. This was a little grander than his mother's house, but not by so very much.

Haroby had been empty for years, as far as he knew, the house uninhabited while (he assumed) Tom's guardian managed the estate from Silworth, several miles west of Norbrook.

He gazed into the courtyard, swept clean and more free of moss and weeds than Holywell's busy courtyard. Clearly Roger Machyn took good care of the place on his ward's behalf.

He dismounted, hesitated. Forward, beyond the gatehouse? Or to his left, towards the range of stable buildings and outhouses?

Leading Ruby, he turned left, walked a little way, halted, his ear struck by an unexpected sound: a voice, a man's voice; another, deeper, answering.

He left his mare to crop a nearby patch of grass and crept forward to where an arch opened into the stable yard. Clean, as orderly as the main courtyard, it was occupied by two men deep in discussion over a horse, a great chestnut courser like those he had seen at Norbrook, powerful, gleaming, a magnificent beast that held his admiring gaze.

One of the men spoke again, as he ran his hand down the horse's gleaming flank: a slim young man with dark hair. Something in the way he moved, the angle of his head, caught Toby's attention, held it.

Too long—the man straightened, turned, saw him. And stood gazing, with a little frown creasing his brow, as if he too was wondering, as Toby was, why the other was somehow familiar, where he could have seen him before.

Should he run away? The second man (short, stocky, his homespun clothes marking him as a groom) had seen him too, and shouted. The younger man laid a restraining hand on his arm and strode towards Toby.

Toby braced himself, waited. An assured young man, early twenties perhaps, well-made, in good clothes, with steady dark eyes. Warm, like his mother's eyes, like his own...

He knew then.

'Tom.'

The dark eyes scanned him, with a question in them that found a hesitant answer. 'Toby—?'

He nodded. The beat of his heart thundered in his ears, set him trembling.

'What? How?'

'You were at Silworth, they said. I thought there was no one here.'

'We moved a month since, I and my wife and my

household.'

Momentary panic: 'Our cousin, your guardian?'

'He remains at Silworth. I am now of age, and come into my estate.' There was still bewilderment in Tom's gaze. 'But you? How do you come here? My mother—how is she?' Voice sharp with anxiety: 'Is all well with her?'

'She's well.' Toby's conscience stirred uneasily at the thought of all those tender letters unanswered, reminders of a repudiated past. 'I'm at Ashby St Ledgers now.'

'Ah, I see.' The frown again. 'Our uncle I suppose: Nicholas Gaunt—his doing? I heard he was there.'

Toby nodded, since he could think of nothing coherent to say. This fine looking young man with his kind eyes, the elder brother who had pledged so heroically to stay true to his faith—who was he now? What had he become? The beloved brother he remembered; or an enemy?

So much to say, no words, a tumult of feelings: unease, doubt, love flooding up from the past, from their shared childhood, swelling his throat so the words would not come. Oh how he longed to be loved again by this lost brother, to find him still the hero of his memory!

He cleared his throat, though his voice cracked. 'You're wed now?'

'Aye.' Tom smiled, a warm tender smile. 'I'm fortunate to have loved where my guardian would have me love. So all are happy.' A pause, while they looked at one another, eyes full of questions, of wondering; then: 'Have you dined, Toby?'

Hardly, but he nodded. He cleared his throat again. 'This horse. Is it yours?' A stupid question, with no bearing on all the things he wanted to ask, to know.

'He is indeed. What do you think? Come, take a closer look at him.'

He steered Toby towards the horse, dismissing the groom as he did so with an impressively authoritive gesture.

Toby, awed, gazed at the animal. 'So powerful! He'd make a great warhorse. There are such beasts at Norbrook, but I think yours is finer.'

'You've been to Norbrook?'

'Aye. I had a message to carry.' He clamped his mouth shut. *A most secret errand. You must speak of it to no one*. A shiver ran up his spine.

Tom's eyes seemed to see right through him. 'I see.'

What did he mean by that? Surely though nothing in what Toby had let slip was truly a betrayal? There could be a hundred and one innocent reasons why he should carry a message from one household to another connected by blood and friendship. From the little he'd said, Tom could have no idea what was the nature of the message, nor was he going to find out from Toby. Duty, loyalty, his new-found faith tugged at Toby, warned him he should not even be here, that to yield to this impulse was a dangerous distraction.

Tom laid a hand on his shoulder, shook it gently.

'Toby, it's so good to see you. I can't find words.' He sounded as full of emotion as Toby himself. 'Let's get

Warrior here inside and take some refreshment. My wife is from home today. Her father is sick. I would wish you could have met.'

Daughter of the man who, by law, was his guardian too. Thank goodness she was away!

'You would like her, Toby.'

'She's not of our faith.'

'*Your* faith, Toby. Not mine.'

He reddened, as if he'd been rebuked. 'You promised once.'

'I know. I meant it too. But—' Tom shrugged and spread his hands. He ought to have been shame-faced, embarrassed, but if he was he hid it well.

'I guess you had to make a show of turning Protestant, to keep the peace?'

'No, Toby, it was my free choice, after long thought and prayer. Otherwise I should still be Catholic in my innermost heart, not—as I am. I was gently reared, encouraged, persuaded; finally convinced. Be sure, Toby, I would not wish for persecution in the name of religion; at least, not of those who live at peace with their neighbours. But I am not a Papist.' He smiled gently, as if aware how shocking the last word must sound to Toby's ears. 'Come now, Toby, don't look so desolate! Let's go inside and you can tell me about yourself, all the years. There's so much time to make up for.'

He fought a twinge of conscience. He ought not to stay, in view of all his brother had said, and his promise to

Nicholas. 'I'd like that.'

Once the horse was returned to the groom's care, and Ruby cared for, they went into the house. In the panelled hall, Toby came to a halt, looking about him.

'It's so small, not like I remember!'

'You're grown up, that's all.' Tom's smile was tender, reminiscent. 'Do you remember our uncle riding his horse into here?'

'He gets angry now if you remind him. He's put all that behind him.'

'Ah, I see.' Again that penetrating look. 'Whose idea was it you should go to Ashby?'

'His, I suppose. But our mother thought it best. And it was, I'm sure of that now. Though at first—well, I didn't want to go. There was talk I'd go to Cambridge. Sir Cuthbert would pay for me.' He saw that Tom had no idea who Sir Cuthbert was, so broke off to explain. 'It seems so long ago now, and such a wordly thing. From heretic hands too.'

Tom broke into an awkward silence. 'Time for refreshment. Come to the library.' He led the way to the book-lined room, pausing to order wine and honey cakes to be brought to them.

Toby was impressed: his big brother, giving orders in his own great house! From a comfortable cushioned chair, he looked around him. 'I don't think I remember this room at all.'

'It's no wonder. It was our father's place. You would

only ever have been in here when you'd displeased him.'

Memory pierced him. 'Oh, yes, I do.' He shivered. 'This is where we got a beating.'

'So you do remember? Best forgotten perhaps. Tell me more about yourself now. How is it at Ashby? How long have you been there? What do you do there? The usual duties? Most of all, are you happy?'

'Oh yes—yes! Master Robert Catesby, the son of the house—he is, well! When he's there—'

'I've met him, once or twice.' Tom's tone was guarded, but Toby seized on the words.

'Oh, you'll know then. He's such a man, like no other!'

'Hmm. That much is true. He has a way with him. But that can be dangerous, used wrongly.'

'Oh, but he is a good man, truly!'

'He's brushed with the law in the past. You do know that?'

'Only because he stands up for what is true, and will not compromise.'

Tom shook his head. 'Just be wary, Toby, that's all. Use your good sense.' His face relaxed. 'How much do you remember, of living here?'

'Only small things. It's our leaving it I remember most. The journey, how you kept us safe.'

Tom shook his head. 'That was Jane, not me. Oh, I made a show of it, but I was terrified really. If it hadn't been for Jane—well!'

A moment came into Toby's head: the drip of rain on

leaves, Jane's arms about them, her soft low voice over their bent heads, soothing, reassuring.

'When we were most frightened, she used to say prayers with us, in English. I doubt she has any Latin. I can still hear her flat warm voice, those simple prayers, from the heart. When I lie in bed, if I can't sleep, I remember the consolation of it even now.' He studied Toby's face. 'How is Jane? You've not spoken of her.'

'Oh. No. She's well.' The loving presence, steady, sturdy, always there alongside his mother, with a rooted tranquillity that his mother had never known. A twinge of homesickness tugged at him, drawing his thoughts back to those he'd left behind, to Holywell, luring him away from where his heart ought to be. He thrust the memory aside.

'My mother took us from here for the good of our souls.' He meant his words to sound like a reproof, but it was clear that Tom did not take them that way.

'I know. I know. For me, so it has turned out.'

Was there not even one tiny hint of bad conscience, of guilt? Toby tried again, studying his brother's face, that open friendly beloved face. 'Tom, if England came back to the true faith, would you return too?'

'Who knows? Probably not. It's not likely to happen, is it? I think there's no appetite for such a change. The King is not by nature a harsh man and has no hatred of Catholics as such. His mother was one after all, and his wife too. But a few hotheads have made him wary. And he has voices on all sides clamouring for harsher measures.

The Catholics are few, though if they live with patience, then easier times will come. But the conversion of England —no!'

'If a few, with fire in their hearts, and vision, if they undertook—?'

'What? Some scheme led by Robert Catesby?' His tone was ironic, but his eyes uncomfortably searching. 'The King has good informants, and most men are loyal, with little love for Catholicism—or for all the Scots at court, come to that, but that's another matter. One thing's for sure: you don't win hearts and minds, or souls, by force. On the contrary. The Spaniards learned that, with their doomed Armada. And now they seek to make peace. That is much more likely in the end to bring hope to the Catholic remnant.'

'Or an end to hope!'

'Is that what your friends at Ashby tell you?' Toby could see he was troubled. 'If that's so, you'd best have stayed at Holywell.'

He frowned at his brother. 'Why? I'm happy at Ashby. It's where I'm meant to be, for my soul's health.' A sudden terrifying thought occurred to him. 'Tom, you won't tell your guardian where I am? That you've seen me? I beg you!'

'I won't tell him. I promise. At least, so long as I'm sure all is well with you. I should wish to be sure of that.'

'You can be, truly!'

'You know Robert Catesby has dabbled with treason in

the past? He was lucky to escape with his life. He was one of the Earl of Essex's rebellion against the late Queen and had a spell in the Tower for his pains.'

'That wasn't anything to do with our faith, was it? People can change.'

'No, but it shows a reckless spirit, willing to risk everything for a dream. You know what the penalty is for treason?'

Toby shivered: to be hanged, drawn and quartered, the fate many a Catholic priest risked every day of his life in the English mission field. He had never seen such an execution, and tried to keep his shrinking imagination from thinking of it. But sometimes, in the night hours...He always tried to tell himself that faced with such a fate he would be unflinching, courageous.

'I am not afraid. I know right from wrong.'

'Use your reason. Don't let your heart lead you astray.'

Tom's words seemed to echo something Humphrey had once said to him. *If the heart's set right it can't go astray.*

'Of course not.'

This chance meeting, which had begun so joyously, promised so much, had descended to a tangle of unease, irritability even. He should never have come here! It was an ill impulse that had led him to turn back to Haroby, a moment of weakness.

'I should go now. I'm expected.'

As they embraced, Tom said, 'If ever you are uneasy or troubled, seek me out. I should in any case wish we might meet again.'

Unsure if he felt the same, Toby rode away with his head full of a confusion he had not felt since he first met Robert Catesby.

As he neared Ashby it cleared, and he felt cheered, hopeful. All would be well with the 'great enterprise' of which his uncle had spoken. How could it be otherwise, when led by Robert Catesby?

He stepped into the hall—and nearly tripped on a small stack of saddle bags. Raising his head, he found himself face to face with Humphrey.

'What's this? Are you going somewhere?'

'Home first. Then overseas, I think.' His friend looked pale with misery.

'For good? But you never said!'

'It's been on my mind. I sent word—I heard this morning. I didn't want to speak of it until I knew. Then you weren't here. I looked for you.' He came and took Toby's arm, bending his head and lowering his voice. 'Toby, I can't stay. Truly I can't. Things are not right here. Maybe you should go too. But if you stay, have a care.'

It could have been Tom speaking. Toby felt his heart thud. A new unease spread through him. He had been so sure—

'Master Catesby will be back soon.'

'The more reason for care.'

Desolate, he watched his friend ride away.

* * *

At Haroby, once his brother had left, Tom went to his room and wrote two letters, which he handed over, separately, to two of his most trusted servants.

The first man left for London immediately, with his message for King James's chief minister, Robert Cecil, Earl of Salisbury, warning, without names or anything more than unspecific hints, that a small group of disaffected Catholics seemed to be hatching some kind of major plot.

The other man, with more elaborate directions for his journey, set out at dawn the following day.

Chapter Sixteen

Kate was in the stillroom, pounding caraway seeds in a mortar to make her tried and tested remedy for stomach ache, from which Philip suffered only too often. Added to milk, sweetened with sugar, it was more palatable to her children than most other medicines. The scent stung her nostrils, pungent, astringent. From the open window a soft breeze reached her; and, inevitably, the patter of summer rain.

'Madam.'

She'd not heard anyone come in. She swung round to see Jane standing there, with something in her expression that immediately alarmed her.

'A man is come. With a letter. He would say no more, but that he must put it into your hands alone.'

Toby! Something's wrong...Nicholas has written to break bad news...

Kate put the pestle aside with trembling hands, covered the part-ground seeds in case of flies. She crossed herself, murmuring a prayer (though for what she was unsure) and tried to walk calmly after Jane into the hall, where a man stood by the fire, muddied and weary from a long ride. She heard Jane slip away, but knew she would be waiting behind the screen, listening in case anything untoward happened, in case she was needed to offer support or comfort.

The man pulled a cloth-wrapped package from the

breast of his doublet. 'I was told to give this only to you, madam.'

Fumbling, Kate unwrapped the cloth, finding inside only a folded paper. She opened it.

'Have a care of your young son, madam. I fear the company he keeps. You would do well to bring him home to your side.'

She read it through twice, then looked up, bewildered, frightened. 'Who sent this?'

'Sir Thomas Machyn, madam.'

She had a sudden picture in her head of the stern face, lined with disapproval, almost heard the reproving voice in the words she scanned again. Then she thought: *Foolish! He's dead, long dead. But—Sir Thomas Machyn?*

She gave a little gasp. *This* Sir Thomas must be her son, her firstborn, the boy snatched from her, the boy who was now a man, with a new young wife she had never seen; the boy from whom she'd heard nothing for ten years. Until now.

Something clutched her throat, so she could scarcely draw breath; tears pricked her eyes.

'You come from Silworth?'

'No, madam. From Haroby. I am of Sir Thomas's household.'

Her son with a household of his own, at Haroby—but of course, he must now be of age!

'And he sent you with this?'

'He did, madam. He said it was most urgent, for your attention only.'

'He told you no more than that?'

'No, madam.'

'So you do not know what lies behind these words?'

'No, madam. I have not seen them. If I had, I cannot read.'

'Does he expect an answer?'

'He said not, madam.'

Thanking him, she sent him on his way to the kitchen for refreshment and to dry his clothes. The moment the door closed behind him, Jane came to her. Kate handed her the letter to read.

'What can it mean?'

'I wish I knew. But for Tom to write to me, after all this time, so suddenly, without warning—it must be for what seems to him a grave cause.' She frowned, trying to make some sort of sense of it all. 'Perhaps Roger Machyn has discovered where Toby is, and aims to set hands on him. Would Tom think that cause for a warning?'

'It doesn't seem to be so, from what he's written. Besides, Master Machyn could have come for Toby at any time these past years, if he'd wished.'

'I suppose he could.'

'So will you send for Master Toby?'

She hesitated. Would that be enough? *'I fear the company he keeps,'* the letter said. What company was that? Someone at Ashby?

And Nicholas: what of him? Could Nicholas be part of the danger, as Tom saw it? Surely not!

Or was the danger of quite another kind, not a physical threat, but a more devious thing? Perhaps Toby and Tom had met, and Tom now longed somehow to convert his brother from the Catholicism that would become more deeply entrenched from years at Ashby. But no, Tom would not then urge Toby's return to Holywell.

Could it be that Toby had never been reconciled to his uncle, never accepted his exile to Ashby, but instead, in an act of rebellion, had found doubtful friends somewhere else, who were leading him into mischief? That was only too likely, she thought, knowing Toby as she did, recalling his mood when he'd left Holywell.

Oh, if only she could question Tom, press him to tell her what he feared, how he knew of it, whether indeed he had seen Toby! If only she had even one letter from Toby to hint at how he was, what he was feeling, what he was doing.

She knew she could not ignore this urgent missive, coming, she felt instinctively, from what remained in her older son of affection for the brother he scarcely knew.

So she must send for Toby to come home; write to him and to Nicholas.

And what then? If he would not come, if Nicholas would not release him?

Surely he would not refuse his own sister? On the other hand, if Tom's anxieties (whatever they were) were without foundation, if the only possible objection to the company Toby kept was their Catholicism, then there was no need at all to extricate him from the place, no need for anxiety.

'Oh, if only I knew more! What if I send for Toby but he won't come?'

She gazed at Jane, saw in her eyes the realisation that was breaking into her own consciousness. There was only one way to be certain, to know what lay behind the message, to ensure that the right course was taken. 'I think I must go to Ashby. At the very least to see how he is. Perhaps to try and see Tom too.'

'I will come with you then.' Jane saw at once the rebuff in Kate's face; the eagerness died from her voice. 'No, I'm needed here, to care for the children in your absence.'

'I think that's for the best. Though God knows I would wish for your company.'

'Better a man, a groom to ride with you. John.'

'Yes. But can I ride so far without papers?'

'Would not Sir Cuthbert give you papers?'

'He would, but what do I give as the purpose of my journey?'

'Say that Master Toby is sick. Is that not enough?'

Sensible Jane. 'Of course! For all I know he's sick in the head with some devilment.' But what; but what?

Beneath her whirling thoughts lay a long buried unease, stirred to life again. Nicholas had taken great pains to persuade her to entrust Toby to his care, but her first instinct had been very different, a mistrust of the man her brother had become, of his sternness, his inability to win Toby over. She had allowed Toby to go with him even though she'd seen how unhappy he was. And now this… Yes, the most likely explanation was that Toby had rebelled against the rigours of his new home and found other more congenial company, of the worst kind, whatever that was; that he was being lured into serious wrongdoing.

She stood gazing at Jane, as Jane gazed back at her; two women linked by anxiety for an unknown threat to the boy they both loved, and by a memory.

'You know now, madam. Master Tom has not forgotten you, or his brother. He's not lost to you.'

Kate was so choked by a rush of tears that for a moment she could only shake her head, though she managed a faint smile. Then: 'No. No. After all these years.'

She felt Jane's hand rub her arm, though the other woman said nothing.

'I'll put things to rights in the stillroom,' Kate said at last. 'Then I'll make ready.' *Holy Mother of God, keep him safe!* she pleaded as she went. *Keep them both safe!* Then, thinking of Nicholas: *All of them.*

It was not Toby who filled her thoughts as she finished preparing the medicine, or even Philip for whom it was designed, but her eldest son, who had lived here for so short a time.

Two weeks, that was all, during which between them the little household had begun to make Holywell into a home again. Day by day memories of their perilous journey had faded and fled, taking fear with them. They'd begun to feel safe again, safer as each day passed.

And then Roger Machyn had come one night after dark, with a score of armed men, like pursuivants in pursuit of a priest. Like them, they had thundered at the door, burst into the hall with torches held high, scoured the house, overturning furniture, tearing off bed linen, terrifying the servants. And they had found Tom. Or rather, he had confronted them at the foot of the spiral stair that led to the attic rooms where the younger children were hidden.

Her dear son, her own precious Tom, looking so young, so small, so unlike the strong protector of their journey, yet holding himself proudly, with no sign of fear.

'I am here. You need look no further. I will come with you, if you let the rest of us alone.'

They *had* looked further, but found nothing. And Tom had been roughly handled, dragged out to the yard and tied to a horse, though he'd protested all along that he would not resist, there was no need for force. Frustration and anger made them the harsher.

She'd tried to run to him, but Roger Machyn had restrained her.

'For now, I will let it rest. But never fear, your husband's will must be enforced, in full. As for that one,' he'd nodded to where Tom was mounting one of the waiting horses, 'he is my ward, as the law demands. There is to be no communication between you, of any kind. You are not to be trusted. Henceforth, he is dead to you.'

She'd watched, sobbing, as they rode away, Tom's last longing look seared on her memory through a mist of tears. And his final cry into the night, 'I'll stay true, mother, always!'

Had he stayed true, at heart? She did not know. What she did know was that he was not dead to her, even after all this time. He'd remembered her enough, cared enough about his brother, to send that warning. Now she must act upon it.

Once the stillroom was in order, she made her way to Meadhope, to see Sir Cuthbert. Her thoughts tipped and turned, churning in her head. She knew well enough what she had to ask him. She could not ride so far from home without the right papers, which he would surely give, even if she told him little of her errand. She could plead the loving mother, missing her son; or sickness—yes, Toby suffering in health, needing his mother's care. But should she tell him anything more? Should she hint at what had been in that note, and her fears?

No, not while she did not know what lay behind it. What if Toby were involved in something illegal? Sir Cuthbert, however much her friend, however ready to turn a blind eye, was still a magistrate, still the arm of the law in this place. He was a kindly man, often flexible in his approach to the law as it concerned her. But she could not wholly trust him to put his conscience, his sense of civic duty, to one side, for the sake of their friendship. No, she must ask only for the papers, giving the invented purpose for the journey, and leave it at that. And she must do it quickly.

But some way short of the Hall, she was caught in a sudden heavy shower. The nearest shelter was offered by the parish church. St Luke's church, filched from the true faith, now tainted by a heretic parson and his heretic flock.

She fumbled with the heavy door, turning the handle slowly, pushing it open. It was very dark inside, so she could not see where she was going, but she stepped forward. Then realised she could hear something, a voice murmuring words, familiar words: *miserere mei...miserere mei...*have mercy on me...

She felt the hairs on her neck rise, a shiver run down her spine, of joy, not fear. She took another step, then saw the light, faint and distant, a candle, two. And the voice, more clearly now, 'Have mercy upon us miserable sinners.'

That was what she'd heard, her sad heart turning it to the consoling Latin. Gervase Langley was leading his heretic worship, a litany she supposed, with responses that had in them somehow a faint far-off echo of the familiar words. She stayed where she was, listening, with an ache at her heart, the tears running down her face. What warped impulse had brought her here?

She turned and wrenched open the door again. A wall of water met her, torrential drenching rain. One step further and she would be soaked through. She hesitated, then caution won and she retreated into the church and sat down on a bench, at a point where the shadow was deepest and a pillar screened her from the rest of the nave.

'That it may please thee to defend and provide for the fatherless children and widows and all that be desolate and oppressed.' That was Gervase Langley.

Another voice (no, two voices) replied: 'We beseech thee to hear us, good Lord.'

She took out her rosary, slid the beads through her fingers, silently mouthing her own familiar prayers to shut out the accursed words. Yet was she not a widow, with fatherless children? Was she not desolate and oppressed?

The voices ceased at last. She sensed that the service was nearing its end and shrank back into the deeper shadow. She would have slipped out of the church, but she could hear the rain still, thundering down outside, splashing from the spouts on the roof.

Steps neared the back of the church, passed her, made their way towards the door. A murmur of voices, increasing, then dying away.

Silence fell like a blanket over her, easing tension, bringing calm. Alone in this building where people of her faith had for generations offered their prayers, her grandmother among them, she could at last feel at home, at peace. After a time, she rose to her feet, to go and kneel before the place where the altar used to stand.

It was still there. No, not still there, for it had been removed last time she'd heard, dragged out and smashed to pieces in a furious act of vandalism by a zealous churchwarden after the death of Queen Mary: that at least had been her grandmother's version of events. But now a simple table, covered with fine white linen, stood again at the east end.

She stayed where she was, gazing at it.

'Madam.'

The word, gently spoken, jolted her with shock. She turned, and looked into the face of Gervase Langley. She could feel herself blush from head to toe. What must he think, finding her here? Was that triumph in his expression?

'I—I thought I was alone.' She could feel tears rising again in her eyes, a lump in her throat making speech difficult.

'Not alone, never alone, not in this holy place.' There was no triumph in his expression, only kindly concern. 'You sought shelter from the rain perhaps?'

She bent her head, for her voice would not form any sort of reply.

'Come, let us sit down until the storm ends.'

Without any conscious decision, she followed him to the front pew, where she took her seat at his side. Somehow she knew that she did not have to speak, and nor did he seem to feel the need to say anything. Once again, the quiet settled over her, but not as before. She felt calmer, less anxious and embarrassed, the peace of the place allowing other deeper anxieties to make their way to the surface of her mind. She tried to pray in the silence, to ask for guidance. Instead she found herself saying, 'I was on my way to see Sir Cuthbert.'

There was no more than the faintest murmur from the man at her side, to indicate that he was attentive to what she had to say.

'I had a message today. From Tom, my son.'

She did not look at the rector as she spoke, but she knew he'd turned to gaze at her. 'Your eldest? The one who was taken from you?'

'Yes.'

'You've had no news of him since?'

'Only that he was wed. No more.'

'It did not give you joy to hear from him?'

'No. Yes, perhaps. No.' Silence again, while she knew he waited for her to fill it, if she chose. She'd often felt like this as she knelt before a priest to make her confession. She had to remind herself that this man was not a priest of her faith, not a priest at all, for he represented a heretic church that did not even believe in the sacrament of confession. She rose to her feet. 'I must go. I have to get papers, for a journey.'

The rector stayed where he was. 'I see, I think. To go to your son Tom?'

'No, to Ashby, where Toby is.' She wanted to walk away, to leave the rector and his stolen church, but something kept her where she was, standing near him. It was raining still, though not so heavily now, the sound more of a gentle swishing, a pattering on the roof. She could leave without risking a complete drenching.

She sat down again.

'You're afraid of something?'

Silence. She wanted so much to tell him all of it, but knew she must not.

'I don't ask you to say what you don't wish to say. Know only that nothing you say will go beyond these walls. Between us and God.'

'As in the confessional?' Her tone was wry, sceptical.

'Exactly so.'

She sighed, pondered. Then: 'I can't tell. In truth, I don't know. Not all of it. Not even a little. But I want to bring Toby home. He's—he's sick.'

'There are many kinds of disease, especially afflicting the young.'

'Yes.'

'I will pray for you and for young Toby, and your journey. That may not reassure you, from a heretic priest.'

She turned a sudden smile on him, surprised at herself. 'Thank you.'

Then she stood up again and this time took her leave, made her way out of the church and continued on the road leading to the Hall.

Putting her case to Sir Cuthbert Featherstone was a simple matter. He accepted her story of Toby's illness without any visible suspicion and provided her at once with the necessary papers. 'So, you'll see how he does and bring him home if he's well enough to travel? That seems like a wise course. I expect they've been working him too hard. Or—' He gave a sly smile. 'They've been demanding too many austerities from him. Not good for the young, or the old come to that. You know, my offer still stands. I would be pleased to see him well educated, set on the right path.'

'I know you mean it kindly, but for him, for me—'

'It's not the right path. I know. But if you should change your mind.' His gaze sharpened. 'How do you travel? You will need a man to go with you, one at least, one who knows the way.'

'John will ride with me.'

'John Emerson? A good man, maybe. But has he ever put his nose beyond the Bishopric? I heard there's plague near York, so there'll be ways you can't take, towns to shun.' He frowned. 'This won't do, my dear madam. I have a coach, little used, and grooms with scarce work enough to keep them out of mischief.'

Just for a moment the thought of such unaccustomed luxury tore at her, brought sudden tears to her eyes. Only: to accept this would mean that her neighbour must know more of her business than she could tell him. 'Thank you. It is good of you, most kind. But no, we shall do well enough.' Then a new idea came to her. 'We'll go first to my cousins in York. They will set us right, I'm sure.'

'Then God speed you, my dear.'

Every instinct told her to leave at once, even though it was already dark by the time she reached home, but she knew that would be foolish. There were too many things she had to put in order before she set out: a message to be sent to the Thorntons in York, to say she would be with them in a day or two (she paid the lad from the Meadhope Inn to take her hastily scribbled note), and another to Andrew Wardle to let him know she would be away for a time, but left the management of her estate in his capable hands.

And then there was Jane.

Jane who ten years ago had brought them through so many dangers to the safety of Holywell; Jane who from the moment she became part of the household had cared for every one of the children with a devotion as steadfast as that of any mother; Jane who had cared for her, Kate, not just as her servant, but as her true friend and companion. How could she bear to leave her behind, to undertake this journey to an unknown conclusion without her?

At evening prayers she announced to the household that she was to go away for a time, and saw how Jane at once put her arms about the twins, gathering them to her like a mother hen sheltering her chicks beneath her wings.

Kate made her way to bed, but not to sleep.

Tense with terror, she lay wakeful for hours, turning from one side to the other, sometimes slipping into drowsiness only to jolt awake again with fear crawling like a living thing through her veins, over her skin. She feared for Toby, for the unknown danger at which his brother had hinted. She feared for the journey she must make, with so many obvious perils of the kind any traveller faced, and a woman more than most, the horrors of that old journey coming alive to haunt her again.

And with all that was the thought that Tom had sent word to her, had made contact however tersely after all these years. One son almost within reach, the other in danger—how could she sleep with all that going round and round in her head?

Some time in the night she heard Jane's noisy breathing subside to quietness, then the sound of movement. And Jane was lying beside her, putting arms about her. She found herself drawn close, held against that soft warm body as her children had been held so many times in the past; a comforting presence.

'All will be well, madam. You'll see.' Jane stroked her hair, murmuring soft words whose sound soothed her, lulling her to sleep for the few hours of the night that remained.

Chapter Seventeen

Fearful though she was of the journey, it was a relief, two days later, to be setting out at last, with one final long embrace from Jane. 'I'll keep the little ones safe, never you worry. And be ready to welcome you back with young Toby before the month is out.'

Throat tight with suppressed tears, Kate whispered, 'I wish so much that you could come with me.'

She rode away in the dawn rain, sitting pillion behind John on their sturdiest horse, its saddlebags packed with the bare essentials in food and clothing.

She and John talked no more than was necessary, John, she supposed, because he was by nature taciturn, Kate because she was concentrating on her errand, her thoughts full of Toby, and of that message from her lost son, wondering still what it meant, what it might mean for Toby and the danger she had been warned about; and what it told her about her other son, who after the long years of silence had suddenly broken into her life again, though whether for good or ill, whether just for an instant or in a way that would bear fruit in later times, she did not know and could not tell.

'How far to this place, where Master Toby is?'

John's voice startled her. She'd told him little more than that they were going to bring Toby home, staying at York for one night on the way. She had given him no other reason for the journey, intending to judge the situation when she reached Ashby, and then decide what to tell John.

'I would guess it's about two hundred miles.' Putting the distance into words set her heart thudding again. So far, so many dangers lying in wait for them.

'Then it could take a week or two, as God wills.' He crossed himself, and she realised he'd sent up a prayer. Asking for a blessing on their journey? Very likely.

What was he thinking? What did he feel about it all? What did he think of her, and of Toby? She had no idea, for she could not see his face and his voice gave nothing away. He had always seemed devoted, if an assiduous attention to his duties was a mark of devotion, but he was not an easy companion. She longed for Jane's company, so calm, so practical, so open with her opinions, so comfortingly familiar.

They'd hoped to reach York that day, but the rain had churned the roads to mud and swollen the rivers, forcing them to make many detours. The August days were shortening too, and by the time they reached the outskirts of Darlington it was growing dark.

John dismounted, reaching up to help her from the saddle. 'We'd best stop here for the night, madam.'

'We've covered so little of the way!'

'I know, madam, but if you weary yourself so soon you'll not have strength for the rest of it.'

As the light of a torch outside a nearby inn fell on his face, she realised he was looking at her with real concern. She felt tears spring to her eyes, but sniffed, swallowed, forced them back.

'Then we'll rest here, if we can find somewhere not too costly.'

She had little sleep that night, sharing a room with a large woman whose snores set their bed shaking. But by dawn, as the travellers set out again, the rain had ceased, giving way to glimpses of the sun, and their outer clothes of yesterday had almost dried, though still caked with mud.

'They say Northallerton's closed off with the plague,' John told her as they set out. 'We'll have to take a long way round. I've learned which road is best to take.'

Once away from the well-maintained highroad, they found the narrow ways clogged with traffic, the villages they passed through posting wary officials to demand where they came from and where they were going. Twice they were asked for their papers, so Kate was glad Sir Cuthbert had made sure they were all in order.

Around the middle of the day, they halted for refreshment at an alehouse, where John left her in the deserted parlour with bread and cheese and small beer, while he saw to the needs of the horse.

A group of men came in, farmers returning rowdily from a successful morning at some distant market, Kate thought. One of them glanced her way, his gaze sharpening. The way he looked her over made her shiver. She shrank as he slid along the seat beside her.

Not meeting his gaze, Kate pulled off a piece of bread and raised it to her mouth. She felt a hand on her knee, a firm exploring hand, hot breath on her cheek, stinking of bad teeth and sour beer and tobacco. She recoiled, but heard a slurred voice rasp, 'I'll wager there's fine titties down here.' His hand slid onto the bare skin under her ruff, moved down.

Kate stood up, sending the table tilting dangerously, so that the bread slid to the floor. The man reached up and pulled at her. He was strong. She wanted to cry out but dared not for fear his friends might to come to join him; then there would be no escape.

'Sir, let my mistress be!'

John! Thank God! The man was assessing the situation; decided that John was not a man to take on, glanced again at Kate. All respectful deference, he pulled off his hat.

'I mistook. Madam!'

'I'll seek a private room. Away from these——!' She could hear the fury in John's voice.

'No. The sun's come out. We can eat outside.'

They found a bench in the sunlight and ate their food there. Kate found that she was shaking so much that she could scarcely direct the bread to her mouth. She turned to John. 'Thank you, John. It was not—I feared—'

'Indeed, madam. He was a vile wretch. He may call himself a gentleman, but he's none.'

It was late afternoon by the time they reached York (yet another demand for their papers, at the city gates). Kate longed for clean linen, good food, warmth, a quiet night's rest. But what if the Thorntons had never received her message? What if they were away from home? She'd had no reply, but then there'd been no time for one.

'If your kin are not at home, there are inns a-plenty in York.'

John, the mind-reader: Kate smiled to herself, reassured.

Her message *had* been received. The family were at home, and Dame Frances—larger, more lined than Kate remembered—gave John and the horse into the care of a servant, welcomed Kate with an embrace and (talking incessantly) led her to a chamber upstairs. 'As soon as you're refreshed, there is supper ready for you, my dear.'

Left alone, Kate looked with dazed eyes at the room where she found herself. Dark hangings, a window facing the bed, a table below it on which a bowl of scented water was placed for her use: these things tugged at her memory. Surely this was the very same room where she'd lain, sick and exhausted, at the end of that other terrible journey, only slowly becoming aware of her surroundings? Even now, after so many years, she felt her stomach churn, her throat dry. Fragments of memory snagged in her mind, but she forced them aside, telling herself that for all she was tired and anxious, this journey was nothing like that impulsive unplanned flight that haunted her still. And even then this place had offered solace, a haven. This time, good food and a night's rest would soon put things right. And tomorrow perhaps they would cover more miles, come closer to where Toby was, closer to bringing him home.

She braced herself, washed hands and face, changed into clean linen and made her way downstairs to the parlour, where Dame Frances waited, together with a beaming, moon-faced young girl.

'Ah, welcome, my dear. Let's to table.' Gesturing to the girl—'My niece Joan'—she led the way to a table laid with pies and meats, and a tureen of soup. As they took their seats, Kate heard the door behind her open and close again.

Dame Frances looked round. 'Ah, here is Richard, come just in time.' There was a note of affectionate reproof in her voice, which drew a smile from the man who took his seat opposite them.

'Your pardon, mother.'

Richard, who had been at school with Nicholas; the boy with grey eyes, whose kindness had stayed in her memory, now a tall young man.

Those grey eyes glanced at Kate, looked again, assessing her, but not in the least as the man at the inn had done. This was different, quite different, though his gaze met hers, lingered there, arousing the strangest sensation. Her breath caught in her throat, the room around her seemed to shrink to this, two pairs of eyes linked by some weird force that reached deep inside her. All her weariness, all her impatience at the length of the journey, all thoughts of Toby, fled from her consciousness, leaving only the two of them, she and this man, here in this place, at this moment.

'Kate! Do you wish me to help you to some of this good pottage?' Realising Dame Frances must have been speaking to her for some time, Kate turned her head, drew breath, glanced at the tureen from which her host was about to ladle a thick pottage, and stammered her thanks. She felt her face flood with colour.

She was scarcely aware of what she ate, which was not much. It was hard to believe she'd ever felt hungry. She heard her host's incessant chatter as a distant blur of sound beyond her reach, while she was conscious only of the brown-haired young man facing her across the table, and the way that whenever she raised her eyes it was to meet his. Sometimes they had a light in them that hinted at laughter, drawing a tentative smile from her in response; then it was as if he had reached across the table to touch her hand.

'So, what is this about your boy Toby? He's under your brother's care, I understand. Richard, you remember Nicholas Gaunt?'

Kate saw that, just for a moment, Richard had no idea what his stepmother was talking about. Was he, like her, held in some place apart? He turned puzzled eyes on Dame Frances, then gave himself a tiny shake. 'Ah, yes, I do, of course. He called here last year, in the spring. A changed man. Not as I remember him from school. Perhaps he thought the same of me. But then we have both grown older.' His voice was deep, warm, and sent odd vibrations through her.

She realised with a jolt that Dame Frances was expecting her to give some explanation for her journey. She'd written only that she was travelling to visit Toby. What should she say now? Before reaching York she'd thought out what she would tell her kinswoman, just enough and no more. Now she had no recollection of what that carefully prepared explanation had been. 'I've had word Toby is sick and in need of me.' Even to her ears, her stammered words sounded unconvincing, though Dame Frances seemed satisfied.

'The very first apricots from our garden.' Kate looked up, saw that Richard was presenting her with a dish of apricots. Someone must have brought them to the table, though she had not been aware of it.

Blushing, smiling, she took one. 'You grow apricots? And they ripen so far north?'

'They do in my garden at Warthrop' She recalled that Warthrop was the country estate Richard had inherited from his dead mother's family; it was there that the infant twins had been nursed after their arduous journey. 'It is favourably situated, sheltered and sunny.'

Kate took a bite of the apricot.

'Do you taste the sunshine?'

She returned his smile. 'I do, though to find sunshine this year—it must indeed be a favoured spot.'

Silly trivial words, yet somehow as she looked at him she felt as if they were heavy with meaning. A little silence, while they simply smiled at one another.

Joan's noisy yawn broke into the quiet. 'I'm tired Aunt Frances.'

The girl's face was innocent of any awareness that she'd committed a breach of manners, and Dame Frances was unperturbed. 'No wonder, my poppet. It's late. I think we must all be tired, just as you are. And if you've well eaten?' She cast an enquiring glance at Kate.

'Thank you, I have eaten very well.' Had she? She had no idea, knowing only that she was no longer hungry. She heard—felt—Richard murmur some similar reply. Did he, like her, regret that this meal must come to an end, that they must part?

They rose from the table. There was a kiss from Dame Frances and from young Joan, along with an impulsive hug; and then briefly, lips brushing her cheek, from Richard. Sensation shot through her, firing colour into her face.

She could feel the kiss still as she climbed into bed and closed her eyes. Sleep eluded her. It was as if she'd never been tired, as if she was still gazing into those grey eyes, while excitement somersaulted inside her, over and over.

Was it possible that Richard was feeling as she did, lying awake in his bed somewhere in this house?

What foolishness! How could a virile young man possibly be attracted by a middle aged widow, mother of six living children? How could she even allow herself to think it?

She found herself wondering how it would be in the

morning. Would she see him before she and John set out on the next stage of their journey? Would she ever see him again once they left York behind? Oh, she hoped so! And yet she feared it too, for it would only force her to face reality.

She slept at last some time before dawn, and fell into the most disturbingly thrilling of dreams, from which she woke to a throbbing body and a mingling of shame and delight.

Richard was there in the parlour when, dressed for the journey, she came down to eat some of the bread and meat put ready for a modest breakfast. He too looked dressed for a journey. Perhaps he was bound for his estate.

Beaming, Joan came and took her hand. 'I'm coming with you, Kate.'

'Is that so?' Puzzled, Kate glanced from Dame Frances to Richard and then back again.

'Richard and I talked this over last night, my dear. He was to set out to return Joan to her family in Peterborough the day after tomorrow, but we think it best to bring his journey forward, to give you company on your way, or for part of the way, at least.'

Kate's heart leapt. She was relieved at the added protection Richard's company would offer, of course she was. But that was not why she felt such a bubbling sense of excitement. 'Oh, that is to trouble you!'

'Indeed no, madam.' His voice seemed to reach right

through her body. 'I merely set out a day or so sooner than I planned. We shall be good company each for the other.'

Later, as he helped her onto the saddle of one of two fresh horses supplied from the Thornton stable, Richard held her gaze for a moment or two longer than was strictly necessary. Or so it seemed to Kate. Could he be feeling as she did? Was it possible?

John, taciturn as ever, rode just behind them. Kate hoped he did not resent Richard's assumption of the role of protector, though he'd seemed pleased that Kate was no longer to ride pillion. 'That will be the more comfortable for you,' he'd said, when he saw the arrangements. They were now a party of six, with Richard's manservant and Joan's maid among them. Joan had her own horse, which she managed with what to Kate was surprising competence, singing to herself as they went. Richard treated her with a gentle kindliness that Kate found rather touching.

'She is too quick to trust,' he murmured to Kate once, when the girl was well out of earshot. 'She has to be watched at all times, for fear lest she should be taken advantage of. There have been a few narrow escapes in the past. She comes to us from time to time, to give her a change of scene and her family a little respite from her care. But we love her, as who could not?'

'She seems a warm hearted, loving girl. What will become of her?'

'Oh I think she will always be at home with her family.

Marriage is not for the likes of her.'

'A convent?'

'I think not. She would not understand what she was undertaking. Unless there is such a place that would nurture her.'

They watched her for a time in silence, then he said, 'I well remember your brother at school. He was a rascal.' There was a wistful smile playing fleetingly about his mouth. 'But as I said last night, he's changed. If he hadn't, then I guess you'd not have entrusted your son to him.'

She felt that old stir of unease. 'No—No, he has seen the error of his ways, thank God. He has grown very devout and turned his back on all that wildness.'

'And you are just a little sorry for it?' His eyes twinkled.

She felt her colour rise again. Why? It made her feel awkward, embarrassed. She wanted to look at him without any rising colour, for he was good to look at and in many ways so easy to talk to.

'I should not say so. Perhaps, just a little. I—it has not always been easy. To find my scapegrace brother censorious of my conduct…'

'Indeed? What terrible sins have you committed?'

The memory of last night's dream slipped into her thoughts, making her colour even more. She tried to push it aside. 'Oh, that I live at peace with my heretic neighbours, too much at peace. He is right, I know that. I think that I've grown lax over the years, as once I would not have been.'

She watched his expression. Would he show the same

distaste and horror as Nicholas had done?

'You have kindly neighbours that care for you? Is that so very bad? We regard ourselves as fortunate to find the same.'

What was it Nicholas had said of his old schoolfellow? *He shows signs of too flexible a conscience?*

'Yet you gave your son into your brother's care, though I think you believe him to be too rigid?' It sounded almost like an accusation.

'No, I believe him to be right. It's I who am wrong. I am weak.'

There was scepticism in his expression. 'Because you are on good terms with your neighbours? That sounds like wisdom to me!"

'The wisdom of this world, perhaps. But it's more than that.' Her colour deepened again. 'I have permitted the rector, the so-called priest of our parish—I have allowed him to teach my sons, even welcomed it. And to assist me with the management of my estate.'

Rather than disapproval, she saw enquiry in his eyes, and interest. Emboldened, she went on, 'He says he prays for the uniting of Christendom. Not under the Pope, but in friendship and mutual trust.' Her rueful smile indicated that this was a foolish hope.

'As indeed do I.'

Her eyes flew to his face. 'Really?'

'I think we are not so far apart—from some of those of the Protestant faith, at least. I am something of an

Erasmian. At one time Erasmus was admired by thoughtful people on both sides of the argument, though less so these days, I fear.'

She'd heard the name, though it meant little to her.

'But you are still a Catholic?'

'I think you would call me a Church Papist, though I would perhaps feel that to be short of the mark.'

Like Sir Thomas. She felt a sense of disappointment.

'You don't approve?'

'It's not for me—No, I think that a—'

'A betrayal? Do you think God is so cruel that he would have us all suffer for our faith, or, worse, kill for it?'

'The blood of the martyrs is the seed of the church,' she quoted, while her memory echoed Nicholas's repetition of the words. They had discomforted her then.

'Indeed. And sometimes that is necessary, and right. I am sure that some are called to that great sacrifice. But in the end, if you look at it carefully, with an independent and rational mind, there is not a great deal that separates us. Small matters of interpretation, that's all.'

'Small!' All those arguments about transubstantiation, and purgatory, and faith and works!

'I know, that's heresy, or close to it.' His smile was rueful. 'Some from one side or the other would have me burned at the stake.'

'You've given thought to these things it seems.'

Was this how Sir Thomas had thought? Somehow she doubted it, for why otherwise would her son have been snatched from her so cruelly?

She saw then that Richard had coloured, much as she had before. 'Forgive me, I do not readily talk so freely of these matters. Not even to my confessor, I fear. They are my thoughts, but better not put into words, I think.'

'I shall not betray you.' Smiling, his eyes held hers, and she felt sufficiently at ease to risk a personal question. 'And you, sir. You are married?' She felt herself colour even more at the very thought, which was ridiculous. There had been no wife seen nor mentioned at any time.

'No madam, not as yet. I was betrothed early, but alas the lady died of the smallpox. To find a wife is one of those tasks I know should be an urgent business with me, but somehow there is always something else. If you hear of a good bride, do let me know. You would be doing me a kindness, to save the effort of searching. I think you would know well the kind of lady who would suit me.' Was there a hidden meaning there? If there was, he quickly changed the subject. 'Now, tell me of yourself. I know a little, for you are part of our family history, on the side of my dear stepmother. But I'm ignorant of much of it. You were once at Haroby, were you not? But now in the Bishopric, at Holywell?'

She told him, hesitantly at first and then easily, happily, talking as if they had known one another for years. Her embarrassment faded; she felt at ease as she had not for a long time. He was excellent company, so that the miles seemed to slip by almost unnoticed, as he talked of books he had read, of ideas that interested him, revealing a questioning, rational mind that treated hers as if she were an equal. He listened to her questions and her concerns and never dismissed or belittled them, as most other men of her acquaintance would have done. That was exhilarating enough; better still were the stories he told, the small things he observed, his ability to stir her to unladylike laughter. Once, she found herself thinking, 'Nicholas would frown at this.' At her laughter, her failure to look away when Richard gazed at her, at her immodesty…But as swiftly as the thought came, it vanished. Somehow it did not matter at all, and Nicholas seemed very far away.

As they travelled further south, she saw how the trees were already starting to turn with the approach of autumn, lit with bronze and ochre in the sunlight. Around midday they halted to eat, not at an alehouse or inn, but at the edge of a wood, looking over a field blazing gold after harvest. Here it was so warm they were able to take off their cloaks and spread them to sit on.

Richard's servant Adam laid out bread, ale, cheese, cold beef, young apples and more of Warthrop's apricots. Joan squealed with excitement, falling on the food with a hearty appetite. Kate was too sated with happiness to eat much, and simply sat looking about her, savouring it all.

Nearby a tangle of brambles was glossy with fruit. She caught Richard's eye as he watched her. 'They're ripe already, much further on than at home. I used to love to gather them.' Fleetingly, she had a memory of Jane picking the last hard withered blackberries to try and stave off their hunger on that terrible winter journey. She shivered, then returned her gaze to Richard, as if in consolation and hope.

He grinned, reached over, plucked a particularly luscious fruit. 'Here! Open your mouth!'

Sweetness exploded on her tongue, through her whole being, the ripe fruit and the intimacy of the gesture bound together with the warmth of his gaze. The past and its memories shrivelled like mist in morning sun.

She caught John watching her with a speculative look in his eyes. What was he thinking? Was he reading something into the way the two of them behaved together? Was there anything for him to read?

Oh yes, for today she felt young again, a girl joyous in the moment, yet with depths undreamed of, brought to sudden life. It was as if time stood still, as if the past and the future had fled, so that she almost found herself forgetting why she was here, what was the purpose of this journey.

Richard, a seasoned traveller, advised a stay that night at an inn at Pontefract, where he bespoke rooms, stabling and a hearty supper of collops, ham, a good game pie, two fruit tarts, cheeses and (to Kate's astonishment) the extravagance of a jug of wine.

'Claret, from Bordeaux in France,' Richard explained as they took their seats at a table in the quietest corner of the inn's busy hall. He poured wine into one of the glasses that stood on a smaller table at his side and handed it to her. 'I know of old what a good cellar they keep here.' He raised his own glass. 'A toast: to you and your journey!'

Candlelight glowed through the wine's clear red, set Richard's eyes sparkling, gave definition to the strong cheekbones, the gently smiling mouth. Kate raised her glass, her eyes on his, then sipped. The wine was good, better than any she'd tasted at Holywell, where what they had was inevitably stored longer than was beneficial, because of its cost and rarity.

Joan, exhausted from the journey, ate little and was soon despatched to bed, her maid with her. Once all the food was served, the male servants too were allowed to retire. But Kate and Richard lingered, replete yet still picking at the remains of the meal, as Richard filled their glasses again and again. Kate forgot all about the dwindling number of travellers in the hall, was aware only of the man facing her in the candlelight, of the talk and laughter they shared; and the moments of silence when each seemed only to feast on the other's face.

The room emptied, the inn was quiet. Richard raised his hand. 'Listen!' A distant bell was ringing. A church clock? 'Two, three…nine…twelve…midnight! And we're to rise early tomorrow—today, already! I fear I've kept you too long from your bed.'

Oh, not too long, not at all, and she would have sat there with him all night if he'd asked it of her!

But he was right, it was late, and they had two more days' journey ahead of them; or she did.

He rose to his feet as, reluctant to move, she watched him. Then she too stood up. The room seemed to sway about her. She giggled foolishly, put a hand to her mouth. 'Oh, the wine!'

Richard took her arm, steadying her as they made for the door opening onto the stairs that led to the bedchambers.

Beyond the door, which he'd closed behind them, it was suddenly dark, though there was a gleam of moonlight from a window somewhere above. She knew Richard had come to a halt at the foot of the stairs—to give way to her, let her go first?

She stepped forward. 'Goodnight.' Her voice came in a hoarse whisper.

She felt him move nearer, knew that he had bent his head close to hers, to her face, her mouth.

She felt his lips on hers, soft, warm, exploring. His arms were round her and she sank against him, her body close to his, exactly as she wanted it to be.

He was pulling her closer, moving back, aside, with a gentle urgency, until he was perched on the stairs, tugging her down beside him. She felt her heart thud, from longing not fear. She felt a turbulence inside her, her whole body aching, tingling, excited; and full of desire. A moment's hesitation, a pause, then she reached up to put her arms about him, urging him nearer. Her mouth opened to his.

She felt his hand push its way below her ruff, down over the bare skin, to close over her breast. She moaned softly, eager for more.

His other hand was struggling with her heavy skirts, pulling them up, finding its way to her stockinged legs, then up, up to the flesh beyond. She seemed to be drowning in a flood of desire, dizzy, suffocating, longing. His hand reached between her legs, into the most intimate part of her, slipping, sliding, fingering her to an agony of longing. 'Oh! Oh! Oh—!'

Words poured out on his breath: 'Oh, sweeting, dear love!' Her body arched against his fingers, urging them on. 'Oh, Kate! Oh Kate!' An ocean of pleasure bore her up, carried her away.

A final crashing wave of delight, and she found herself beached in a place where passion was satisfied, her body at peace, content, relaxed as she had never known it before. She could hear his rapid breathing close by, though he pushed her gently away from him, while he held her still, her head resting on his shoulder as he stroked her hair (her coif had long since fallen off).

'Forgive me. I should not—'

Should not what? There was nothing to forgive, no reluctance on her part, not even the faintest tremor of guilt. She was his willing accomplice, wishing only that this could go on, go further.

He dropped a light kiss on her forehead. 'Oh, Kate, I have not felt like this, not longed for…Oh, if we could be wed!'

She gave a gurgle of laughter. 'Two days together and you'd have us wed! And me an old widow with scarcely the means to live? I hardly think that's what your family would want for you. Or what you would want, if you give it thought.' Yet her heart said, *Oh, if I could have a husband like this, tender, kind, one who talks to me as an equal…*While her head knew that it could not be. This was not how the world was.

'You are not old, not to me.' His mouth had found hers again, and she felt once more that stir of fierce desire, of longing; just as he drew back.

'No. No, dear heart. Not now.'

The words, gently spoken, brought her to her senses, as he had come to his. She remembered where she was, how she had come here, what lay before her tomorrow and in the days to come. The whole purpose of this journey—the message, the unknown danger that threatened her son—came crashing down on her, chilling her, crushing all passion. A moment of madness, that was all this had been, something she must put aside, learn to forget.

What she had allowed him to do to her was a filthy thing, a sin. She should not have trusted herself alone with him. She should have stopped him, long before he kissed her, hurried up the stairs ahead of him. She should not have allowed herself to drink so much of that good wine. Yet a part of her felt that she'd done nothing wrong, nothing even that she must bring to confession when next she knelt before a priest.

She drew back, struggled to her feet (her legs felt feeble, trembling), pulled her skirts into place, replaced her coif. She let him take her hand for a moment, caress it, then she drew it away. 'Goodnight,' she whispered.

His whispered response followed her up the stairs, to the door where John lay stretched in protection, keeping out—what? The danger was out here, with her; in her.

They set out before dawn the following morning, in silence. Stealing a glance at Richard's face, she thought he looked stern, withdrawn. He seemed to avoid looking at her at all, still less speaking to her. Was he ashamed of last night's impulse, which had led him to make advances to a woman who was utterly ineligible to be his wife?

As the sun rose she felt a little more cheerful, but not a great deal. This, she supposed, was the thing called love, the thing poets wrote about that was irrelevant to any respectable gentlewoman, unless she happened to be particularly fortunate in the man she married. Well, she would have to put it aside, for it could have no place in her life.

Mid-morning, a sudden heavy shower caught them in the most open part of their ride, where there were no trees to offer shelter, no inns in sight. She heard Richard ride up beside her and felt him fling something heavy over her shoulders, covering her head; his cloak. 'Here, I've no need for this. It will keep off the worst.'

She turned to thank him, but at first no words would come. She smiled through the painful beating of her heart, her insides turning to water at the glance of his grey eyes, so kind, so concerned. Her voice husky, she said, 'Thank you, sir.'

His eyes lingered on hers for longer than necessity or even courtesy demanded, before he urged his horse into greater speed.

She watched him, a rider at ease in the saddle, strong, graceful.

'Madam?' It was John at her side. She turned to look at him. 'You are troubled.'

'No, not at all. Just anxious to get to Ashby, that's all.' Was John, who knew her so well, fooled by this assurance? From the long look he gave her she thought not.

They reached Newark after dark. The last part of their journey had been slow and difficult, though there was a fitful moon. 'I know of a comfortable inn there,' Richard had assured them.

Kate, genuinely exhausted, asked for supper to be brought to her room and ate alone, without temptation of any kind, except that she found herself wanting to weep. She lay awake for much of the night, with Richard's face swimming into her consciousness; and when fitfully she slept, she dreamed of last night, of those moments on the stairs, and woke to find her body aroused and aching.

Tomorrow, she thought bleakly, *we should get to Ashby, if all goes well.*

The last day in Richard's company.

Perhaps he was thinking much the same, for as they gathered outside the inn in the early light, she saw how his eyes rested on her, thoughtful, sad. But it was still too dark fully to read their expression. She told herself it was all imagining, and urged her horse forward.

She heard Richard come up beside her, turned and caught his smile, sweet, tender, then a little rueful. She had not noticed before how it brought out dimples in his cheeks.

'You look tired. I think you were as wakeful last night as I was.'

Was it so obvious? Perhaps, for her head ached too.

She noticed through the day that whenever he could—when they halted to eat, when they sheltered under trees from the rain—he seemed to find any possible excuse to touch her. He would move so close that his hand brushed hers, or he'd flick a fly from her cheek, or reach out to tug her cloak closer round her, or when they were ready to move on, to lift her into the saddle. It thrilled her and brought anguish and longing all at once.

Once they talked at length, as they had the previous day, forgetful of awkwardness in the interest of what they were discussing. She found herself telling him about her children, about her fears and hopes for them, while even now keeping silent on the real reason for her journey. Until she knew what it was that threatened Toby, if it was a real threat, then she did not want to speak of it to anyone else.

Though she did tell him of Edward, gone to be a priest, and how she knew her son Toby was not called to that vocation. His response surprised her.

'I thought once to be a priest. When my betrothed died, it seemed a sign. But I soon saw that I was too far from orthodoxy for that to be possible. You cannot give your life in all honesty to something you only hold to be true in part.'

'Are you sad about that? Would you have liked to be a priest?' After what happened that first night, surely not!

He gave her a smiling sideways look. 'What do you think?'

She felt herself blush and the talk ended, as he urged his horse into a canter and then halted further off for her to catch up. When she reached him she was as breathless as if she had run the distance.

Then they came to Stamford, and she knew this was the parting of the ways. Richard gave John careful instructions about the route to take, in her hearing, so they both had the details clear in their minds. And then they shared a meal of bread and meat, after which he helped her into the saddle. He leaned closer, saying softly, 'There'll be a way. I'll find a way. I give my word.'

She rode away from him with a strange confused mixture of misery and joy warring inside her.

He had gone. It was over: a dream, a taste of what might have been if life had somehow been differently arranged, or what perhaps one day would be, in Paradise—no, that was a shameful, unholy thought, which at once she pushed from her mind.

She resisted every urge to look back as she and John took the narrow rutted road away from the others, as the thudding of many hooves faded and woodland noises augmented the sounds of their own solitary mounts.

Flooding back into her consciousness, repossessing it, came the goal of this journey, the thing that had brought her here: her anxiety for Toby.

She had set out from Holywell consumed by the need to see her son, to discover what, if anything, threatened him; intending always to go straight to Ashby St Ledgers, in the hope that there she would find reassurance. But now, all at once, she hesitated. It was Tom who had written, the son she'd thought lost for ever. His message had told her little, but he lived not much further away from here than did Toby. Even starting so late in the day she thought they could reach Haroby by nightfall, if they took no wrong turning.

She drew rein, considering. John came alongside. 'Madam?'

What should she tell him? Nothing; or everything? Haroby, or Ashby?

She longed to see Tom again, to put her arms about him, her son, her lost son, for whom her heart had ached since she'd watched him dragged away from Holywell. But she feared it too. His message had been so brief, so cryptic.

He'd not wanted any reply. She did not want even to suspect that there might have been malice behind it, but it was a possibility. Might it even have been a ruse to lure Toby into Roger Machyn's clutches?

No, she must go to Ashby first, to see for herself if Toby was threatened in any way. Later, when she knew the truth of it, then perhaps she could allow herself to seek out her firstborn.

That decision made, she made another, here in this woodland clearing where John watched her in bafflement. She must tell John the truth, for she would need his help, once they reached Ashby. So, she told him everything: the message with its stark yet hidden meaning, her fears, even her suspicions.

'I need you to be my ears and eyes, when we get to Ashby. I can only see and hear so much, and that only on the surface. Servants often see more than their masters, I think.'

When she'd finished speaking, John paused for a moment, as if taking in what she'd said, pondering its implications. Then: 'I will do so, madam, as far as is in my power. You shall know everything I learn.'

'Thank you. Then let us go on our way.'

Chapter Eighteen

One summer night, long ago, she must have ridden to Ashby St Ledgers, for a celebration of the Mass. Her memory of the occasion was hazy, but this afternoon, approaching the half-timbered gatehouse, Kate was stabbed by recognition, not just of the house, but so much else of that forgotten past, the constraints, the husband she feared, who had been at her side that night, her faith the only thing she had to cling to; and her children. She thought Tom, just breeched, had also been of their furtive little party.

She gave herself a shake, thrusting aside the shadows of the past. It was over, forgotten, as far as it could ever be. This was now, bringing her here on quite another errand. The one cheering thought was that once, in this place, she had known the consolations of her faith. Surely that must bring reassurance that Toby was safe here, if anywhere?

Yet she was churning with anxiety. It had seemed so simple when she first set out. She would arrive at the house, blaming a mother's anxiety for her unannounced visit: there had been no letter for so long (which was quite true), she felt the need to reassure herself that all was well with Toby. After what had happened to Tom, wasn't that understandable?

Now it all seemed rather lame. To come so far, to risk so long a journey for so small an excuse? Would anyone believe her, or even make her welcome?

Well, she was here now. It was too late for second thoughts. She would somehow need to sound convincing.

So she slid from the saddle, stumbling as she stretched cramped limbs. John went to hammer on the door, until a servant came. Having explained who they were, he led the horses to the stables, with a parting glance in Kate's direction that said as clearly as any words, *Trust me! I know what I have to do.*

Kate stepped into the house.

'Madam, if you will be so good as to wait here, I will take word of your arrival.'

She passed through the door the servant held open for her, finding herself in a parlour, shadowed but for a good fire, hung with tapestries, a little threadbare in places, telling of a struggle to survive as in many Catholic homes.

She had asked to see Toby, told the servant that this was the reason for her unexpected arrival. Soon, please God, she would know the truth, know how things were with him!

But when the door opened again, it was not Toby who came in, but Nicholas; who stood for a moment looking at her, before coming nearer.

'Kate!' He embraced her, but not before she'd seen something in his eyes that looked like dismay. 'They told me you were here, but I could scarcely believe it. Why no word that you were coming? What brings you here? Is something amiss?'

He sat down facing her, holding her hands, his eyes

piercing, so she felt he already knew the answer to any question he might ask, had already read what was in her thoughts and her heart. She felt her colour rise.

'I am here to see Toby.'

'So I was told. But I don't understand. I must know why.'

She had thought she might feel able to tell Nicholas the whole story, once they were face to face. Now some unsettling instinct told her she could not, *must* not.

She drew a deep breath. 'It's foolish, I know, but having lost one son I feared for the other. And I have heard nothing for so long, not one letter after the very first, nothing. I felt that all was not well. Tell me that Toby is here and in good health?'

'Indeed he is! Foolish Kate!' He stroked her cheek. 'Would I not have sent word instantly if anything was wrong?'

'I thank you for that.' She wondered why she did not feel more relieved at his assurance. 'Then may I see him?'

'Of course. He is occupied at this present moment, but he will shortly join us for supper. I would guess you are hungry. How far have you come today?'

She was swept by a sense that she had travelled a whole lifetime since leaving Holywell. Yet the journey was already fading against the reality of being in this place, at confronting whatever it was that might be threatening her son.

She did not want to eat, felt repelled by the prospect of

sitting at supper with the entire household. She was too anxious for hunger, too torn by unease at keeping so much from Nicholas, at being less than open with him, at feeling that this was how it must be; and she wanted to see Toby now, this minute, and in private, not among others before whom they could not talk freely.

But there was something in her brother's face and his voice that warned her to say no more, simply to acquiesce.

Nicholas went on to question her about those she had left behind at Holywell, about the estate, about her health, all things that were far from uppermost in her mind, remote from this place, things she had no wish at all to discuss. At last he said,

'Now, a room has been prepared for you, I believe. I will have you shown the way, then you can make ready to eat.'

She tried to take note of the way to the room, though there seemed to be so many other rooms to pass through, far more than at Holywell. Sometimes they met others, on a stair, emerging from a doorway, servants, men and a few women, but never Toby; or John. Where was John? How would she ever find him to know what, if anything, he had discovered?

Supper was served in the hall. As Kate took her place at the high table, she glimpsed John among the servants at the far end of the room. She thought he looked her way, but could not be sure.

Then she saw Toby, one among the young men and

boys bringing food to the tables. He had grown—taller even than his uncle, she thought, and thinner too—and was there something a little careworn, anxious, about his face? As he approached their table, he came to an abrupt halt, stared at her as if she were a ghost, before one of the other boys prodded him into resuming his duty. No one, then, had told him she was here. She wished she knew what he thought, seeing her, what he felt. Was he glad to see her? She tried to catch his eye, but he passed close to her without once looking at her, and then was gone.

She found herself seated beside Lady Anny Catesby, who welcomed her, 'For the sake of your dear brother and your son, who are most valued members of my family here,' and apologised for the absence of her son Robert. 'He is called away on some business. A restless soul, my son.' There was, Kate thought, a faint note of asperity in the other woman's voice. 'And it is *your* son who brings you here, so I understand.'

'Forgive a mother's misgivings, but I had not heard for so long.'

'Ah, I understand you so well. We mothers have little power over our sons, but that does not ease our care for them. It could be that yours is still young enough to be guided by you.'

Was that a warning that her fears were not misplaced, that there was indeed something from which she must rescue Toby? She told herself she was likely reading far too much into Lady Anne's words. 'When I have spoken with him I will hope to have my fears put at rest.'

'It is hard to find quiet time for talk, in so busy a household.'

'I shall find time, somehow.'

She thought she saw scepticism in her companion's eyes, before she turned her attention to an elderly female relative ('my cousin Agatha') on her other side.

After that, the meal seemed interminable. She tried to eat, while her insides churned. She tried to listen to what was said to her by those around her, to make sensible answers to men and women whose names she was too weary to take in. She felt only bewildered, exhausted, more anxious than ever. Nicholas, seated opposite her, talked animatedly, but not in any way that made sense or interested her. He introduced her to this person and that, tried to involve her in conversation, but in a formal and mechanical way. He seemed a stranger, unknowable. It all seemed unreal.

When they rose to leave the table, she hung back, hoping that Toby, clearing the tables, would come to her.

'Come, sister!'

'I wish to speak to Toby.'

'All in good time. He has duties to perform.'

She saw her son standing still, watching her, but Nicholas gave her arm a tug. To protest, to disobey his urging, would cause a disturbance. 'We gather again for Vespers in an hour. I know you will wish to join us.'

'Toby will be there?'

'Of course.'

But with the rest of the household…She felt a rising sense of frustration. 'I will go to my room and rest a little.'

Nicholas parted from her outside the door to her room. Inside, she found John, standing by the window.

'Forgive me, madam. I brought your things up.' An excuse, she knew. He could have given them to someone else to bring, or simply left them and gone on his way.

'Thank you, John.'

He waited until she'd sat down on a stool by the newly lit fire, her eyes on his face. The gravity of his expression alarmed her, though when was John anything but grave, dour even? 'You've heard something, so soon?'

'I can't be sure, madam. There's something afoot, that I'm sure of. But what it is, I don't know. The story is Master Catesby's gathering a company to fight in the Low Countries. There are a good many would follow him to the ends of the earth from what I hear.'

Not something that would be welcome to the government, and it might even be illegal for all she knew; and not what she would want for Toby, who would likely be only too eager to form a part of it, seeking danger, adventure. Was this what his brother had feared, as a threat to him? Was it enough to justify her trying to take him home with her? Possibly, from Tom's heretic viewpoint. Fighting with the armies of Spain could well seem treasonable to him. Except—had Nicholas not told her last year that there were negotiations for a treaty between

England and Spain; that peace between the two old enemies was King James's dearest wish? Had anything come of it?

Yet if this was all, if this was what threatened Toby, she could only feel relieved; and a little embarrassed that she should have come all this way for so little cause.

She saw that John was frowning, his eyes on her face.

'That's not all of it, madam. There have been deliveries, passing through to other houses under cover of night, weapons, it's said. And there's other talk, whispers. One hinted the story's a cover, to hide—I don't know what. Not all are in on it, but most I think know there's something. And, there's some are afraid.'

She felt her heart thud. What could it be, this thing that could arouse fear even in those who did not know the whole of it? Or was it all just rumour, servants' talk? She must not jump to unwarranted conclusions.

'Thank you, John. Please keep listening and looking. I need to know the truth.'

And to speak to Toby: that was the most urgent need. She saw him again among the household gathered for Vespers, and this time managed to reach him before he left the room. 'Walk with me in the garden, Toby, if you have time. It's a beautiful evening, and so warm.'

'Allow me to join you.' That was Nicholas, behind her.

She forced a smile. 'May a mother and son not have a little time to themselves?' She tried to make her tone light, teasing, but thought it simply sounded forced.

'Would you exclude me then, your own brother?'

There was something in his voice that sounded almost like a threat, at once unexpected and disturbing. Having no choice in the matter, she allowed him to insert himself between them.

Outside, in the soft air, grey but lit with furtive beams of sunlight, they took the path that wove a pattern through a small herb garden. At first no one said anything, then Toby came to a halt, turning to face her.

'Why have you come, mother? Is someone sick at home?' She was not sure if he was anxious, or embarrassed that she should have come at all. His voice, with the rough uncertainty of his approaching manhood, was no longer so familiar to her, so easy to interpret.

'No, Toby. Everyone is well. But we'd had no news of you, none at all, even after Edward left. I would guess you had my letters? And Mariana wrote too. For all we knew something was wrong, you were sick or worse.'

'Oh, mother!' He sounded exasperated. 'You didn't have to come all this way to find out!'

'How then were we supposed to know?'

He shrugged, though she could see that he'd coloured a little. 'I beg your pardon, mother. There was so much to do, so many new things.'

'But you are happy here? You are pleased with the life?'

He glanced at his uncle before replying, though she could not read his expression. 'Of course. Truly, mother, I am glad you made me come. I like the life. I have learned so much.' Kate thought the tone too forced, too emphatic, but she could not be sure. If they had been alone…!

But they were not alone and Nicholas took control of the conversation, encouraging Toby to tell his mother of the things he'd been doing, the improvements she would have been able to detect in his horsemanship, his handling of a sword, even his Latin, if only she had been accomplished enough in those fields herself.

They were just emerging from the herb garden to the more formal area beyond, where a woman was weeding around the roses planted there, when they heard hurrying steps behind them.

'Master Gaunt!' A servant, red faced, gasped out between breaths, 'There has been a delivery, sooner than expected, with word from Master Catesby. I am asked to bid you come, sir.'

Nicholas frowned, seemed about to say something, then apparently thought better of it. He turned to Kate. 'I am sorry. It seems I must leave you. Toby, you'd best get to your music. I believe you have a lesson this evening.'

'Tomorrow, uncle. I have been practising.'

Nicholas took an uncertain step away, turned back as if about to speak, then at the servant's murmured 'Sir—' followed the man back to the house.

Kate felt as if a threatening shadow had been blown away, leaving the sky clear. As soon as Nicholas was out of sight and they were beyond the hearing of the weeding servant, she placed her hands on Toby's shoulders and turned him to face her. He bent his head, avoiding her gaze.

'Toby, I want to know. Look at me! Look me in the eyes. Now, tell me. Are you truly happy here? Is everything well with you, in truth?'

Mutely, he returned her gaze, then looked down; then up once more. Was it her imagination, or was there a plea in his eyes, an appeal for her to help him?

'Toby?'

'I have been very happy, mother.'

'But—? Now?'

He shook his head. 'I don't know.' He hesitated, and then burst out: 'I—I had a friend. Such a friend! But he left, six weeks gone. I miss him…' His voice sounded, she thought, as if he were on the verge of tears.

She ran her hand consolingly up and down his arm. 'What happened? Was he dismissed?' Could this be the danger that had threatened him: dubious company, now brought to an end? If so, she could only be thankful that those responsible had cared enough to act on her son's behalf.

Toby shook his head. 'No, he left of his own free will. He was—uneasy. I miss him so!'

She considered what he'd just said. 'And you are uneasy too?'

A long silence, while again he avoided her gaze. 'When Master Catesby is here, the lady's son—then it all seems right. But when he goes—'

'As at present?'

He nodded, head bent again, feet shuffling.

'There's something troubling you. Not just you either. There's something in the air of this place. Something furtive, secret. What's going on?'

'I don't know.' This time, she sensed he was telling the truth, up to a point at least. 'Not all of it, anyway. At first, I thought it was for a company of soldiers for the Low Countries. I thought they would let me go with them. But I heard…I don't know, but I think it's something else. I heard whispers. My uncle did not deny it, but he says only that it's a great enterprise, for the bringing of this land back to the true faith.'

Why did that make her shiver? Was that not what she wanted too? Did she not daily pray for it? 'But you know nothing and have no part in it?'

'No. Yes. Only that I have been sent to carry messages sometimes, secret messages. I should not even have told you so much!' Then: 'There's something else. I've never told my uncle, or anyone. I saw Tom.'

Her heart lurched: so they had met, these two sons of hers!

She drew a deep breath, seeking the right words. 'How did that happen? By chance?'

'Yes—No—I found myself by Haroby. I did not know he was there. I went in, just to see—'

She listened in silence, resisting any urge to interrupt as he told her of the meeting, watched his colour rise and fall, heard the emotion in his voice, sensed the love revived for the brother he'd adored; the hope dashed.

'Mother, he's truly apostate, bound for Hell! But oh, I wish…!'

She took his hand, her voice gentle. 'Did you part in anger then?'

'We did not agree. I said what I ought not, things I should have kept to myself.'

'About what is happening here, what you know of it?'

Mouth clamped shut, he gave an almost imperceptible nod.

'What did Tom say to that?'

'That I should go home, to Holywell.'

And then he'd written, to warn her of Toby's danger. It all now made sense, a horrible, frightening sense.

'Is that what you'd like, to come home?'

He shot her a startled look. 'No! I must—!' A pause, while he swallowed hard; then a whisper, 'I think so, yes.'

'You're afraid of whatever is purposed?'

'I think—I believe it's what some would call treason.'

She shivered. 'But not your uncle? And this Master Catesby?'

'No. He (Master Catesby, that is) he says it's God's work, for the good of our immortal souls. That all else has been tried and this alone remains.' Again that anguished plea in his eyes. 'Perhaps I make it more in my imagining than it is.'

'Or perhaps not. Toby, you *shall* come home. I will take

you back with me.'

'But—no, I can't! I've said too much anyway. It would be a betrayal, cowardly too. I could never look Master Catesby in the eye again.'

'You wouldn't have to. You've told me nothing. I have simply watched and listened and drawn my own conclusions. I will—' She realised that Toby's gaze had been caught by something behind her. Turning, she saw that Nicholas was almost upon them.

Toby grabbed her arm, his voice low. 'Mother, my uncle must not know, about Tom, about anything! I beg you!'

'I shall say nothing, I promise.' She turned to greet Nicholas, her smile faltering as she saw how sharply he looked them both over, as if assessing the depth of their betrayal. She felt an odd mixture of guilt and anger.

'Still here, sister? And you, Toby? It's time for Compline. We are already late.' His voice was crisp, full of disapproval.

There was no more time for talk that day, either with her son or her brother. Kate watched Toby as he stood with the household at prayers, wishing she could smooth away every last troubled line from his face, wishing too that she could be sure she'd convinced him of the need to come home with her.

She had no idea how she was going to extricate him, unless she could persuade Nicholas to let him go, and she was very far from sure she could do that. And without his uncle's agreement, or better still that of his hero, the absent Robert Catesby, she did not think she could persuade Toby that it was not a kind of desertion to leave.

So the most urgent task before her was somehow to convince Nicholas of the necessity for Toby to return to Holywell. In bed that night she lay awake for a long time, turning things over in her head, planning what she might say, seeking any possible argument that might win her brother over, without betraying what Toby had told her; and praying that she would find the right words when the moment came.

When at last she fell asleep, she had the oddest dream, that Richard came to lie beside her and took her in his arms, not with passion, not in any way to rouse lustful feelings in her, but tenderly, with consolation and what she knew were words of reassurance. She woke to the dawn with an unexpected sense of hope renewed and a conviction that she would be able to do what had to be done.

She began to think Nicholas was avoiding her, for she had to hurry after him when the household dispersed following morning prayers. She caught his arm as he was on the point of leaving the room. 'Nicholas, I must speak with you!'

He was so long in replying that she thought he was going to refuse her. Then he shrugged. 'Very well, so long as our talk is brief. I have much to do.'

'Not here.' She looked round the hall, busy with activity. 'Somewhere private.'

He led the way to the parlour in which she'd waited the previous day, where he turned to face her as she took a seat by the fire.

'Well then, what is it? I would suppose your mind has now been set at rest. You have seen how content Toby is here at Ashby. You will be anxious to return home.'

'So long as Toby comes with me.'

He stared at her as if he thought her insane. 'Why? What possible reason could you have to return him to Holywell? Has he told you that's what he wants?'

She mustered the first of several possible arguments she had settled on last night, as being the least contentious. 'You say he is happy here, but I know him better than that. He misses the friend who left. Humphrey, was that his name? More than he would admit, except to me. He's not well, not himself. I can see how thin he is. He needs some time at home, for rest and reflection. A few weeks, perhaps until after Christmas, and he would I think be ready to return.' Which was not what she intended, but she thought it offered the only hope of convincing both her brother and her son that it was a good move. Once safely back at Holywell, Toby would again be under her influence. Relieved to be there, he would surely have no wish to leave.

'That's nonsense, Kate. That is to mollycoddle him, allowing him to yield to a minor disappointment; even a large one, if such it is. He has to learn to take life's knocks or he will never truly become a man. I'm sure that's not what you want for him, if you reflect.' He studied her face for a moment, frowning a little, as if struggling to read what he found there. 'I see what it is! You miss him, which is natural enough in a mother. You lost one son and don't wish to lose another. Yet you must know that to be merely a mother's whim, to which you must not yield if he is to grow to manhood as we would both wish, and to stay true to our faith. It is not like you, Kate, to be so swayed by an earthly impulse!' Half-smiling, he lowered his voice, though there was, to Kate's ears, more of menace than of tenderness in it. 'Do not forget: at your request, Toby's welfare was placed in my hands.'

'And now, at my request, I will take him back into mine.' She drew a deep breath, forced her voice into calmness. 'I will not discuss this, Nicholas. I have decided.'

'You are a woman. You cannot have command over the life of a man.'

'Toby is a boy still.'

'But you are not his guardian, legally speaking. He is in my care.'

'Your *care*, yes. And nor are you his guardian by law. And it was never meant that you should put him in danger.' Speaking on impulse, without premeditation, Kate realised at once what she had done, before ever the words were out. Well, it was too late to draw back.

There was a silence so complete that it seemed to swell and fill the room. Nicholas stood quite still, watching her, taking in what she had said, his gaze icy, hostile.

Minutes seemed to pass, while, heart thudding, she watched him take control of himself, drive back whatever emotion filled him (anger? fear?), assume an expression of mild concern; and at last, when he spoke again, force his voice to calmness, indifference. 'Danger? What are you talking of?' Then, as if struck by a new realisation, 'Ah, so there was a letter, after all! Toby wrote to you. That's what brought you here!'

'There was no letter and he's told me nothing.' She rushed on, to hide the lie. 'Oh, call it a mother's instinct if you like, a mere 'earthly impulse'! I was convinced that all was not well, though I did not know how or why. Now I'm here, I know I was right. It's nothing certain, nothing solid, but I can tell there's something going on.' She steeled herself to meet his gaze. 'Tell me, what was the delivery you were called to so urgently last evening?'

He waved a hand. 'Men's business. Nothing to concern you.'

'Men's business that you have to hide from view?'

'Is that not often so, with the world of men, and especially for those of our faith?'

'We're not talking about visiting priests or celebrations of the Mass, are we? You would never have kept that secret from me. This is something quite different.'

'It requires secrecy. Women talk.'

'Did you not see me face the pursuivants, years ago at Haroby, when Sir Thomas was from home? Did I talk then, for all their threats? But this—I have to know, for Toby's sake. How deep in this is he? What have you embroiled him in?'

'I can tell you only that we're doing God's work, that it is no easy task, that it must be done. And that I have not *embroiled* Toby in it, as you put it. He has a small part only, from his own choice.'

'It is not lawful, this men's business.' It was a statement rather than a question.

'God's law is above that of man, as you know full well. The priest you shielded at Haroby was not there lawfully, was he?'

'I knew it was right to shield him, and would do it again. But what is happening here—you won't tell me of it, you can't, because you know it's not just unlawful, but wrong. As Toby does in his heart, or so I believe. He is uneasy, to say the least. I have seen it in his face. Does he know the whole of it?'

'No, indeed not. He is too young and untried.'

'Then he is too young to be involved at all.' She rose to her feet. 'I leave at first light tomorrow, and Toby goes with me. That's all I have to say.'

As she turned away, Nicholas caught her arm. 'Sister, don't do this! Wait, do not be so hasty!' He drew a deep breath, as if collecting himself. 'I have perhaps been too impatient of your frailty. I understand you, while I do not commend you for it. And if indeed Toby is unhappy— which I doubt, but we shall see. If he wishes to return to

Holywell for a time, then I shall accept it.' She watched him, wary, mistrustful. 'I ask only one thing: that he does not leave until after Master Catesby returns. If nothing else, I know Toby would not wish to leave without saying farewell. That would seem gross ingratitude after all he owes our master here.'

It sounded so reasonable, a concession with one small condition, a delay not a refusal. But she mistrusted him all the same. 'When do you expect him home?'

'We can't always be sure. But I had word yesterday that he hopes to be back within the week.'

A week. It was not so very long, and would give her time to make thorough preparations to take Toby home; time to convince him, if he needed it, that this was for the best. At present she could not be completely sure that he would agree to her plan. She was certain, too, that he would want to take his leave of the man he so clearly revered.

'Very well. So long as his return is not delayed beyond that, I will wait until then.'

She saw how Nicholas relaxed, the tension falling away. 'A wise decision! I rejoice that you too will meet Master Catesby. I know you will love him as we all do. He is a man with the power to change the world for the better, drawing all after him.' He smiled and patted her arm. 'Meanwhile, enjoy what this place has to offer. This afternoon, my Lady Anne will be at her music with her friends. I know you will find pleasure there, and be made welcome. It will calm and cheer you.'

As she returned to her room she had, momentarily, a sense of relief that the matter was decided without a thorough disagreement with her brother. She made her morning devotions and then sat by the window, considering all that had been said. A week's respite, a week to prepare, to mould Toby's doubts into a firm decision to return home…

Or a week in which Nicholas could mould Toby to his view?

Was this not how Nicholas always brought an argument to an end, by turning all at once from anger or severity to a calm and reasonable reaching out? Had he not done exactly that this morning, bending her gently, unobtrusively, to his will? Even as they parted, as if concerned for her welfare, he had directed her activity for the day. Something that would take her mind off her anxieties, and keep her away from Toby.

And meanwhile he'd won time to work his will on Toby too. A week, at the end of which the master of the house would return; the man of whom Toby had spoken yesterday, in the garden. *When Master Catesby is here, the lady's son, then it all seems right. But when he goes—*

She sprang to her feet, shaking. What a fool she'd been! It should have been obvious to her why Nicholas had insisted Toby wait for Robert Catesby's return—because he was convinced Toby would not wish to leave once he was securely back under the older man's influence. He would not need to work on Toby himself, for he could be sure Catesby's presence would be enough to do it for him. Had not Nicholas wished her to meet him, so she too would fall under his spell? Toby, already enthralled, would surely not be impervious to that influence.

A man with the power to change the world for the better, but with fearful secrets, hidden caches of arms. No, that was not the way!

She knelt down by the bed, seeking a means to escape, to extricate Toby from this place. There must be no delay. They must leave as soon as humanly possible, well before the return of the master of the house. But how to do this, without her brother's knowledge? He would surely thwart her if he knew.

It came to her: her other son, Tom, who lived only a short distance away, who had written to warn her of Toby's danger; who, now come of age, the head of the family, would surely count in the eyes of the law as Toby's rightful guardian.

Thinking fast, she made her plans.

She made her way, slowly, warily, downstairs, trying to appear as if she were simply taking exercise, while she looked for John. She found him checking their horses in the stable. She glanced round. There was a groom laying straw in a stall nearby, within earshot.

'Are they well rested from the journey?' What innocent excuse could she find to draw him away from here, to a place where they would not be overheard?

'It seems so, madam. They did us a kindness at York, lending us such sound animals. They're as fresh as the day we set out.'

'That's good!'

Ah, the groom, task completed, was wandering off into the yard, whistling to himself. She lowered her voice, just in case: 'John, there's something I need you to do, urgently! A message to take, by memory, in person.'

She passed a restless day, trying to suppress her anxiety, wondering how John's errand was going, whether it would work out as she hoped and planned. The afternoon of music, which at another time she would have enjoyed, seemed interminable.

She had no opportunity to speak to Toby that day, nor did she wish to, in case Nicholas became suspicious. But whenever she glimpsed her son—waiting at tables, busy with some outdoor activity—she wondered what he was feeling and thinking, and ached to have him safe, away from this place.

It was after evening prayers, as they were dispersing to their beds, that she saw John step from the shadows to speak to Toby. He had returned then, and his speaking to Toby suggested that, so far at least, all had gone according to plan. She forced herself not to watch, to turn away and climb the stairs to her room.

Coming to morning prayers next day after a sleepless night,

she saw that Toby was absent; as was John, though that would likely not be noticed by anyone but herself. Once prayers were at an end, she went to Nicholas. 'Where's Toby? Is he sick?'

She could tell that he too had noticed Toby's absence. His eyes were full of suspicion. 'You don't know? He's said nothing to you?'

'I've scarcely seen him, and not today at all.'

'One of the lads said his horse had cast a shoe and he went last night to have it shod. But that could have been attended to here. It does not make sense.'

She tried to look like an anxious mother, to introduce a note of panic to her voice. 'I hope nothing is wrong. An accident, a fall...'

'So, sister, do I. A search will be made. I will let you know when there is news.'

She sensed that he did not trust her. She was going to have to be very careful with her next move.

'I shall be in my room, at prayer,' she told him.

She waited there just long enough to allow her brother's search party to get underway, wishing she knew which direction they would take. If Nicholas suspected Toby of making for Holywell, then they would go north or east, she guessed. On the other hand why would they think that, while she was still at Ashby?

She thought she managed to slip out to the stables unobserved, where she found the place deserted. She saw that John's horse had gone, as well as the sturdy mount

Toby had received from his uncle; only her own borrowed animal remained. It was a long time since she'd saddled a horse herself, but she managed to do it, listening all the while for any threat of interruption.

Constantly watchful, looking about her, she rode out of the stable yard and took the westward road, towards Haroby and the son she so longed to hold in her arms again. In just a few hours, if all went well, she would be with them both, her two sons, reunited; and safe.

So many memories slid to the surface as she neared the place from which she'd fled ten years ago, brought to life by a row of cottages, a farmhouse, the lush summer green of the woods, the gentle hills. And then the hamlet, houses clustered about the gatehouse of Haroby itself, glimpsed just beyond the *Red Lion* Inn. Outside which John was watching for her.

She knew at once that something was wrong. 'Sir Thomas is here?'

'No, madam. I've said nowt to Master Toby, but I found he was from home. His guardian is very sick, they say. But I thought it best to bring word to Master Toby that he wished to meet, just as we hoped he would. It was the only way to bring him here. I hope I did right?'

'Yes, yes, I'm sure you did.' She slid from the horse. 'Where is Toby now?'

'In his room, upstairs, waiting for Sir Thomas.'

'Then we'd better let him know.'

She felt a weight of disappointment and anxiety

churning inside her. So it had all gone wrong, from the very start! She had trusted that Tom would agree to invite his brother to a meeting, a matter of urgency, asking him to take a room at the village inn where they would meet the following morning. True, John's initiative had got Toby safely away from Ashby, but there would be no help from Tom to ease their flight; no lost son to clasp in her arms.

She gave herself a little shake. It all depended on her, and John. There was no one else. It must be done.

She made her way to the room where Toby waited, lying morosely on the bed. He swung round to face her. 'Mother! What are you doing here? I thought Tom was to come?'

As gently as she could she explained what had happened, while sensing Toby's growing anger at the deception. Terrified that all would be lost, that he would insist simply on returning to Ashby, she sat on the bed beside him and, urgently pleading, tried to impress on him the need to go back to Holywell. 'Just for a few weeks, that's all. A little time to draw breath and clear your head. That's all I ask.'

She was reminded of Tom's resistance to the flight from Haroby all those years ago. She'd won him over in the end. Could she do the same now, with his brother?

'I'm sorry I deceived you in this, but I know that in part at least it's what you wish for, to go back to Holywell, just as Tom counselled you. I'm afraid there's no time to be lost. Your uncle has already sent a search party to look for you. I would have us go on our way most urgently.'

'So he doesn't know of this plan of yours? He would try to stop you if he did?'

'He knows what I wished. He knows I am concerned for your welfare. We disagreed, and he hates to be thwarted. But once we're away, then I think he'll let it be. He's too wrapped up in whatever this enterprise is to trouble more than a little about your going.'

He was silent for a long time after she'd exhausted all her possible arguments. She watched him, wishing she knew what he was was thinking, though he had his head bent, staring at his hands as they twisted restlessly in his lap. She sent up urgent prayers that he would agree to leave, while repressing every instinct to say any more. She had done what she could. Now it was for him to choose.

He raised his head, met her gaze. 'I will come. For a short time, a week or two, a month at most. No longer.'

'That's all I ask.' Though it was not all, as she knew full well. But swept by a huge sense of relief she led the way downstairs to where John waited.

They were not followed, and the last few days of fine weather had firmed the roads to their horses' hooves. If she had been without anxiety, Kate would have enjoyed the journey, the more so as they were to call at York on the way north, to return the borrowed horses. She would see Richard again—oh, she must not allow the thought to fill her, for what after all could it bring in the way of happiness, this love without hope?

All went well that first day, but the following morning she could see that Toby's mood had changed. He was silent, morose, sitting hunched on his horse, so absorbed in some gloomy thoughts of his own that she often had to say something several times before he realised she'd spoken to him. She tried to probe his frame of mind, to encourage him to tell her what troubled him, but he dismissed all her efforts with a brusque coldness.

Another day, another night at a decent inn, and it was no better. They mounted their horses as the sun rose, ready to leave. But instead of urging his horse forward, Toby simply sat motionless in the saddle, staring into the distance.

'Toby? We should be going. I'd hoped to reach York by tomorrow at the latest, while the weather holds.' Her heart fluttered at the very thought: *Richard*.

Toby shook his head, as if dispelling some unwelcome mental intrusion. He dug in his heels and his mount moved forward, but slowly, as if she sensed her rider's reluctance. They had gone no more than a few paces when he halted again, looking directly at his mother. 'This is the coward's way, mother. I should never have agreed! I ought to go back, I know I ought.'

She tried not to let him see her dismay. 'It's only that you are confused, my dear. That's why you need some time away, to be sure what is right. You are still too close to everything to judge it rightly.'

Again, he shook his head. 'That's not it. Oh, I was afraid, but I should not have given in. I did not even bid farewell to Master Catesby. If I had, he would…'

He would have talked you out of it, she thought. As well he did not know Nicholas's condition for allowing him to leave! She searched her mind for the right words, for something to prevent him from turning back the way they had come and riding away from her, beyond her reach, into the very danger she thought she'd snatched him from.

'Tell me, what did your friend Humphrey think of Master Catesby?'

That (thank goodness!) had struck home. She saw how he coloured, and his gaze fell before hers.

'He—he loved him, as I do, as we all do. But: he said we should let conscience be our guide, not the heart.'

'And his conscience warned him against Master Catesby? As I think yours does, if you are honest.'

His silence answered her as clearly as if he had spoken, even before he said at last. 'I don't know. When he's not there, then—'

'Don't you see, that's why you need to take time for reflection? I think perhaps your conscience needs refreshment.' She smiled, reached out a hand to caress his. 'You are full of confusion, torn all ways. At Holywell you will see clearly again, one way or the other. Or so I hope.'

And tomorrow they would reach York, and there would be Richard, who could talk so fluently of serious things, who would listen and argue with a gentleness that Nicholas had never shown. She imagined Toby confiding in him, hearing his views, being guided into a better way of thinking. Richard too was a man who could win others over, who could reach their hearts, as he had reached hers. What better example for her troubled son?

But oh it wasn't only Toby's well-being she was thinking of as she waited for his decision! She longed so much to see Richard again, for all the pain she knew that would bring.

Another long silence, then Toby drew a deep breath. 'Very well. I will come with you. For now.'

At York they were welcomed warmly by Dame Frances.

'So this is Toby! Well, a fine lad I see, though a bit peaky, in need of a few home comforts. Come in, come in!' Then, devastatingly: 'Richard will be so sorry to have missed you. He's had to go to Warthrop. Some trouble with a tenant. You'll know the kind of thing. He'll not be back for a good few days.'

Kate managed to keep the tears away until she was safe in her room, where she felt like howling in anguish. This was more than disappointment, a pain that cut through her, draining light and colour from the world.

It seemed to take an age before she had herself under control. She scolded herself for her weakness, washed her face, forced herself to a degree of composure. It was, she told herself, just as well they were not to meet again, in the circumstances, though sad for Toby's sake. Those few blissful days in Richard's company were over, in the past. Ahead of her lay the duties of a devout widow, with a family to protect and nurture.

That night she dreamed that she was back at the inn, in Richard's arms on the stairs, while her body throbbed again with all the passion of that evening; and she went on to dream that they were wed, man and wife as they could never be in life.

Waking to a deeper heartache, she was glad that their little party would soon be on the way home.

Three days later, they rode at noon into the stable yard at Holywell, so familiar and yet somehow so strange. Kate felt as if she had been a lifetime away. There was no one about, apart from a rough looking donkey tethered by the house door, his saddle bags still on his back as he nibbled at the sparse tufts of grass growing at the base of the wall.

Kate had expected someone, alerted by the sound of their horses, to come from the house to welcome them. But all was quiet, unnaturally so at this time of day. Where were they all? She searched her memory, in case there was some local festivity she had forgotten about, something to take the household away for the day, but could think of none. She glanced at Toby, and saw that he like her was uneasy.

John led the horses to the stable, while Kate and Toby went into the house. The hall was deserted, though they could hear sounds from the kitchens; and someone was coming downstairs, a stocky man in a fustian coat: Peter Nattras, the barber surgeon from Meadhope, with Mariana close behind him.

'Oh Mother, Jane is sick, very sick!'

Running to Kate's arms, the girl burst into tears.

Chapter Nineteen

She did not look like Jane at all, the woman who lay on the truckle bed in Kate's chamber, flushed and shivering and gasping for breath.

'I fear she is like to die,' Master Nattrass had said before he rode away, promising to call again before nightfall.

A low moan behind her made Kate turn and draw Toby into her arms, his face blurred to her view by her own tears. She kissed him.

'Come, my dear, let's do what we can!'

Within an hour Jane, gently washed and dressed in clean linen, had been moved to the comfort of Kate's own bed. The stench of sickness had lessened, retreating before the bowls of lavender-steeped water, the rosemary and marjoram burning in the hearth. Kate moistened Jane's cracked lips with wine, watching with fruitless longing for the least indication that she knew they were there.

On the other side of the bed, Toby held the hand of his old nurse, stroking and stroking it in an anguish of tenderness. Still in his travel-stained clothes, he had gone at once to kneel at her side and refused to leave. Urgent prayers stumbled from his lips, pleas to the Blessed Virgin to have pity, in a confusion of Latin and English.

Mariana had told them how the whole household had been sick with a slight fever, all of them cared for by Jane with her usual tireless competence. And then she too had been taken ill, and grown quickly much worse, lying for days now in the grip of this terrible fever, no longer recognising any of those around her.

Kate sent her exhausted daughter to bed, did her best to reassure the other members of the household, saw them fed and rested, while her mind was filled with the need to care for Jane, who seemed to be sinking ever further into unconsciousness.

She managed to persuade Toby to change his clothes, though he was gone only long enough to pull on a random selection of garments, a clean shirt, breeches, hose but no shoes. He knelt once again by the bed, taking Jane's hand. His gaze left her face only once, to reach his mother.

'Thank God I didn't turn back! It would have been too late.' His voice cracked and fell silent.

There was little enough to cheer Kate today, but this let in a tiny chink of light, however fleeting.

Peter Nattrass came again, to apply leeches (as he had already done twice before, so Mariana had said) and force an ill-smelling potion between Jane's resistant lips.

'Will that do her any good?'

He shook his head. 'I hold out no hope, madam.'

'Then please let her be!'

Kate paid what was owed and saw him ride away, praying that she'd not dismissed Jane's one hope of healing.

Some time after midnight Toby fell asleep, there at the bedside. Kate tucked a cloak round him and sat on, gazing at the face of this woman who was so much more than a servant to them all. It was clear that Toby loved her more than he'd ever realised until now, faced with losing her.

Kate herself recognised what she had always known: Jane was the rock who had sustained her, been at her side through so many troubles, shared her joys and her sorrows. Constant, practical, dependable, loving, she had kept her alive on that long-ago flight, supported her through the years, her friend and confidante; the person she would have told of her feelings for Richard, but who now would never know. How could she bear to lose her? She could not imagine life without her, could not bear to think of it. She would be losing a part of herself. Yet the time was fast approaching when she would be faced with that loss.

She longed to send for a priest, but knew of none within reach. Holywell was not like Ashby, with the constant coming and going of priests of which Nicholas had told her. Their own prayers would have to be enough. She, like Toby, murmured all she knew, all that felt right, her fingers slipping over the beads of her rosary. She wished she could recall some of the prayers for the dying, words she'd heard whenever a priest brought the last rites, but only the most familiar prayers came to mind: *Sancta Maria, Mater Dei, ora pro nobis peccatoribus, nunc et in hora mortis nostrae...Holy Mary, Mother of God, pray for us sinners, now and at the hour of our death...* They would have to do.

When the first light of dawn crept into the room, there had been no change, just the sound of Jane's rasping breath, the gentler crackle of the fire. Death was crouching at the door, and there was nothing they could do to keep him away.

Toby woke, stretched; remembered. He leaned over to stroke Jane's cheek. 'Don't leave us, Jane! For the love of God, don't leave us!'

Kate shook herself, brought to mind her duty to the rest of the troubled household. She left Toby to keep watch while she summoned them all to prayers downstairs; the briefest of prayers, but no less heartfelt for that. A weight of grief seemed to fill the hall. Kate wished she could hug every one of them to her, drive away the heavy sense of imminent loss. But all she could offer was to send them quietly about their tasks, as far as possible finding something that would distract them and yet contribute to Jane's well-being: spreading straw in the yard to deaden the sounds of animals outside the window, washing soiled linen, gathering herbs, preparing nourishing broth in the hope that the sick woman might soon be in need of such things. The love every one of them felt for Jane was clear from the eagerness with which they all set to work.

As Kate crossed the hall on her way back to the sickroom, Cecily ran after her.

'Oh, madam, tell me she won't die!' Her eyes, large in her white face, were full of unshed tears. 'She tended me so kindly when I was sick. So kindly!'

'We can only pray, my dear. It's in God's hands.'

She waited for the girl to return to the kitchen, but the anguished face was still raised to hers. 'Before, at home—

no one was ever kind, not like Jane, and you, madam. The sickness—I was the last she tended, then she fell sick.'

And now you blame yourself. Compassion warred with impatience: *Oh, not now, please Cecily. I want to think only of Jane!* She took a deep breath. 'Don't blame yourself. It's not your fault. It's no one's fault. Just do your best to help, as I know you will. You can make a good broth. It was Jane who taught you.'

She was on the point of turning away when she realised the girl had still not moved, but stood there, her head bent. 'Cecily. What is it?'

'I did wrong.' A faint colour washed over her face. 'Not lately. Long since.'

Kate took her hands. 'Tell me, my dear.'

'My Dad. He said I was to tell him, anything. Wrong things, unlawful. Anything that happened here.'

Kate felt a chill. So Cecily had been Henry Stobb's spy, his informant, allowing him to carry word of any breach of the law to the authorities! Some instinct had once warned her that this might be so, but she'd not acted upon it, and had even come to trust the girl.

'And did you tell?'

'I made things up. That Master Gaunt was a priest. I knew he wasn't.'

So that was how Henry Stobbs had come to inform on them to Sir Cuthbert! Except that the man had seen her with Nicholas, and could simply have made up his own mind as to his possible identity; and to no effect, as it happened.

'After that, what else? When the Holy Mass was celebrated here?'

Cecily shook her head vehemently. 'No! No madam. I told him nothing more. Just that once. He used to beat me. I'm glad he's gone, so glad.' She sounded utterly sincere.

'Then think no more of it. You're safe here. I only ask that you let me know if your father ever approaches you again. Promise me that!'

'I will. Thank you, madam.'

As she made her way upstairs, Kate forced all thought of Cecily from her mind. Time enough for that another day.

In the sickroom the only change was that the noisy breathing had ceased. Toby still sat stroking Jane's hand, gazing at her gaunt face. He had been weeping.

'Toby!' Kate put down the dish she'd brought with her, went to the bed, her own breath caught in her throat. There was a faint pulse fluttering beneath her fingers. *Thank God!*

She held out the dish with its hunk of bread and cheese. 'I've brought you this. You need to eat.'

He shook his head. 'I couldn't.'

She persisted, until he broke off some of the bread, chewing it slowly, as if every movement of his mouth required a massive effort. He refused to take any more. 'It's no good. I'm not hungry.'

Toby, not hungry! Yet he'd had nothing since yesterday

morning.

'Have *you* eaten, mother?'

The question startled her. What was that to him? She was his mother, the one who looked after them all.

'You'll sicken too, if you don't eat.'

His concern brought tears to her eyes. She laid the dish on a stool beside him. 'Then let's finish this between us.'

It could not be said that either of them took any physical pleasure in the bread and cheese of that shared meal, and both found it hard to force down the food. Yet to Kate there was something almost sacred about it, so enfolded were they by their love for one another. It was a new strange thing that Toby should be caring for her, as she had for him all his life long. She realised with a little shock that he was no longer a child. Whatever had happened during the past year it had brought him to manhood.

Around midday Mariana came into the room, refreshed from her first long sleep for many days. 'I can sit by her now, mother, if you want to rest.'

Another child who had suddenly grown up, though so much younger than Toby: perhaps it was always so with women, on whom the burdens of the household fell from an early age, so that very little of their lives was given over to childhood.

She did not want to leave Jane, but her practical self told her she needed rest. She persuaded Toby to go to bed too, and made Mariana promise to call her if there was any change, but did not then go to lie down on her daughter's bed in the adjoining room. She knew she would not be able to sleep and was too restless to lie quietly, so instead she made her way out to the garden where the wind chilled the sunny day. She walked aimlessly along the paths, now and then pulling a weed from among the herbs. The roses were past their best; autumn would soon be here.

Autumn without Jane, the seasons passing without her? It was unthinkable! So often they had walked together along these paths, pondering the needs of the children, Jane listening attentively to her worries, nudging her with gentle advice. Though it had been winter when Jane first came into their lives, a grieving widow, cruelly made childless; reaching out to nurture Toby with all the love that fate had denied to her own flesh and blood, and in doing so nurturing them all.

Remembering, Kate shed harsh tears that did nothing to ease her pain, for they could change nothing.

By the time she returned to the sickroom, Toby had already resumed his vigil at the bedside. 'Have you slept at all?'

'A little.' He gave a faint smile. 'More than you, I guess.'

Much later, after evening prayers, Kate lit candles well away from the bed, so that their glow would not disturb the sick woman, while longing for any sign that Jane was capable of being disturbed, by anything at all.

She sent Mariana to bed, though Toby refused to go. Mother and son resumed their vigil in the silent room.

Another hour of earnest prayer, and Kate felt as if she might fall asleep, there at the bedside. But if the end was near—? She felt her eyelids droop, heavy with exhaustion, tried to force them to stay open. She must not miss that aweful, solemn moment.

'Mother!'

Toby's whisper jolted her into full wakefulness. Jane had not stirred. But her eyes were open, bewildered blue eyes gazing ahead, to one side then the other, coming to rest on Toby's face.

Her lips moved. 'Toby…Safe home!'

The words were so faint, forced out on a sighing breath, that they would have been lost altogether among the sounds of daytime. In the quiet of the night they were just audible to the two watchers at the bedside.

Toby bent and kissed Jane's hand. Kate stroked her forehead, brought a cup of wine.

The moment had passed. The eyes were closed again, the haggard features still, exactly as they had been for so very long. Was this her *nunc dimittis*, with Toby returned to Holywell, the moment when she felt free to let go her hold on life? Was this the end?

Fearful, Kate felt for a pulse. Yes, it was there! Was it even a little stronger than before? She could not be sure.

She caught Toby's eye, shook her head. 'I don't know. But she's living still. I think the fever's left her.'

Aound dawn Jane's eyes opened again, and they caught that faint voice. 'Thirsty.'

As she held the cup to Jane's lips, supporting her (so thin, every bone sharp through her skin!) Kate felt a leap of joy. Please God, she was over the worst, she would live!

Jane took a few sips, then was made comfortable again. 'I thank you.'

Toby made a choking sound, and then broke down in uncontrollable sobbing. Kate held him, stroking his hair; and Jane's hand reached out, just touching his sleeve, offering her consolation too.

It took a little time before Kate felt able to summon the household to morning prayers, but there she told them the good news, offering thanks for the miracle of Jane's recovery. That morning the kitchen was filled with song, Mariana's eyes shone, Philip laughed and did an ungainly dance that set him coughing, John whistled as he went about his work. The storm had passed, the heavy weight of grief dispersed; the sun shone again, though it was a dark morning, with heavy rain.

After so grave an illness Jane's recovery was slow, but it was steady. When a few days later she was able to take two or three shaky steps across the room, it was all Kate could do to prevent her from immediately trying to resume her duties. 'I've been lying in bed long enough.'

'You must submit to being cared for. I'll have no argument!'

There came a day when Jane was strong enough to want to hear Kate's account of her rescue of Toby. They were sitting by the fire, late in the morning. Toby had been despatched to make use of his improved knowledge of Latin in the instruction of his sister, an arrangement that Kate suspected would please neither of them, while keeping them both occupied.

'He's changed, young Toby. A man, yet not a man. Now, I want to hear all about it, how you brought him safe home. What you found at Ashby, whether Master Tom was right, as I guess he was. All your adventures!'

Kate told the story, in fits and starts, disjointedly, with diversions and many interruptions to answer Jane's questions. But she kept nothing back, at least as far as it affected her sons.

'So the bad company Master Tom feared—that was your own brother?' Kate nodded. 'That's hard to take.'

'You always doubted him.'

'I take no satisfaction in that.' She paused, took a sip of wine. 'This Master Catesby: you didn't meet him?'

'No. But those who had—they were like men bewitched. Toby too.'

'You think he's thrown off the enchantment?'

'I don't know. Time will tell. Once or twice, coming here, I thought he'd turn back. If we'd not found you so sick, then…' She shrugged. 'We shall see.'

'And your brother? He's still in thrall?'

'I guess so. There's been no message, nothing. I thought there might be a letter.' She had been sewing while they talked, but now her hands lay still in her lap as she pondered all that had happened.

'It's not only Toby who's changed, is it?'

Kate looked up, startled.

'This kinsman from York, this Master Richard Thornton. You've said little of him, but I've watched as you did. I heard in your voice.'

She felt herself colour. 'There's nothing to tell, not really.'

'And you blush like a young girl speaking of her first love, whenever you say his name.'

Kate laughed. 'I can hide nothing from you, can I? But indeed it means nothing, truly.' Her smile faded. Speaking of him, of her feelings, only brought the truth home to her. 'It cannot mean anything.'

Nothing, but an ache of longing that could never be assuaged.

She told Jane everything. She had seen the essential truth that the Kate who had set out to rescue her son from an unknown peril, the mother anxious for her son, had somehow found a new Kate, the woman with a physical body whose longing she could not ignore, driven by need—and something more?

'Are you so sure naught can come of it?'

There'll be a way, he'd said as they parted. *I'll find a way.*

But there could be no way. When she'd told him she was no wife for him she had simply been stating an obvious truth. If he did not see it, that was his blindness, not hers. *She* saw clearly enough. Older than he was, with a very different experience of life and its barriers and restraints, she had the clearer vision. She could do no more than accept that this interlude had happened, to accept the agonising mixture of joy, pain, loss and guilt, and offer it up in prayer as a small part of the suffering that must be an essential part of a holy life.

Jane patted her hand. 'Maybe you shouldn't give up hope. Life can do strange things.'

'It brought you back to us. God restored you.'

'Indeed he did. All things are possible.'

'But not this, I know. Believe me.' She forced a smile. 'At present it's enough that we're all safe home, here together.'

Jane's eyes were full of a calm happiness, sharing the thought.

'What now for Master Toby? Have you plans for him?'

'There's been no time to make any. I don't know. He can't just kick his heels here, doing nothing. That will only lead him into more mischief.'

'Maybe first of all he needs time to think on what's happened, set his feet on the right road.'

'I'll send him to talk to you. He'll hear what you have to say.'

They smiled at one another, at ease, content; restored.

Chapter Twenty

'How can you be so stupid!'

Mariana glared at him, lip quivering, and then burst into tears; unconvincing, forced tears, out of which she was quite able to find a furious riposte. 'I am *not* stupid! Latin's stupid. What use is it to me?'

'The Holy Mass—'

She cut him short. 'I didn't have lessons when Mother was away. I didn't need them. When Jane got ill it was me looked after everyone. I sent for Peter Nattrass, I kept the house. Jane would have died without me. I'm not a child any more, to be ordered around by my stupid brother who had to be sent away he behaved so badly.'

'You're ten years old! And you should be sent away yourself. Most girls of our rank are, just as I was. It's usual, the right thing.'

'Then why are you back here? Mother said you were sick, but you don't look a bit sick to me.'

'You're an impertinent brat! Shut your mouth and open your book!'

By way of answer, Mariana flung the Latin primer across the room.

Shaking with rage, Toby retrieved the book, returning it to the table by which they'd been sitting for an interminable half hour. 'That does it! You can stew in your ignorance. I shall tell Mother you're beyond teaching. I'm going out.'

Once mounted on Ruby, cantering down the road from Holywell, his anger began to slip away. In its place—what? Frustration, uncertainty, guilt?

Jane's sickness had temporarily pushed aside all his confused feelings, held them in a state of suspension, with the fevered woman the centre of all their attention, their hopes and fears. And when against all the odds she'd recovered, after the first wave of relief Toby had found himself back where he'd begun on first coming within sight of Holywell: stranded in a desolate place, battered by a confusion of thoughts and emotions. Even in this familiar beloved dale, he felt lost, no longer a part of it, no longer at home.

Part of him felt relief, and not only at Jane's recovery. His mother had snatched him away from something that had kept him wakeful for hours at night, given him nightmares when he did sleep, troubled his appetite and filled all the activities he'd once so loved with a gnawing anxiety. Yet—he'd felt all the same that he was at the heart of great things, privileged to be entrusted with even the little information he'd been given, willing to endure fear and worse in a cause led by the person he most trusted and loved in all the world: not his uncle, not even (as it should have been) God or Our Lady, but Robert Catesby. Yet he'd allowed his own weakness and his mother's pressure to lead him into betrayal, of a kind; or if not betrayal, desertion, which was just as bad. He'd proved himself a coward. He'd thought that at Ashby he'd found himself. Instead, he'd turned his back on what was good and true, returned to his old wayward, aimless self.

His mother had promised that his return to Holywell was a temporary arrangement, that he was free to return to Ashby at any time. He saw now that this was a trap. How could he possibly return? No one would ever trust him again. He would be shut out from the enchanted heart of the place, no longer admitted even to its outer circle. Very likely they would refuse to have him back.

He felt torn in pieces. Humphrey had told him to put conscience before the beguiling of the heart. He'd thought he felt as Humphrey did, when he looked dispassionately at what he knew of what was happening at Ashby. Now he realised his conscience was split in two. Was it not rather his fearful, cowardly heart that had led him to flee from the place? Would it not have been right to take his courage in both hands, play his part as he was asked to do, and face whatever the consequences might be? If they were to succeed in their project, he would feel even worse for having turned his back on them. If they did not succeed, he would feel ashamed beyond words that he was not with them to share their bitter fate.

Even this horse he rode, so much better than the poor old beast put out to grass in the field beyond the orchard— even that stirred his sense of guilt, for had Ruby not been a gift from his uncle, a generous gift? Was he not guilty of theft as well as ingratitude in using her to flee from Ashby, in riding her still?

But it was good all the same to be riding. He urged the mare into a gallop so recklessly fast that he could not think, felt only the speed of the horse, the thud of her hooves, her power beneath him.

He paid little attention to where he was going, only following instinctively the less frequented ways, until he eased the mare to a halt on a steep hill and there turned at last to look back the way he had come. From here, on the northern slope of the dale, he could just see the trees that sheltered Holywell, the fields of oats almost ready for harvest stretching from the house to where the river gleamed between its wooded banks; the hill beyond. He could see Meadhope village, a huddle of grey houses about the church, and Ashburn Mill to which a cart was moving with grain to be ground to flour; and to the west the further hills rising gaunt, angular, so unlike the soft hills, the dense woods, the lush landscape around Ashby. The light was clear, sharp, cold. He loved this place, yet today he hated it. How could it be his home any longer, after all that had happened? How could he ever feel at home again anywhere?

He swung his horse round, took the track through the little wood behind, on towards High Intake Farm. Before ever he reached it, he caught in memory the stench in his nostrils, saw the half ruined walls, the mouldering heather thatch, the scrawny cattle, the vicious dogs.

Then he reached it, and had to rub his eyes to be sure. This was nothing like he remembered, the house newly thatched, the yard swept clean, without weeds, the sturdy cattle grazing in a well-tended meadow.

He shrugged, rode on. What did it matter? Why should he care? Nothing mattered any more.

He followed the track over the fell, passing the occasional fellow-traveller at speed, without offering or acknowledging any greeting. He was in no mood for courtesies. The early rain had ceased, the clouds were breaking, the air was cold, bracing after the soft sweetness of Ashby.

Someone was coming towards him, another rider: a good horse, decent riding clothes, red face and a fringe of ginger hair just visible beneath the brim of his hat. Hal!

There was no way of avoiding him. They were already almost upon one another. He urged Ruby to one side, drew rein, waited, head high. Remembering how they had parted, he assumed his haughtiest expression. He would not meet Hal's gaze. It would be as if they had never met, never even been acquainted.

'Toby! By all that's wonderful!'

His defences collapsed. Hal's unfeigned delight was irresistible. He found himself shaking, blushing like a girl.

'I didn't know you were back. Are you here for good? When did you arrive?'

Toby stammered out a reply, more or less coherent. Then, abruptly, 'Hal, last year—Bess.' Even speaking her name stirred his body to shameful life.

Hal waved a hand. 'Oh, that! Think nothing of it!'

'You were angry, with reason.'

'Maybe, at the time. I didn't know the whole of it. I should have known you can't trust a woman, even your own sister. It's in their nature. Bess told me afterwards, it was all her doing.'

Woman the temptress, like Eve, leading man astray: that was what they had taught him at Ashby too, as had every priest who had guided him from childhood.

'That's all in the past. Where are you bound?'

'Nowhere. Just riding, to clear my head.'

'Then let's ride together. I'm bound for home. I've promised my father I'll go through the accounts with Master Steadman; you know, our steward. My father has this thought he might suddenly die and I wouldn't have the first idea how to manage things. No idea where that comes from. He's as hale a man as ever lived, I'd say. But—' He shrugged. 'I did promise, otherwise we could have taken the hawks out. I don't get to go hawking at Cambridge, and there's no one much here to ride with.'

It took Toby a moment or two to grasp what his friend was talking about. 'I'd forgot. You'll have had a whole year there by now.' Then, though it did not interest him and seemed utterly irrelevant: 'How was it?'

Hal's face lit up. 'Better than you could ever imagine! I must tell you all about it. Come back with me and pay your respects to the family. You haven't called since you came home?'

Toby shook his head. 'Did you tell your father? You

know, about Bess, and me?'

'It never went beyond the three of us. You needn't fear his wrath.' He laid an entreating hand on Ruby's bridle. 'Come, they'll be glad to see you, I know.'

'They'—Bess? Again that stirring in his loins, the thud of his heart. He'd thought it banished for ever, that shameful passion, done to death by the holy influence of Ashby, of Robert Catesby. He tried to school his voice to nonchalance. 'How is your family?'

'They're well. We've got Bess visiting just now.'

'Visiting? She lives there!'

'Oh, she's been wed this twelvemonth. Did you not know?'

Of course! The man from Houghton-le-Spring. He felt a fierce pang of jealousy. 'Is her husband here too?' What was his name? Will something?

'Will Fenwick. No, he has work to do. Something, I don't recall what. Bess was in need of rest and a change.'

'Is she not well?' Pregnant: that was the most likely explanation.

'Oh well enough, I think. But that Fenwick is a poor thing, when all's said and done. I'd have thought my father could have found better. He had his reasons, I suppose. Money, land, those sort of reasons.'

'She isn't happy then?'

'Oh, she has a husband and a household. It's what every woman wants. She's well enough.'

Should he go with Hal to pay his respects to these old

family friends—heretics, who had caused him to be led astray? No, that had been his doing, his choice. They had for the most part been unfailingly kind to him. And Bess was now a married woman. That shameful interlude was over, so what better moment to face her, accept what had changed, put it once and for all behind him?

He turned his horse and they set out, slowly, in the direction of Meadhope. The way took them past High Intake Farm, where Hal explained its transformation. 'Henry Stobbs was turned out. Not before time, from what I heard.'

'What became of him, and the family? Did I not see Cecily in the kitchen yesterday?'

'She's living at Holywell all the time now, I think. Your mother found places for some of them, and Master Langley looked after the rest. That cottage on the rectory land, that's where they are now, I think. All but Stobbs himself. I heard he went to Durham, but that could just be a rumour. He's gone anyway. Good riddance!'

At the once-so-familiar house, Hal led Toby inside. 'I'll have to leave you now, but we'll meet again. Tomorrow perhaps? I've a few weeks yet before I go back to Cambridge. You'll find them in the parlour, upstairs.'

Trying to repress his anxiety, Toby turned towards the stairs; and met Bess coming down.

She had a tired troubled look and had even lost weight a little, but she was still alarmingly pretty, and he thought her face lit as she saw him. In spite of everything, in spite of his resolution to lead a devout life, the attraction tugged at him. After all that had happened, he had a fierce longing for an uncomplicated physical release. 'Oh, Bess, how are you? Hal says you're wed now.'

She pulled a rueful face. 'Aye. A married woman, with a household.'

'That must be a fine thing for you.'

'It's well enough.' Then she smiled. 'No, it suits me fine. Only—' She gave him a sly sideways look which set his heart thudding. She came closer to him, on the same step, raised her face to his, her chin almost touching his chest, lowered her voice to a whisper: 'In bed—he's not like you. He hasn't your…' She paused. Then, so he scarcely heard: '…touch.'

Startled by her directness, his heart thudding, he stammered, 'We've never been in bed together.'

'Would you like to?'

'Bess!'

'Don't look so shocked!' She looked down, away. 'I don't think he has much taste for me. I ache for…' raising her eyes to his face, so that he saw at once what she meant, then: 'I want children, Toby.'

'What's stopping you—? Oh!' His body in turmoil, he coloured more than ever. 'You're married. They'd have to be his children.'

'Would he know the difference?'

'I don't know. Surely?'

'I can get him to do it, after a fashion. So he thinks he

has anyway. He likes to drink deep before bedding me, or trying to bed me. But he doesn't then remember what he's done. He believes he's taken my maidenhead.'

'You're still a virgin!'

She nodded.

'What's wrong with him?' Those sweet luscious lips, the round smooth breasts, the trim waist, the delicious curves he could only guess at: how could her husband possibly resist?

She gave a quick glance round, to make sure no one was near, then she was reaching up, slipping her arms round his neck. 'Take me, Toby! Let's find a private place and you can pleasure me.'

He was shocked, appalled—and wildly excited. It was terribly wrong, a great sin that she was inviting him to commit. She was Eve, the eternal temptress, shameless, alluring, leading him to wickedness. And yet: after so much disappointment, why not? Why should he not have some pleasure after all? 'Where is private enough?'

She thought for a moment. 'You know the byre at Home Farm? The house is empty, but the byres are used, for storage and the like.'

'The hay byre?' The place in his dream, the one that had made him so ashamed; afterwards, Robert Catesby had spoken to him by the well. A sacred moment.

'Meet me there at dusk today.'

Toby made his way to the byre on foot, so there would be

no tethered horse to betray them. By the time he reached the place it was still light enough for him to make her out when he stepped inside. She was leaning down from the hayloft, gesturing to him to use the ladder to reach her.

Once in the loft, he found himself drawn into her arms, tugged down to lie beside her on a fragrant bed of hay. With a great sense of release, he fell into the old familiar routine, the caressing, the loosened lacing, the bodice falling open. Only this time there was no barrier beyond which he must not pass. This time she let his tentative exploring hand reach down to her ankle, up her stockinged leg, on to the warm moist hidden place. He heard her gasp, her breathing quickening in tune with his.

'My first time too,' he murmured.

'Oh Toby! Come, now!'

'Oh Bess! Oh Bess!'

He pushed up her skirts, tugged at the ties of his breeches, his hands clumsy with eagerness. She had her legs parted, was pulling at him. 'Come, Toby, come now!'

He was there, throbbing flesh to throbbing flesh, thrusting, entering her. She gave a moan, a gasp, her fingers clutching at his back. Calling his name over and over through ragged breath, she gave a last ecstatic cry, at the very same moment as he was flooded with a pleasure more intense than he could ever have imagined.

Afterwards, in complete darkness, he heard her give a little sigh.

'Toby, my joy!'

My joy! My joy! The words repeated themselves in his head as he rode home. He felt as if a burden had been lifted from him, as if happiness was at last within his grasp. Yet he knew he ought not to feel happy. He should be feeling appallingly guilty. He had just committed an act of adultery with the sister of his oldest friend, the daughter of their generous neighbour.

And he knew he would do it again tomorrow if she asked; as she had. And every day for as long as she wanted him.

Chapter Twenty One

For the few weeks of her stay at Meadhope, Bess gave Toby all the purpose he desired for his life. He was consumed by thoughts of her, her sweet body, the things they did together in those hours snatched in the hayloft. He had no idea how she managed to escape her family, what excuses she gave, but it didn't matter. It was enough that she was there, in his arms, sharing the growing delight they found in one another.

Only once did they fear discovery, hearing footsteps outside, then the door creaking open below, a man whistling as he moved around. They lay utterly still, breath held, praying he would not mount the ladder. There was a clattering sound, a grunt as of someone lifting a heavy weight. Then the door creaked again, the steps moved away, more slowly than before. Bess let out a long breath. 'That was a near thing!' Somehow it only made their times together the sweeter, to know the risk they took.

Between those blissful hours, he went for an occasional ride with Hal, his enjoyment shadowed by guilt, and even found time, playing the dutiful brother, to give lessons to his siblings (Latin for Mariana, horsemanship for Philip), little though he enjoyed the experience. Mariana consistently refused to cooperate, so that every session with her was a battle of wills, and as for Philip: 'He just sits there like a sack of turnips,' Toby grumbled to Jane. 'He's never going to be free of the leading rein.'

Gently, Jane told him to be patient with his sickly brother. 'It's not his choice to be so weak. I know it's hard for someone as strong as you to understand, but promise me you'll try!' Thinner, still frail after her illness, Jane seemed to speak from the heart in a way that touched Toby the more. But that didn't make his task any easier.

When he tried to persuade his mother that Mariana was beyond teaching, she was sympathetic, but equally unhelpful. 'I know, Toby. She likes to think she's a grown woman.' Then, in an uncharacteristic moment of intimacy, 'I wish I knew what was best for her! It can't go on like this.'

But at least there was Bess, and the prospect of their meetings to lift his spirits through all the frustrations of family life.

It could not last. The day came when she broke it to him that she was to return to Houghton and her husband, as he had known she must. They considered the possibility that he should ride over to her new home so they might meet there, but she told him it was too risky, that she knew of no safe place as she did here at Meadhope. 'I'll come back again, of course I will.' They had a last long afternoon in the hayloft—long, but ended far too soon—and he watched her ride away.

At supper that evening he drank too much ale, followed by wine pilfered from the cellar when no one was looking; and woke next morning with an appalling headache, to be lectured by his disappointed mother, who seemed to have thought him a reformed character. 'What's got into you, Toby? You seemed happy. I thought you'd resigned yourself to our modest way of life.'

He was a very long way from being resigned to anything. He felt angry with everyone, with his mother, his uncle, the twins, even with Bess; and especially with God. Each time he thought he'd found some purpose in his life, something that truly mattered to him, it was snatched from him, as this had been. It was not fair. It was cruel!

It was unfortunate that Father Fielding made one of his infrequent visits to Holywell that very same day. Memories of Ashby revived in Toby, of the intelligent, impressive priests who came there; and the utter contrast between them and the shabby, uncouth figure of this priest. He made a confession, of a sort, leaving out anything to do with Bess, mentioning only his own impatience with the twins, and his intemperance. He was uneasily aware that an incomplete confession made for an incomplete absolution. But though this niggled at him he did not really care. Even the Mass that followed seemed a poor affair, recalling the rich music, the beautiful vestments, the order and reverence of Masses at Ashby; the men there with him.

What were they doing now? Was Catesby in the house again? And how did he think of Toby, the deserter? Very likely, thought Toby, he did not think of him at all. He would have other matters on his mind.

There was that other question too: could he pray for the success of the great enterprise they had entered upon, whatever its precise nature? For success, he was sure, would mean the return of the Catholic faith to England, in government, in the lives of all Englishmen, the complete reversal of all the years of persecution, something they had prayed for as long as he could remember. Those of their faith would no longer be a barely tolerated faction, but in power, in control. That was why it was so hazardous a thing, because the stakes were so high, the ultimate goal of such burning importance for all of the true faith.

And for Bess and her family.? Did he really want the world turned upside down, so they should be made to suffer in their turn? He knew from Hal that among Protestants there was a bitter recollection of the fires of Queen Mary's reign. Catholics might venerate her memory, but she was 'bloody Mary' to his Protestant compatriots. *Gentler by far than the fires of Hell that face them after death,* had been Father Fielding's dismissive observation, when he'd spoken of it.

If only there was someone he could confide in about all this, tell of his doubts and fears and hopes! Jane, dear loving Jane, was the best person to advise on good behaviour and practical everyday matters, but not, he felt, this massive thing that hung over him. And he knew already what his mother thought about it.

Oh, it was all too much for him! Better to drink and eat and hunt and try not to give a thought to any of it. He rode with Hal (*I thought you'd forgotten me,* his friend joked on their first meeting following Bess's departure) but even that once enjoyable activity had lost its savour. Hal was good company, most of the time, but he could never be a friend like Humphrey. In any case, he would soon be on his way back to Cambridge. Toby felt adrift, lost.

A week after Bess left, his mother drew him to one side after morning prayers.

'Toby, I have an errand for you.'

Fighting his headache, squinting against the painful gleam from the window beside which his mother stood, Toby braced himself. *What now?* 'Yes, mother?'

'I wish you to accompany Mariana to Newcastle.'

'Newcastle?'

'That's what I said. To the house of one Mistress Lawson.'

The name chimed somewhere in his memory. 'The lady who paid for Ned to go abroad, and Margaret?'

'The very same. She is willing to take Mariana into her household. It is just what I would have wished for her.'

He thought of all his recent confrontations with Mariana, her difficult moods, and wondered how she felt about being sent away. Perhaps another household would be able to manage her better. Then there was her twin: for all their very different abilities, they were still close. 'What of Philip?'

'I am still considering. Father Fielding had a thought, but I'm not sure.'

So Toby set out for Newcastle, escort to his sullen resentful sister, who'd wept at parting from her twin. Her older brother exerted himself to cheer her, which at least stopped him from thinking of his own misery.

It was no use: Mariana did not even try to respond to Toby's light remarks, his attempts at distracting her. In fact she said nothing at all, did not even look at him, but simply sat on her lumbering horse in stubborn silence until they had ridden the length of Holywell's drive and gone some way on the road beyond. Toby gave up. It was not going to be a comfortable journey, and they still had many miles to go.

All at once Mariana reached over and grabbed his arm, gesturing with her head towards a thicket that bordered the road. Toby was just in time to glimpse a figure half-hidden there, though it slunk back into the shadows as they passed. Mariana spoke at last, her voice a rasping whisper.

'That was Henry Stobbs!'

'Can't have been, Mariana. He's gone long since, so Hal said.'

'I know. I'm sure it was him. Certain!' She gave a little shudder. 'I never did like him.' After a moment's thought, she added, 'I hope he's not going to see Cecily. She's scared of him.'

Toby turned his horse, rode back a little way, rejoined his sister. 'No one there. Not a soul. You're imagining things.'

'I'm not! I saw him. So did you, didn't you?'

Irritated, not willing to humour her after his spurned efforts at kindness, he shrugged. 'Not Henry Stobbs.'

'It was! You know it was!'

As he did, uneasy though it made him. But he was not going to admit it. It was his turn now to say nothing, to ignore his companion. He'd had enough of her contrary ways. He would do his duty today, but no more.

It was only too obvious that Philip was miserable at his twin's departure. He refused to do anything but sit by the fire with his head resting on Trusty, who seemed as disinclined as the boy for any activity.

Kate felt for her youngest son. She reminded him of what Father Fielding had often said to him during his short difficult life, how this present suffering was just a small taste of what our Lord and the blessed martyrs had suffered. It was, she guessed, advice as ineffective to him as it had often seemed to her.

Meanwhile she pondered the other advice the priest had given. 'Why not write to your cousins in York? It may be they know of a household that would take in a young lad for his education. Master Thornton himself, for instance. He has a considerable estate I believe. His stepmother, when younger, had a reputation for welcoming girls of good family into her household. Might he not do the same, if he is of the same mind?'

Master Thornton, with whom, like any heedless country girl, she'd shared an intoxicating (and intoxicated) embrace on a stairwell at a village inn, which shamefully she did not regret as she ought.

'I don't know. We've not had very much contact with

them of late.'

'Permit me to send word to a priest I know, who serves their neighbourhood. I will ask him to make enquiries. We must be sure that it's a fit place for the boy, perhaps even for both of your sons. But if not him, then they may know of others. The Jesuits have a hold on parts of Yorkshire, and I would prefer that your son should not be within their influence.'

When she'd hinted at what had brought Toby home ('It was not after all the right place for him') he'd readily laid the blame on this detested faction.

'The Jesuits have the great households in their avaricious grasp. Living in comfort undreamed of in my experience. Too assertive, too risky. Better to live quietly according to the laws, as best one can. But we shall see.'

She did not know how to refuse his offer, or even if she'd wanted to. She was unsure of everything.

Toby returned from Newcastle with his mood as difficult as ever.

Holywell's oats were ready for harvest, so he joined Kate and every available member of the household in the sheltered field near the river, where they were gathering in the meagre crop that would help feed them through the winter. Toby set to work with a savage truculence that prevented anyone from engaging him in conversation, shutting him apart in an intangible circle of hostility.

'He's right out of sorts.' Jane was sitting with Kate at

the edge of the field, during one of the necessary short breaks for refreshment, welcome on this unusually hot day. Toby had refused to halt his frenzied activity. Alone in the distance, his progress along the rows was marked only by the rhythmic swinging of his sickle, the fall of the crop following him like a wave.

'I wish you would try and discover what's turned him to such bitterness. All at once, when he'd seemed glad to be home, or so I thought. I can't get him to talk to me.'

'He'll not talk to me either.' Which only told Kate how deeply troubled he was.

At least, as far as Kate was concerned, the vigorous activity of harvest prevented her from wondering whether Father Fielding's intervention would bring a response from Richard. When she had a moment of quiet, she wondered if he would grasp this opportunity to revive their friendship. Was that even what she wanted, for the pain it would bring? Daily, she expected, feared, a letter or some kind of message, if only through the priest.

What she received was a visit, heralded only a few hours ahead by a servant sent to tell her that Master Richard Thornton would be at Holywell that very evening, together with his mother, Dame Frances.

There followed a confusion of preparation, sweeping, sorting linen, cooking, gathering herbs and vegetables, hurrying into dairy or pantry and forgetting why she'd come, giving orders twice over for fires to be lit in the bedchambers, bedlinen to be aired (she assumed their guests would spend at least one night at Holywell), finding she kept dropping things, falling over furniture that was standing where it had always been.

Once, she caught sight of her reflection in a shadowed window on the stairs: wild hair escaping from her crumpled coif, a smudge of flour on her cheek. She glanced down at her gown, the skirts dusty, her bodice stained. He must not see her like this! But what to wear, how to find time to tidy herself?

She ran up to her room, found clean linen, a neat ruff, a crisp white coif.

There came a shout from below, the clatter of hooves beyond the window. Should she delay, change her clothes, make sure she was fit to be seen? No, better he should see her at her least prepossessing, know what she was really like. Then he would understand, as she did, that there was no future for them.

Besides, it would waste precious time, when they could be together. She dropped the linen, apart from the coif into which she stuffed her bedraggled hair, and hurried down the stairs, almost losing her footing on the way.

He was there, out in the sunlit courtyard, dismounting, doffing his hat, as the two Thornton servants assisted his mother from her sturdy horse. Then he was bowing to her, the man she remembered, more alive, more vital, more beautiful than in her memory.

She moved forward, somehow no longer the lady of the house welcoming her visiting kinsfolk, but more like a foolish love-struck maiden, hot, flustered, blushing furiously. Taking a deep breath, she said what she hoped were the right things, ushered her guests into the house, where she had a simple supper served, since there'd been no time for anything else. She was glad that at this time of year there was ample food in the house.

Then, as they ate, she found her awkwardness falling away. Richard was as she remembered, a man with whom she felt at ease, as if she'd known him all her life; her friend, in spite of the fierce undercurrent of attraction beneath it all that told her he was so much more than that.

At supper their talk had been general: the weather, the state of the harvest, the health and well-being of their respective families. Making it clear to Kate that Father Fielding's message had reached him, Richard engaged Philip in conversation, clearly trying to discover what kind of boy he was, to judge if they might suit. It seemed to Kate that Philip liked him well enough and quickly lost any shyness. Richard even managed to engage Toby in conversation, drawing from him a courteous response, with little sign of his usual truculence. He was good with children; he would make a good father.

Once evening prayers were at an end, Dame Frances embraced Kate. 'I'll bid you goodnight, my dear. I thank you for making us so welcome.'

Kate watched her make her way upstairs, her maidservant at her heels. Did she know of her son's feelings towards her? If there was anything left for her to know...

There had been no sign in Richard's manner this evening that any of the passion of their last meeting still remained. It was only too likely that he'd come to see how impossible their love was and forced himself to acceptance. As she had always known she must do too.

Once the household and family dispersed to their beds, Kate lingered in the hall, her head too full of questions for sleep, her body too restless.

'Kate.' His voice behind her made her swing round.

'I thought you'd—'

He came to her, took her hand, his touch piercing her with delight.

'Gone to bed? Before we've spoken together, where no others can hear us?' His face, lit by a single candle and the glow of the fire, was full of tenderness. 'You know why I'm here?'

'You hear we seek a suitable household where Philip may be educated, as far as he is able.'

'So my dear stepmother believes.'

'Then, she does not know…?' She could not finish, for fear he would not grasp her meaning.

'That I love you? I think she guesses something, but that's all. Kate, there is no hindrance there, I'm sure of it. It might not be what she would most wish for, but she would seek my happiness before all else.'

'Yet: I am a poor widow still, no longer young. It's been so short a time.'

'Did you not know, as I did, from the moment we sat at

supper, that day in York?'

'Oh, I felt—' Of course she did! How could she ever forget? 'Oh yes! But that's not enough is it?'

'Why not?'

'For all the reasons I've told you. I am old, a widow, and poor. There is only Holywell.'

'I have means enough. That's no hindrance either.' He brushed her lips with his finger, setting her body on fire. 'You'll have to do better than that.'

'I'm too old to bear more children, I'm sure of it.' She studied his face, saw that he was considering what she said as if it was new to him. 'You will be a good father, one day.' Her voice broke on the words. 'A good husband. To a young wife.' She pulled her hands free of his. 'Let's talk of Philip, I beg you.'

She thought he was about to protest. He even reached out as if to embrace her, but instead shook his head, took a deep breath. 'Then let us sit down.'

She saw him pause to collect his thoughts, as she was trying so hard to do.

'I understand young Philip is missing his twin. I could hear it as we talked at supper.'

'That's true, but not all of it.' He could not have failed to see how damaged the boy was, in body and mind.

'I know. We shall have to try what a change of scene will do for him, and a more active life. I know he will never be as his sister and brother, but it may be he is stronger than he seems, or could become so, and better able to

357

learn. I would have liked to say that his sister could come too if she wished it, but my mother is too advanced in years to receive her at York, and I—I have no wife.' He fell silent, his eyes held by hers. Then he said, 'What of young Toby? It was not sickness that made you bring him back from Ashby, was it? I always suspected there was more to it than that.'

'I do not think I gave you any reason.'

'Oh, I know you well, my lady Kate! I could hear it in your voice, see it in your eyes. Besides, there was something about your brother, when he stayed on his way to you last year, something I mistrusted.'

'You told me you thought him very hot for the faith.'

'And angry, full of anger. There were things he said—nothing I could put my finger on precisely, but…well! Am I near the mark?'

'I think so. Oh, it's a tangle, and even I don't know the whole of it, nor Toby either I think. More a feeling that it wasn't right. And a warning I had.'

She fell silent, wondering if she'd said more than was wise. She felt instinctively that she could trust Richard (of course she could!) but there was so much one could not know about another person; even someone so near and dear as a brother.

'Would Toby perhaps wish to come to my household, with his brother?'

'Oh, that's a kind thought!'

'But?'

'I don't know. I have been thinking a great deal about his future, but this time it must be right for him, whatever it is. He's had some strange contradictory moods since he came home.'

He stood up, and she felt his lips brush her brow. 'Sweet Kate. What I would give to take that troubled look from you!'

'Oh, but you are doing so much to help!' The words sounded forced, foolish.

'That's nothing, unless I can convince you to be my wife.'

'Without hope of children?' She watched his face for any trace of doubt or hesitation, but could not be sure. 'Oh Richard, we cannot be wed, I know that. I am certain of it, from the bottom of my heart.' Grief, pain, longing swept through her. 'I wish it were not so! I want so much—so very much!'

His arms were about her, drawing her close. Oh how she loved the smell of him, the feel of his body against hers, the passion of his kiss!

'I too, my dear heart, my darling. I will wear down your resistance, convince you it's possible, some day, somehow! I promise you that.'

She came very near to giving in. But not quite. She knew she must not, knew she could only allow herself to savour this moment and be ready to face the pain that would inevitably follow.

* * *

Two bittersweet days, filled with tumultuous emotion, and Richard and his mother went on their way. It was agreed that Philip should become part of Richard's household at Warthrop, as soon as the Christmas festivities were over. 'It will give me time to make all ready,' Richard said. 'Then I will come for him myself.' His face lit with a new thought. 'Better still, why not come to Warthrop for Christmas, all of you? We will celebrate together, with the Holy Mass too if it can be arranged.'

She felt a shiver of delight that had nothing to do with the sacred mysteries. Against her better judgement, she found herself accepting his invitation.

Kisses for them all, and he was gone. Beside her, Toby said, 'I like him. He's—different.'

Kate caught Jane's eye, full of meaning. Jane put a hand on Toby's shoulder. 'You had a lot to say to him yesterday, I noticed.'

Richard had invited Toby to ride with him, and Kate too had seen how long and earnestly they talked together on their return.

'He takes heed of what you say to him. There's not many men like that. Only—' He gave himself a little shake and fell silent, as if remembering something lost, irrecoverable.

Kate had a brief heart-wrenching vision of the two of them together, she and Richard, guiding Toby to a happy manhood, caring for all her children. She gave herself a little shake, repudiating the impossible idea, and turned to go back into the house.

That evening, in their bedchamber, Jane perched on the edge of the bed where Kate lay.

'Where's the impediment that keeps you apart? I saw clear enough that he loves you, yet your heart's breaking for want of him.' She studied Kate's face. 'Maybe he's not spoken of it?'

'Oh he has! I've known him so short a time, but that's no barrier. Or not much of one. As for—well, you know how the world looks on a widow who takes another husband. But even that—Jane, you know my courses have all but stopped. There will be no more children.'

'You can't be sure of that. Does he see it as an impediment?'

'In his heart, I think so, yes.'

Jane stroked her hair. 'Oh my dear madam. I would so much wish for you to know happiness, true wedded happiness. I knew it with my Jack. A long time ago, but I have good memories still, for all the grief when he died. I know you had none of that with Sir Thomas. Sometimes being poor and landless brings greater freedom.'

'But not now, to me. Not if you're a gentlewoman, and the man you love a gentleman.'

'No, I see that.'

Later, in the dark, she murmured, 'Jane I came so close, so close to begging him to take me, to bed me. I wanted to say: let's have this moment, if we have nothing else, ever. And if by chance I'm found afterwards to be with child, then I will marry you.'

'Then why not? What have you to lose?' She could hear from her voice that Jane was smiling in the tender knowing way she had.

A good question. It would be a sin. Yet—

'What I feel, is it just lust? Wantonness? If I could once lie with him, then afterwards would I be free of this longing? Would it cease to hurt so much?'

'There's only one way to be sure of that.'

Kate shivered, in a way that set her body alight.

Chapter Twenty Two

The summer browned into autumn, the nights grew colder, edging earlier into darkness. They gathered apples and nuts against the winter, salted meat, stored oatmeal and a small amount of barley. Sheep were brought down from the fell to the shelter of the riverside meadows. Sharp winds blew leaves to turn the tracks and roads to gold and bronze. A spell of fine weather prolonged the daylight just a little.

There was work enough to keep Toby occupied, though he seemed more restless than ever. He rode with Hal as often as he could, which was not as often as he'd have liked, with his friend busy preparing to return to Cambridge.

'My mother's making such a pother about it all,' Hal complained. 'God knows why! I've had a year there already. She knows I've lived to tell the tale.'

'That's mothers for you.'

'This is *my* mother we're talking about! If you're a horse, yes, she'll fret over you night and day, for the least little thing. But her own whelps, us, we've thrived with neglect. And now, she's fretting about this and that. The plague's the latest thing.'

Toby shivered. 'Is there plague in Cambridge?' It was a horrible way to die, from what he'd heard, pierced by a memory of Jane as they'd found her on the day of their return, laid low with a lesser sickness. The plague was even worse.

'Not as I know. It's easing in these parts too. It's bad in London though. They shut Parliament down and now it won't open again till November, so my father says, the second time it's been put off for the plague. Though why he should care, I don't know. He grumbles enough that Durham has no voice in Parliament. Gentlemen like him should have a voice, and so on and so on…Are you listening, Toby?'

'Oh—what? Yes, of course!' Though he'd been thinking that at least Sir Cuthbert had a voice in other ways, as his son would too, one day; while he had none, nor the prospect of one.

'Let's have a gallop.' So they did, for the last time.

The following day, Hal left for Cambridge.

Kate, desperate to rouse her son from his misery, found him in the hall, mid-morning.

'Toby, I'm about to look over the accounts before the All Hallows' rents are due. Come and look them over with me. It will be good training for you.'

'Training for what? I'm never going to have land of my own, am I?' He sat hunched by the fire, scowling into the flames. 'Anyway, it's weeks away, All Hallows.'

'A month, that's all. And one day you may find yourself with Holywell in your care. Meanwhile you can help me.'

Toby did not stir. Exasperated, Kate shook him. 'If you won't help me, then go and ride with Philip! He's been shut indoors too long, while you've been gadding about with

Hal.'

Philip, as moody as his brother, lay curled up with Trusty at the other side of the hearth, but at this he raised his head. 'Oh, I'd like to ride! Please, Toby!'

Toby gave in, though he led the way scowling and muttering under his breath, Philip and the dog at his heels. It was not going to be an enjoyable ride for the younger boy, Kate guessed, but what else could she do?

Jane, on her way to the kitchen, had come in on the tail end of the exchange. 'He's like a baited bear, poor lad. I'd send him off to your friend Richard if I were you.'

Kate blushed. 'Oh, I wish I could! But no, it will have to wait for Christmas. He's a busy man, with other calls on his time.'

'Aye, I reckon so.' Jane sighed. 'Well, this isn't getting the dinner made, and I don't trust Moll, with Alice laid up with her monthlies. I've given her a dose of—' Half way to the door, she came to a halt. 'It's got very dark all of a sudden. Must be a storm on the way. Who'd have thought it on such a bright morning?'

'It's a weird light.' They went to the window. The sky was clear of clouds, yet a yellow-grey half light turned the land to something strange and sinister. 'It's not a storm. It's like nothing I can recall.'

With a clatter of hooves the riders returned to the yard, dismounted, shut the horses in their stalls and ran into the house. The shivering dog slunk to the fireside, whimpering.

'Mother, the sun's gone, darkened over!' Toby's voice

was excited and awed at once.

Kate crossed herself. Beside her, Jane, steady, practical Jane, whispered, 'A portent. The heavens are out of sorts.'

Somehow, without any summons, the household gathered in the hall, murmuring their fears. There was never much natural light in this place, with its ancient slits for windows, its tapestry-hung walls, but now it grew ever darker, dark almost as night. Toby, on the floor near the hearth, held frightened Philip in his arms, while his brother stroked the head of the whining dog. Sarah and Molly, in tears, clutched one another. Alice, torn from her bed by a terror that obliterated her pain, pulled white-faced Cecily in to her side, huddling close to the other girls. John knelt near the door, head bent, eyes closed, with his arm round the trembling stable lad; Will was muttering over and over, 'What is it? What is it, Master John? What's to become of us?'

Kate, as frightened as any of them, her heart thudding, led them in a prayer from the night service of Compline, for all that it was nowhere near bedtime. *Visita, quaesumus, Domine, habitationem istam, et omnes insidias inimici ab ea longe repelle: Angeli tui sancti habitent in ea, qui nos in pace custodiant; et benedictio tua sit super nos semper.* Visit, we beseech thee, O Lord, this dwelling, and drive far from it the snares of the enemy; let thy holy angels dwell herein to preserve us in peace, and let thy blessing be always upon us.

Afterwards, her voice quavering, hesitant, she began to sing the evening hymn,

T*e lucis ante terminum,*

*Rerum Creator, poscimus…*Before the ending of the day, Creator of the world we pray…

One by one, other voices joined hers, a small sound swelling in defiance against the dark.

*Hostemque nostrum comprime…*Tread underfoot our deadly foe…

As she sang, she found herself wondering what Richard would say, that rational, easy-going man. Would he laugh at her fears, or was he also awed into prayer by this veiled sun? Would he, like her, wonder if this was some kind of judgement on them all, some warning of darker times to come?

Even hours later, when the light emerged, the sun shone again, Kate wished that someone could have teased her out of the sense of foreboding that hung over her, over them all. They had returned to their everyday tasks and concerns, but the air was heavy with a tremulous silence and Kate was still shaking, unsettled, anxious.

'It feels as though something bad lies in wait for us, something truly evil is about to happen. A warning.'

'I feel it too.' Jane took the tureen Kate held out to be taken back to the kitchen, most of its contents untouched, though the entire household had sat down to dinner and mutton stew was usually a popular dish. Kate could see that she was trying to assume her usual matter-of-fact manner. 'But there have been other times like this, and nothing worse came on us afterwards. Mind, those girls are good for nothing, sobbing at the least thing and paying no heed to what anyone says to them.' A pause, then she added, 'All will be well, madam. You'll see!'

By nightfall, the wind had risen, the sky clouded over and for days afterwards storms buffetted them, swelling the river, tearing branches from trees, toppling walls, mutilating roofs. It scarcely seemed to get light from dawn to dusk, though this was no eerie darkness without obvious cause, simply a disheartening obstacle to any outdoor activity.

Kate reflected gloomily that the All Hallows' rents would have to be offset by all the repairs needed around the estate, to farms and stock. It was going to be a hard winter.

Holding anxiety at bay, she told herself that in less than two months it would be Christmas, and they would all be on their way to Warthrop, for a feast lit by a celebration of the Mass—and the presence of Richard.

There was no Mass said for All Hallows, November the First, though they celebrated as best they could. The next day a message came from Newcastle, to say that Mariana was not thriving in her new home. She had lost her appetite (Mariana, who loved her food!), was at odds too often with other members of the household and had now become quite seriously unwell. *We think it better,* Mistress Lawson wrote, *that she return to your care, where in due time another place may be found for her, more suited to her fractious spirit.*

Kate showed the letter to Jane. 'Do you think she's pining for Philip?'

'Maybe. But if the place had suited her, I think she'd

have been happy enough. You said it was a rigorous household. I'd guess it's all been too much for Mariana. She needs something a bit more worldly, if you don't mind my saying.'

Kate might have minded, had she not recognised that Jane was quite right. She went in search of Toby, to send him to bring his sister home.

It was obvious enough that Mariana had not been eating properly for some time. She had lost all her girlish curves, and much of her rosy colour. But she returned to Holywell in high spirits, running into the house in an unseemly manner and hugging everyone in sight, her mother, Philip, Jane, even the dog.

'Where's Toby?' He'd had more than enough time to hand over the horses to John's care.

Mariana pulled a face. 'He's sick. He puked all over Mistress Lawson's workbox. She had to pretend to be concerned for him, but I could see she was very displeased. He's said not a word all the way here. I thought I'd never get him home.'

Kate moved to the door in search of her son, just as he came in. He stood leaning on the doorpost, his face drawn, ashen.

'Toby, my dear!' She put her arms about him. 'Are you able to walk upstairs?'

He slumped against her, which gave her answer enough.

'I'll send for John to help.'

'No—no, mother. Please!'

Jane's voice cut in: 'Come, Mistress Mariana, and you Philip. I think I saw Moll making comfits this morning. Let's go and find out if they're ready.'

As Jane led the children away, Toby groped for a stool and collapsed onto it, haunted eyes raised to his mother's face.

'Newcastle—a man, came to the house…It's all over, the news—'

Kate knelt beside him, took his hand in hers. 'Tell me now, Toby. What news is this?' She braced herself for his answer.

'In London—Parliament. The King and Queen, the royal family, Lords and Commons, every one, every single one—outside too, houses for miles, families, children.'

Head spinning, breath caught in her throat, Kate tried to grasp what he was saying. 'What's happened? Who—?'

He shook his head. 'They were discovered…' Words spilled from him in broken anguished phrases. 'Just at the very last moment, just one day before the King came to Parliament…Great barrels of gunpowder under the place, ready for the match. Enough to destroy the city for miles around, not just Parliament. If they hadn't, if they'd been too late, a few hours…' He shook his head as if trying to clear a terrible vision. 'They arrested one, someone I don't know, Guy Fawkes. They are seeking the rest. Catesby, Master Catesby—'

The man who could charm all he met, Toby's hero; and Nicholas's.

'Your uncle too?'

'I think so.'

Horror chilled her to the bone. Like Toby, she was trembling. One terrible thought: 'Did you know—?'

'Only what I told you. No more than that, I swear to God and Our Lady! If I'd known—this—oh, it's evil, beyond evil!'

But the little he knew might be enough to implicate him, even threaten his life.

His gaze held hers, his voice came in a whisper. 'Mother, I'm afraid!'

As she was, for Toby, for her brother, for all of them. A Catholic conspiracy, so very nearly brought to fruition, threatening to overturn the whole government of the country and destroy so many innocents in its wake: it was obvious enough what the repercussions would be, on all of their faith, even on those who had nothing to do with the plot, who lived peaceful lives in accordance with the law. But Toby, who was connected to the very heart of it, even if he knew nothing…Only he did know something, a little, she was certain of it. She had snatched him away from Ashby, brought him to Holywell, to safety. Was that enough to keep him clear of the taint of treason?

The news spread, so there was no way of keeping it from the household. The horror of it hung over the place, touching them all with fear. Even Jane seemed unable to find any words of comfort or reassurance. Toby avoided everyone, not even appearing at meal times, though he took scraps of food from the kitchen to eat in his room or carry with him on his solitary rides.

Mid-morning two days later Kate was in the garden gathering sage for the kitchen, her cloak pulled close about her against the rain and the chill wind, when she heard the sound of horses' hooves approaching along the drive; a whole company of horses..

She made her way to the yard, heart pounding. Who were they? Dangerous friends—or enemies? They wore some kind of livery, and most were armed. Not friends then, for sure.

The leading rider dismounted as she went to meet him. He removed his hat, but his expression was cold, grim. 'Madam, we seek Master Tobias Machyn.'

Just as she most feared! 'Who wants him?'

'We have a warrant from his honour Dean James of Durham. He is required to answer questions.'

Her thoughts raced. Where was Toby now? He'd passed her on the stairs an hour ago, mumbling something about going for a ride. Had he gone, or was he still about the house? Was there some way she could warn him?

Too late! At that moment Toby rounded the corner from the stable, halted for a moment, looked about to retreat, furtive, wary, guilt written all over him. If they'd had no idea what he looked like, they would know now for certain who he was.

A shout. Two men seized him, hit him as he struggled to break free. Kate saw his eyes meet hers, imploring help.

They had him bound, mounted on a spare horse, ready to move away. She ran to the leading horse, barring its path. 'What is this outrage? What possible business can the Dean of Durham have with my son?'

But she knew quite well of course, and they must know she knew.

'Good day, madam.' The rider replaced his hat, dug in his heels, urged his horse forward, so that Kate was almost knocked to the ground.

Helpless, she watched them ride away.

Chapter Twenty Three

Taking only the outdated papers that had protected her on her journey to Ashby, Kate rode through the rain to Durham, down the hill into the city, up again to the great Cathedral on its prominent peninsula in the river: the shrine of St Cuthbert, their greatest saint. Her grandmother used to tell her of the old days, when the place was full of light and colour, the shrine hung with jewels. Not that she herself had seen it, for no woman was ever permitted into the body of the Cathedral: St Cuthbert himself had decreed it so, the monks said. Women had to make do with the beautiful chapel at the west end, where the Venerable Bede lay buried. But there'd been colour enough there, in that place lit by many fine stained glass windows, the walls painted with episodes from the life of Christ, Bede's tomb hung with rich offerings. Then had come King Henry's break with the Church, followed by King Edward's rigorously Protestant reign.

And all gone, broken, burnt, trampled, destroyed. Kate had no wish to see the Cathedral in its desolation, and in any case her errand was with the Dean, housed now in the former Priory, part of the Cathedral precinct, the College, where once the layworkers of the monastery had lived and guests been welcomed.

The Dean's house seemed to grow from the Cathedral itself, a fine stone building with a sheltered garden. It felt very far from the bleakness of home.

She hammered on the great door, which was at last opened to her by a servant with coldly disdainful eyes.

'I would speak with his honour the Dean. It is urgent, most urgent!'

'So is all his honour's business at this time. He is at present much occupied and has no leisure to see any but the most necessary, on matters of state.'

She took a deep breath. 'This is a matter of state.'

He looked her over, as if trying to gauge the likelihood that this shabby gentlewoman, arriving unattended, could have anything of importance to offer. But he asked for her name, and some details of her errand—she told him only that she was the mother of Toby Machyn, at present in the Dean's custody—and left her.

She waited anxiously, looking about her at the room where she stood, this room that had once been part of the lodging of the prior of the great Benedictine monastery, where once her own forebears, a great aunt on her mother's side, had served the needs of the place. How much had it changed since then, or would that last prior (the Cathedral's first dean, so her grandmother had said) have found it just as he remembered it?

'Mistress, if you return this afternoon, early, his honour will see you then.'

The voice speaking just behind her made her jump. She turned, slowly taking in his words. 'May I wait here?'

'No, you must return.'

So she left, having remembered to thank him, for she

might need his help later. What now? She was too churned up, too anxious, to be hungry, though it was a long time since her early morning bread and small beer, snatched in the darkness before dawn.

She made her way through the chill of the cloisters, on into the Cathedral.

There was now no bar to the admission of women into this unadorned space. She had expected to be grief-stricken, appalled. But pausing at the back of the nave she was struck into immobility, her breath caught in her throat. It was so vast, so massive beyond imagining, the great round pillars marching off like giant forest trees into the dimness. Far off, she glimpsed the delicate tracery of a screen, where once the high altar had stood. Moving slowly forward, she saw that it had niches where there must once have been statues, now empty. And on the further side, the desecrated shrine of the great northern saint, now marked only by a plain marble slab set into the ground. Yes, it was a place of desecration, but not somehow desolation, not quite, not while the great pillars stood, and the beautiful marred screen, and echoes hung in the air of all the prayers that had been offered over the centuries, all the chanting of the dispersed monks.

She found a quiet corner and furtively pulling her rosary from under her gown slid the beads through her fingers, offering the ancient prayers as they had so often been offered in this place, mingling with the Latin words other prayers for her wayward, misguided son, urgent, anxious fervent prayers.

She wandered along the aisles, past side chapels where once other altars had stood and where there were sometimes still traces of the colour that had lit up the place, before so much whitewash had been daubed on its walls. She lingered in the Quire, watching the way the light moved over the ancient stones, restoring colour to them as the sun shone through what remained of the stained glass.

When she sensed that it was afternoon she made her way back to the Cathedral close and the gaunt door of the deanery.

There, she was admitted at last to the Dean's presence, in a whitewashed room that felt as if it might once have been a private chapel. He was writing at a long table, and for some time continued to write, ignoring her. Should she say something, try to attract his attention? But the servant had given her name when he admitted her. The Dean must know she was there.

Then: 'Well, madam?'

A long nose, a dark auburn beard, a frowning face: she was not encouraged. But Toby's fate depended on this meeting, so she drew a deep breath, looked him directly in the eye.

'Your honour, I come to plead for the release of my son, Toby Machyn.'

'Indeed.' It was all she could do not to falter at the sharpness of his gaze. 'It is only by God's divine providence that we have been spared a most deadly blow against this kingdom and all who live in it. Those who conceived this treasonous plot must be brought to justice with all speed. You can have no quarrel with that.'

'My son had nothing to do with it, your honour.' Was that the right way to address a Dean? She had no idea.

'Is that so? Then what was he doing at Ashby Saint Ledgers? You do not deny he was resident in the establishment of Robert Catesby for more than a year?'

'But not lately. I brought him home with me some months gone.'

'Indeed, so I understand.' How did he know all this? Someone must have informed him, someone who had been watching, even a neighbour whom she'd thought a friend. Or someone from her own household?

'What reason did you have to bring him back to Holywell?'

'He was sick, sir.' If Toby had been questioned like this, what reason had he given for leaving? She wished she knew.

'Indeed.' She felt her heart thud faster than ever, so that she could scarcely breathe. Had she made things worse? 'You do not answer my question: why was he sent to Ashby? What was the reason for his going there?'

'I am a widow, your honour, of small means and poor estate.'

'And an obstinate Papist!''

She raised her eyes, met his gaze, fearlessly (she hoped). 'Yes, sir, but a loyal subject of his majesty King James, a true English woman.'

'Unless the Pope decrees otherwise!'

'I had not heard that His Holiness gave his blessing to this enterprise. Nor would he have done.'

'And if he had?'

She had not considered that question, dared not even think of it; or not yet. There was only one possible answer she could give. 'It would have been wrong in any circumstances, your honour.'

'Hmm. Then why Ashby?'

'Because my brother offered to take him there. I trusted my brother.'

'Your brother Nicholas Machyn? Do you deny he had a part in this horrid treason?'

That was a terrible thought. Oh if only she could be sure he was as little involved as Toby! But then she could not even be entirely sure about Toby.

'I do not know. We are estranged of late. If he had a part, I did not know of it. I had not realised how much he had changed. We had not met for many years, but I trusted him. As God is my witness, I wish I had not.'

'Tell us where he is now, and I will believe in your loyalty.'

So Nicholas was still alive, and free! She struggled to hide her relief from those watchful eyes. 'I—I do not know. I have heard nothing.'

'How can I trust the word of a Papist? Your Pope decreed that it was the duty of any Papist to destroy our late Queen Elizabeth. The Jesuit faction make no secret of their wish to overturn the state. Is that not still the wish of all your kind, to destroy those they miscall heretics?' He stood in silence, glaring at her. She hated his eyes, the way they seemed to bore into her, seeking out treacherous thoughts, accusing. 'You say you took your son home because he was sick. Is that indeed all it was? Or was it rather that you had word of what was afoot and sought to shield him from the consequences? In the which case your duty was to send word of what you knew to those in authority.'

She held her breath, praying that her face gave no sign that he'd hit on any shadow of the truth. 'I have told you how it was, your honour.' Silence, as his eyes still fixed on her, as if reading her thoughts. 'I beg of you, your honour, please let him go, so that he may prove himself a loyal subject of his majesty! I will vouch for him.'

'Do you expect me to trust the word of a papist? No, madam, that is too much to ask.' He shuffled the papers before him, as if anxious to return to work on them. 'Besides, it is no longer in my power to release him, even if I would. He was this morning despatched to London.'

A cold hand clutched her heart. She felt the colour come and go in her face, the room spin about her. She reached out to grasp the back of a carved chair, to steady herself while she drew a deep breath. She would not give him the satisfaction of seeing how very afraid she was.

'Go home, madam, and consider where your superstitious faith has led you, into what evil paths.

Consider, pray, and change your ways, before it is too late. As for your son, that is now a matter for my lord Salisbury.'

There was nothing then to be done but to make her way home; though she went first into the cathedral and paused beside the ruined shrine. 'Blessed Saint Cuthbert, help us!'

Shivering, distraught, she made her way down the hill to the inn where she'd left her horse. Part way there some instinct made her look round—to see a man following her a little way behind. There was something purposeful about his stride, as if it was not chance that brought him there, but a deliberate purpose.

A moment more, and then with a shock she realised she knew him: Henry Stobbs.

Catching her eye, he turned aside into a nearby doorway, but not before she'd glimpsed a knowing leer. She walked on with shaking limbs, looking back once at the now-empty street. So that was how the Dean knew so much!

And where did Henry Stobbs get his information, now he was no longer her tenant? From his daughter Cecily? That was an unbearable thought.

She reached home at dusk, exhausted, drenched, cold, and utterly miserable. Hope had abandoned her. She fell into Jane's arms, weeping out her fear and desolation.

In her head the thoughts circled, battering her brain: *He's been sent to London...I must go and find him, beg them to let him go…*

But what could she do or say, what power had she to change the hearts of a King who had almost lost his life, of the men who protected him? *I rescued Toby from danger, as I thought, but that was all. I knew something was wrong, but I did not seek to warn anyone in authority. They will use that against him, against us all, just as the Dean did.*

Yet to go to London offered the one single shred of hope; at the very least she might be able to see Toby, to comfort him. For that, she would need new papers, ones whose authority no one could question.

First thing next day, following a sleepless night, she took the well-trodden path to Sir Cuthbert's house, asking to see him. Shown to the parlour, she heard steps approaching, looking up in disappointment as Dame Juliana entered the room.

'I was expecting—I have to see Sir Cuthbert. It's of the first importance.'

'He's not at home. He left yesterday.' He too, gone beyond her reach!

Her heart thudded, faltered, her breath stopped in her throat. 'When will he return?'

'He'll return when he returns.'

For the first time, something in the other woman's voice caught Kate's attention: a sliver of ice, repelling her, quite unlike Dame Juliana's usual friendliness. She had always been brusque in manner, not wasting words, yet with a warm cheerfulness that allowed one to forgive the lack of polish. This morning, that warmth had gone. She had not even offered her neighbour any refreshment.

Kate fumbled for a chair and sat down, uninvited. Dame Juliana simply stood gazing at her, saying nothing.

'You have no idea when—?'

'Did you not hear me? He has business of some kind, I know not what.'

Kate knew then: her errand was hopeless. How could she go to London without papers? And who but Sir Cuthbert would give them to her? The other magistrates near at hand would be certain to refuse such a request from so notorious a Papist, especially at this time. At best she would meet with refusal, at worst with suspicion, questioning, even imprisonment. That would not help Toby at all.

She rose to her feet. 'I will leave you then.' At the door she paused. 'Please, I beg you, send me word when Sir Cuthbert returns!'

Dame Juliana seemed to relent a little. 'I heard your boy is in trouble. If he had aught to do with this—well, he merits whatever falls on him. If not, then God give you both a good outcome.'

On the way home, she saw a group of women gathered on a corner by the rectory wall, one of them, she thought, Henry Stobbs' down-trodden wife. They fell silent as she passed, watching her. One of them spat on the ground. 'Popish bitch!'

They laughed at this suddenly permissible breach of

due deference. For the first time in her years at Holywell Kate felt alien, outcast, hemmed in by enemies.

Back at the house, she summoned Cecily to the parlour, and there sat while the girl stood facing her, full in the light from the window. She looked anxious, fearful of a rebuke perhaps. Or afraid she'd been found out?

'Cecily, I have some questions for you. I wish you to answer me in all honesty.' She studied the girl's troubled face. 'Tell me, your father now lives in Durham from what I hear. He must have some employment there. Do you know what it is?'

'I don't know for sure. There's a Master Fowler he spoke of, a lawyer I think.'

William Fowler, her husband's steward at Holywell, her ancient enemy. Had Henry Stobbs always been his ally, even when he was her tenant? It would explain a great deal.

'I see. And has your father made any move to see you of late?'

Cecily shook her head; her gaze did not falter. 'No, madam.' She shuddered. 'Thank God!' A pause, before she said slowly, 'Mam told me he'd called on her, a few times.'

'For what purpose?' Was that a foolish question? Might a man not visit his wife simply from affection? Not that Henry Stobbs had ever appeared to show any affection towards his wife.

'I don't know for sure. Mam doesn't want him calling. She's best off without him. Last time, he beat her.' Then:

'Sunday, she sent word not to visit. Not while I'm living here. She wants me to leave this place.'

Because of the taint Kate's own brother had brought upon them, through Toby; that was obvious. 'Do you wish to leave?'

Cecily shook her head vehemently. 'On no, madam! Never!' Her eyes brimmed with tears, her voice roughened. 'It's my home. I was only a burden to Mam. Please, don't send me away!'

Kate reassured her, saw how relieved she seemed to be. She looked and sounded utterly sincere, but how could one be trustful of anyone these days?

Toby had lost all sense of time. He knew when it was day because then the high barred window let in a furtive light, enough to illuminate the dank stones of the walls, the thin blanket that formed his inadequate bed, the heavy door that shut him in. Then he could just make out the marks left in the stone by other prisoners: initials, a roughly scoured crucifix; *Domine, salvum me—Lord, save me!*

When night came the darkness was complete, interminable. Then that scrawled Latin phrase turned over and over in his head, became his prayer. What had been the fate of the captive who had scratched those words in the walls of his cell, painful stroke by painful stroke? Had the Lord heard his cry? Or were they the last words that escaped his lips on the scaffold?

At first, locked in this place at the end of the long

terrifying journey from Durham, he'd curled up in a corner, shivering, nauseous, haunted by the memory of Dean James' parting words to him: 'They'll get the truth out of you, be sure they will!'

He had no doubt at all what that meant. Enveloped by terror, he could think of nothing else, unable even to take in his surroundings, or search his mind for something, anything, to turn his thoughts away from listening for the steps on the stair of the men who would take him for 'questioning'. Dean James had been harsh enough, the soldiers of his escort brutal, handling him as no one ever had in his life before, as if venting on him all their fear and anger at what his erstwhile associates had planned; but what awaited him now—no, he must not think of it!

At the end of the first night, he'd heard steps approaching the door, heavy with menace. He'd forced hinself to his feet. He must face his fate with courage, showing no fear. *God help me! God help me!*

A key turned, bolts were thrust back, the door opened.

A hand thrust a bowl towards him. Shaking so much he spilled some of its contents, he'd taken it, as the door was slammed shut, barred again; the steps receded.

A thin ill-smelling broth. He retched. His stomach was in any case churning too much for hunger. He put the bowl down in a corner (well away from the one where he'd relieved himself an hour before) and resumed his crouching against the wall.

This happened each day without fail, this moment

when his gaoler brought the unappetising broth.

He wished he'd found some way of marking the passing of the days. Had it been days, or weeks, or the long months it felt like, when the steps on the stairs were different, not the single heavy tread of his gaoler, but many steps, clattering in his head long before the door was thrust open? Hands grabbed him, manhandled him down the stairs into the cold air.

A barge this time, along the river to what he knew from its vast impenetrable walls must be the Tower of London. His terrified brain registered only fleeting impressions: steep stairs, long passages, more stairs, a room with three men at a table, three pairs of cruel searching eyes—and sounds, horrible sounds that punctuated all of the seemingly endless interrogation: moans, screams, anguished prayers. Somewhere nearby, the torturers were at work, their victims likely men he knew. His skin crawled, he felt sick, he could not think.

All he knew was that he must try to clear his head enough not to be trapped into betrayal. 'I do not know.' 'I knew nothing of this.' Repeated over and over. For the most part it was the truth.

'Where is your uncle?' (so they had not got him, he was still free!) 'I do not know.' They must have heard how his voice shook.

He wished he knew what they already knew, what tale the other prisoners had told. One thing shocked him: 'You have a brother, an honest gentleman. You called on him.

We know what was said.'

So Tom had betrayed him! No, worse than that, he, Toby, had betrayed his fellows by speaking of things he should have kept hidden, things his uncle had warned him not to speak of. He tried to recall what had been said at that meeting, but it seemed lost in a past beyond recovery.

At the end of what felt like hours, days, they let him go, with the parting words, 'We have other means of getting honest answers from you.'

Since then, he daily expected them to come for him again. Sometimes, with disgust, he found himself weeping from fear. A snivelling coward, that was what he was. Fear was almost as bad as a real hurt, the naked terror at what he might face, which he'd confronted with the shameful realisation that he was unlikely to have the fortitude to endure without telling tales. The only slight consolation was that he had very little to tell that was not guesswork or hearsay. But that might be enough to harm one of those he loved. He forced himself to earnest prayer, not to betray them, to confront his fate with courage.

Whatever they'd done, or wished to do, those men had been his companions, had trusted him. Sometimes he hated Robert Catesby, enraged at what he'd brought on him. The next moment his mind would be full of memories of the man's smile, his voice, those eyes that read his soul and seemed to love it. What was become of him now? Was he in the hands of the torturers? And those others, his uncle among them?

Yet they'd done wrong, planned what he could never have approved. Why should he suffer for them?

Because for all their faults they were of his faith.

If they had succeeded, what then? Would he have felt otherwise? The question niggled in his mind, unsettling him.

Where did the truth lie, what was the right way? What awaited these men in the life to come—Hell? Or the Paradise they longed for? And for him?

Once, slipping briefly into sleep, he dreamed he was staring into a pit of fire, trembling on the brink of falling headlong into it. The Hell that awaited him, for betrayal? For calling evil good? He feared torture in this life; he feared Hell in the next. The one would be horrible, unbearable, but it would end, somehow. The other would be eternal endless torment. And he did not know how to escape it.

Oh why could he not order his thoughts, calm himself, offer his fate to God, to hold it in His hands, for good or ill? Instead, he spent each day waiting, waiting; hearing the steps, screwing up his courage, swept with relief when it was the familar gaoler with the unappetising bowl. Some days, better days, he was hungry enough to take a few sips of the disgusting broth. Mostly his stomach turned to water at the very thought.

Light-headed, he found his head thronged with weird images, monsters, moments of relief swinging over to horrors that set him shivering. He wanted it all to end somehow, but feared how it would.

Steps again: the bowl. But in it, a crust of bread—and meat! Disbelieving, he tore at it with his teeth, forcing himself to chew slowly. Ingrained in him from that long ago flight from Haroby was the thought that the starving should eat slowly, cautiously. But it was good meat, roast beef, and bread fresh from the oven.

Why though, why this now?

Then he knew! Chill fingers shivered down his spine; he pushed the last of the food aside.

They wanted him strong enough, clear enough in mind to withstand the torture while he told them everything they needed to know.

It was the very next day, towards evening, that he heard the steps again, not those of the warder with the food, but many steps, the heavy military tread he awaited with dread.

Chapter Twenty Four

'You must go to London, mother! You must! It's cowardice to slouch around here while Toby, while he—' Mariana broke off, shaking her head, lip trembling.

Jane put an arm about her, her tone gentler than her words. 'That's no way to speak to your mother. And she's right not to travel without papers, in these times. It would be madness. She'd be locked up herself before she ever got anywhere near London, and what good would that do?'

Mariana drew back from the shelter of Jane's arms. 'Then I'll go! They'll not lock up a child, will they?'

'Oh Mariana!' Kate felt tears spring to her eyes. 'You're generous and loving, but you don't understand the dangers. And how would you know the way? How would you get help if all went awry? It would take an age too.'

Yet she was every bit as enraged with her own inaction as was Mariana. Two long weeks had dragged by since Toby had been taken from them, two weeks of sleepless nights and days passed in a haze of exhaustion and fear. She was haunted by visions of Toby, cold, hungry, afraid, worst of all, undergoing torture: her dear son, the child she'd loved and nurtured, suffering unspeakable agonies. Her stomach churned endlessly, so she could not eat.

Each day, Mariana had come down to the hall for morning prayers to ask, as she had again today, if there was any news of Toby, any hope. Yet Kate was still here, waiting helplessly to hear that Sir Cuthbert had returned.

Mariana did not know that she'd once set out for Bishop Auckland to try and find another magistrate who would authorise her journey to London. Braving insults hurled at her by a group of Meadhope villagers on their way to market (she'd only with difficulty prevented John from turning aside to scold them) she'd reached the town; to be confronted by soldiers who, finding she had no papers, ordered her home, repelling her pleas for help, threatening her with arrest.

She'd thought of appealing to Richard, but had no idea how he felt about what had happened. What if the news had turned him against her, knowing as he did that Toby was somehow involved in it all? Besides, tainted as she was by this connection, any contact between them might hurt him too.

So she'd waited, and hated herself for doing nothing, for not simply mounting her horse and riding south, alone, just as she was, braving all dangers.

'I'll call at the Hall again today,' she said. 'Just in case Sir Cuthbert's home and they've forgtten to send word. And if he's not there, I'll think of something else, I promise.' She took Mariana's tear-stained face in her hands and kissed it. 'Will that content you, my pet?'

Mariana shrugged, saying nothing.

Dame Juliana was in the stable yard, mounted and ready for a morning ride, and clearly impatient at the interruption. 'He's not here, and I know not when he will be.' Then, grudgingly: 'I will send word as soon as I have news.'

On the way home Kate met the rector, seized a momentary hope: perhaps he knew what had taken Sir Cuthbert away and when he might return?

'He said nothing to me, madam. I'm sorry. That in itself is unusual. I wonder if he had some secret errand, on affairs of state. In view of the late troubles...'

She shivered. Had he been summoned by the authorities to try and further implicate her son? And what might he say, that could bring greater danger on him? She could not bear to think of what the consequences might be.

'You know I pray for you, for you all.'

She made a grimace. 'That we will be converted to your faith?'

'That you will be kept safe and your child brought home.' His words were quietly spoken, but she heard them as an accusation.

'I'm sorry. I know...'

'You are in torment. I understand.'

'What they might do to him, what they have already done. I can't bear—'

'Try not to think of it. Keep hope alive. And pray.'

Words, words...they could not bring Toby back to her.

More days dragged by, another week, into the first days of December. More rain, darkness, cold.

Then an afternoon worse than most, when nothing

went right. Mixtures spilled in the stillroom, crocks broken, the fire sluggish and smoky with wet wood, Molly struck down with a fever and rash, which might be smallpox, though proved, Thank God! not to be. Kate's head ached from the moment she rose from her bed until dusk.

As darkness fell, she heard horses outside, in the yard.

No! No! Let it not be soldiers!

It was Sir Cuthbert who stepped into the hall, shaking his drenched hat, so that the light caught drops falling like scattered jewels to make dark spots on the stone flags of the floor. Behind him came a small group of men, lost in the shadow beyond the screen. Her eyes flew to his face, his smile; saw his head turn, followed his gaze.

'Toby!'

Her son ran from the shadow into her arms, clung to her. She held him, enfolded him for a long long time, as if she wanted never to be parted from him ever again.

When at last she drew back, full of questions, she looked from Toby—thinner, drawn, looking older than when she saw him last, so short a time ago; so *long* a time—then to Sir Cuthbert, his ruddy smiling face. 'Sir?'

She saw it now: the sudden absence, so hastily made, no reason given, no word to anyone, as if there was a great secret concealed: 'You were in London?'

'He spoke for me, mother. Made them see I meant no harm. I did no harm.'

'With the help of your son Thomas.'

'Tom was in London! You saw him?' She looked

questioningly at Toby, who shook his head. It was Sir Cuthbert who replied.

'He would have stayed longer, but he was summoned home. He was in London to answer questions, concerning young Toby. What he said was of help to me, when I spoke up for the lad.'

Without releasing her hold on Toby, Kate reached out to grasp Sir Cuthbert's hand. 'There are no words, sir, none warm enough, nor full enough of gratitude.'

'I couldn't see a neighbours's child destroyed for no good reason. There have been too many deaths, and ruin, and more to come I fear. I could not see them added to. But it was as well your other son was there. Without him, I might have failed.' With his free hand he pulled a package from under his cloak. 'He asked me to convey this to you.'

Her head spinning, Kate made no attempt to open the letter. She gazed at Sir Cuthbert, trying to take it all in, trying to admit the joy that was starting to burst within her.

Instead, the practical housewife reasserted itself. 'Forgive me. You are drenched and cold, and hungry too I'll be bound. Come to the fire. I'll have them bring food and drink. Toby, go and put on dry clothes and come down to eat.'

Sir Cuthbert gave a little bow. 'I thank you, but I must be on my way home. I'll take no harm to be wet a little longer. And I think you'll have things enough to say to your returned wanderer. We can talk again, you and I, another time. For now, I'll bid you good night.' He bent and kissed her cheek, before turning away, followed by his small retinue.

Once he'd ridden out of sight, she broke the seal and opened the letter.

Madam my Mother,

I write to inform you that my dear guardian and cousin, Master Roger Machyn, departed this life on Michaelmas Day last, after a long illness, at peace with God and Man.

I am thankful that I have lately been able to be of assistance to my brother Tobias, and would if it is in my power be of further service to him. I am minded to welcome him into my household, where with God's help I may hope to cure him of all traces of the infection that has lately afflicted him. I am this day summoned home where my wife is fearful of miscarrying, but when time allows I will write further to you on this matter.

With all deepest respect, dear mother,

Your loving son, Thomas.

So much to take in! But here was Toby returning to her side, dressed in dry clothes and looking thinner, more drawn than ever. She folded the letter and tucked it into her sleeve. Had he seen? She thought not. He seemed dazed, bewildered, as if he still had not quite grasped that he was home, and safe.

She took his hand in hers, feeling how cold it was. 'Let's go and eat. And then to prayers, for we have much to thank God for.'

Between them, she and Jane kept the younger children from displaying too much excitement at their brother's return, though Mariana was clearly longing to bombard Toby with questions.

'But I want to know what happened. What's wrong with that?'

'He's very tired and needs to rest. Be patient. There will be a better time for talk, tomorrow perhaps. Now, it's time for quiet thankfulness.'

It was not until they were all in bed that Kate was able to show Tom's letter to Jane.

'Have you told Toby of this?'

She shook her head. 'There's been no time. I need to consider it.'

'And your thoughts, so far?'

'I don't know. What do you think?'

'He seems to like his brother. It might be a good thing. The right thing.'

Kate scanned the letter again. 'He hopes to cure him of 'infection'. What does he mean by that?'

'The influence of your brother, and this Master Catesby who had such a hold on him? Isn't that clear enough?'

'So I thought, at first. But what if he means our faith, Holy Church?'

'He speaks of the infection as having afflicted him 'lately'. That does not sound to me as if he speaks of Holy Church.'

'Perhaps. Oh, Jane, I hardly know who to trust these days, who are true friends—beside you, as always! Those who seem most holy have betrayed Toby, and me. It is the heretics who have saved him. In a worldly sense at least. But what if that's a snare of the Evil One?'

'Dear madam, you're weary beyond words. You cannot hope to think clearly just yet. Leave it a while, let things get back to normal. Best of all, wait until Master Tom writes to you again, as he says he will. Then you'll be better able to judge what's best.'

It was good advice, but for all her relief and thankfulness that Toby was safe, she knew that nothing could ever be as once it was. Their secure and comfortable world had gone for ever, and they none of them could be sure what lay ahead, Toby least of all. In this short time he too had been changed, by experiences his mother could only guess at.

He had a haunted look, but he told her little about what had happened in Durham and in London, though it was a huge relief to know that he'd not been tortured. Yet in his mind he was clearly in torment. He did not say so, but it was obvious he was not sleeping well. He came dutifully to prayers, morning and evening, was punctual for meals and hardly left the house, though now and then went for solitary rides—or she supposed them to be solitary, since no one ever reported seeing him in company. She guessed he rarely left the bounds of the Holywell lands. Just as well perhaps, for there was still hostility out there towards anyone connected to the late conspiracy, though the insults, spitting, hurling of eggs and stones had lessened since Sir

Cuthbert returned.

Her heart ached for Toby, longed for the lively mischievous boy who seemed lost for ever. Once, he said to her, 'My uncle. Have you heard?'

'I have heard nothing, nothing at all. Was he not taken with the others?' She yearned to know herself, though the very thought filled her with dread.

'I don't know.' Then he added in a undertone: 'Robert Catesby is dead.'

She could see the anguish in his eyes. 'In London?'

He shook his head. 'They're not brought to trial yet, the others...He died trying to resist, somewhere in Worcestershire.'

The next time she saw Sir Cuthbert, Kate asked her neighbour if he had any news of her brother.

'I hadn't heard he was taken with the rest,' she was told. 'I think they're still seeking him.'

Perhaps, she thought, he was already overseas, overlooked as a mere minor player in the horrible drama, if that was what he had been. She hoped it was so, but at the same time was filled with anger whenever she thought of him. He had got himself involved in a dreadful thing and entangled her son, entrusted to him, in his conspiracy. For that, she thought she could never bring herself to forgive him. But she would have liked to be able to tell him so, to hear his contrition—for surely he must now regret the part he'd played?

A week after Toby's return, she came on her son in the

orchard, standing beneath the apple trees and staring into the distance, as if lost in some grim thoughts of his own. 'Tell me truly, how much did you know of all this?'

It was a moment or two before he swung round, as if her words had taken some time to reach him. 'What I told you. That there was a plot afoot. I guessed some things. But no one told me, not outright. Just what I told you before.'

'Do you wish the plot had succeeded?' She held her breath, waiting for his reply.

'Oh now, mother, how could I think that? It was wrong, wicked.' He turned anguished eyes upon her. 'What would have become of my friends, of our neighbours?'

'Then you don't think the great end would justify any means to achieve it?'

'You don't think that, surely?'

'No, I don't. I too think they were wrong, whatever their motives. I thank God it did not succeed. But oh I know that we shall all suffer because of it! Even those of us who are loyal subjects of our King, who would never stoop to treason. The conspirators will pay with their lives, certainly, but many who had not a treasonous thought in their heads as well.'

'I know.' He sank down on a nearby bench, and she sat beside him, though it was cold and wet. 'I can't bear that, the thought—It's been hard enough, it was hard enough in the past.'

'We shall need courage, Toby, and strength to endure.'

He had his head bent now, so she could not see his face.

At last he said softly, 'I wish I knew. I want; I don't know...'

She laid her hand over his. 'We can only be faithful, and prayerful. It's the only way.'

'Is it?'

'What other way is there?'

'I really thought, when I first came to Ashby, it seemed —well, like a little paradise. I felt that I had come home, that I'd found the place for me. That I could serve the true faith with all my heart and fear nothing. And now I find that at the very heart it was poisoned. That it was all built on a lie. I don't know where I am now. It all seems so hard, so pointless.'

'It will get better, and come clearer. In time. Give it time, Toby. Be patient.'

He stood up, began to wander restlessly about the garden while she kept up with him. 'If being true to your faith means doing such terrible things, then is it better not to be true?'

'They were not true. They did wrong.'

'But they were the most holy people, full of prayer and devotion. There were priests too.'

She felt a sense of shock. Could there really have been priests involved? She struggled with her thoughts, wondering what to say for the best. 'With the conspirators? In the plot?'

'I don't know for sure. But they must have heard confessions. So they would know.'

'Even if they did, they could not break the seal of the

confessional. Perhaps the conspirators, knowing what they planned was sinful, were ashamed to confess it.'

'They didn't think it was wrong. I know they didn't… You always said the worst sin was to call evil good or good evil. They did that.'

She slipped an arm about his hunched shoulders. 'Oh Toby, I don't know. I don't know what to say for the best, or what to think.'

'But if you can't trust your own uncle, people you look up to, always looked up to…'

'I know.' She sighed. 'We're going to have to be brave, and strong. It's going to be very bad for a long time.'

He turned troubled eyes on her. 'I'm not sure. I don't think…' He shrugged. 'We shall see.'

She felt as if a hard lump had developed inside her, a cold sense of dread and helplessness. A little later Toby saddled up his horse and went for a ride.

In riding, Toby always used to be able to drive out the worst of the thoughts that haunted him, but these days it was not so easy. There were so many conflicting emotions, things he could not speak of to anyone. There was guilt, because his release had been secured on the strength of his conversation with his brother Tom. Sir Cuthbert, by some chance meeting with Tom in London, had learned of that encounter at Haroby, and had then been able to paint it as a deliberate act on Toby's part, a way of alerting the authorities to what was planned, albeit in a circuitous manner. Sir Cuthbert's cheerful assumption that this would please Toby did not help at all. He'd already felt guilty about what he'd feared could be seen as a betrayal. Now it looked all the more certainly to be such, and something that had worked to his advantage. He was hugely relieved to be free, but full of shame at the manner of his release.

At other times he found himself consumed by a furious anger at what his uncle had led him into. Nicholas must have known, even as they rode away from Holywell, what he was going towards; must have had some inkling as to what was being hatched in that pious nest.

He thought perhaps he'd begun to hate not just his uncle, but all that he stood for; all that Ashby and Holywell stood for. Yet the very thought shocked him.

Since coming home, he'd tried to be attentive to prayer, hoping to regain some of that sense of a holy presence that had so uplifted him at Ashby, in the early days. He would think of Humphrey, who had seemed to embody all that was good and true, if anyone did. And then memories of Robert Catesby would intrude, tearing him in pieces, reminding him that what had seemed good, what had moved him most to love and reverence, was tainted at its very heart. There would always be an odd detached part of his mind looking on, mocking, deriding, passing judgement on what once had been sacred. He knew he was close to rejecting all of it.

Then there had been those days on the way back from London, when Sir Cuthbert, who had saved his life, engaged him in solemn talk, the memory of which disturbed him even further.

On his way home a few hours later he found himself passing the church just as Master Langley emerged from it. He doffed his hat, as did his old tutor. 'I am glad to see you safe home, my boy.'

'Thank you, sir.'

'We live in troubled times.'

'Yes. They'll get worse too I think, for us at Holywell.'

'Have you news of your uncle?'

'No, nor do I care.'

'He did wrong, certainly.' The rector sighed. 'But he is still a child of God, however utterly led astray, however greatly he has erred.'

Toby stared at him. 'You can't surely think he deserves your pity?'

'His fate in this life is unlikely to be anything but horrible. And in the next—well, that's in God's hands. But...'

'Yes.'

'Such waywardness. Such misguidedness. How could he be so blind? How could any of them be so? It is a weight on the heart.'

That was certainly true. 'Yes.'

'Will you take a glass of something with me, my boy?'

He hesitated, recalled that there was nothing in particular awaiting his attention at home, and went into the rectory.

The following Sunday, Toby came late home for dinner. He took his place, hurried, flustered, with an apology but no excuse.

Afterwards, as he was about to leave the room, Kate caught his arm. 'Where were you, Toby?'

'Do I have to account to you for my every moment?'

'No, but you were absent from prayers. And do I not have reason to be concerned, after all that has happened?'

He said nothing, simply gazed mutely at her, with an expression she could not read. Then he turned and walked away.

In the days that followed there were no unexplained absences, no signs of furtive behaviour; but the next Sunday it happened again, exactly as before. This time she would not allow him to evade her questioning. 'Toby, I must know where you've been!'

'You won't like it.'

'Try me!'

'Very well. I've been to church, to the parish church.'

It was as if she'd been struck to the heart.

'I said you'd not like it.'

'But why, Toby? Why?'

'That's easy: I'm taking no chances. I want everyone to see I'm a law-abiding subject of the King. I don't ever want to go through all that again.'

'So you'll take chances instead with your immortal soul?'

'Oh, I don't know mother. I just don't know any more.'

'What don't you know?'

'What is the truth. Master Langley is a good man, I think.'

And so she thought too, in his way, as far as any heretic could be. It was not enough.

So this son she had kept safe, as she thought, kept near her, protected and cherished, had gone the way of his brother with less cause. And yet: some small voice deep inside her acknowledged the wisdom of it, was even glad that he was taking these steps to safety. What mother wanted a martyr for a son, if there was a choice, for all she must know that was the better way? Yet he was placing himself in deeper peril, eternal peril.

What could she say? Only one thing, after a long pause: 'I will pray for you, Toby.'

She had surprised him, that was clear. 'I thought you already did.'

'So I do, every day. But I will pray the more, for the health of your eternal soul.'

He swung round then, grasped her arms, gently enough, but firmly too. 'Tell me, mother, do you truly believe that men like Master Langley, or Sir Cuthbert—do you truly, wholeheartedly, believe that they will be condemned to eternal torment, without hope?'

That question she had so often asked herself, and never yet been able to answer to her satisfaction—though Richard had given her an answer, once.

'That's in God's hands, not mine,' she said. 'But there is one difference with them. They are not apostates, casting off the true faith in which they were raised.'

'Sir Cuthbert did.'

She'd forgotten that.

'Then there's Tom. You would like him, mother. He's grown into a fine man, from what I saw of him.'

And one she had every reason to be grateful to. She shivered still at the thought of what would have been Toby's fate without his brother's intervention, aided by Sir Cuthbert. 'Except in that one thing. He could have kept true and been a finer man by far.'

'But then I'd be held in London now, facing a traitor's death. Or dead already. But I'm alive, and I owe my life to a heretic, an apostate.' He raised her hand then and kissed it. 'My most dear mother! Don't grieve for me. I must follow my conscience.'

'Is it your conscience or your self-interest?'

'Some of each I think. I don't know. If I find it's all self-interest then I promise you I'll turn my back on it. But I need time.'

'Then please God you have time!'

The following Sunday he came home from church to find the yard full of horses, watched by a handful of men; one of whom he recognised. Inside the house, all was in disarray. In the hall, his mother sat white-faced, tense, by the fire, Jane with her, trying to calm the terrified servants, while soldiers tramped all over the house, emptying coffers onto the floor, thrusting swords through already threadbare hangings, examining cooking pots and barrels, overturning churns in the dairy, casks in the brewhouse.

'What's going on?'

'What does it look like?' His mother sounded weary beyond words. 'They're looking for your uncle. It seems someone claimed they'd seen him near Bishop Auckland.'

'You've not seen him?'

'No, of course not. I hope to goodness he comes nowhere near us.' Her voice was tense with anger. 'They're the Dean's men.'

He felt sick. 'I thought they looked familiar. You know that Henry Stobbs is with them?'

'I didn't, no.' She shivered. Cecily, crouched nearby, gave a little cry.

'I saw him out there. Smirking, the bastard!' Toby's face was grim. 'But they'll find nothing, will they?'

'Just leave us with hours of work, putting things to rights. How could my own brother do this to us?'

On a sudden impulse Toby put his arms round her. 'I'm sorry, mother, so sorry. It's all my fault.'

'No, my dear. I was as misled as you. It was I who sent you away with him. I thought—Oh, Toby!'

Chapter Twenty Five

The wind howled about the house, rattling the windows. Hangings shook and trembled, strange whines and whistles caught Kate's ear as she passed through the rooms. She hoped everything had been well fastened down outside; the stable door that wouldn't stay closed, the hay in the byre… Of course they would be! She could trust John to see to them.

She felt unsettled, weary yet not sleepy, lacking the blessed tiredness that comes from work complete, the end of a satisfying day. When would her days cease to be eaten away with anxiety? When would she know peace again?

The doors were safely barred; she'd checked them, back and front. Fires in hall and kitchen were damped down for the night, the peats barely glowing. Toby and the children had gone to bed as soon as evening prayers were over, the servants too, and even Jane had gone upstairs. 'You look tired,' Kate had said. 'Go to bed. I'll be up soon.'

'You're tired yourself.'

'If I go later to bed, perhaps I'll sleep for once.'

Jane stroked her arm, but said no more.

Alone by the fire but for the slumbering dog, Kate tried to calm herself, but the tumult of the storm seemed to find its echo in her mind and body. She felt restless, miserable. All these years she'd tried to nurture and protect her children, to keep them safe in body and soul. And now she saw all too clearly that she was losing the battle for Toby's soul. She did not want him to suffer harm, but what use was it to keep him safe from torture or death in this life if he was then to face eternal torment in the life to come?

What was it Richard had said? Something about not believing God was so cruel as to ask us to suffer for our faith, or kill for it? Oh, how she wished he were here now, to reassure her with his rational arguments, his deep calm voice; to put his arms about her and hold her close against the storms without and within!

The dog woke, raised his head, growled.

'Hush, Trusty! It's just the wind.'

Or was it? She listened. Nothing.

The dog growled again; barked, once.

Quiet.

Not quite. Surely there was something; something new, even above the sound of the wind. A horse? No, imagination, surely, at this time of night, or she hoped so. She stroked the head of the now silent dog, rose to her feet and moved towards the stair, carrying a candle to light her way. Time for bed, rather than to sit here brooding. Perhaps Jane would be awake still, to soothe her with her calm common sense.

She put a foot on the first step, moved towards the second. Paused again. There *was* something out there!

She returned to the hall, listening, the thud of her heart pounding in her ears, rivalling the wind.

The scratching of the branch on the window was loud tonight, louder than she remembered it had ever been. The pear tree growing in that sheltered spot had become straggly with neglect. She must get it cut back before the next storm came, or there'd be a broken window. Or was it too late? That was worse still, a fierce rattle.

She turned to glance at it; and froze. A face, distorted by the uneven pane and the rain running down it.

She caught her breath, clutched her throat. A hand reached up, to tap on the window, gesture. A dark bearded face, pleading.

Then she knew. *Nicholas.*

She stood where she was, fighting the urge to turn away, ignore him, simply to continue up the stairs to bed. She owed him nothing but anger and reproach.

She could not do it. She went to the door, slid aside the bars and opened it, almost thrown back by the power of the wind, flinging him in with it. He was drenched, but more than that, he looked utterly dishevelled, dirty, haggard beyond anything the storm could have done to him.

It took some time to bar the door again against the force of the wind. Nicholas made no move to help, and when she turned round she saw that he'd sunk shivering on the settle by the embers of the fire. The dog, knowing him, was licking his hand, though he seemed unaware of the animal's attentions.

His eyes met hers. He said nothing but she knew what their message was: *Help me!*

'Where have you come from? Where are you going?' Though she knew; the answer to the first part at least.

Anger surged through her. 'They came looking for you yesterday. I was able to say with a good conscience that I'd had no word of you at all. It's likely they're watching. I'll give you food, but then you must go.'

He looked as if he did not understand what she was saying. He rubbed a hand across his face. She saw there was blood streaked through the dirt.

'Are you hurt?'

'No, not—It's not my blood, I think...I don't know.'

Better not to ask any more. She hurried to the kitchen, brought cheese, bread and beer. He snatched at the bread she tore off for him, devoured it as if he'd not eaten for days, gulped down the beer. As he reached for more, she caught his wrist.

'Enough. I'll wrap up the rest for you to take with you.' Shutting her ears to his exclamation, she reached for a linen napkin she'd brought with her, folding it about the food. She put a stopper in the flask and thrust the package into his hand. 'Here, take it, but go! Go now!'

'May I not—?' None of his old certainty, only pleading, fear even. 'Just a few days, two nights, no more. Until I'm rested, until they've stopped watching the ports. I can get a boat.'

'No! No!'

'For the love we have, for our shared blood!'

'That's why you must go. For the sake of the children. I cannot risk their lives, when it's you that have done wrong.'

'Wrong!'

'Yes, Nicholas.' Her gaze was steady, though her heart thudded. Did he really not understand what he'd done? 'What you tried to do, what you plotted, that was evil. You and your friends—you've ruined the lives of every Catholic in England, turned us into strangers, aliens in our own land. Made sure that the true religion will not be restored for generations, perhaps for ever.'

'Because we were betrayed. If we'd succeeded—'

'If you'd succeeded, you would still have sinned, destroying innocent lives. Life and death are not in your hands, but God's. We may not have the king we hoped for once, but he's the king still, to whom we owe allegiance. Render unto God the things that are God's!'

'Would you quote from the Protestant Bible?'

'If I say it in Latin does that make it more true?' She thrust the package at him again. 'Take it! I won't have you starve, but you must go, now, at once!'

He laid it on the bench beside him. She glimpsed a flash of anger in his eyes, immediately veiled; as if in a moment all the weariness and desperation left him. He took her arm, drew her down beside him.

'Kate, you and I, we have shared so much. Remember how we rode together, you as eager as any boy? The stories you told me, to console me in grief? The laughter we shared?' His voice, soft, even tender, tugged at her memory, drawing out glimpses of their childhood, of how she'd cared for him, nurtured him, prayed for him; loved him. 'Think how we danced, here in this place, just a year or so gone. Just two days, two nights, that's all I ask. Then I'll be gone, I give you my solemn word. We will not meet again until better times come. And they will come, my dear sister, one day they will!'

Another man too had made such a promise—*one day*. The thought came unbidden, breaking the spell.

'No! You are my brother, we've shared so much, that's true. But you broke that bond. You've destroyed it by your own hands, by what you did. I'll not put this place and all of us at risk for you, not for a moment longer. You must leave, now!'

She knew that if he refused, she could not force him to go without summoning help; and that would all too likely end with soldiers at the door. A step too far…

They faced each other, Kate fighting the urge to lower her eyes before her brother's burning gaze, though it seemed to scorch her. 'Go, now!'

What seemed an age, neither moving. Waiting, two wills opposed.

He rose to his feet.

'You, you are a coward, an apostate! You'd save your own skin at the cost of your immortal soul. You are no different from your husband, in the end. For this, when we come to power—as we shall, one day!—you will suffer with all the rest who betrayed God's cause, you and all your stinking heretic family.' The words poured from him like liquid fire, low, fierce, hissing with menace. 'Remember this, Katharine: you are no sister of mine, for I have no sister.

414

Not from this moment, not as long as I live. I curse you for your shrinking, craven heart. May you burn in Hell with all heretics! As you surely will, in endless bitter agony!'

He swung round and reached for the door. She saw with a pang how he staggered, but resisted every impulse to hold him back, to beg him to unsay those dreadful words, to reassure him that in spite of everything she loved him still. To do that would be to retract what she'd already said, and she could not in all honesty do so. She lowered her voice, her eyes sombre. 'I pray that one day you will know in your heart that what you've done was a mortal sin.'

He gave her one last terrible look, tugged the door open, stepped through it into the storm and was gone. She stood staring blankly into the dark, hearing, faintly, the first sounds of his departing horse, and then only the wind and the rain. At last, shaking, sobbing, she barred the door, took the candle and ran up to her closet, to kneel in incoherent prayer until the daylight ventured into the room.

Why, Lord, why do you ask all this of me? It's more than I can bear. I should not have to choose between them, between those I love...

In the morning it was as if it had all been a terrible nightmare. No one else seemed to have heard anything, because of the wind, she supposed. She said nothing to anyone, not even Jane. How could she ever explain that she had turned her own brother from the door, when he'd appealed to her in his utmost extremity?

Five haunted days passed, burdened with memories, her thoughts tossed this way and that, filled with guilt and misery, swinging back to anger at what he had brought on them all, what he'd become. Haunted, always, by echoes of his voice, cursing her…Her little brother, whom she'd cared for, protected as long as she was able. She'd prayed for him, loved him as if he were her own child. Or almost as much.

How must he have felt, to be spurned in his hour of need by the sister he loved, whom he thought loved him? Oh, how it must have pierced him to the heart! No wonder he'd cursed her. It was no more than she deserved, or so she felt now.

Yet she had done it for those others she loved, for her children, for Toby above all.

Would Nicholas one day come to see why she'd acted as she had, to understand; even to forgive? By now, please God, he was well on his way to safety, to a new life overseas. She prayed through her pain that there'd come a time when, putting the past behind him, he would be free to seek her out and they would be reconciled. In time perhaps, he would have learned wisdom from all that had happened, come to understand that the rigidity of his faith had led him into loveless, uncaring paths, that there was a better way. Perhaps she would even begin to see things from his point of view, to understand what drove him. And then brother and sister would learn to live in harmony, as she had always hoped they would, one day.

But for now she struggled to forgive him, to forgive herself, though she offered tearful prayers, hour after hour, hiding her grief as best she could, even from Jane.

* * *

It was Jane who greeted her as she emerged from her closet on the morning of the sixth day after Nicholas had left.

'Madam.'

'What is it?' As Jane's face slowly came into focus, its grave look frightened her.

'Over by the…they found…madam—'

Fear clutched at her heart. She stared at Jane's troubled face. He'd been gone five days; he must have reached the coast long since, found a ship to take him away to safety. Surely, by now he was beyond their reach?

'A body. Dead. In a ditch. A man. From his clothes, they think—'

She knew then, felt the chill of it. 'Where have they taken him?'

'To the Hall, to Sir Cuthbert. After that I don't know.'

She pulled on a cloak and went at once to Meadhope, where she found Sir Cuthbert and Dame Juliana in the entrance hall, heads bent happily over a letter.

'We've good news of Bess, the very best,' Sir Cuthbert announced, before appearing to realise how inopportune a time it was to lay his own happiness before Kate. 'Forgive me. I was…'

He passed the letter to his wife and came towards her, the smile entirely gone from his face.

'I heard that you had someone here, who might be—'

'Your brother.'

'May I see him?'

417

'Of course. If you think yourself strong enough. He has already been identified. You don't need to see him.'

'I would wish to.' Would she? She did not know, only that this had to be faced.

He led her to a small room off the family parlour, where a shrouded figure lay on a trestle. He drew back the cloth, and she saw the face, cold, still, lifeless. Nicholas, yet not Nicholas, for the troubled soul had gone. Only the husk was left.

Kate pressed her hand to her mouth, stifling a rising sob. 'I had hoped—but it is him. My brother. *Was* my brother.'

Sir Cuthbert laid a hand on her shoulder. 'Would you wish to be alone with him for a while?'

She shrank at the thought. 'Thank you,' she said, for want of anything else to say.

But when he'd gone she wanted to run after him, to run away from what she'd done. For wasn't that the truth? She had brought Nicholas to this: a lifeless corpse, battered, bruised, marked with dark smears of blood, a damaged body in which once had dwelt a damaged soul.

She reached out a hand and laid it on the cold cheek, stroked the lank hair.

'Forgive me, little brother. God forgive me! I should have taken better care of you, all my life, and yours. I should have done something, said something, when you came here that spring, when I took Toby from you.' *But you did say something*, murmured a voice in her head. *You did say, and he would not listen.* 'I should never have turned you away!'

What else could I have done? asked her heart. *For my children's sake, for what was right; if it was right?* How could she tell, in this world of murky allegiances tearing at her heart and her conscience, shadowing the path that once had seemed so clear, so brightly lit? Now all was doubt and fear.

She tried to pray but no words came. She found she was shivering. She went to the door and was relieved to find that Sir Cuthbert stood just the other side of it, waiting.

'Can I take him for burial?'

'I'm sorry. In any other circumstances. But in this matter, no.'

'What will happen to him?'

'That is not in my hands. They will come for him tomorrow. Better not ask too much.'

She did not probe any further. She knew they would not deal gently with the corpse of a man guilty of treason. Perhaps it was better that he was dead. Perhaps.

Unless she could have hidden him at Holywell, keeping him rested and fed, until it was safe for him to flee abroad...

As she rode home questions, doubts tormented her endlessly.

Oh, had she done wrong? Had she been the sinner, in turning him so cruelly from her door? Would she ever know, in her heart?

That night at Holywell they prayed for his soul. No need for secrecy any longer, for the whole household knew of the body in the ditch, and its identity. As the prayers ended she looked at their faces: her children, the servants who had been part of her household for so long, of whom only Jane and John remembered the boy Nicholas; others who had never known him, except as a guest welcomed to this place.

In the quiet of her room that evening, Kate told Jane of Nicholas's coming, and how she'd turned him away.

'Why did you not say? I saw that something was wrong that morning, but I did not think, never…'

'I thought it best to say nothing. How could I? If they came looking for him you would not be able in all conscience to say you knew nothing of his whereabouts. It had to be kept secret, for all our sakes. Yet—' Tears sprang to her eyes, unchecked. 'Oh, if I'd not turned him away, he'd be living still!'

'You could do nothing else, now could you? You could not have given him shelter. That would have put everyone in danger, and for what? He is, he was, a traitor. Your only other course would have been to take him in and call the authorities.'

With a sharp intake of breath Kate stared at her. 'Is that what you think I should have done?'

'No, my dear madam. To do that to your own brother? No, you could not have done it. That would not have been right either.'

'I know some would have said it's what I ought to have done. Please God no one finds out he was ever here!'

'Amen to that.' Jane took her arm. 'You need rest. Let me help you to bed. I'll bring you a posset to help you sleep.'

But she did not sleep, that night or for many nights afterwards, more than a little, fitfully, soon waking to nightmare thoughts of Nicholas turned from her door, riding in terror through the night, lying in a ditch, fevered, in pain.

When she did sleep it was in brief snatches filled with disordered dreams: Nicholas, her small brother, all tousled brown hair and wide brown eyes, nestled in her arms as she strove to console him for their grandmother's death; only somehow he was Toby, so like his uncle, so much in need of the comfort she could not give. She'd wake to other scenes from the past, other long-buried memories—the funny little ways she'd forgotten, the impish smile, the irrepressible giggle, their shared happiness in the loving home at Holywell.

She remembered how she'd tried to carry that love with them to the chilly austerity of their Uncle Gaunt's house, tried to help the bewildered, angry child to avoid the harsh words and beatings that fell on him when he rebelled. How painfully she had missed Nicholas when he was sent away to school and she was left alone, and lonely. How, later, visiting Haroby after her marriage, he'd brought love and laughter into the place, into a life that was barren of either of those things. Sometimes she'd been angry with him, because of something he'd done or said. But always she'd been sure of his love, as sure as she was of anything; as he was sure of hers.

As he'd been sure when he turned to her for help.

Again and again his blazing angry eyes filled her head, his final curse echoing and re-echoing…the very last words he had spoken to her, with no hope now of reconciliation, ever.

Night after night, the same, so she seemed to sleepwalk through the days, her limbs aching, her eyes sore, her whole body longing for rest, a rest without end from which she would not wake, ever again, to this nightmare world.

'I would wish to have a Mass said for him,' she confided once to Jane. 'But no priest is going to come here now, in these times.'

'This Christmas coming, with your kinsman, at his place—didn't he promise there would be a priest?'

Only two weeks, and it would be Christmas. She had longed to see Richard again, to feel his arms about her.

Now, she thought only: Nicholas would not approve, he would not go. If he sees me from wherever he is now (*Oh, don't think of that!*) he'll be tormented the more by my betrayal, my lewd thoughts, my lack of resolution; my utter frivolity.

She was beginning to understand that though his burning faith had led him astray, in some things Nicholas had been right: too often she had compromised her faith, for an easy life. A new resolution took shape within her: she would be steadfast, set her feet on a purer path.

She raised her head, looked Jane in the eye. 'We shan't go. It would be wrong. I shall write and tell him so.'

Jane took both her hands in hers. 'Oh my dear madam, why not?'

From the confusion of her mind, Kate grasped at a possible excuse. 'As things are, in these times, it would put him in danger, and his family. To be associated with the likes of us.'

She could see at once that Jane was not convinced. 'You know he'd not heed that, for a moment.'

'Then I must heed it for him.' And take the first difficult step to a new and better life...

Sir, she wrote, *I thank you for bidding us to pass the days of Christmas with your family, but I fear I must decline.*

Further, I think it best if we do not meet again unless circumstances compel us to do so. I write this with regret and much gratitude for your kind attentions towards us. I will make other arrangements for my sons.

Your servant,

Katharine Machyn

'It's done,' she told Jane, when she'd sent it on its way; and then fell against her, racked with sobs.

Chapter Twenty Six

Shrouded in a grey mist that sucked all joy from her life, weary beyond words, Kate intended to shrink Holywell's Christmas celebrations to the barest essentials: a modest feast for their tenants, some carefully chosen music to be sung at the worship that must take the place of the Mass, perhaps a few green boughs to adorn the hall.

In the end she could not bring herself to inflict such austerity upon her children, who were already volubly disappointed at the abandonment of the promised celebration at Warthrop.

'The times are not right,' was her unconvincing explanation for this. And: 'We are still in mourning for your uncle.'

'We owe him no tears!' Toby exploded. 'He brought only disaster on us. I could have died!'

'I know. But it's customary.' Her weary tone robbed the excuse of all conviction.

'Then can we go to the Hall on Christmas Day? You don't have to come. I know Sir Cuthbert's invited us. He told me last Sunday.'

'Please, mother!' implored Mariana.

Kate could not find it in her heart to refuse. At least it would leave her with less to do at home, and she would not have to dance and sing with the company if she did not feel like it.

It hurt her that on Christmas morning Toby slipped

away to the parish church; though at least he'd first joined the household for prayers, taking his part in the singing with a show of enthusiasm.

Kate, watching him ride away, with his careless, 'I'll see you later, at the Hall!' felt helpless, discouraged. But what could she do? She could not lock him in his room.

From his seat half-hidden by a pillar, Toby could just see the Featherstone family pew, right at the front below the pulpit. He watched them come into church, last of all the congregation, dressed in their most festive clothes: Sir Cuthbert and his wife first, as usual. Dame Juliana's maid would follow soon, to sit beside her. But no, this morning it was Hal's stocky flame-crowned figure who strode at his mother's heels, home from Cambridge for the holiday. Toby felt a mixture of joy and apprehension: would Hal know what had so nearly happened to him, would he feel sympathy, or distaste? Would the student even condescend to greet his old friend?

Then there was that other question, only half-admitted: would Bess be home for the feast? She was not here this morning, for Dame Juliana's maid took her seat next, and after her the other servants filed onto their backless bench in the south aisle.

At the end of the service, as was customary, the Featherstone party left the church first. Toby found his way out barred by a slow-moving bunch of his fellow-parishioners, and thought Hal would be long gone before he reached the churchyard. But his friend was hovering among the gravestones, watching for him, and came at once to clap him on the shoulder. 'Toby! I thought it was you! You old scapegrace! They tell me you've been in trouble.'

Toby shivered, as he always did when the episode came to mind. 'Not any more.'

'I did think I'd have to shun your company, but I'm told you've turned into a good upstanding citizen, in church every Sunday. Good for you! We must go hawking soon, then you can tell me all your news. I'm sick of being shut in with my books. Not that I've been the model student this term. I've a deal to tell you. You're coming to us for dinner today, aren't you? Then let's walk together.'

Hal chattered on in a way that made Toby's head spin. So much had changed since they'd last been together that it felt impossible to recapture the old ease in his friend's company. Hal was as full as ever of the delights of university life, and Toby heard him with a twinge of envy mixed with something like disapproval. He found himself thinking of Humphrey and his grave gentleness. Hal seemed somehow so much younger now, fixed in a past that Toby had long since left behind.

Meadhope Hall was fragrant with the scents of Christmas, pine branches, spices, wax candles, roasting meats, and its sounds: laughter, music, lively chatter. Toby and Hal arrived there at the same time as the Holywell family, all welcomed in to the great hall where a massive log fire blazed in the hearth and the vast table was already spread with good things. Everyone was greeting everyone else with embraces and kisses and the friendly warmth Toby had missed so much, yet found hard to cope with today.

The usual family members were there, along with a thin pale young man whom he did not recognise, though from his rich dress he must be a close relation rather than a servant; and behind him, emerging into the thin winter sunlight, a young woman in green and scarlet. Bess. She saw him at once.

'Merry Christmas, Toby!' She embraced him, decorously, one neighbour greeting another.

After all that had happened, she still had power to rouse him. He could see in her eyes that she knew it too. She was just as he remembered, though perhaps a little plumper. 'Merry Christmas to you, Bess. You look well.'

'I am very well.' She came a little nearer, lowered her voice. 'I'm four months gone with our child.'

The room seemed to sway about him. *Our* child?

She glanced behind her at the pale young man. 'Our firstborn. Will hopes for a son.'

So that was Will Fenwick, the man she'd married. Who had not been able to consummate their union.

Had he learned how to do it, taught by his eager wife; or—? *Four months,* she'd said. Through his confusion Toby just managed to work out that the child must have been conceived at the end of summer, or early in the autumn.

September perhaps, when they had lain together day after day in the byre at Meadhope's Home Farm. Colour flooded his face.

Our son. Not hers and Will Fenwick's, but hers and his, Toby's. Could that be so? Did her husband have any inkling of the truth, if it was the truth?

She linked her arm through his and steered him towards the fortunate young man. 'Will, this is Toby Machyn, from Holywell. Hal's oldest friend.'

Toby muttered something incoherent which he hoped sounded polite enough. The other man made some sort of clumsy bow. It was a relief when an awkward silence was broken by Sir Cuthbert's booming voice summoning them to the table.

Noise, laughter, an excess of food and drink engulfed him, forced Bess's news from the forefront of his mind. Perhaps he'd imagined it all; it seemed so unreal.

It was late in the afternoon when a great bowl of flaming brandy was set in the middle of the table and they were summoned to a game of Snapdragon, to see who could snatch the most raisins from among the flames without getting burned. Competing with Mariana (who proved very adept at it) Toby felt a tug at his sleeve, and saw Bess behind him, urging him into the shadows away from the noisy crowd.

He followed her, and she drew him further into the corner.

'You know, don't you? It's our child, yours and mine.'

He drew a deep breath. 'Your husband doesn't suspect?'

She shook her head. 'He thinks he's done it. I told him he'd got it right. He believed me.' Her smile was warm, enticing, full of meaning. 'So, if we want more children, I know where to come.'

A curious mixture of excitement and resistance shivered through him. Was this what he wanted?

He knew he ought to feel guilty, deeply ashamed of the sin that had led to this moment. They had committed adultery, and now there was to be a child; and Bess, it seemed, would gladly sin again in exactly the same way. Could he take it so lightly?

If no one ever guessed the truth, if her husband was happy to believe he'd fathered a child, and Bess to bear the infant she'd feared she would never conceive, and to bear more in future: how could that truly be a sin? He'd loved Bess, had given her pleasure in taking his own. If things had been different, if he'd been as eligible a husband as Will Fenwick, they might even have married.

At that moment a new resolution crystallised within him. It had been coming for some time. Now he was sure, absolutely sure. He'd become regular in his attendance at the parish church, even more than the minimum required by law, but it had been simply a matter of outward show. Now he resolved to take the next logical step. His mother's love had nurtured him from infancy, Humphrey had shown him that goodness could be captivating, but what had others of his faith ever given him? Lies, wickedness masquerading as holiness, deadly danger for a cause he could not defend. And from the heretics that he'd been told were bound for Hell? Friendship from Hal, wise counsel from Gervase Langley; his very life from Sir Cuthbert and his brother Tom—and this now from Bess. The moment had come to make his choice, for good or ill.

The following morning he waylaid his mother very early, as she was descending the stairs.

'Mother, I need to speak with you, most urgently.'

She could not make him out clearly in the shadowed stairway, but his voice told her enough. 'You sound very grave, Toby.'

'Can we go to your closet?'

She led the way back up the stairs, and once in the room with the door closed turned to face him. 'What is it? Is something wrong?'

She could see him straighten, brace himself. He took a deep breath, then: 'I've asked Master Langley to give me instruction.'

'Instruction? In what?' Then she knew, with a blow to the heart. 'Toby!'

His eyes held hers, unflinching. 'I shall become fully a member of his church, our parish church; *my* parish church. I will attend prayers here at home, but I shall not go to Mass any more.'

'Oh Toby, that you should do enough to be safe, that's

one thing, though God knows that's still wrong. But this—
to throw it all away for worldly advantage!'

'I'm sorry. I know how much it hurts you.'

'It hurts God, Toby. Christ and Our Lady.'

"I don't believe that any more. Not really. I've seen
what such things can lead to, the extremes, the hate…'

'Not all on one side. What of your friend Humphrey,
whom you spoke of so tenderly? And,' she felt herself
blush, 'our cousin Richard Thornton.'

She sensed that she had touched him, just for a
moment. 'I know. There are good people. But I think each
of them would see that there is truth on both sides. I have
to find the right way for my conscience.'

She tried to remonstrate with him, but her arguments
fell against the adamantine wall of his decision. He'd made
up his mind and that was that.

In the end, she gave up. 'I'll pray for you, Toby, as
always. That you will come back where you belong.'

He put his arms about her. 'I haven't gone away,
mother, not really.'

He knew she did not believe him.

Later, he told Jane of his decision, watching all the while to
see his mother's pain and disapproval reflected in her face,
feeling that in some way this would be even worse. If so, it
was slow in coming.

'I know you'll condemn me.'

'Why should I?'

431

'For the same reason as my mother. Because of the danger to my soul.'

'As I see it, God's a good bit more merciful and loving than we give Him credit for. It's we silly humans make the rules, Popes and Bishops and what's in bread and wine.'

He stared at her. 'Jane! What would my mother say?'

'She knows I'd die for her faith. She doesn't know it would be for her sake, not for any Pope or creed. So you'd best keep that to yourself. I'd tell her if she asked, but she never has. Better that way.'

He laughed and gave her a hug. 'Oh, Jane, you're wonderful. And I love you so much! What would we do without you?'

Two messages were brought to Holywell in the following days. The one, delayed by the weather, reached Kate from Tom, her son.

My dear wife is safely delivered of a daughter, thanks be to God.

This comes to convey to you and all your family our warmest wishes for the Christmas season. When the spring comes, we hope to make the journey north to visit you, in the hope that my brother Toby will then return to Haroby with us to become part of our household.

And to make doubly sure that his straying from the Church became fixed and permanent....*No, Tom, no! I long to see you, but not as Toby's guardian and mentor.*

Two days later a man came to Holywell, with a different message for Kate: a letter, and a small box, bound with red ribbon.

'A gift from my master, Richard Thornton.'

She took it with shaking hands, just remembering to send the man for refreshment before she made her way upstairs to her closet. There she pulled off the ribbon, opened the box. A ring, simple gold. She turned it this way and that until the light caught an unneveness inside it. She took it to the window to see better: words engraved inside, four words: *Two Hands, One Heart.*

Oh Richard! Tears sprang to her eyes.

The letter...! Hands shaking, she broke the seal, unfolded it.

Dear Heart,

If you return this gift to me, I will understand that you wrote those words in all sincerity, and I shall know you will never be mine.

But if by Twelfth Night I have not had it back from you, then I will know your heart is indeed one with mine. I will come to Holywell, to make arrangements for young Philip to come to Warthrop, and perhaps Toby too. And for you and I to be joined in marriage, if not at once then as soon as may seem best, when all due formalities are done.

Believe me, your own

Richard

She held letter and ring to her lips and then to her breast. She knew what she ought to do: return the ring to its box, wrap it carefully and give it to the messenger to return to Richard. That had been her decision, to put aside the lascivious urgings of her body, her longing for a companion in her life. To choose chastity and holy widowhood, exactly as Nicholas had wanted for her.

She knelt to pray, with the ring still clutched in her hand, but no words came, only memories of Richard, his voice, his smile.

She gave up, threaded the ring on the ribbon that had bound the box and hung at about her neck.

'I shall consider what to do in a few days,' she told Jane.

'Of course, my dear madam,' said Jane, with a smile.

Chapter Twenty Seven

Twelfth Night, the end of the Christmas festivities—and Kate still carried the ring about her neck, night and day. She had not written to Richard, still less returned his ring. This day, he would know the choice she had made.

If it was a choice. She had thought her choice was made after her brother's death, but as the days of the Christmas season passed the nightmares had lessened, she had ceased to be constantly haunted by visions of Nicholas's face as he cursed her. And into this time had come Richard's letter, in which she seemed to hear his voice, tender, considerate, undemanding. She longed so much to feel his arms about her, to hear him speak to her, to laugh with him; to feel cherished, loved. But was that enough to make her turn her back on a holy widowhood? Was it not rather the womanly weakness of which Nicholas had so often accused her? Could she stand firm, if Richard were to come to Holywell, or would she simply melt into his embrace, unable to help herself? She told herself she must not do it. She must stay true to her resolution.

That morning, she dressed with greater care than usual, 'in honour of the day,' she told Jane, who knew qute well that she still wore Richard's ring about her neck.

Helping her to put on the dark green velvet gown she'd worn for Nicholas's arrival nearly two years ago, Jane made no comment, only murmured, 'Yes, madam,' her expression, like her tone, belying the meek words.

'Don't look like that, Jane! I'm in earnest. What other reason could I have? If anyone was going to call today, we'd have had word of it. I'm not even expecting Sir Cuthbert or his family. I told him we'd have a quiet celebration today.'

Yet all day, as she went about her routine tasks, Kate found herself straining for the sound of Richard's horse clattering into the yard, for his cheerful greeting; or at least for a messenger sent by him, with word of his imminent arrival.

Instead, just after dark, Father Fielding came stealthily to the house, just in time for tomorrow's Feast of the Epiphany.

Suppressing her disappointment, Kate helped him out of his wet cloak and ordered food and drink to be brought. 'This is indeed a blessing, father. It's so long since we saw you and I have so much wanted your ministrations.'

He looked, she thought, utterly weary, as if the shadow of the times had fallen on him as on all of them. She realised with a little shock that he was an old man, though he'd never seemed so before.

What he said next took her by surprise.

'I have to tell you that I'm to go overseas, to embrace the contemplative life. It is time for new men to serve the Church in this land in these difficult times.'

She felt bereft, as if yet another of the things that had supported her faith, her struggle to nurture her children within the Church, was being torn from her.

The priest must have sensed her dismay, for he was quick to reassure her.

'Someone else will take my place. I don't know who, but you will be informed in due time. You are not forgotten, in my prayers if nowhere else. So tonight this will be the last Mass I shall celebrate at Holywell.'

'Then will you offer it for the soul of my brother Nicholas?'

'Of course, though we must principally observe the Holy Festival. I heard of your brother's death, and the circumstances. A tragic business. I will offer the Mass also for the poor souls who will soon face a cruel public death, and for their fellows who have been spared as your brother was.'

There was something in his tone and his expression that made her shiver.

'You cannot think that what they planned was good or right, surely?'

'In that they failed, with consequences that will I fear be disastrous for us all. But if they had not—'

She felt as if her heart missed a beat. 'If they had killed so many, and set the Princess Elizabeth on the throne, as we've learned they meant to do, then you would have applauded them?'

'Would you not? Is there not any price you would pay for the return of this land to its true allegiance?'

'Not any price. To me it seems there are some means that would go against all right ways, that must be of the devil.' If they had been standing here in an England ruled by Catholics, through the figurehead of the young princess, with Nicholas part of the government, would she feel differently? Would she still feel a shiver of horror at what they'd planned, if it had succeeded? How could she know?

'It did not succeed, just as in the late Queen's reign the Armada from Spain was defeated, to the grief of all of our faith. So we are where we are.'

She remembered her late husband's dismay at that event, which in the end had led to his apostasy. And now, that same pattern was being repeated in their son.

The priest refused her offer of refreshment. 'Later, when Mass is ended. Now, we must prepare.'

That meant confession. She summoned the household, but went first herself. There were the usual sins: impatience, self-indulgence (though little enough of that in these stringent times) and a reluctance to trust in God. She was on the verge of confessing to having refused her brother shelter at Holywell, but something held her back. Which after all was the worst sin, to have driven him away, or to have failed to betray him to the authorities? And had she not paid for any sin, in the anguish of losing him? Fearful of what the priest's response would be she kept silent.

But there was one other thing: 'I find myself tempted to take another husband.'

There was a prolonged silence, while she waited, tense, fearful.

'Ah! That I did not expect. I thought you safe from this

at least. You must resist this temptation, my daughter. For a man whose children have need of a mother, that's one thing. Likewise, for a woman with very young children and no other protector, it would be a wise move, should the husband be a fit person. But in general, no. It is best for a widow to lead a chaste life of holiness and prayer, devoted only to God. There are many who would say to do otherwise is to commit adultery.'

So Nicholas would have said—Nicholas, who had done a terrible wrong. Except that it seemed Father Fielding did not quite see it like that, not as she did.

In the past she had always accepted the priest's advice and guidance, in everything. He represented Holy Church and its authority, the force that had ruled her life from infancy. How could she do otherwise than hear him and heed what he said, especially as in this he was simply repeating what her conscience told her was the right course for her to take?

She pushed away the defiance that was bubbling away somewhere deep inside her. She must be true, she must be obedient: it was what she asked of her children, one of the many links in the chain of authority and obedience that made her world, and theirs, an ordered place.

Her confession over, her penance prescribed and forgiveness offered, she went in search of Toby, finding him in his room, making ready for bed.

'Toby, did you not get my message? Father Fielding is here and awaits your confession.'

Toby, sitting on the bed, pulled off his stockings and folded them neatly, the good tidy son. 'I told you, mother. I will not take part in the Mass. The same goes for confession.'

He *had* told her, of course, but a part of her had not quite believed he would stand firm when it came to the point.

'The intention of the Mass is for your uncle, and also for all those who were once your companions.'

'They can rot in Hell where they belong!' He saw how shocked she was. 'You know they did wrong. It's for God to judge. No prayer will change that.'

He had strayed so far, much further than she'd thought. Close to despair, she tried a little longer to persuade him, to no avail.

It was without Toby that, after midnight, the household gathered in the attic room as so often before, hearing the familiar Latin words, but this time with Nicholas's name repeated over and over. *Will it make any difference?* she wondered. *Will it save him from eternal damnation?*

She had hoped it would make her feel better about the way they had parted, but it did not. She thought her brother's dreadful curse would haunt her for ever, and his loss was a perpetual ache at the heart, made worse by her fear that he'd died unrepentant, in a state that was beyond the help of any prayers.

After a dawn breakfast, the priest gave them his blessing and went on his way. When he'd gone, Cecily came to confide in Kate. 'Madam, I told the Father. I wish to be received into the church. He says I may, when there's a new priest.'

It should be a matter of rejoicing, but it did not feel like compensation enough for Toby's apostasy.

The next day snow swept down from the north in the teeth of a bitter wind, obliterating the roads, cutting them off even from Meadhope. It was three weeks before the thaw began and the ways were open again, and another week before Richard rode into the stable yard, with Adam his servant.

He came to her. A brief cousinly kiss, then calm greetings for Toby and the twins and Jane.

They went indoors.

He was shown to the best bedchamber, where warm water was brought so he could wash and change out of his travel stained clothes. Then he joined them in the hall for supper. Kate saw how his eyes followed her, held her. She saw him look at her hands, and knew he sought the ring. What was he thinking?

She could not tell. He was the perfect guest, affable, courteous, talking to each one of them as seemed fitting; easy light-hearted talk over the meal. Afterwards, when the twins were out of earshot, he brought the news that the snow had kept from them.

'You know the conspirators were executed this last week, in London?'

441

It had been inevitable, expected, but Kate still felt a little shock. She glanced at Toby. Was he too chilled by the vision of the agonising deaths these men must have suffered, thinking how very easily he might have been among them; and Nicholas too?

'I think perhaps you knew some of them?'

Toby looked momentarily startled by Richard's question. He was silent for a moment, frowning. Then: 'Most of them, though not well.'

'You know Guido Fawkes was a fellow pupil of ours, of your uncle and myself, at school in York? Older than I, so I never knew him.'

'They talk as if he was the leader, but he wasn't.' Toby sounded almost angry. 'I never knew him. It was Robert Catesby who led them all. And he's dead.'

'Blown up by his own gunpowder, so I heard.' He studied Toby's face. 'I can see that you have regrets still.'

'I —he had such a way with him.'

'The most dangerous kind of man, when he goes to the bad.'

'I know that now.'

To Kate's surprise he told Richard of his arrest, of his fear, even of his sense of guilt at the means of his release, not all of which he'd even confided in her; and Richard listened attentively, saying little except to offer an occasional gentle note of sympathy and understanding, without condemnation. Toby seemed to see, as she did, that here was a man he could trust.

Evening prayers ended, the household dispersed to bed; and Kate lingered at the fireside with Richard.

'I had no word from you. And no ring returned.' There was a question in his tone.

Reaching beneath her ruff, she pulled out the ribbon, with the ring hanging on it. She held it in her hand, saying nothing, her eyes on his.

She saw his colour rise, his eyes fill with light. 'Then— then you will be mine?'

Would she? Oh, how much she longed to be, not a holy widow, but a wife, loved and loving as she'd never been in all the years of her marriage!

He took her hands in his. 'You are still unsure. I would not press you, if you need more time to consider, to decide. It is your choice. Yet I know—I think I know—that you love me. Would it be so wrong for us to marry?'

Swept by desire, longing for him, torn in pieces, she could find no words.

'Kate, I have given all this much thought in the days since I sent the ring. Let us be practical, if that will help. Your son Toby needs guidance. Why should I not adopt him as my son, so that I am his father as surely as you are his mother? He would in time inherit all I have. Meanwhile he could learn all I can teach him about the management of an estate.'

She stared at him, astonished at so unexpected, so generous an offer; yet wary of allowing herself to be carried away by it. 'But—if there were other children, ours together? I think it unlikely, but it could happen. What then for Toby?'

'We would make sure, in law, that it would make no difference, or at the very least that he would have enough of an inheritance to know he is a valued son. We will ensure that all the formalities are in place.'

He'd watched her all the time as he spoke, trying, she supposed, to read her reaction, to understand what she felt.

But how could he, when she did not herself understand? She had known that in coming here he would talk of marriage, even expect it. She had not anticipated that he would have thought it out in so much detail.

'Kate, times are going to be hard for those of our faith, after what happened. It may be harder for you, with your close connection to the conspiracy. My conscience will allow me to conform enough to keep us both safe, and to protect you from the worst the law might do.'

To be as Sir Thomas had been, perhaps ultimately to foreswear his faith, as Toby had already done? No, for Richard was not Sir Thomas, nothing like him. 'Won't it put you in danger, to be close to me and mine?'

'I don't think so. And I noted what Toby said, after supper. He's already turning his back on the past, more I think than you would wish. I see how it hurts you. It could be that I will be able to help him find a middle way. Would you not rather he became such a flexible Catholic as I am, than a downright apostate—or such as your brother?'

Was this the escape route for her conscience, to marry

for the sake of Toby's soul?

Oh, who was she fooling? She was clutching at his offer because it chimed so precisely with what she longed for!

She looked up at him. 'Yes, Richard. I would wish us to be wed.'

He folded her into his arms. 'I am yours, Kate, eternally.'

'And I am yours.' She raised her face to his, felt his mouth on hers, reached up to draw him nearer.

'Let's to bed, dear heart.' He cradled her face in his hands, looking into her eyes. 'I shall go to my room. If you go to yours, I wish you good night and a tranquil rest. It is for you to choose.'

She watched him go, heard him mount the stairs. Shaking so much she scarcely knew what she was doing, she waited a few minutes, ran her fingers over her rosary, wordlessly, without thought, and then softly, warily, looking about her, made her way to his room. She pushed open the door, stepped inside, closed it behind her. She felt dizzy with desire.

Dressed only in his shirt, he came to her, held her, scanned her face. 'You are sure?'

She nodded. He led her to the bed, eased her down, lay beside her; reached over to unlace her clothes, free her from their restrictions. He loosed the ring from its ribbon and slipped it onto her finger, kissing her as he did so. 'My bride!'

Soon all but her chemise were cast aside.

Then: her mouth, her neck, her breasts, caressed and kissed, his hand again finding that place discovered before on the stairs of the inn.

But this time, there in the bed, he brought her to a peak of longing, entered her gently, then fiercely, so they travelled together to that wave of pleasure breaking on the shore.

A short while, as they lay in each other's arms; then: 'We are one Kate, as surely as if we had sworn our fidelity in church. All that remains is the final blessing.'

Chapter Twenty Eight

'Toby!'

Mariana's hiss reached Toby as he descended the stairs on his way to the hall for morning prayers. Wide eyed with excitement, his sister caught up with him, lowering her voice so much that he had to strain to catch what she said.

'Mother stayed all night in Master Thornton's room. All night!'

Toby stared at her, trying to make sense of what his sister implied, feeling his colour rise at the very thought of it.

'Don't be foolish, Mariana. She'd never do such a thing. How can you even think it?'

'It's true, Toby. I swear on—oh, anything you like! I got up to pee. It was just getting light. I saw her, our mother, coming out of his room. She didn't see me, but I saw her, clear as anything.'

'You imagined it, you must have done!' She gave a vehement shake of the head. 'Even if you didn't, how do you know she was there all night? What if he was taken sick, and had need of help? Or maybe he asked her to wake him early. There's sure to be some simple explanation.' Anything, to still the uncomfortable sensations that were creeping through him at this moment.

'I know it's not that! Didn't you see the way she looked at him last night at supper? She couldn't take her eyes off him.'

'I didn't see anything different from normal.' Which was true, but then he'd not paid much attention either to his mother or to their guest, except when Richard had taken a friendly interest in his own thoughts and feelings.

'You watch, today. You'll see, I wager you will!'

He put on what he hoped was a look of adult severity. 'You should clear those filthy thoughts out of your head, Mariana. This is our mother you're speaking of!'

She shrugged, pouted. 'Oh, you don't see what's in front of your nose. No wonder you got into trouble!'

He bit back an angry retort. 'It's time for prayers. You need to put these fanciful ideas out of your head.'

But when they were gathered in the hall, Toby found himself casting furtive glances at their guest, and at his mother, who did not appear to be looking at Master Thornton at all. Though she had a little smile, as if hugging some secret joy to herself…Oh no, surely not? He found himself squirming with embarrassment at the possibility that Mariana could be right.

Later, after breakfast, as he rose from the table, he found Richard at his side.

'Toby, there's something I wish to discuss with you, if you have a moment.'

The tone of voice was nothing like his uncle's used to be, less imperious, gentler, but Toby was still struck with unease, as he had been whenever Nicholas had suggested a private conversation.

'Shall we go to the parlour?'

He followed Richard up the stairs, his anxiety increasing with every step. Instinctively, he'd warmed to this man, but instinct had led him astray before, as Mariana had so unkindly reminded him.

'Shall we sit down?'

'I'd rather stand, sir, thank you.'

Richard took a seat facing the window so that the morning light fell full on his face. 'Don't look so distrustful. I would hope that nothing I shall say will discomfort you.'

But he *was* distrustful, though he said nothing, simply gazed back at their guest. After what Mariana had said, now this! It was impossible not to suspect that the two were somehow connected.

'First, I have to tell you that your mother has consented to become my wife.'

At that, staggering, flooded with a mixture of astonishment, embarrassment, dismay, Toby did sit down, heavily, on the cushioned window seat. 'Sir!'

Richard smiled gently. 'I see you're startled by this news. You had not then guessed anything? I expect it seems strange to you to think of your mother in such a way—she has been alone so long. But I give you my word she will be loved and cared for to the utmost of my power, and respected in all things.'

He knew then: she *had* lain with him last night! Mariana was right. But he could not say so, could not find the words to say anything.

'You'll need time to take this in, I see that. Let me put

to you other matters that your mother and I have considered and propose to put into effect, if you are happy with them.'

Into Toby's bewildered mind the words seeped in fits and starts. Richard would, he understood, go soon to his estate at Warthrop, taking Philip with him. There, he planned to put things in order and to arrange the legalities for the marriage. 'I would suggest that you come there with me, to see that all is done as it should be. And we both of us hope and trust that you will put aside your aversion to the Holy Mass long enough to serve as a witness for our marriage, when it takes place there, as we hope it will.'

And then what was he saying? Something about naming Toby as his heir, in law, to inherit that prosperous estate…?

But this was his home, where they were now. 'What about this place, what about Holywell?'

'It will remain your mother's property as long as she lives. She will continue to manage it as she sees fit. Afterwards, we propose that it will pass to your sister, for her life, whether she marries or no…You are wondering if you will lose from all this? Warthrop is a much larger property, with many tenanted farms. There will be a great deal to learn about the management of such an estate. But to know that it will one day be yours—that should I think help you to take a real pleasure in the work.'

It was all too much for Toby, who stammered out meaningless phrases, uncontrolled, incomplete.

Richard rose to his feet.

'I know this has come as a shock to you, that there is much to consider. I do understand something of what you must feel, and I put no pressure on you. You will not be forced into doing anything that does not sit well with you. We ask only that you ponder this, come to us with any questions or doubts that you have. And then we hope you will be content to rejoice with us. I love your mother very much, you know. One day I trust you will know such true love for yourself.'

Toby thought of Bess, but in the same context as his mother it was too much. He even felt a little sick.

'I'll give it thought, sir.' Then: 'Who else knows of this?'

'Your mother is at this very moment writing to your brother Tom. As for the rest of the household, and your sister—let's leave it until you have had time to consider it all at length.' He grinned. 'But don't leave it too long, I beg you!'

Toby managed a faint smile before Richard left the room. He sat there a little longer, trying to still the turmoil in his head and body, trying to make sense of it all.

His mother, that pure widow, example to them all of the holy life, their guide, protector, their example, suddenly become an ordinary woman, with a woman's desires...like Bess...It was too much to grasp, too much to bear!

But there was the other side of it all, the proposal that he should become Richard's heir, with an estate that would one day be his; no longer a landless alien without prospects, trying to forge an uncertain path through the world, but a young man with a firm future before him, a man of means.

He had from the first liked Richard, who took him seriously, listened to him, treated him as someone worthy of his consideration; understood him, as far as he could tell. He was no Robert Catesby, who would lure the very heart and soul from you, inspire the most fervent devotion, as to a saint; a man whose loss, even knowing all that he'd done, had yet left a place of anguish deep inside, still unhealed. If not a Catesby or anything like, Richard seemed a decent man, kind, thoughtful, considerate, and offering both friendship and something more.

So long as he was first wed to Toby's mother.

Toby's mother, the holy widow, who last night had shared Richard's bed. Toby shuddered. That was the stumbling block, the massive barrier to accepting what was offered.

As soon as he could trust his legs to carry him he ran down the stairs, out to the stable, saddled Ruby and rode away over the frosty ground, hoping the cold air would clear his head, help him make sense of it all.

Was there someone he could talk to, confide in, some wise and kindly person who would listen and advise? Master Langley? No, for it was not for him to tell the rector what his mother planned to do. The same applied to anyone else he could think of. He was alone in this; he had to find his own way through the fog of embarrassment, doubt, hope, to whatever lay beyond.

As the sun rose, the frost thawed and rose thickly into mist, chilling him even through his warm cloak. Today, the ride was not helping at all. He turned for home, feeling as queasily bewildered as ever.

Stepping into the house, he came to an abrupt halt. At the far end of the screen passage, outlined against the light from the narrow window behind them, his mother and Jane were talking together. He was about to hurry on to the stairs, when Kate's voice reached him, gentle yet commanding. 'Toby!'

He wondered whether to ignore her, to express his disapproval (if such it was) by pretending he had not heard. No, this had to be faced, somehow.

He approached the two women, expecting Jane to slip away, but she did not. Did she know what was planned? Was she in on this alarming secret?

'I understand Master Thornton spoke with you this morning?'

Wondering what Richard had told her of their meeting, Toby admitted it.

'I know it will be strange for you, to think that I should marry again. Perhaps you think it wrong?'

Did he? He really didn't know. 'It is for you...I think...'

'He told you the rest, what we plan to do? For you, if you're happy with it?'

'Yes.'

The two women glanced at one another, then Jane

said, 'You should go with Master Thornton to his estate, get to know the place—and get to know him better. You're old and wise enough now to be able to judge what sort of man he is, if he is fit to be your mother's husband, and your stepfather.'

He flung his head back, looked her in the eye. 'What if I decide he isn't fit?'

'So long as your reasons are sound, then I am sure your mother would take heed of your concerns.'

Looking at her face, he knew his mother had no doubts about the outcome. Well, he would see. It made a sort of sense.

Chapter Twenty Nine

In the garden, Mariana was playing at cat's cradle with Joan, whose clumsiness had reduced them both to helpless laughter. The sound lifted Kate's spirits as she passed the open window on the stair.

She'd been unsure about Richard's recent suggestion that his mother's niece should come to live at Holywell, as a companion to Mariana, to be educated and guided, as far as was possible, by herself and Jane. She'd agreed only to a trial visit of a month or so, a little holiday for Joan. Now, she smiled to herself. Their laughter showed how right he'd been, not just for Joan's sake, but for Mariana's too, distracting her from her gnawing anxiety about her twin.

Kate continued on her way to look in on Philip, propped on pillows in the bed he'd once shared with his brothers. Trusty lay alongside him, taking up rather more of the bed than was comfortable, but Kate knew the child would not want it any other way.

The plan for him to go to Warthrop had come to nothing, for early in February he'd been struck down by a severe illness that took him close to death. Four months later he was a little better, but his progress had been painfully slow and the racking cough lingered. There were few days when he felt strong enough to leave his bed, even to sit in a chair by the window.

She gave Philip his medicine, lingering to let him talk if he wished, simply being with him. Jane would do the same later today, and Mariana always ended the day in his company.

She was just leaving the room when word came that Sir Cuthbert had called, and was waiting to see her in the hall.

One look at his grave expression was enough to fill her with alarm, though when he spoke it was at first simply to make the usual neighbourly enquiries, while refreshment was brought to them.

'How about young Toby? Have you news of him? He's still with your husband, at Warthrop?'

'He is. He's doing well, learning much about the management of the estate, and working hard, I gather.' And after a difficult beginning, he was by now happily reconciled to her marriage. 'Richard thought he might benefit from some study of the law at the Inns of Court, but the times are not propitious for that, as things are.'

'A pity. It would have been good for him. Perhaps in time—If you need my help, you have only to ask.'

She smiled. 'I thank you. That's kind. But you know how my circumstances have changed.' Joy ran through her as she spoke of it; such a change, so much more happiness than she'd ever thought possible, even at this time of heartache for those of her faith.

It had all gone so smoothly, so calmly: the legal documents drawn up for her betrothal to Richard, making Toby the legal heir to Warthrop, ensuring that Holywell remained her property for life, to pass afterwards into Mariana's hands. And then, best of all, the secret nuptial

Mass at Richard's estate, where, witnessed by Jane and Toby and Richard's servant Adam, they'd been married just after Easter. She'd been astonished how much more secure this had made her feel, how protected and supported. Yet Richard had left her free to organise her life in her own way, to remain here at Holywell as it suited her, to manage her estates as she chose (though he was willing enough to help and advise if she asked it of him), to come to Warthrop whenever she wished. He had even once or twice conferred with her over some aspect of the management of his own property. This marriage was so very different from her first, in every possible way; her husband so unlike any other man she'd known, in his respect for her, his consideration.

Sir Cuthbert, who'd met Richard often enough to grow to like him, had been delighted by their union, when she'd told him of it.

But now, this morning, she saw that grave look return to his face.

'It's as well you have that protection, my dear madam. I have been putting off what I have to say to you, until I was sure. But no longer. It will I think be law before the end of June, next month.'

She understood him. 'The new oath that all of us are to swear?'

'The very same. It saddens me greatly to have to warn you of this, on top of all the rest.'

All the rest, as she knew full well, being the severe new

recusancy laws brought in this year, just as every peaceable Catholic must have feared. Sir Cuthbert had warned her of them as soon as the Christmas festivities were done.

'I fear that I shall be forced to put the magistrate before the neighbour and friend,' he'd said. 'If it had not been for —well, you know, of course! Last year's dreadful outrage changed everything, for all that it failed, thank God. I can no longer take so flexible a view of the law.'

And the law required her to receive the so-called sacrament of Holy Communion in her parish church at least twice a year, on pain of a crippling fine, even for the first offence. For that, if nothing else, he'd approved her marriage.

'You now have two places of residence,' he'd said. 'It will be the less easy to observe your behaviour. And I guess that your husband will take a less stringent view than you do.'

She was sure of that, for Richard had made it clear that he would observe the law, while adding, 'What you do, dear heart, is for your own conscience. I will support you whatever you choose, and' (with a grin) 'so long as you take due care, I will pay any fines that fall due.'

Would this new development bring still harsher penalties on her and her fellow Catholics?

'This oath now,' Sir Cuthbert was saying. 'I shall be obliged by law to offer it to you and all your household.'

'I understand. Until I know the words, I shan't know if I can in all conscience take it.'

'It will command you to swear allegiance to King James as our lawful King.' He saw she was about to speak, and raised his hand to silence her. 'Wait, that's not all. You must deny the right of the Pope or any other foreign ruler to depose or excommunicate the King, or permit any of our sovereign's subjects to plot against him or seek to depose or kill him. Could you swear such an oath? You would be denying the power of the Pope over your conscience in this thing.'

She'd thought her own brother had done wrong; was that not enough to allow her to take this oath, if it should be presented to her? 'I think perhaps I could.'

She saw Sir Cuthbert relax into his usual smiling self. 'Then I'm content. It would pain me to have to commit you to prison, or hand you over to those who might be less willing than I to treat you with leniency. But I'm sure you see how things have changed, since…And in your particular case, considering your brother—well!'

'I know. I understand.' Then she looked gravely at him. 'But I shall have to see precisely what the words are, when the time comes. I can't promise anything without that.'

'Then I'll hope for a happy outcome.'

She bent her head, drew a deep breath, then looked up at him. 'And now I have some news for you, which I think will please you very much. I had planned to call on you to warn you, before the banns were read for the first time.'

'Banns?' She saw bewilderment give slow way to a dawning delight. 'Here at Meadhope, in the parish church?' She nodded. 'That is beyond wonderful! I would never have thought—'

'Nor I,' she confessed. 'Richard convinced me that it was right. Yet I am still not quite easy about it. He urged me to see that it is a way to invite our dear friends, our *heretic* friends, to witness our union in public and to share in our rejoicing.' She knew her tone sounded mechanical, as if reciting something she'd learned by rote. 'Next month, June 10, the feast of St Margaret of Scotland, as soon as the banns are read.' It still felt to her like a betrayal, for all that her reason had accepted Richard's argument.

It was obvious at once that Sir Cuthbert had no such qualms. Laughing, he embraced her.

'Let me kiss you! I cannot enough express my delight! This will make life so much easier for you in these times, and for we magistrates too. It will bring so much joy to our lives.'

To make life easier should never have been her aim, if Richard's gentle urging had not persuaded her. And that final element, intruding in so timely a manner: 'My son Thomas will be here, to be our witness. We heard from him two weeks since.'

When she'd first written to tell Tom of her marriage she'd sensed disapproval beneath his formally worded felicitations. She had feared it was to be Toby all over again. But invited to make a visit to coincide with their second and public marriage, he'd accepted readily enough. In two days time he would be here, at Holywell, with his wife and child. She would hold him in her arms again, after eleven long years.

'I am delighted beyond words, my dear! Truly happy! You will I hope wish to invite this old friend to your wedding feast?'

'More than that, sir.' She looked up at him, touched by his obvious delight. 'I have no one to give me away. Will you permit me to ask that service of you?' Seeing how his face lit up, she could have no doubt of his response before he gave it.

She saw him on his way and went in search of Jane, to talk over his visit and its implications, and to make further plans for next month's celebrations.

Richard took the ring blessed by the rector and slipped it onto the fourth finger of Kate's left hand; the ring she had worn round her neck every day since he gave it to her— and every night but one—now marking their union for all to see. Her eyes met his, felt the tenderness in them, the depth of his love for her; and for that moment all her reservations about this ceremony fell away. It felt right, as holy as that other secret marriage, just as it should be.

'With this ring I thee wed: with my body I thee worship: and with all my worldly goods I thee endow.' His eyes sparkled at those last words, as if to say, *You have the best of this bargain!* 'In the name of the Father and the Son and the Holy Ghost. Amen.'

Instinctively, she made the sign of the cross, as he did

too. Another prayer and then, over their joined hands, Gervase Langley's pronouncement: 'Those whom God hath joined together, let no man put asunder.'

Prayers and blessings poured over them, somehow enfolding them in love. But unease edged into Kate's mind as the formal marriage service drew towards its close.

Master Langley had prepared them for the service, going through each stage of it with them, so they knew what to expect. Trying to push aside her resistance at the very thought of this alien ceremony, Kate was at first reassured to find it was in many ways not so very different from the Catholic rite. What she had not expected was one crucial resemblance: once the vows and prayers were over, came the words, 'Then shall begin the communion.' Simply to be present in the Protestant church had been hard enough for her to accept, for that alone would count as a sin. But this…to be faced so soon with this extreme test of her faith. Reading the sentence, she'd cried out. 'Oh, I cannot, will not! Not this!'

Richard had laid his hand over hers, while the rector said gently, 'Hear me, my dear madam. I know that this would be to ask too much of you. I understand. I shall not ask it. I shall simply speak the words you see at the very end, as an instruction. That is all.'

She'd raised her eyes to his kindly face. 'Will that not get you into trouble with the law?'

'I'm prepared to take the risk, and trust to the leniency of my good friend Sir Cuthbert. And the mercy of God, who would not ask any of us to face a test beyond our endurance.'

Now she found herself doubting him. Had his promise been simply a ruse to lure her into the church, to force her into a conformity she did not want? Would this day end in guilt and bitterness?

A sermon whose words she was too troubled to take in, and then she heard him declare the final words she'd read in the prayer book: 'The new married persons, the same day of their marriage, must receive the holy Communion.'

And he moved calmly on to the blessing, while her heartbeat steadied, her hand relaxed in Richard's grasp, and tears of gratitude filled her eyes.

Hand in hand they stepped out of the cool dimness of the church into the sunlit churchyard. There, before the company gathered outside, Richard kissed her.

'Three times wed, dear heart,' he murmured. 'It could not be more sure.'

'Three times?' Kate frowned. 'I recall twice only.'

His voice grew softer still, so she scarcely heard him. 'That first time, in your best bedroom, in January last.'

How could she ever forget? She felt herself colour, gave a little shiver of delight. 'Oh! Yes!'

'Was that not truly a marriage of two loving hearts?'

'The first and best,' she whispered.

And then Tom stepped forward to embrace his mother; her lost son returned to her.

'You've found a good man, mother. I had my doubts when you wrote. But now I see.' He gave a little bow in Richard's direction. Over the past days, since his arrival at Holywell, they'd had time to get to know and like one another. 'I'm happy for you, truly.'

Joy filled her. She exchanged a glance with Richard, sharing their happiness. He took her hand. 'Come now! Let's to the feast!' He gestured to the company to follow.

They ran forward to where a worn stone barred their path: the base of an ancient cross that had once stood in the churchyard. There, like many a bridegroom before him, he lifted her up and carried her over to the other side. She clung to him, laughing.

Then on to the gate, which was tied shut with ribbons, a clamorous group of boys at the other side. Richard reached into his pocket, drew out a handful of coins, flung them over; and the gate was opened to let them pass.

They picked their way through the boys scrambling for the coins and climbed onto the flower-decked cart waiting to carry them back to Holywell. Their guests followed, riding alongside, running after them, singing and laughing, some throwing corn (though not much at this time of year, when stocks were low and harvest far off). After the solemnity of the marriage ceremony, it was all noisy revelry.

At the door of Holywell they were met by the gentle fair-haired young woman who was Tom's wife Lucy, their infant daughter in her arms. 'We called her Katharine,' Tom had said when first they met.

No one had said, 'Perhaps she will one day have an aunt or uncle younger than she is.' Kate guessed that they all assumed this could not happen. Only Jane and Richard knew she'd miscarried of a child just last month. It was still possible there would be another conception, next time carried to full term. She did not much wish to be a mother again, but she would like Richard to have a child of his own, one day.

Indoors, the servants, most of whom had been at the ceremony, were bustling around bringing food to the tables. By the fire, Philip, downstairs for the first time since his illness, sat nestled up to the dog. Richard went to him, crouched down beside him. 'Good morning to you, my brave gentleman. It's good to see you downstairs.' As always, the tenderness in his voice as he spoke to the child moved Kate beyond words.

She turned to welcome Sir Cuthbert, who had just come into the house. 'I thank you for your kindness this day, and the great service you rendered.'

'My dear Katharine, it has been a pleasure to share in your happiness, in these dark days. I hope for you this is the beginning of a more tranquil life.'

Much later, when everyone had eaten and drunk to excess, the company took themselves to the garden, where sweetmeats were brought to tempt them further—Mariana had spent a large part of yesterday in the stillroom preparing them.

The air was heady with the scent of box and roses. Kate sat in the arbour in the most sheltered and sunny corner, the infant a heart-warming weight on her lap: baby Katharine, smiling, looking about her with all the intentness of a lively seven months' old.

'She's a happy little thing,' said Jane beside her. 'See how she takes everything in.'

'She will be a capable and learned woman, one day.'

'Like her grandmother.' A little pause, then: 'I thought today, in church, if only it could always be so, that those of every faith could use each other kindly. To be able to join together, without rancour.'

'Yes. It was a time to be treasured.' She was surprised to realise that for her this was true.

From her seat, Kate could see all those she loved best, her small realm gathered here in this place. Not far away, Richard was deep in amicable discussion with Sir Cuthbert and the rector—and Toby, happy confident Toby, holding his own as a young man among equals, a young man who had found his place in the world.

Walking towards her along the path between the low box hedging came her other son Tom and his wife. The child on Kate's knee gave a crow of delight as her mother approached.

'Time for the little one to be in bed,' Lucy said, lifting her into her arms. 'Bid goodnight to your grandam.'

Kate watched them walk away, back to the house, the next generation of her family.

'I think I have never been as happy as I am now. I know there will be hard times to come, that life can never be easy. But this day will stay in my memory for ever.'

'And mine too,' said Jane.

Lightning Source UK Ltd.
Milton Keynes UK
UKHW012013100221
378572UK00001B/244